TȟUNKÁŠILA
GREAT SPIRIT, ARE YOU THERE?

MICHAEL FOSTER

Copyright © 2018 by Michael Foster

All rights reserved.

No part of this book may be reproduced in any form or by any electronic or mechanical means including information storage and retrieval systems, without permission in writing from the author except in the case of brief quotations embodied in critical reviews and certain other noncommercial uses permitted by copyright law.

This book is a work of historical fiction. Some names, characters, places and incidents existed during the time period this book describes but their appearance in this book are strictly products of the author's imagination and are used fictitiously. Any resemblance to actual persons, living or dead, events or locales is entirely coincidental.

Book cover and design by Aaron Foster

Cover photograph 'Acoma Bell Tower' by
Edward Sheriff Curtis

ISBN: 9781729159071

Dear Reader,

The fiction and non-fiction sections of libraries and bookstores are clearly labeled. They are kept separate as if one might corrupt the other. Our basic premise is that one is fact and the other made up - imaginary. A typical definition of fiction is - *literature in the form of prose, especially short stories and novels that describes imaginary events and people.*

I would argue that the line between fiction and non-fiction is so blurred that all written word is a form of fiction. What I mean to say is that the author adds impressions and interpretations to the work. For example, pretend that five of the most respected reporters in the world witness the eruption of a volcano. They are all standing at the same vantage point and experience the phenomenon together. When asked to objectively describe what they saw, heard and felt, their written accounts will not be identical. Fiction? Non-Fiction?

When writing about the birth and death of Jesus, Mathew, Mark, Luke and John each described these events in their gospels a bit differently. If the world can believe these slight variances in the Bible then hopefully you, my reader, can accept the liberties I've taken with the history within this novel.

Black Elk is not a fictional character. He was born in 1863 and died in 1950. He was second cousin to Crazy Horse. Black Elk was also an active participant in both the battles we know as Little Big Horn and Wounded Knee. As a young boy, he was deathly ill for more than a week. It was during those days of high fever that he had many visions – visions that guided his life. Black Elk was employed by William Cody as a performer in the famous Wild West Show – he traveled throughout the United States and Europe as part of Cody's troupe. Black Elk converted to Catholicism later in his life and worked diligently to share the gospel with his people in their sacred Paha Sapa, the Black Hills. He is currently designated *A Servant of God* by the church which is a step toward being named a Saint. Harney Peak, the highest point in South Dakota, was renamed Black Elk

Peak in recognition, symbolizing the significance of the mountain to Native Americans.

When the U.S. Cavalry officer defected to the join the Lakota in the middle of *Wakanisha Is Love Enough*, the author named him John Dunn plagiaristically in honor of John Dunbar, hero of Michael Blake's novel *Dances With Wolves*. But one morning shortly after the release of *Wakanisha Can We Stand*, my brother David called and asked if the John Dunn from my novels was the same John Dunn that exerted a major influence on the growth of Taos, New Mexico during the latter part of the 1800's. After doing minor due diligence, I found that the birth and death dates from the John Dunn of Taos matched precisely with the character I'd created. Fiction? Non-fiction? Or something more?

Scholars of Buffalo Bill's history or any employee or volunteer at the Buffalo Bill Museum and Grave in Golden, Colorado would surely cringe if they read the fictitious liberties I took. My descriptions of the show, how it operated and the acts presented are complete fiction. I used Cody's show to present to you, my reader, some history of white – Indian encounters of which you may not have been aware. I was, however, as true as possible to the dates and locations of those shows.

Technically, Itunkala, Hanna, and the rest of the characters that populate these three novels are inventions. The books, if they ever find a larger audience, would be found in the Historic Fiction section of your local bookstore. But to me, the characters and their stories are real. Itunkala, little Mouse, came to me in a vision in 1985, gave me her story and wanted it told. I tried unsuccessfully to ignore her for over two decades.

I know that to the rational mind, visions are passé'. But I just cannot ignore the string of coincidences that led me to write these words. My son Aaron, also a writer, was born in 1976. My wife Mary and I had a stained glass studio in Colorado at the time. A local gallery featured our work. Shortly after Aaron was born, the owner of the gallery presented us with a pair of beautifully beaded child sized moccasins. I had the moccasins appraised twenty years later – they were quite old, authentic and Lakota Sioux.

In the late 1990's, Mary and I attended the opening of a local winery – one of the attending vendors was selling unframed prints and lithographs. I found a signed print by Bruno Bruni titled *Solitude*. I obsessively bought it on the spot. Much later, the image became Itunkala to me!

In the September 9th 2001 edition of our local paper, an article titled *She Seeks Justice* was featured on the front page of the Parade Magazine. The picture on the cover of Elouise Cobell triggered some obsessive feeling – the rest of the Sunday paper went unread. Her Blackfoot name is Yellow Bird Woman. If you're curious at all, pull on that thread and it will lead you to Cobell vs. Salazar.

This spring, I read the opening scene from *Wakunisha, Is Love Enough* to a small gathering. Three days later, a man from the reading showed up at my front door unannounced with a box. He didn't want to come in; he just wanted me to have the contents. Inside the box was a bowl made by Deloris S. Sanchez from the Acoma, New Mexico pueblo near Taos. I tried to refuse but he was insistent. He told me that the bowl had been in his family since he was a child in the 50's. His name is Derrick. He said, "When I heard your story, I knew the bowl had found its home."

The word *obsessive* appears several times in the preceding paragraphs because it best describes how intensely this story has gripped my life. My family would probable choose words from a thesaurus with a little more oomph like *fanatical, possessed* or even *neurotic* – they've had to put up with me during this process.

So dear reader, as you experience this third novel in the series, it is your choice to decide – fiction or non-fiction. But no matter what you choose, what's most important is what you believe.

Michael Foster - 2018
Canwapegi Wi - Moon When the Leaves Turn Brown

Also by
Michael Foster

WAKANISHA IS LOVE ENOUGH
Book 1

WAKANISHA CAN WE STAND
Book 2

Tangent – An Unusual Romance

Through Time and Other Stories

Gauntlet

On the train in Pennsylvania - 1897

Life is not a problem to be solved, but a reality to be experienced.
Soren Kierkegaard

Science investigates; religion interprets. Science gives man knowledge, which is power; religion gives man wisdom, which is control.
Martin Luther King, Jr.

The human brain contains a powerful relic from its prehistoric past. That remnant is the desire to dominate, to be the alpha. Coupled with intelligence, that need is our greatest flaw. Upon first meeting, whether individuals or nations, we judge the other to ensure our own survival.

When women meet for the first time, their challenges and judgments are usually gentle. They likely share the soft things of life like children and the beauty they see in each other. Yet women can be fierce and territorial with each other. Then banishment is usually their violence.

When men encounter each other for the first time, physical strength is gauged before intelligence.

Yet the spirit that resides within us all seeks equality.

Black Elk and John Dunn had coexisted as equals for years. In a very tribal way they recognized and accepted the strengths of the other. Dunn was physically larger and stronger. He would have been a perfect Akíčhita, head of tribal security, much like a sheriff. Whereas Black Elk was highly spiritual and most likely would have been accepted by the tribe as their Shaman and religious leader.

Tribal governance relied not on a single leader but a group of leaders with distinct skills for the very survival of the people. Black Elk and Leftook would surely have been part of a tribal council had they lived before the disruption caused by the onslaught of European culture.

But in Cody's troupe, Dunn and Black Elk had risen to positions of authority, as they would have in a Sioux tribe. Call it what you will - big dog, survival of the fittest, top of the pecking order - these two men were respected and followed as leaders because they possessed the traits that enhanced the probable survival of the entire group. Their friendship, strengths and dominance had served the troupe well until now. Then Hanna and Ben arrived. The delicate web of relationships within the troupe was shaken by old joys and fears, loves and losses.

When Hanna left the dining car with Abe Hubert, the three men that loved her were left behind to sort things out. If there were a word that was the opposite of synergy, it would have perfectly described the interactions between these three men that had a claim on Hanna's love. The primal need to be the alpha male warred with their need for acceptance.

John Dunn, Leftook, was by far the largest and physically strongest of these three men. By default, he should have been the alpha male. But he deferred to Black Elk because the man was Hanna's father.

Black Elk thought of his daughter as Happy Seed. He had only held her for scant hours before she had been taken from him and sent off to live in a white world. His heart wanted her back to fill the last seventeen years of searching, wondering and pain. But when Black Elk saw his daughter and her love of this young Sioux man called Ben Gregor or Iron Eagle, Black Elk deferred to him.

Ben was barely a man but secure in the knowledge that Hanna loved him. He felt much less courage than he showed. He stood tall as he talked to these two men from Hanna's distant past yet he deferred to them because of the images Hanna held in her heart. In her imagination, these men were god - like, perfect.

The train slowed as it passed over a bridge. The span crossed the Susquehanna River, a waterway named for a people long defeated. The Susquehannock nation was called Conestoga by the English, another irony. A large wagon by that same name brought settlers west to further push the First People aside as European culture spread west across the continent.

But misfortune, like joy, does not last forever. Time diminishes both. These human interpretations of events become lost in oblivion. Life is much like any bridge; it does not change with the years in spite of the pain or joy for those who pass across it. The river, like time, passes beneath regardless.

For Hanna and Ben, time was a very different story like their own pain and joy. It was morning and they were on a train headed north into a new and unmapped life. The day before, Hanna had been held prisoner by a white preacher accused of sins the man himself owned. Today, she was free and reunited with a man who most certainly was the father she'd never known but had dreamed about her entire life.

When breakfast was finished, Ben, Black Elk and John Dunn sat in the dining car unsure of how to proceed. It was Ben that broke the stalemate. "That man that just left, Mr. Hubert. He's your boss, right?" Ben looked back and forth between the two older men. "Maybe you can show me the ropes?"

"Hubert was very clear." Dunn said. "He wants everybody and everything ready to go when we step off the train in Erie. That means all the horses have to be in tack, everybody in costume, everything. We're probably two or three hours behind the first train. We have to be ready the moment we arrive." He looked at Ben and smiled. "But look what we gained!"

An impartial observer might have viewed this scene of indecision as comic. Yet again the question of who was alpha kept the three standing in the dining car aisle shuffling their feet, looking at each other. It was Ben who said, "This way. Right?" By being the first male to pass through the doorway he established, at least for the moment, who was alpha.

When the three entered the next passenger car, all the occupants looked up - conversations stopped. Hanna and Ben's story had passed from person to person through the train like gossip travels through any small town. Black Elk and Big John Dunn were heroes in this tale. In this epic story, Ben and Hanna were the victims, saved from gross injustice. And as the story was retold, it grew. Their story resonated with this group of roustabouts, animal handlers and performers because they also were victims of a prejudiced society.

Black Elk stepped to the front. "Please welcome Ben Gregor. You may have heard that I have found my daughter." He stopped for a moment to calm his voice; his emotions threatened to overwhelm his ability to speak. "Please welcome them."

As they passed through the car, there were handshakes, backslaps and hearty greetings. After being at the Carlisle School Ben was awed by the joyous acceptance into this diverse group. To be openly welcomed by the four colors of men was an overwhelming experience. Men shook his hand and gave warm greetings. Women hugged him and offered him shy compliments.

They were nearly to the door of the next car when and older Indian man stood and took Ben's hand. He looked into Ben's eyes almost aggressively. "How coula." he said in oddly accented Sioux. "Are you a Human Being or are you a radish raised by the whites?"

Black Elk and Dunn stiffened at this crude remark. But Ben met the man's gaze and held the handshake. "I am a man. I am young and have much to learn. If you have wisdom of value, we will talk again." Ben met the other man's gaze assertively enough that the older man dropped his eyes. Then Ben released the man's grip and passed into the vestibule separating the cars.

Inside the gangway connection between the cars, Ben turned and faced his new father-in-law and Dunn. "Hau kola! I do have much to learn. Tell me when I need to know something. Be honest. And yes, I would give my life for you as I would for Hanna. You are my Ate' and Leksi'. I hope to learn much from you!"

Ben did not see the look that passed between the other two men as they passed into the next car. Had his back not been turned, he would have seen that their acceptance of him was growing.

Ben lost track of time and the names and faces of the people he met. In each car, every person greeted him warmly. He also saw the great respect that Black Elk and Dunn received. He heard them both called Naca' (Chief) and boss. In each car and on each face, Ben saw respect and admiration for the two men that had become his relatives. His own respect and admiration for these two men grew with each new encounter.

Likewise, the two older men watched how Ben interacted with this diverse, extended family. It was as if Ben were meeting a tribe of his own people for the first time.

At last, the three men approached the door to the first stock car, the car where Black Elk and Dunn spent most of their time. Even though Ben had been consciously judged on his interactions with humans, the test to come was more elemental.

"Welcome to our humble abode," Dunn said as he led Ben into a car that was filled with the smell of horses. The aroma of good green hay and manure was like a homecoming to Ben.

The horses were housed in narrow, diagonal stalls. Water and feed were in tubs at the head of each stall and were tied to their stall door. Dunn's large chestnut Morgan and Black Elk's Cayuse Appaloosa stood untethered in an open area.

The horses nickered as the men entered their space, their eyes bright and alert. Dunn nodded toward the big chestnut and said, "That's Kangee and" pointing to the Appaloosa "that's Wasica."

Ben smiled as he approached the horses. "Raven and Spirit Guide. Good Lakota names."

Black Elk smiled as he corrected Ben. "A wasica is a guardian spirit. Your Lakota is good."

Both the older men watched as Ben approached the horses. The horses' ears were forward listening curiously, not laid back in fear or aggression. They watched the young man approach them, their body language saying, "I like him."

Ben touched Kangee but then moved on to Black Elk's horse. "Beautiful! A real Indian horse." Ben reached under the horse's neck and touched the soft fur on the opposite side as he made eye contact. Then using his other hand, Ben rubbed along the horse's withers and down its flank. Wasica leaned in against Ben like an old friend.

Dunn and Black Elk again made eye contact. The slight smile they shared was small but the joy that passed between them was enormous. An unexpected puzzle piece had slid into place that neither man knew was missing.

The train slowed and seconds later leaned slightly as it entered a long sweeping turn. Ben looked up startled at this change but the two older men adjusted their stance automatically like sailors on the deck of a rolling ship.

The morning light streaming in the windows ceased at the same time there was a profound change in the sound. Ben gasped and looked up at the other two men.

"Just a tunnel. We're probably pulling into Emporium Junction." Dunn looked out the window as the tunnel masonry slid by. Moments later the train emerged back into the light. "We've got to stop and take on coal and water for our run into Erie."

"It just wasn't the tunnel. Didn't you feel it?" Ben still had his hands on the horse; the look on his face was serious. "It felt like Hanna called me. I know she's not here but it felt like she just called to me."

Dunn looked at Ben with concern but when he turned to Black Elk, he realized his friend had felt something also. "Go find her. I'll stay here and get the crew organized for tonight's show."

Even before the engine had come to a stop under the coal tower, townspeople began to gather around the train. Every car was emblazoned with advertising and lurid pictures. Crowds always gathered when the trains stopped in small towns.

Black Elk looked out the window disgustedly. "Kacha'!" Shook his head sadly.

Ben joined the two men at the window and asked, "What does Kacha' mean?"

Dunn laughed. "There really isn't an English word like it. It can mean really stupid or bad. It can also be used to express a contradiction or irony." He pointed to all the people trying to look in the windows. "Look at all of them! To them, we're famous. They treat us like royalty when we're in costume. But if you walked down their street away from the show, you'd be called radish or worse. You might even get thrown in jail. I'll tell you about Jack Johnson sometime."

"Later!" Black Elk looked distraught. "I felt her too!" He pulled a beautifully made porcupine quill breastplate down from the wall. "Here! Put this on. If any of the rubes try to stop you, just tell them you're Chief Iron Eagle and keep walking."

"Why do I need this?" Ben asked.

"Look! If Hanna gets off the train, there could be trouble. Dunn, you take the side of the train with the crowd. I'll walk the aisle inside. Ben, you take the other side. Who ever finds her, just be sure she's on the train and safe."

"Why do I need to wear this thing?" Ben asked.

Black Elk put his hand over Ben's heart. "In here, this is our world. Out there is their world. Out there belongs to them. We make believe in their world."

Ben shook his head sadly. He put on the breastplate and walked to the door on the opposite side of the gathering crowd as Dunn pushed through the crowd on the other.

"Go in the back of the first car." Black Elk said anxiously. "Open the door and ask for Hanna. Abe won't yell at you too bad because he knows you're the new guy. If she's not there, work your way back. I'll start from here and meet you somewhere in the middle." Ben nodded his head in agreement and stepped down into the land of the whites.

He began to jog toward the front of the train when four young men about his age stepped out of a copse of trees near the tracks. Ben continued to jog and consciously tried to ignore them as they formed a line between him and the front of the train.

Ben had seen this formation many times before - the scuffed boots, the dirty jeans and the confidence that comes with superior numbers. He attempted to walk around them but the largest stepped into his path. Ben thought to himself, "Why is it always the biggest and never the smartest?"

"Hey! Redman! Wach yer hurry?" He put his hands on his hips and did his best to look important.

Ben smiled up at him and asked, "You boys looking for work? My name's Iron Eagle." He held out his hand as if to shake hands.

The big one sneered. "You ain't gonna be much of a job for me." The others began to box Ben in.

"Hey Chief! Ask your friends if they want to come on board." Dunn stood on the top step one car back, an easy smile on his face.

"Sure thing Mr. Dunn." Ben watched as a bit of the bravado leaked away from this group of locals. "You boys want to come up and see what goes on?"

The four had their hands in their pockets and were shuffling their feet as they looked at Ben sheepishly. One of the smaller ones asked, "What do ya think? I wouldn't mind." They were mumbling between themselves and had not seen Dunn move until he put his hands on two of the young men's shoulders.

"Chief, you need to get about your business. I can help out guests." Dunn smiled around the circle than tilted his head toward the front of the train. "Go on, the big man needs you."

"Sure thing Boss." Ben approached the biggest of the four until he was nearly touching. The bully fell back a step. Ben smiled and said, "You might want to be nice to Mr. Dunn here - he was in the war and has a bit of a temper." Ben walked off whistling.

Ben found Hanna sitting with an ancient woman in one of the passenger cars. The two were happily chatting away in Sioux when he arrived. "How coula," he said almost as if asking permission to sit with them. Ben sensed an ancient connection had opened again between generations of women. The two women before him were so different yet so similar. Physically the old woman was wrinkled and nearly toothless where as Hanna was young and flawless. Yet the energy that flowed between them made them the same, identical in spirit.

Hanna seemed to be nearly vibrating with excitement. "She tells me we are going to have a boy!" Hanna looked so happy. The worry around her eyes was gone. She was so animated. She vacillated between speaking Sioux and English. "Please sit. She's called Kanj Coonshi. She says we're having a boy! Soon! She thinks he will be a reader of dreams!"

The old woman patted the seat next to her and said in broken English. "Sit! We talk."

"She told me of The White Buffalo Woman. Ben, it's amazing!" Hanna's eyes were wide-eyed with wonder. "Many of the Bible stories my step-father taught me and our Sioux legends are nearly identical. Did you know that both Christians and our people worship a trinity?"

Black Elk stepped into the car with a concerned look but when he saw the three sitting together, he smiled and sat across the aisle and listened.

"Our Sioux legends tell of a flood! We believe in judgment and a heaven!" The beauty and passion of her expression completely overshadowed her obvious pregnancy.

Black Elk reached across the aisle and took his daughter's hand. "My daughter. My Wakanisha."

Hanna had a look of absolute wide-eyed wonder. "Ben! Ate'! Do you understand? The White Buffalo Woman and Christ could be the same person - or at least the same legend. Don't you see?" The intensity of Hanna's feelings was so strong, it was as if her spirit was a great light shining through her tears. "All of us! The four colors of men! We're all brothers!"

No Man's Land
July, 1897 – Corry, Pennsylvania

Parents can only give good advice or put them on the right paths, but the final forming of a person's character lies in their own hands.
   Anne Frank

Children must be taught how to think, not what to think.
   Margaret Mead

The first sign of trouble was *the old boot on a stick* signal. The engineer of Buffalo Bill's second train saw this prearranged warning in the middle of the tracks. The tripod of heavy tree branches held an old boot with a bit of red cloth flapping in the breeze. The engineer throttled back the massive locomotive as it crushed the hastily tied together signal. He pulled on the steam whistle just as the train entered a long sweeping left-hand turn.

The dense hardwood forest on either side of the tracks made it impossible for the engineer to see around the curve. But when the train reached a straightaway, standing near the tracks was a man waving a flag. The engineer throttled back even more until his train was chugging along at a speed that a man could jog easily. As they approached, the engineer recognized the man on the ground as a brakeman he knew well. The two had hoisted many a beer in the decade or more they'd been working the Buffalo Bill Show.

As the engine passed the brakeman expertly grabbed the ladder and climbed into the cab with the engineer and the fireman. "Derailment bout two miles up. Gunsel drivin' lumber tried to switch too fast. Lost five cars. Gotta mell of a hess." Both men poked their heads out. Behind them about mid-train they could see the conductor swing his light.

"Hey, you know our conductor Frank?" The engineer pulled the rope on the steam whistle twice.

"Yea. I'll tell em." The brakeman climbed down the ladder and climbed aboard again where the conductor was outside riding the ladder. "Derailment just past Corry. Got a freight ahead of us. Could take a day or more."

"Damn, gonna miss our show in Erie. Stay aboard. We'll take ya forward and I'll get our brakeman to walk back to signal." The conductor dropped from the slow moving train to the ground and then climbed aboard the caboose. Moments later, the brakeman dropped to the ground with his kit and started walking back up the tracks to warn any oncoming train of the danger ahead.

Corry, Pennsylvania had grown to a population of over six thousand people in the mid-eighteen hundreds. Abundant timber, the discovery of oil in nearby Titusville and the railroad literally put Corry on the map. Corry was an important junction. Thirty miles to the north lay Erie and the shipping lanes across the Great Lakes. South was Pittsburg. Corry sat at the intersection of the rail line going to Harrisburg, the state capital. All rail traffic between Buffalo and Cleveland passed directly through Corry, Pennsylvania.

In the distance the engineer could see the outskirts of this small city. The track was straight as a string and before him were at least two trains parked on the track. The land on either side of the tracks was open ground covered with green grass hip deep in some places. There was a meandering copse of trees far to the northeast where his map showed Brokenstraw Creek. He throttled the locomotive back until the loud chuffs of vented steam were nearly a second apart. He pulled the rope twice sharply and gave two toots of his whistle, which was answered like an echo from the train ahead.

The conductor from the first train stepped down from the first train's caboose and waved as he walked up the tracks. When the two trains were less than a hundred yards apart, the conductor signaled by pantomiming cutting his throat.

The engineer gently pulled the throttle lever all the way closed and let his train slowly coast to a stop. He then pulled the brake lever that sent steam pressure to each car to set the brakes. Almost before the hiss of steam escaping from beneath the cars set the brakes, people of all ages and sexes stepped to the ground in full costume.

"Hey! Big E. Ya sees what I sees?" The fireman leaned out the right side of the engine compartment and looked forward.

"Hey yourself Bakehead!" the engineer barked. "This hog ain't gonna shut herself down!" He continued through his mental checklist of switches, levers and gauges that had to be just so before he let down his guard.

The engineer absolutely loved his job. He controlled a massive machine that weighed thousands of tons that was the epitome of technology. He was also aware that hundreds of people relied on him for their very lives. He checked the last gauge, breathed a sigh of relief and mentally relinquished his power.

Outside his window the engineer saw hundreds of people. Near the edge of the field townspeople milled around drawn in by their curiosity. Yet they didn't mingle because the occupants of the train were outsiders, foreign and exotic. And some were colored!

The occupants of the first train, all four colors of men, visited happily in their fellowship and the ability to be off the train on a lovely summer day. They viewed the town's people as the rubes, the suckers born every minute.

But when the costumed occupants of the second train poured out into the field, a critical mass was reached.

It was the children from the second train that began the miracle. Some were dressed as Indians while others were dressed as sodbusters with bonnets or bib overalls. They began playing tag, running and laughing with those from the first train.

As with an avalanche, it started with one pebble. Two young girls, one red and one white, both about the same age noticed each other across the empty expanse of tall grass. Both were similarly dressed; their gingham dresses were simply made and no-nonsense. Each carried a doll. In any other setting they could have been friends from a first or second grade classroom across a playground from each other. Only later would a comment be made about their skin color. One was fair skinned while the other a coppery red. But to them, the important thing was to play dolls together. What else could be more important?

Becky Little Horse was the first to wave. She clutched her very blonde haired doll to her chest and wagged her fingers across the short distance that separated the two. To Becky the distance was just that, a brief walk to a new friend, not some metaphysical barrier.

Maddy O'Connor waved back shyly. Before either of the sets of parents could intervene, the two girls unconsciously and innocently met in the no-man's-land that separated these two cultures. The irony that Maddy's family members were recent immigrants was completely lost on these two new friends.

Both Maddy's parents and Becky's mother saw the two girls and hustled forward to save their daughters from what seemed to be some form of peril.

Becky's mother was dressed in gingham and wore a matching bonnet. From a distance she appeared to be the part she played, a brave white settler woman.

When the three adults met beside their daughters, the O'Connor's gasped when they saw the other woman's features. Her skin was a darker red than her daughter's and she had high cheekbones and black, intelligent eyes. The O'Connor's faces became even paler when, from across the field, they saw a large, bare chested red man in war paint and deerskin breeches striding directly toward them.

The two little girls were much too busy introducing their dolls to notice the existential drama playing out just over their heads. To them, their friendly interaction was much more real and certainly more fun.

The very brief but intense silence was broken when the frightening Indian man, in perfect Connecticut accented English, said, "Good afternoon." He put his hand on his daughter's head and continued, "My name is Avery and this is my wife Abigail." He tilted his head back toward the train. "We work for Mr. Cody, Buffalo Bill." The way the man held out his hand and the intonation of his voice was so normally white that Maddy's father returned the handshake before he realized that he had done so.

To her credit, Maddy's mother plucked up her courage, offered her hand first to the Indian woman and said, "Hello, my name is Cora. I really like your dress."

Ben carefully helped Hanna down the steps onto the cinders lining the tracks. She stood in the shade of the railcar as Ben assisted *Kanj Coonshi*. Ben disappeared into the train again and reappeared moments later with an armload of wooden bingo chairs. Hanna and Old Grandmother sat down and continued to visit happily in both Siouan and broken English. Ben sat down next to Hanna and listened. He was dressed in some faded denim trousers and a simple deerskin pullover given him by the ladies in the wardrobe car.

Moments later, Black Elk and Dunn joined them. Hanna's father was wearing his Sioux Chief's costume but was bare headed; the ornate headdress he had left in his locker. Dunn was dressed as a Colonel in the U.S. Cavalry but without his coat and hat. His shirt was unbuttoned showing a bear claw necklace he'd won in a poker game.

Several of the women from the wardrobe car joined them and asked what was happening. Ben jumped up and returned minutes later with more chairs. Black Elk had claimed the chair next to his daughter and had joined in the conversation. Ben made two more trips to the supply car for chairs and soon there was a large number of performers, roustabouts and family members sitting slightly elevated from the drama happening below.

Children of all colors were playing tag and Red Hand. One of the performers was showing off his rope tricks to a large, appreciative crowd. An open space appeared at the center of the field and two trick riders were wowing the crowd with their acrobatics.

Ben disappeared back into one of the cars and reappeared carrying a football. He was about to ask the group if anyone wanted to play catch when Abe Hubert walked up to them from the direction of the first train. "Cody, Arizona John, Annie Oakley, her husband and several others headed into town. Cody's on Isham and the rest of them got a ride in some fancy wagon arranged by the mayor. If you need me, I'll be at the St. Nicholas Hotel having a decent meal." He walked off looking for someone who would take him into town.

Not one person sitting in the shade wanted to play football with Ben so he walked out onto the field. Almost immediately, he made eye contact with a boy a little younger than he was. Ben pantomimed throwing and the other boy nodded. Within minutes, the crowd playing catch had swelled to that of more than two football teams. It became quickly evident that there were too many boys vying for the ball.

When Ben got the ball finally, he held it up and waved all the players in to listen to his plan. "I'm going to teach you a game we played at school. Its called Touchback." He sent one of the boys from the train to fetch four more bingo chairs while he explained the rules.

"The object of Touchback is to throw or kick the ball over your opponent's goal line. Your team gets one point if the ball hits the ground without being caught. Everybody understand?" He looked around and saw lots of nodding heads.

"Here's how you play! The teams face each other at the fifty-yard line. The first kicker kicks the ball from their own thirty-yard line. Where the other team first touches the ball is their line of scrimmage; that's the spot they kick the ball back from. Got it so far?" Most there nodded their heads.

"When one team kicks the ball and the other team catches it, the receiving team gets five paces towards their opponent's goal line. You can save them up if you want and take as many paces forward as points. Got it?" He looked around. "If someone throws the ball instead of kicking it and it's caught, the other team gets fifteen paces. Everybody understand?" Ben looked around at all the faces. Some he knew, some he didn't. Some were red, some white. All the four colors of men were there in the crowd, happily waiting to play. "Let's play to five then maybe we can change the teams. OK?"

There was a muted roar of approval from the boys and some men in the crowd. "Let's form teams, OK?" Ben yelled. He sent four boys off with the chairs and formed a rough rectangle approximately the size of a football field. "Find a partner. If you can't find one, pair up with me." In less than a minute, most of the participants had paired up and those without Ben hooked up with others without partners. Almost exclusively, town boys chose town boys and the boys from the train were partners.

Ben took off his shirt and put it on the ground near at the imaginary boundary line. "This is the fifty yard line. If a ball goes out of bounds, where it goes out is the line of scrimmage. OK so far?" There was lots of nodding.

"Face your partner across the fifty yard line." Ben watched as a double line formed across nearly the entire width of their field. "Now, everybody take two steps back." Ben smiled to himself. "These are the two teams."

For an instant, there was a look of shocked indignation on each face when they realized that the partner they'd chosen was on the other team. Then, easy laughter rang out.

"Group up, choose a captain. Then the two captains come to me for the coin toss. Got it? Oh, and one more thing. Who ever touches the ball first after a kick is the one that gets to kick it back. Or, he can give the ball to someone else if he wants, but the ball has to be kicked from behind the line of scrimmage."

As the game progressed, several food carts from the train appeared selling pretzels, sausages and root beer. More food carts arrived from Corry selling roast beef sandwiches, wieners and one cart sold penny candies. But when a large wagon arrived from a local brewery with kegs and bottled beer, it seemed that color and class dissolved at least for that one magic day.

When the shadows lengthened and the day cooled, Ben came with a plate for Hanna and a glass of water. She gave him a look and gave her plate to *Kanj Coonshi*. All the men including Dunn and Black Elk left and brought back enough plates for all. There was a companionable silence as the group ate. As they looked across the field, they could see small knots of people visiting and children playing. Somebody near the brewery wagon was playing some spirited fiddle music and several couples danced. Even though there seemed to be some segregated groups, many were mixed. For a short period of time, the four colors of men seemed to be at peace.

Hanna leaned over to *Kanj Coonshi*. *"There is a story in the Bible called the loaves and fishes."*

"I know this story. Your Jesus was a powerful shaman." The old woman looked into Hanna's eyes and asked, *"Do you know of our ceremony called the Throwing of the Ball?"* Her eyes were questioning. *"Do you think any of these boys caught the Great Spirit today?"*

Reflection
Corry, Pennsylvania – July 1897

Dreams are today's answers to tomorrow's questions.
  Edgar Cayce

"Tell your folks to get cozy. We may be here for awhile." Abe Hubert delivered this update in his usual matter-of-fact tone. He stood in the doorway to the stateroom Ben and Hanna shared. But those that knew this little man also could tell his volcanic temper was ready to erupt at the slightest provocation. "There's one train in front of our two and now we've got two or maybe three behind us by tomorrow." He stuck an unlit cigar in his mouth and clamped down. "The two behind us are freights. The boys at the yard want them to go first."

Ben looked at Hubert quizzically. "That doesn't make sense. It seems that the most efficient way would be to just move all the trains through once the mess is cleaned up."

Both Black Elk and John Dunn cringed inwardly. They had learned long ago to choose their battles with this intense little Jew. He saw the bigger picture and tended to plan long-term. To question him often brought a blistering rebuke for short-term thinking. "Young man," Hubert said evenly, "the freight companies own this railroad. Freight pays the bills. So a freight train gets priority. The brass hats at the yard can do whatever they want! And that my friend is to make money! They will probably shuttle us off onto a siding once the repairs to the tracks are done and let the freight roll through."

"What about the show in Erie?" Ben asked.

When Hubert didn't explode on Ben, both Dunn and Black Elk heaved a sigh. They realized that Abe was humoring Ben for his ignorance.

"It's covered! We got lucky. Last Sunday was the fourth. The fairgrounds were totally tied up last weekend. But the place was available next weekend. Thank God for the telegraph. We can play Saturday the tenth and even Sunday if the boss thinks we won't upset the church going folks." Hubert looked at Ben almost as if he wanted to be challenged. He looked up at Dunn. "Get the word out to your crew. We've got some down time so let's do maintenance. Good night. Sleep well. Tomorrow may be a long day." Hubert smiled at Hanna and turned to go when Ben asked yet another question.

Had Dunn been standing close enough to Ben to put a hand on him, he would have. Instead, he waited for the outburst he knew was coming.

Hubert spun back with a scowl on his face, but his expression turned to one of speculation and grudging respect when he heard what Ben had to say.

"What if we hauled some freight? I mean do our locomotives have the power to haul a few more cars? It seems to me that if we also hauled freight, it would kill two birds with one stone. The show could bring in more money and we'd get some priority with scheduling, right?"

"You know young man, I never thought of that! I'll pass your idea on to our general manager." Hubert gave Ben an odd smile, turned and walked forward to his car at the front of the train.

With Hubert gone, the space the four of them were sharing somehow seemed to expand. Their attention had been on the doorway and Hubert's larger-than-life personality. Now the four of them sat facing each other, two-by-two on narrow couch seats. There was an unconscious realization that even if they were very closely related, the two sets of people in this tiny room really didn't know each other very well.

The day had been more than pleasant. The townspeople of Corry and the large extended family of Cody's Wild West Show had spent the day as equals, sharing a rare fellowship. So often the occupants of the train had felt the strong *them – us* mentality that made today seem like a dream. But for Hanna and Ben, they had no basis of comparison.

Also unresolved were the relationships between these four people. Except for blood ties and long friendships, Ben and Hanna and the two men from Hanna's distant past really didn't know each other. All they really had was only one day of interactions between them. Whereas the last seventeen years of Hanna's life had been only daydreams about the two men on the other side of her room.

As with many meaningful and profound conversations, this one started with the simplest of questions. "How is the baby?" Black Elk looked at his daughter, concern in his eyes.

"I had the one contraction earlier today but I feel fine now." Hanna smiled back at her father. "Its sort of funny. I've felt tired and achy for a long time but right now, I feel really good. I have this nervous energy like I want to clean and get blankets ready. I feel like I need to organize all of you, give you things to do so we'll be ready when the baby comes. Does that seem strange?"

"Your mother was like that just before you were born." Black Elk smiled sadly and continued in Sioux. "*She said she was like a bird. Hohpiya is the word she learned from her aunties. It means to nest or make a nest. Many women do this just before the baby comes.*"

"I wish I could have known her." Hanna reached across the space that separated them and took her father's hand. "*Our lives would have been so much different.*"

"*You are very much like her.*" Black Elk looked down bitterly for a moment then continued. "*We have lost so much. In the life we had, we always had a village to go home to. That doesn't seem like much but it means that our strength came from our culture, our people. You were raised by the whites yet you seem so...*" He hesitated, trying to find the words. "*You walk the Red Road. You are a Human Being.*" He stopped again, the look in his eyes faraway and pained. "*The color of your skin doesn't make a Human Being, it's what's in your heart.*"

Hanna had the strongest desire to climb into her father's lap and disappear back to a time when the whites hadn't taken so much. "*Ate, I know so little, I wish–*" She choked back a sob and couldn't continue.

Black Elk tilted his head toward Dunn. *"This man learned to be a Human Being. He learned when he was much older than you. He was John Dunn; then he became Leftook. He was both when our people needed him. You can also learn."*

"Hanna, our life here is an irony." Dunn said sadly. "Do you know what that means in English? The Sioux don't really have a word for it. *Kacha is* the closest word. In Sioux it means something really stupid or bad." Dunn pointed outside. "To the whites, our people are not human. They are seen as inferior, something to be rid of. But in here on the train, all of us, all the four colors of men live as equals. We all get paid the same and we are brothers. But only in here. The whites that buy the tickets to see us only see us as characters in a fantasy where they are the heroes, the conquerors. The true irony is that when we perform, we perform the famous battles where the cavalry defeats their Indians. We have to reenact these scenes for them every time we perform. Your people are only free when they're locked up in this traveling village."

Hanna looked around her angrily. "Count your blessings!" Hanna defiantly made eye contact with each of the men in her life. "That's what my Poppi told me. I was just a little girl when he died. My mother, I thought of her as my mother then, threw me away – put me on a train when I was eight. I spent the rest of my life until now in that horrible school." She smiled at Ben and took his hand. "But Ben was there with me. And now, I've found you. I could have been one of the girls at school who was the director's plaything, then was punished for having his baby. I'm here and I'm thankful!"

Black Elk smiled at his daughter sadly. "You are so much like your mother. You have her spirit, her sense of good. I am so glad I found you." He stood and kissed her on the cheek. "Its late. Promise me we'll have some time together tomorrow. We need to really get to know each other again."

While Hanna was in the bathroom, Ben pulled the two couches into a bed and spread out the blankets and fluffed the pillows. When she saw the bed, Hanna pulled Ben into an uncomfortable hug and held him tightly. Her belly was so huge that their arms almost didn't reach. Then she sighed in relief as she lay on her side. Ben lay beside her and protectively held her stomach with one hand.

"Ben." she said softly. Thank you. I love you. He kissed the back of her neck as she began to pray.

Look upon your children that they may face the winds and walk the good road to the Day of Quiet. Grandfather Great Spirit, fill us with light. Give us the strength to understand and the eyes to see. Teach us to walk the soft Earth as relatives to all.

Then, as she fell asleep, she said, "Kanj Coonshi taught me that prayer."

In the distance, she heard a sound. It was maybe a train whistle or the call of a hawk. Curious, she threw off the covers and climbed to the roof of her railroad car. The train was moving dangerously fast but the wind in her hair felt wonderful. She felt a sense of total freedom, release. The moonlight streamed through the trees as the train sped through the forest, strobing like lightning. She looked down at her body; her belly was flat and covered with feathers. She held her hands up and was amazed her feet ended in claws and her arms were wings. The train jerked hard to the left as it rounded a corner; the steel wheels shrieked and rumbled as all the cars struggled to remain upright. Her strong feet held on tightly as the train straightened again and gained speed on an impossibly long straightaway. The wind was stronger now, impossibly fierce. It whistled past her ears. She could hear the hiss as the wind passed over her wings. Tentatively, she lifted her wings and felt the immediate pull. She wanted to fly; she wanted freedom. She clung to the top of the rail car that held all that she loved, as somehow, if she remained, her family below would stay safe. Faster and faster the train went picking up speed as if the engine would explode from the manic energy it expended in its effort to reach some destination she could not quite see. The wind increased more and more and as it did, the temptation to fly free came closer and closer to overcoming her need to protect those that she loved. The desire to fly and the desire to shield her loved ones reached a tension so balanced that her perception of herself began to bleed away. Then, in the distance, she saw the impossible. A light was coming, the headlamp of another train approached on the track ahead. Both trains screamed their whistles at each other but neither slowed. The trains accelerated as if somehow the fastest would defeat the other in a mad race to nowhere. She extended her wings, hoping to somehow carry her loved ones out of danger but the weight of her responsibility was just too much. Closer and closer the trains came, barreling through the night, bent on single-minded destruction of the other. Then, when the inevitable came, when the huge locomotives touched and began to merge into flame and steam, her only perception was of her strong clawed feet holding useless metal. She awoke not knowing if she held or flew free.

Water

Corry, Pennsylvania Train Yard – July 1897

We are water. Water is life.
   Standing Rock Sioux

Hanna woke in a sweat. She was tangled up in blankets, feeling anxious. She tried to sit up but couldn't. Her body wouldn't work. She panicked then looked down at herself. Her swollen belly hid her legs. She'd forgotten how pregnant she was. She'd forgotten she was pregnant.

Hanna grunted as she rolled onto her side then pushed herself up to a sitting position. She smiled at Ben, amazed at how young he looked in sleep. She had always envied his ability to fall asleep anywhere, any time. It was like he had no problems, nothing to bother his ability to sleep the sleep of the innocent. It wasn't fair. She worried enough for both of them.

She swung her legs off the side of the narrow bed needing desperately to pee. She found the deerskin shift she'd been given by the wardrobe girls. She slid it over her head. Even in her discomfort, the almost manic need to make it to the bathroom at the end of the car and the nearly forty extra pounds that made her ache, the feel of the deerskin on her body gave her a frisson of delight. Just days before, she'd worn the horrid, itchy uniform from the Carlisle School. She could barely remember wearing anything else.

Hanna finished her toilet and smiled as she flushed. Technically, the train was not within the city proper so water on the tracks shouldn't bother anybody. But still she smiled. Her memories of her first train trip with Ben were still fresh.

Hanna stepped into the vestibule between hers and the next car and watched the sky lighten to morning. There was not any movement, no sound but something drew her eye. A solitary railroad signal pole sat between the tracks not far from her. Sitting on a strut was a hawk, looking directly at her.

A feeling of familiarity swept over her so strong she gasped. The hawk continued to watch her yet the sensation Hanna felt was as if she were in the presence of a person she knew and loved. The feeling was familiar, like a snatch of song or a smell that she just couldn't place. The more she stared the narrower her perception became. Hanna felt as if she was looking through a tunnel with the hawk as the only salient point in her perception. She tried to look away but couldn't. Then Hanna got the most real sensation. She felt that the hawk had smiled. But it was more. She received a feeling of love, acceptance and a peace in her heart that was nearly painful in its intensity.

She involuntarily sobbed and held out both her arms, palms extended toward this vision. She felt hugged and in return wanted to return the love that she felt. It was at that instant a breeze parted the branches of a tree. The hawk was bathed in light, backlit and transcendent.

This magnificent bird flew directly toward her and seemed to stop at eye level completely filling her consciousness. Its wings were outstretched, the tip of every feather flamed. This apparition formed both the symbol of the cross and the sacred hoop. With this vision burned into her memory, she knew nothing more until Ben found her, semiconscious on the floor between the cars.

"Hanna!" "Hanna!" Ben frantically called her name as he put his hands behind her head and gently shook her. Her hands were tightly clasped together against her chest. He pulled the fingers of one hand aside. Her black rock was clenched close to her heart.

"Wee Pea!" Ben was nearly hysterical as he shook her harder. "Suthung!" *"Happy Seed!"* he said again in Sioux.

Slowly, her eyes opened but there was no recognition there. Ben looked deep into those beautiful, familiar eyes and seemed to fall into infinity. Slowly, the person he knew and loved began reassemble, to swim back from a place he'd never been. "Ben?" Her voice was timid, full of wonder. "What? Where am I?"

He sat on the top step and pulled her up and held her. "Is the baby coming? Are you alright?" The worry in his voice and face was evident.

Hanna held out her rock and looked at the carving on its shiny surface. "She visited me. I was flying with her." Her voice was odd, dreamy. She gave Ben an unreadable look. "I was so happy, so complete." She looked around with a look as if she might cry.

"Who? You weren't flying. You passed out right between the cars. I was worried so I came looking for you and there you were, lying right here."

Hanna shuddered momentarily then took Ben's hands. "You were still asleep. I got up and went to the bathroom. Then, instead of waking you, I came here. The sun was coming up. It was so beautiful. Then, I saw her. A hawk. She looked at me for a long time. I felt like I knew her. Then she flew to me."

"She?" Ben looked at her questioningly.

"I could just tell. She felt like a woman, a friend but more. It felt like I've know her all my life but she was still a stranger." Hanna choked back a sob then continued. "We flew together. She showed me how. We flew to a place where I could see a line of women. The line went forever and somehow I knew they were my relatives, all the mothers in my line. They went from the past to the future. I could see my place in this line Ben. It felt like the hawk was my mother's spirit." She looked into his face then collapsed in sobs.

Ben held her as she cried herself out. Then Kanj Coonshi arrived.

"She make water?" The old woman looked intently at Ben.

He answered in Sioux. *Only her eyes. She had a dream or a vision.*

"I know! I feel!" She crooked one boney finger at Hanna and commanded, "Bring her family car!"

Ben stood and began to protest. "But, she –"

"LEHA'NJN!" (Now!) The tone of the old woman's voice and the look in her eyes left no doubt of her authority.

Ben helped Hanna to her feet then they followed Coonshi forward. Several of the women in attendance trailed behind.

The old woman led Hanna through two cars into what was known as the nursery car. She sat on the exact bench that had been her seat before.

Hanna smiled grimly at the memory. The old woman had pulled Hanna onto the seat next to her and presented her with a choice. In her heart, Hanna had chosen the stone.

Kanj Coonshi patted the seat next to her and Hanna sat with a grunt. *"Did your baby water come?"* The old woman's eyes glittered with intelligence and curiosity.

"No. I sometimes have contractions but no water has come."

Coonshi looked closely into Hanna's eyes. *"You had a visit from chanjska."* (Hawk – generic)

Hanna gasped. The look of surprise in her eyes would have seemed comic in another situation.

"I see her!" "You had a spirit visitor. I saw her, Upizica." (Red tailed hawk)

Hanna forgot her pregnancy in that moment. Instead, the memory of her experience seemed to burn deep inside her. She had images and feelings but no context in which to understand them. Hanna pulled out her rock and turned the side up with the carving. *"It was her!"* She fought for control then continued, *"I felt loved. She lifted me. She showed me things."*

Coonshi smiled gently and for an instant, Hanna could see the young woman behind the wrinkles, the beauty of her age. *"Tell me child. What did she show you?"*

"She flew to me then changed. She showed me the sacred hoop and the Christian cross together in one vision; they were the same. Then we flew over a river and beside it were many women. She told me without words that these women were my ancestors behind and my children and their children stretching out as far as I could see." Hanna looked to the old woman for answers but only got another question.

"Was there an opening in this line, a gap where you might stand?"

Hanna closed her eyes and pictured in her mind what she saw. She looked down and saw a space between all the women; they all were looking up, smiling. "*Yes!*" Hanna opened her eyes and with wonder, she repeated softly in English, "Yes."

"*Did this opening in the line have room for just you or could two women stand there?*" The old woman's eyes seemed even brighter.

Hanna's eyes shown with wonder. "*There was room for me and my mother to stand together.*"

Coonshi smiled, the meaning of her questions was clear. "*In the direction the river flowed, did the woman next to where you would stand seem familiar?*"

Hanna closed her eyes again and focused on her vision. "*She was beautiful but sad. Her face was unfamiliar but I recognized her spirit. I felt like I've known her all my life. Like my mother.*" Hanna sobbed these last three words.

The old woman took Hanna's hands in hers gently and said, "That is your daughter. You will have another child." Coonshi smiled. "I tell story." "*The river you saw is the river of life. Women make this water to bring Wakanisha to our world. The Great Spirit made this world with water and women make it to give birth. We create life with water and the Great Mystery. Listen child.*"

First, there was another world before the one we know. The people of that world did not cooperate with each other. This displeased the Great Spirit who set out to create a new world. He sang many songs to bring the rain. Each song brought stronger showers.

When the Great Spirit sang the fourth and most powerful song, the world split and water poured up through the many cracks and there was a flood. When the rain finally stopped, all the people and most of the animals had perished. Only Kangee the crow survived.

Kangee begged and begged the Great Spirit to create a place for him to rest because he was so tired of flying.

Then the Great Spirit decided the time had come to make his new world. He opened his bag where he kept his pipe herbs. The bag was so big it held all kinds of birds and animals. He called forth four animals he knew could hold their breath and stay under water for a long time.

The Great Spirit told these animals he needed mud from beneath the waters to make his new world.

Loon was first to dive deep into the dark water but it was not able to reach the bottom. Next, otter tried but even with its webbed feet and strong legs, he failed. Beaver used his powerful flat tail to dive deep but he returned with nothing.

Finally, the Great Spirit called turtle from his pipe bag and said, "Without mud, I cannot make a new world. You are the last and only hope. Do not fail!

Turtle dove deep and stayed under the cold waters so long that the other animals were sure he had drowned. But the Great Spirit had chosen well. There was a great splash and turtle came to the surface with mud in his claws and the spaces between his lower and upper shells.

With a joyous song, the Great Spirit took the mud and shaped it with his hands into a place on the water just big enough for him and crow to stand. He then took two great eagle feathers from his headdress and shook them over the mud until the mud spread wide, covering the water.

Then the Great Spirit felt lonely and cried tears that became the oceans, lakes and streams. He thanked the turtle and named the land after him. He took many animals from his huge pipe bag and spread them across the land.

The Great Spirit took red, white, black and yellow earth and made men and women. He gave the new people his sacred pipe and gave them his holy knowledge to live by. He even warned them by telling them about the fate that befell the people that came before.

The Great Spirit then told the people of his promise. He promised all living things that their lives would be good and happy as long as the four colors of men lived in harmony. He also promised that the world would be destroyed again if the people did not live in peace with each other.

Dichotomy
Corry, Pennsylvania Train Yard – July 1897

Change is the law of life. And those who look only to the past or present are certain to miss the future.
 John F. Kennedy

Slowly, Hanna came back to reality. The old woman's story had resonated in her spirit so directly that Hanna could visualize perfectly the world covered in water. Her own distant memory of Noah, the ark, and the way her adoptive father had told the Christian flood story meshed perfectly in Hanna's heart.

She had a brief bitter memory of Reverend Stitt's sermons. He vehemently believed that his version of faith was the only true way. Then a small sadness touched her as she realized that she had accepted both flood stories as metaphor. Her sorrow was for those whose narrow thinking kept them from grasping larger truths. To her, the flood was allegory for personal consequence of choice. "We are responsible for our own behaviors." she thought as she came back to the present.

Surprised, Hanna saw that a small crowd had gathered to hear Kanj Coonshi's story. The end of the nursery car where Coonshi always sat was nearly filled with people. Black Elk squatted in the aisle next to her and across the aisle was John Dunn. Two of the women Hanna recognized from the wardrobe car sat behind her. All four colors of humans were there listening raptly. Children and adults sat spellbound, the wonder of Coonshi's story showing in their faces.

There were murmurs of thanks and many there touched their hearts and smiled at Kanj Coonshi as they walked past her bench. She acknowledged each with a smile and a meaningful glance. But when Ben and Hanna stood to leave, the old woman touched Hanna's swollen belly and said, *"Your baby comes soon. He has a big spirit."* Then the old woman stood and looked intently at Black Elk. *"Teach this boy our ways. Tell him our stories. Help him find his spirit guide."* She smiled at Hanna and continued. *"Suthung has hawk to guide her, a powerful teacher. But this boy will be born with only this."* She gestured at the train car and the people in it. *"He will have only this owapanzo thipi, this traveling village to call home. He may never know what it is to be a true Human Being."*

Black Elk smiled sadly at her, glanced at Hanna and said, "With your help Mother, we will have Wakanisha in all things."

Ben helped Hanna down the aisle as they walked to their small stateroom in the sleeper car. Black Elk and John Dunn followed. There was pleasant chatter among themselves and those they passed. When they finally reached the stateroom, Ben helped Hanna to her seat then sat next to her. Dunn and Black Elk squeezed in and sat across from them.

There was a happy, contented silence between them for a few moments then Dunn asked, "May I see your stone?" The look on his face was hard to read; he looked both happy and mournful at the same time.

The stone was a common black piece of granite, scoured by glaciers and millennia of being rubbed smooth by rushing water. In geologic term the twenty-two years the rock had been carried by Human Beings was but the blink of an eye. But those twenty-two years represented a tectonic shift in the lives of men on the American continent. The time between the battle at Little Big Horn to the incident at Wounded Knee knelled the change in who was called master of The New World.

Hanna pulled the stone out of a simple pouch Ben had made her years before. It was warm to the touch. She placed it into the big man's hand with the etching of the hawk facing him.

"I was wearing a dirty cavalry uniform when your mother got this stone." Dunn said. "I was thirty and she was ten." He looked at Hanna with a look that was unreadable. "She was a child and I was a man, but she taught me what it means to be human." He rubbed his thumb over the hawk symbol engraved on it. "Kangee, the old Shaman who first gave your mother this stone told me once that Hawk flies above and can see our path; can see our future." He closed one huge hand over the stone, clasped his other hand over his closed fist and pressed his hands to his lips. He blew gently into his fists then opened them, holding the stone out before him. "I feel her. I feel like she's watching over us, guiding us." He placed the stone in Hanna's palm then gently squeezed her hand.

Hanna solemnly reached for her father's hands. When he reached out, she placed the stone there and in a soft, affectionate voice said, "*Ate.*"

Black Elk starred at the stone for a long time. He looked up into Hanna's eyes then down at the stone again. "*There were eight stones to begin with. You know the story. Your mother and I won them together. We were partners in a contest.*" He hesitated, a far away look in his eyes. "*What you don't know is that I carried these stones for two years. They were a heavy weight. I carried them during the Battle of Greasy Grass. I carried them when we were forced to live by the white man's rules. They were in my dreams of your mother that finally led me back to her. When I finally found her, she had also dreamed of me.*" Black Elk smiled sadly. "*When I gave her back her four stones, she just laughed then forgave me. She said yes to me even before I asked. We threw our stones in the river and were married. Kangee, the man that put us together as children married us.*"

"*Ate, why did you dive into the river after you had thrown the stones away? I thought the two of you did that together sort of like you were throwing away your past.*"

"She had three things she treasured. She had her mother's cooking stone. It's gone. She had a silver cross and a large knife given to her by the white woman that taught her to speak English." Those things are gone. This stone is the only thing that connects us to her."

"I have a little to add to this story." Ben said. "On her tenth birthday, I took her stone from under her pillow. A friend of mine carved the hawk on it. She was so sad that day. I didn't know that she thought it had been stolen. She was sobbing when I gave it to her, and then she was the happiest I've ever seen her." He smiled warmly at her and continued. "I think that's the day I started to love her. Not just as a friend but for her spirit." He reached across and took her hand.

The look on Black Elk's face was pained yet joyful when he said, "*Your mother was ten winters when I first loved her. I was angry with her because she made us win second place so she gave me the stones, her prize. She said, 'Your face tells me we are on different paths. Winning these stones was important to you. My prize was the laughter and friendship we shared. We both have our reward.' Then she turned and walked away. I didn't see her for two years.*"

"There are so many stories you should know." Dunn said. "Your mother taught me how to snare rabbits. I've cooked and eaten many a rabbit thanks to her."

"Speaking of eating, I think we missed lunch." Ben stood and stretched. "I'm going forward and I'll get us some sandwiches. Maybe I can find out if we're moving out today. I'll be right back." He gave Hanna a quick kiss and headed up the aisle. Instead of walking through the train, he exited the car and started walking along the tracks toward the dining car.

Black Elk began telling Hanna the famous story about Itunkala and the rattlesnake when Hanna looked out the window. Two cars up, a large group of young white men walked out of the trees and had surrounded Ben.

"Ate! Mr. Dunn! Look!" Dunn and Black Elk stood and joined Hanna at the window.

Both men hustled forward through the car calling to other men that were close at hand. Hanna could hear them gathering more men as they passed through the next car forward.

Hanna stood, horrified as she watched the group close in on Ben. She tried to open the window and shout his name but the window wouldn't budge. She began to cry as she banged on the window, calling his name.

Moments later, Dunn, her father and several other men from the train boiled out of the adjacent car. She watched helplessly as the two groups of men confronted each other with Ben the center point between these two lines of men.

Hanna was sobbing, watching helplessly when she felt a contraction and an odd sensation. Water poured down between her legs. She felt a momentary dizziness then another intense contraction. She sat, stunned, and began to realize that her baby had chosen this moment. Alone and terrified, she leaned back and began to pant.

Moments later or hours later, Hanna wasn't sure, Ben was beside her. He'd entered smiling, carrying a football and was talking about another game with the boys from town when he grasped what was happening. "I think the baby is coming!" he shouted down the aisle. "Somebody bring *Kanj Coonshi!*"

New Life
Corry, Pennsylvania Train Yard – July 1897

All women become like their mothers. That is their tragedy. No man does. That's his.
  Oscar Wilde

A baby is God's opinion that life should go on.
  Carl Sandburg

Years later, Hanna would realize that the birth of her first child went smoothly. That was her view in reflection. Her vision was perfect in hindsight and luckily pain can't be remembered. But on that day, Hanna did not have the luxury of hindsight; she had no mother to coach her or to reassure her.

Her labor began in terror, not for herself but for Ben. Even when Ben came in happy, laughing, ready for a game, her fear did not subside. Except for Ben, strangers surrounded her. Worse yet, Hanna had only her adoptive mother as a role model who made her question her own ability to be the mother she'd never really had.

Kanj Coonshi arrived minutes later during one of Hanna's intense contractions. Behind her several Sioux women followed the old woman. Two of them Hanna had met briefly but the others were complete strangers. "*Come child. We go into the forest for your baby.*" She looked at Hanna intently with one boney hand outstretched.

Hanna felt almost hallucinatory. She was aware of herself from two perspectives. Inside, she was terrified, in shock and pain with an old woman trying to take her away. She briefly remembered a story her Poppi had read to her about a witch with a poisoned apple. What she wanted most was privacy with Ben to hold her. But somehow he had been pushed to the back of what seemed like an impossible number of people crowded into her sleeping compartment.

Her other point of view was as if she were floating above herself observing the drama happening below her. Looking down, Hanna could be strangely objective. From that viewpoint she realized that the only person on the train she knew was Ben. The rest of this bizarre collection of people were strangers some of whom she'd met only days before. Even her father and the man she thought of as her uncle, John Dunn, were almost complete unknowns.

When Hanna didn't move, Kanj Coonshi pushed in closer to her and said, "*I will look, child.*" as the old woman reached for the hem of Hanna's shift.

Hanna was nearly feral with fear. Her eyes were huge as she pushed back against the spot where her bench and the wall met. The old woman reached again and Hanna scrabbled backwards as if she were attempting to climb the wall. She made eye contact with Ben who was peering around the corner. In her mind she screamed his name but it came out of her mouth as a whisper. "Ben!" she said again, the pain and fear so evident in her voice that the crowd stepped back.

None to gently Ben pulled and pushed until he was sitting next to Hanna; he held her with both arms while he glared at the gathered group. "The women want to take you into the forest for a traditional birthing." Ben's voice was at odds with his behavior. Outwardly, he was the physically aggressive, heroic Ben. But his voice trembled. Hanna could also see the fear in his eyes.

"Don't leave me – stay! Please?" Hanna whimpered then grunted loudly as another contraction took her. She resembled an animal in a trap. Nearly all rational thought had left her leaving only the need to escape.

"I'm here. I'm not going anywhere!" Ben put his hands on her shoulders and turned her to face him. "Hanna, please, I need you here with me!"

Gradually Hanna came into focus. Her eyes, instead of being jittery and blank, finally saw him. It was as if her spirit had fled then returned because he called her. "Who are these people?" she asked shakily. "Why can't we be alone?"

Ben was about to ask for privacy when the commotion in the aisle became even more chaotic. Black Elk pushed through the crowd and looked down at his daughter. The smile he gave her was more in his eyes than his expression. He touched his heart then began giving orders. "PhiláyA, please everybody go back to your space. We are a small village. You will know when we have a new member. Please?" He stood aside as the crowd subsided then he came in and sat next to Kanj Coonshi. "Please stay Grandmother. We need your wisdom."

"Breathe child. Breathe deep and feel The Great Mystery." The old woman sat across from Hanna. The tone of her voice became less insistent and more calming. She put her gnarled hands in her lap and leaned forward. "This is a sacred time. Your baby wants to come to meet you. Try to remember this day – hold these memories in your heart. Then, you can tell your son his story when he is ready, the story of his birth."

Another contraction gripped Hanna. From the expression on her face to her feet, the physical effects seemed total. She groaned as her whole body reacted to the clenching within her. The old woman's words didn't seem to have any result on Hanna's mental state. Her eyes still looked ferine and terrified.

"Child, these contractions will get closer and closer together until your baby comes. Breathe. Be strong and find peace. As we wait together, tell us your birth story. It will help you understand your place in The Great Mystery."

"I have no story!" Outwardly, Hanna's expression didn't really change - the fear that had poured out of her changed to anger. "I know only what my Poppi, the white man who raised me knew. My Ate has told me some and Leftook, my leski' (uncle) told my white family some." Hanna sobbed bitterly. "My story! White soldiers killed my mother. I was separated from my tribe and given to whites. I grew up with red skin in a white town that hated me. Here strangers surround me and you want me to be at peace. She glared around her. "Thunkashila, where are you?"

Suddenly, the doorway was filled with John Dunn. His face was a mask of pain. It was obvious that he had been in the aisle listening but not wanting to intrude until now. "We called you

Happy Seed. You were a happy baby. But never think that you are the only one who feels pain. I was there when you were born. I took the life of the man who killed your mother." The big man struggled to control his voice. *"But never think that Thunkashila, our God, is not there. None of us knows His plan but think of this miracle. Somehow, you found your way back to your family. You must believe that there is something in the sacred hoop of life, some thing you are going to do that will make this world better."* Dunn stopped, looked at Black Elk then continued. *"You do have a story. To give life, to be a mother is the most important thing any Human Being can do."* Dunn sat in the aisle across from the door and gave Hanna a faint smile.

As another contraction racked Hanna, Black Elk stood and took her hands. The two looked into each other's eyes as the intensity and pain nearly swept her away. Yet something in his spirit calmed her, connected her to a larger picture that she was just beginning to grasp. *"Daughter, we were separated when you were just a baby and you grew up with the whites. But we were never truly split apart. I dreamed of you, had visions. Somehow, you walked the Red Road always. I could feel you. And perhaps, if you look deep in your heart, you will remember dreams of us together."*

The sound of the door opening at the front of the car went unnoticed until Dunn stood and cleared his throat. "Hey Boss! You heard?" Dunn stepped aside as Abe Hubert stuck his head into the compartment.

Hubert stood in the doorway, put his hands on his hips and smiled down at Hanna. "Your story has spread through both trains. It's amazing! I wish we could work it into the show somehow. Great stuff! Make the women weep!" He laughed. "Seriously, Mr. Cody, Arizona Jim, Miss Oakley are all talking about you. They want to visit you after the baby comes if it's all right with you. Miss Oakley says she has the perfect gift for your baby, if it's a boy." He winked at Hanna and smiled again. "Oh by the way, your idea about having the porters arrange our food supply is working out great. You've saved us lots of money. When you're feeling like it, I want you back helping me with the books." He turned to go then stepped back. "Good news – bad news. The mess up ahead of us is being cleared away. We might be moving out later today or maybe early tomorrow." Then he was gone; his tuneless whistling was cut off mid-stanza when the door closed behind him.

Kanj Coonshi stood and addressed Hanna. "*I go with the women. We will make a place for you to have baby.*" She turned to leave.

Instantly, the terror returned to Hanna's eyes. "Ben, Ate – I'm afraid. I don't know anybody. I want to be here with you."

"*No men! The women will help you bring this baby.*"

Black Elk nodded and briefly made eye contact with the old woman. "*Suthung that is how you were born. The women took your mother away from the village. They made a lean-to and built a fire. Our old traditions go back thousands of winters.*"

"I don't think I want to do this anymore. I just want to go home." Hanna looked from face to face. Her panic was obvious. "Ben, can we just –" An intense contraction squeezed her rigid. Her words became a sustained grunt as the air in her lungs was involuntarily forced out of her. When the contraction released her, Hanna's head fell back against the seat. "Momma!" she whispered but in her heart, it was a scream, a plea, a primal call for help that would never come.

For Hanna, the following hours or days was like a delirium, at times a fantasy and others a nightmare. The contractions came closer and closer together much like huge waves pounding a beach. She vaguely remembered people around her arguing – outside – inside. The old woman told her to hold her black rock and do what the spirit said to do. There were moments of peace between contractions when no one spoke then at other times sharp words were spoken about tradition and the old ways. People came and went, sometimes speaking Sioux and others speaking English. The words and their meanings melded into background noise as the contractions became almost non-stop. She had a vague memory of Ben yelling at somebody then feeling claustrophobic. There were too many voices, too many people all unhappy with each other.

She had a distorted memory of holding her rock in one hand and pulling herself to a standing position with the other. The faces around her were shocked as she pushed through the crowd and stumbled down the aisle. She was barely aware of her clothing being removed. Then there was nothing but pain, pressure – a roaring in her ears and more pain. At last, there was one last pressure so intense it seemed there was nothing else.

Her next perception came when a woman she didn't know placed a baby in her arms. Her hands shook as she took the baby. She was dimly aware of her nakedness. She had a blanket around her shoulders and many blankets under her. She looked at the child in wonder then noticed she was squatting in the vestibule between cars, her back against a wall. There were people in both doorways and on the ground looking up the stairs at her smiling.

A child! Her child! He made a noise like a murmur but inquisitive. He moved his head back and forth, listening, searching. He instinctively put his mouth to her chest, close to her left breast, near her heart. She smiled almost involuntarily then reached down and touched his cheek. He turned, took the tip of her finger in his mouth and looked up at her.

Hanna experienced an instant sense of tunnel vision but more. It was as if her entire being focused on the eyes of her son. Her son! The words took on layers upon layers of meaning. She seemed to fall into his eyes. There was a tingling where her skin touched his like a mild electric shock, like there was no barrier between her spirit and his. She knew in that moment a love like she'd never known. It was fierce and tender, completely encompassing yet forgiving in the sense she knew she would have to release him someday.

She felt Ben's presence and looked up. He stood above her smiling with his hands extended. He helped her stand then hugged her with their baby; their son safely huddled between them.

Reluctantly, Hanna gave the baby to Ben to hold. Instead of cradling him like she expected, Ben examined the baby closely. Then, he held the baby close and said, "He's perfect. Thank you."

Hanna had no experience in her life to prepare her for this moment. Her instinct told her take the baby to a safe, quiet spot and let him nuzzle her, but Ben was the proud father.

Ben held the baby as Black Elk and John Dunn made very unmanly noises. They both were completely lost in the experience as was Ben. Ben finally saw the look in Black Elk's eyes and passed the baby to his grandfather. Black Elk cried briefly then passed the baby to Dunn who was just as proud, just as happy as if the child was of his blood. Then Kanj Coonshi presented the baby to the many women there that had helped with the birth.

And with each new person handling or fussing over the baby, the more Hanna became possessive and upset. The old woman seemed to hold the baby forever. Hanna was torn between respecting the old woman's authority and her own need to hold her son. Finally, when the baby began fretting, looking for the milk he sensed was somewhere and the heartbeat he knew, Hanna could stand it no longer. She demanded the baby be returned with more force and less respect than she intended.

The old woman relinquished the baby then commanded, "*Iron Eagle, take your family to your spot.*" She smiled knowingly. "*Your bebela (baby) needs milk.*"

Their sleeping compartment was blessedly empty. Hanna sat with the baby and Ben wrapped them with a blanket, but the baby continued to fuss then cry. He wouldn't take Hanna's nipple or even her finger again. The more upset the baby became, the more Hanna began to worry.

Hanna looked over at Ben and saw that he also was upset. Soon, the cycle reached a point where Hanna was in tears, Ben was pacing and the baby cried non-stop.

Without knocking, Kanj Coonshi entered and held out her arms. Hanna handed the baby to the old woman and the baby stopped crying immediately. "*Suthung, hold him close. Kiss his belly. Listen to his heart. He wants you to know him.*" She handed the baby back to Hanna, smiled and nodded her head.

The baby began to fret the instant Hanna held him but she lowered her lips to his stomach and kissed him. She put her ear to his chest and listened to his tiny heartbeat so fast and so sure. Then a warm feeling seemed to wash over them. A holy calmness flowed between them.

Kanj Coonshi stood beside Hanna and began to rub her temples and softly pull her fingernails through Hanna's hair. For an instant, Hanna felt irritated at the intrusion in this private moment then powerful feelings swept through her. The intimate contact made Hanna feel mothered, cared for, protected. Then, as Hanna's perception of the baby she held intensified, she also could picture generations of women caring for each other. She dimly saw a linage of women together; aunties, grandmothers and sisters all pouring their love into a single child, yet all the children that ever were.

Hanna lowered her child to her left breast and immediately the baby took her into his mouth and began to suck hungrily. The connection between the two was almost painful in its intensity. She gasped at the love that she felt and when the baby looked up and seemed to smile, she nearly lost contact with the present. Her disconnect from reality was nearly as intense as when she and Ben completely lost themselves in each other. It was then that she saw herself in the dream. She stood in the great-unbroken line with her mother behind her and her mother behind her and in front, the Wakanisha of their future.

Childhood
On the rails toward Erie, Pennsylvania – July, 1897

Children reinvent your world for you.
  Susan Sarandon

As the sun set on yet another extraordinary day Hanna was barely aware of the changes within her. People came and went. Kind comments were spoken from the door of their sleeping compartment. News updates about the movements of trains were discussed. Hanna heard the voices, saw the people but she felt isolated like she, Ben and the baby were shielded inside a warm bubble of love and protection. For her, little else mattered.

The locomotive called out its familiar, two shorts, one long and one short blast on the steam whistle. Like a restless animal, it had set idle too long and called for its passengers to return. The engineer and the fireman worked, stoking the boiler, building steam because the track in front was to be cleared within the hour. Levers were thrown, the throttle pulled softly and the engine gently tugged all its cars, taking up slack. The noisy tug of the cars further informed performers and crew that departure was imminent.

Ben and Hanna sat on one bench together. Their shoulders touched, her head rested on his shoulder. And between them the new baby slept contentedly. The feelings were so intimate, their contact so complete it was as if they were a single being. When the train jerked the baby awoke and gazed up at them with a look of trust and concern. Ben and Hanna saw their baby's expression, smiled reassuringly then smiled at each other with a look of almost sublime contentment.

From the inside, neither one of them realized what a profound shift had happened to the way they viewed their world. Whether some evolutionary button had been pushed or the Great Spirit commanded them to protect this new life, both Hanna and Ben accepted this responsibility with no awareness of the change. It was as if the moment both of them saw their child, their own childhoods ended.

Hanna glanced up when a soft knock came from their closed stateroom door. One of the kitchen porters stood outside, two brown paper bags in his hands. She didn't know the man's name yet, but he had treated her very kindly every time she had passed through the dining cars. She smiled up at the porter and with a slight toss of her head she gave him a wordless permission to enter.

"You's missed dinner Miss Hanna. Thought you could use some vittles after bringin' this here baby to us." He stepped in and grinned down at the baby. "Fine lookin' little chap! Whole train be talkin' bout him." The porter set the bags on the bench across from them and said, "These a couple ham sandwiches and some cinnamon buns we batched together for breakfast. When my Misses had her babes, she be powerful hungry after. We wants you to keep strong, Miss Hanna." He touched the brim of his hat and stepped into the aisle.

"Thank you –" Hanna said, the tone of her voice made it obvious she didn't know the man's name.

"Amos mam. Folks just call me Amos."

"Thank you, Amos. Everybody has been so kind to us. We feel like we have a family here."

"You be welcome, Miss Hanna." Amos then spoke to Ben. "If you's comes with me, I think I can scare up a sleepin' basket and some soft little blankets for your youngen. You be wantin' some nappies too. When we gets back, I'll make up the bed."

Ben touched the baby on the cheek, smiled briefly at Hanna and was gone.

Hanna experienced a brief emotional vacuum when Ben left. She sighed knowing that the world would intrude but these past moments had seemed perfect. Then the sweet cinnamon smell reached her and she looked down at the two bags. One of them bulged and had a grease stain seeping through the paper. Suddenly, Hanna was ravenous – even hungrier that she'd ever been at school She put the sleeping baby down and reached for a bag.

When Ben and Amos returned a few minutes later, Ben gasped and Amos laughed good heartedly. The baby was asleep on the bench next to Hanna. Both bags were ripped open. One cinnamon roll was gone as was one of the huge ham sandwiches. Hanna was nearly half finished with the second sandwich.

Ben put his hands on his hips and looked down at Hanna. He was slightly irritated. He'd expected to share a meal. It was at that moment that Ben felt a change in Hanna. He saw that she was embarrassed, but there was more. It wasn't defiance, not exactly. That wasn't Hanna. For an instant, there was an almost animalistic look in her eyes, fierce and protective. The message that Ben received was not cognitive or even emotional but at almost a cellular level. He sensed that the new baby had replaced him as the primary focus of her love.

In the hallway behind Ben stood Amos, quietly observing. He cleared his throat and stepped into the stateroom between them. "Miss Hanna. This here's the basket I tole you about. Baby can sleep here and you can carry him from place to place. Why don't you go to the bathroom and clean up – check the baby's diaper while Mr. Ben and I make up the bed?" He gave them both a sad, knowing look and began pulling bedding out of the overhead cabinet.

Ben stood in the aisle and marveled at the efficiency in which Amos transformed their cabin. The benches were converted into a bed near the window and sheets, blankets and pillows were put in place with sure, practiced hands.

Amos snapped the overhead cabinet doors shut, stepped into the hallway and with a flourish and a smile, held his hand out, palm up and pointed to the finished bedroom. But when Ben started to enter the stateroom, Amos stopped him with a hand on Ben's shoulder. "Boy! You's got a choice to make. I know it seems like she's maybe takin' the baby over you. You'll feel the change – just know she still loves you. But you gotta share. That boy needs his daddy and in a year or two, he's gonna make you real proud. You gotta share her! Got it?" For a moment, the older porter looked much more like a dominant father. Then Hanna reappeared.

"Miss Hanna. Bed's made up." Amos smiled nodded to her graciously then said without a hint of a smile, "Can I bring ya'll some dinner befores you turn in?"

Ben and Hanna shared an embarrassed look while Amos smiled indulgently.

"I can make up a nice roast beef or ham sandwich for ya'll – still have some fresh cinnamon buns. Have a bit of that stew Mr. Hubert likes if ya'll want that. And Miss Hanna, my Missus always had a bottle of beer when she was nursing our kids. You be eatin for two now so just let me know what ya'll want."

Hanna was barely aware of the long pull on the train whistle, the loud "BOARD" called out by the conductor and the jerk as the train began to move. The sleeping basket was under the bed and their child was snuggled between them. The sound of the rails beneath the floor was like a lullaby as the new family drifted into a blissful sleep. Hanna lay on her side, both arms and her forehead cradling the baby. Ben had one arm over Hanna and his chin rested on the top of her head.

The rhythmic pulsing of the steel wheels over tracks becomes drumming. She is aware of dancers moving around a fire. A lovely soprano chants songs in Sioux, songs of family and children. She feels the warmth and connectedness of thousands of generations; they are there with her in an unbroken line. She does not question her perspective; she sees far into the past. The line of women stretches to infinity to a place where her ancestors recede to an invisible point but she can see each face, feel each heart beat, know each story.

Behind Hanna stands her mother Itunkala, familiar and fierce, dressed in the red feathers of a hawk. With her are her mother and two aunties. They smile and love her with approval. One is dressed as a buffalo, strong and determined. The other is a meadowlark, mournful but beautiful. Hanna looks further back and sees her family back through the ice and sun to another continent.

She feels warmth and a feeling as familiar as her mother's womb. Beside her, one on each side, her children lean against her. Hanna's daughter looks up, laughing. She is happy, attentive, very much connected. She is dressed in the clothing of the whites but beneath, Hanna can see, can feel the spirit totem of a butterfly in this girl. Hanna feels the girl's spirit and knows she will follow, will hold the lineage of family. Hanna's son is also happy; he is also dressed in the cloth of the whites but he does not look at her. He looks away; his spirit seems subdued and divided. Beneath, Hanna senses his totem as otter: laughter - changeable, but too trusting.

Hanna follows the boy's gaze into the future. She sees women, the descendants of her daughter also dressed in the clothing of the whites for a few generations. Then there is an unbroken line of women dressed in the beautiful skins of animals each decorated in beadwork with pride and love. When she looks back, her son is gone.

Hanna experiences a stab of pain and loneliness. She looks for her son only to see the unbroken prairie. Her perceptions change. The colors become monochromatic yet her vision is sharp, perfect. She looks down and sees her forearms, strong, covered in dense spotted fur. Her color blends with the shades of the surrounding prairie. She flexes her hands and powerful claws emerge from their protective sheaths. Silently, she kneads the damp prairie soil under her feeling the intimate connection to the earth that feeds her, feeds all of creation.

She pauses a moment to give thanks for her existence. She is exquisitely tuned for this life she lives. The tufts at the end of each ear sense exactly the shifts of wind; the air brings her the scent of her prey. She hears movements in the rabbit's warren. Her hearing is so acute she senses that a doe and many kits are in the underground shelter. Hanna can even hear the many heartbeats, one of which she will silence when she feeds. But feed she must. Her kittens wait for the life giving flesh she will bring to them.

She tenses! Each of her senses tells her it is time. The rabbit smell fills her consciousness. She hears movement. Ears long and brown emerge slowly from the hole, turning listening for any threat. She tightens every muscle, firmly places the pads of her feet into the soil, claws extended for maximum traction. She computes the attack route and is poised to spring, to tear the throat, drink the sweet, life giving blood.

The mother rabbit looks her way. Hanna is coiled to spring only waiting for the rabbit's attention to vary. She stills her breathing; her heart almost stops. She waits. Then, an explosion of feathers and talons pulls the rabbit clear of its lair. The rabbit shudders, kicks then lays still. The red tailed hawk stands atop the rabbit, talons through the rabbit's neck.

The hawk lowers its head as if in thanks then looks directly into Hanna's eyes. There are no words, only primal understanding. "I care for you still." Then, the hawk is gone, crying shrilly overhead.

Hanna returns to her natal den, an abandoned badger hole. She places the rabbit carcass on the ground near the opening and calls softly for her two kittens. As they watch she eviscerates the rabbit, eats a small bite of liver then moves away for her children to feed. She purrs loudly as she watches her children partake in the sacred hoop.

Something more primal than sound or movement awakened Hanna. Her child awoke and nuzzled her chest. In the darkness, Hanna saw the gleam of his eyes. She uncovered her breast and held her son to her. He looked up once again then began to nurse. The sensation was both familiar yet new and exquisite; the pleasure and pain so intense Hanna gripped the railing with her free hand to connect her to her current reality. Then the memory of her dream entered her consciousness full force. She saw, she felt, she knew that she was not alone.

Victory or Massacre, Truth or Fiction
Erie, Pennsylvania - July 10 and 11, 1897

Indians contemplating a battle, either offensive or defensive, are always anxious to have their women and children removed from all danger...For this reason I decided to locate our [military] camp as close as convenient to [Chief Black Kettle's Cheyenne] village, knowing that the close proximity of their women and children, and their necessary exposure in case of conflict, would operate as a powerful argument in favor of peace, when the question of peace or war came to be discussed.
   My Life on the Plains (1874)
   Lt. Colonel George A. Custer

Every June 25th we gather to commemorate the Battle of Greasy Grass when Custer wore an arrow shirt.
   Debra White Plume
   Lakota Sioux Activist

The first attack came from the south. John Dunn, playing the part of Major Marcus Reno, led a squad of cavalry toward the Sioux encampment at full gallop firing indiscriminately. There were loud cheers from the crowd of ticket holders as the first Indians in the village succumbed to the withering fire.

Another cheer went up when General George Custer led another squad of men and attacked the Sioux village from the rear. The cavalry circled the many tipis firing at braves, women and children as the Indians stepped from inside their homes.

Then, as if the crowd of spectators expected it, a large number of Sioux warriors in vivid war paint appeared in the battle. Simultaneously, scores of warriors, women and children appeared from the tipis all carrying weapons.

The battle raged. Sioux braves shot from below their ponies' bellies. Trick riders did cartwheels jumping on and off their horses. A cavalry officer stood on horse back at a full gallop, firing at the Indians. Hand-to-hand combat broke out. It was swords against tomahawks – arrows against the famous Colt 45's.

General Custer seemed to be everywhere at once, firing from the back of Comanche, his favorite horse. His blonde hair flashed in the sun. When his first pistol ran out of ammunition, he threw it dramatically and pulled the second. Custer fired his second pistol until empty, clubbed a young brave with it and then drew his sabre.

By ones and twos, the soldiers fell, dying with great drama. General Custer fought on alone until he was completely surrounded. The throaty cheers from the audience seemed to keep him energized and on horseback. Finally, he was pulled down from his horse but still he fought on. The buckskin shirt he wore was cleverly made. Spring-loaded arrows seemed to appear in his chest. And with each arrow strike, the great man would stumble then fight on.

Then a hush fell across the battlefield. The audience let out a collective gasp. Slowly and with great grandeur, Sitting Bull strode across the killing field. He walked directly to General Custer who was held from behind by many braves.

General Custer appeared nearly dead but when Sitting Bull approached, the great general stood tall and defiantly thrust out his chest in a show of bravery and masculinity.

Very slowly, Sitting Bull pulled out his knife and held it poised to strike. Then, as the warriors cried out in joy and the audience wailed in protest, Sitting Bull stabbed Custer with a downward stroke of his knife. Custer fell.

The warriors swarmed around tight to this scene, hiding Custer's body from the audience. Then, Sitting Bull leaned in, and there was a great cry from the warriors as Sitting Bull waved the blonde wig above his head.

As the audience surged to their feet and booed and hissed loudly, the entire troupe, cavalry and Indians alike returned to life. They stood, faced the audience and bowed to both catcalls and bravos.

Always the consummate showman, William Fredrick Cody appeared on his famous white horse Isham. Wild Bill had waited behind the tipis until the troupe had taken their bows. Then, with perfect timing, Cody rode toward the audience just as the applause for act one died down.

The crowd from Erie and its environs surged to their feet in esteem. The cheers and whistles were louder than the howls of protest they'd made when witnessing perhaps the worst defeat the American military would ever experience.

Cody sat on Isham and projected both humility and dominance as the adoration of the crowd washed over him. He let the audience have their way with him until the adulation was just about to climax. Then, with a single hand in the air palm facing the crowd, he tamed them with an act of will. "Ladies and gentlemen!" he said and stood in the saddle.

The entire crowd sat compliantly with their hands in their laps as if they were a kindergarten class waiting for birthday cookies. The Erie fair grounds were so quiet that one could hear the call of a meadowlark from a mile away.

"This afternoon, you witnessed the reenactment of a great American tragedy. The Battle of Little Big Horn will appear in the history of this great country for the ages to come." Cody paused dramatically and made eye contact with the crowd. Many there felt as if the great man was speaking directly to them. "Tell your children what you saw here today so that a calamity such as what you witnessed will never, ever happen again!"

While Cody was mesmerizing the crowd, the troupe of players, their horses and gear were all being moved toward the train to make room for the next acts.

"Before the amazing Miss Annie Oakley and her sharpshooter husband Frank Butler come out…" The crowd began to cheer but quieted obediently when Cody held up his hand again. "Yes, Miss Oakley is up next, but let me first invite you to join us tomorrow afternoon when we present an American victory oft misunderstood and certainly worthy of your consideration – The Battle of Washita River." A wild cheer went up from the crowd then Cody yelled over the audience, "Ladies and Gentlemen, Miss Annie Oakley!"

Black Elk and Dunn almost always spoke in Sioux during these moments. For reasons neither could explain, they both felt was easier to question their existence in a language that had a better vocabulary to define it.

Their practice of not speaking English around locals began years ago. Curious town folk always snuck into the venue and waited on the grounds near the train. For these *Hoksika*, immature people or children as Dunn and Black Elk called them, waited and watched from the troupe's staging areas rather than experience the show. They were mostly curious but also usually a bit rougher than the gentile town folks that paid full admission. These intruders normally fell into one or more of three types: they were trouble-makers and wanted to heckle or steal, they were curious and needed to talk or they that wanted to join up. Black Elk and Dunn found that by talking in Sioux, these *Hoksika* let them be.

Dunn and Black Elk walked slowly for they were in no hurry. Their horses plodded along behind them contentedly without a shred of existential dread. The horses, unlike humans, were happy and satisfied when their needs were met.

"*Wichowe,* (brother) *do you think Cody walks the Red Road?*" Black Elk looked over at Dunn. "*He makes his speeches to the Wasicu* (white people) *but his words mean two things. They hear him and think he honors them but his words also honor The People.*"

"*The Naca* (chief, boss) *is a strange man. I have talked with him many times but he hides his spirit. Maybe he reveals himself to his friends but with me, he is the man on the poster – Buffalo Bill the famous showman.*" Dunn glanced at Black Elk and shook his head. "*I think he may prefer to believe this fiction we live.*"

"Tomorrow we do Washita." Dunn said bitterly in English. "Sometimes I wish I had the honor of killing Custer myself."

The two men walked together in silence, lost in thought.

"Mind if I join you two?" Both men had been dream walking, thinking of spending time with Hanna and the baby when Ben walked between them. "Quite the show!"

Hanna, her father, Ben and Dunn began the evening after the show by sitting in the fading light talking and enjoying each other's company. They all sat in wooden folding chairs in the meadow near the train. They took turns holding the baby until he began to fuss. Hanna covered herself and nursed the baby and the easy conversation continued. But when Ben commented on the Wild West Show and its depiction of Little Big Horn, Black Elk gently tried to change the subject.

"But Ate', what you are doing is important. The people need to know their history. My teacher read to us out of an old newspaper. I remember feeling ashamed to be an Indian – the newspaper story said the Indians massacred all the soldiers."

"Hanna, there is much of your history you don't know." Dunn blurted out; he then glanced nervously at Black Elk, hoping he hadn't intruded into the conversation.

Black Elk smiled sadly. *"Listen to Leftook. He knows the history of our people and the whites."*

"Hanna, your mother was ten when I came to live with the people." Dunn paused as if to collect his thoughts. "She lived the truth. I learned to be a human being from her." He paused again, looked at his friend Black Elk in a way that all there could see the pain on his face.

"Your mother was born in the early spring after a very bitter winter. Just before she was born, soldiers came to a camp very near hers and killed many Indians that were there. The chief of that camp was Black Kettle, a very respected and wise Cheyenne. He and his people were camped where the cavalry told them to be. He even had a white flag and an American flag flying from his tipi. The soldiers killed many of them anyway. Some of the survivors pledged their lives to defeat the whites – those went to join with Crazy Horse and Sitting Bull. It was the massacre at Sand Creek that set up the Battle of Greasy Grass, Little Big Horn." Dunn made eye contact briefly with Black Elk then looked directly at Hanna. "Your father knows the true history. He has lived it. He fought at Little Big Horn."

The sadness on her father's face penetrated a little deeper into Hanna's understanding of the human suffering her people had endured. She looked between these two men she'd just met and was about to speak when their conversation was interrupted.

Two men from the show walked past and stopped to say hello. The two were so different the contrast was almost shocking. Both were about the same height but one thin and wiry with coppery red skin and long black hair tied into a single thick strand down his back. The other man was fair skinned, blonde and very broad. His enormous head framed a large flat nose, and prominent ridges above deep set eyes.

Dunn shook the men's hands and introduced them. "Great show today guys. Hanna, I'd like you to meet Morty Wiseman and Standing Wolf – Sitting Bull and General Custer." Dunn smiled again at Hanna's expression.

The two men made pleasant small talk for a few moments, excused themselves and walked on.

Hanna was wide-eyed and still processing when Ben entered the conversation. "If I was part of the show, could I play the part of a white person?"

"I usually play the part of a military type because I was in the cavalry in another life." Dunn answered. "We're very tribal about who does what – the best person for the job does the job. But yes, it is ironic. A white man plays Sitting Bull and a Human Being plays Custer."

He turned and spoke to Hanna. "The audience sees what it wants to see. This is fiction – make believe. We're no better than the newspapers. The headlines called Little Big Horn a massacre and the horror that happened at the Washita River a victorious battle. It's just a matter of which side you're on as to which words fit. They say that history is written by the victors."

"But many white people are honorable. My Poppi..."

"Hanna, excuse me for interrupting but you should know about the make-believe we present to the whites." The pained look on Dunn's face made Hanna almost look away. "There is so much of your people's history that you don't know." The sadness in his eyes was almost unbearable. "And much of what you've been taught is not true." Dunn opened a folding chair, sat down next to Hanna and began to speak.

"Black Kettle, like many of the other chiefs, realized that fighting the whites was futile. Even after his people were butchered at Sand Creek, he went to the government again and asked where his remaining people could live in peace. They were sent to the Washita River in Oklahoma." Dunn stopped for a moment, grimaced and continued. "Custer and his troops attacked and killed most of Black Kettle's tribe including the chief and his wife. They were shot in the back trying to escape. It was Custer and his men that discovered gold in the sacred Black Hills on the land given to your people forever. It was this greed for gold that brought thousands of whites onto the reservation. Not only did the government not stop this, they finally broke up the land and gave much of it to the whites."

Hanna looked stricken. "And tomorrow, you have to pretend that Custer and his men were heroes?"

Dissonance
On the tracks west of Erie, Pennsylvania - July 11, 1897

How often it is that the angry man rages denial of what his inner self is telling him.
   Frank Herbert

The rightful claim to dissent is an existential right of the individual.
   Friedrich Durrenmatt

Dunn's horse Kangee nickered happily when the big man returned to the stock car. He rubbed the horse affectionately then lay on his usual hay bale surrounded by the familiar. The sweet aroma of dried grass mixed with the smell of horse failed to calm him as it usually did. His prized collection of Twain's short stories lay on his chest, unopened. Even the gentle rocking of the train and the occasional whiff of coal smoke through the open window did nothing to ease his angst.

For some reason he couldn't quite explain, reenacting the Washita River Battle completely unsettled him. Dunn knew the show was fiction. He knew it was meant to entertain and instruct. He couldn't quite get his head around the idea - he could feel that his subconscious was about to present him with an uncomfortable truth.

He was glad he was alone. Had there been anybody with him, they would have thought John Dunn was in a foul mood and they would have been right. But what he showed outwardly didn't begin to touch the inner pain that had flooded to the surface. He was much too far into examining his self to even suspect that the appearance of Happy Seed and a new baby had forced his past into his here and now.

Schizophrenia was not a word that Dunn considered as he looked back at his life. It would have been far easier to blame his pain on that flaw, on some outside source rather than face the choices he'd made.

Dunn had played heroes and villains in the years he'd been with the Wild West Show. He also realized that perspective – hero or villain - were dependent on which side of the conflict you were on. It was, after all, conflict that made history. And the audience loved to witness reenactments of historic events. He'd worn the grey of the Confederacy and the blue of the Union. In the South, the audiences loved to watch battles like Brice's Crossroads or Bull Run. For Northerners, Gettysburg was a favorite. Dunn had played soldiers from both sides and had never given much thought to the job he did. What was most important to him for years was that he belonged to a group, a tribe.

It was a lie! The abstraction that had been swimming just below the surface of his consciousness for years struck him like a hammer blow, like a knife in the heart. The life he'd lived with Cody's Wild West Show was a falsehood.

"No, not completely!" Dunn rationalized. "The relationships, the tribe I belong to are real." Then the image of the tracks, the narrow ribbon of steel that defined and narrowed his existence forced itself into his rationalization. "I work for a white man that entertains white men with stories from the past – stories that are not true." he thought bitterly.

He had never needed to lie to Itunkala, Little Mouse. It was her hugeness of spirit and her total forgiveness – total acceptance that helped the man John Dunn become Leftook, the human being. He had been John Dunn the Quaker who compromised his beliefs and went to war. He had been Lt. John Dunn who lost his altruistic principles and committed atrocities. Then he had become Leftook, the Human Being, a place and time where he'd been fully alive, happy.

Dunn compared his life to a trajectory - it was as if his spirit had been fired into the air like an arrow. When his family had been massacred on the Kansas prairie so many years ago, when Itunkala had her life extinguished by a single bullet, the trajectory of his life reached its peak then began to fall. Spoon Woman, his mate, had fallen with him for a while.

There was a lot of lively conversation in the dining cars as there usually was after a show. All the tables were full and more people streamed through to the second dining car; it was set up buffet style.

Amos worked his usual magic. He had a friendly word for everybody as they passed through. He bussed tables – he served food, took orders and when need be, moved folks along.

When Ben opened the door to the dining car and Hanna walked in, holding the baby, conversation ceased briefly replaced by a collective "Aw!" Black Elk followed them in with a proud smile on his face.

"Why Miss Hanna! It be good seein you up and around." Amos gave her a gracious smile and at the same time, he rapped his knuckles on a table where several performers were lingering over their coffee. "Come on over. These gentlemen just be leaving. Right!" He gave the four men a look that could only be described as the expression a father would give his sons who were late finishing their chores. Within seconds, the table had been cleared, wiped clean and Amos pulled out one chair for Hanna with a flourish.

Before she sat, Hanna gave Amos a one handed hug and a peck on the cheek before she sat down. "Amos, thank you again for the food you brought me. It was the best meal I can ever remember." Before Amos could comment, Hanna continued. "I mean it. I spent over ten years at the Carlisle School - the meals were awful! Those sandwiches and rolls are the best food I can ever remember."

Amos looked around the car then asked, "Where Big John? I spected him be with you. He so proud of that babe."

The look on Black Elk's face arrested them all. Even though he was dressed in faded denim pants and a blue work shirt, his bearing seemed both regal and tragic. "John's been through some changes. Today was a hard day for him. Sit – please." He sat and indicated that Ben and Hanna should sit across from him.

"I's bring you somthin' from the kitchen. Spect you all needs to talk." Amos left and almost immediately returned with plates heaped with roast beef, potatoes and steamed cabbage. "Tomorrow ain't got no mistakes in it yet." He looked at each of them briefly then turned back to his duties.

As they ate, Black Elk spoke in Sioux. "*John, Leftook and I have lived lives that are much the same. But in a way, he has lost more. We both lost our women and the lives we had.* He paused, looked at Hanna, and then continued. "*I lost you – that was hard. But I got you back so I am lucky. You lost, too. You grew up white with red skin and you were hated for it.*" He looked at Ben and smiled wistfully. "*Perhaps you were the most lucky. You had a white family that cared for you and you had your Ate' to teach you. You were also good at sports – the whites liked you for that. And they learned to respect your courage.*"

The baby fussed so Hanna put him over her shoulder and patted his back. She was rewarded with a surprisingly man sized burp which elicited good-natured laughter from all around.

"*Leftook lost his o'agle. It means foundation in English but more. It's a place of holding, a solid place. He grew up learning the teachings of the white Jesus. His people didn't believe in killing or violence. Yet he joined the fight to stop slavery. When the killing became meaningless, he spoke out against it and was almost sent to prison. He was sent to kill the red man but instead, he learned to walk the Red Road. He lost everything. All he has now is,*" he pointed around the room, "*this.*"

The train slowed for a few minutes. They passed through a small town with the name New Castle painted in gold lettering on the station. The engineer blew the whistle twice and then began to accelerate again.

"We goin' to stop in a half hour or so - take on water and coal." Amos announced. "We pick up the main tracks goin' east and west in Kenwood. We have an hour or so there. If you get off and walk around, don't be goin' alone. It be full of crackers!"

Ben gave Amos a look that said, "I'm not afraid of rednecks." Amos raised one eyebrow wisely and returned to work. Ben looked across the table at Black Elk and asked, "How did Leftook get that nickname?"

The man looked at his son-in-law for a moment then got a far-away look in his eyes. *"The short answer is that he knocked a Sioux warrior to the ground with a left hook."* Black Elk stood and demonstrated, then sat down again. *"The Creator was very busy with us then. Many tribes of Human Beings came together to discuss the White Man. He brought your mother and I together there."* He looked across the table at Hanna and held out one hand. *"He gave us your stone that day to remind us."*

Hanna was wide-eyed in wonder. Almost without thought, she pulled her stone from her pocket, rubbed it across her son's cheek then placed it in her father's outstretched hand.

Black Elk rubbed a fingernail across the carved image of hawk. He felt the warmth of his daughter's body in the stone. Then, almost as if a spirit had touched him, he remembered the teachings of the White Buffalo Woman.

This fire is like the love that burns forever in the heart of the Great Spirit. It is the same fire that warms the heart of every buffalo, every eagle, every rabbit and every human. The spirit of Wakan Tanka is in all things.

This fire that burns at your center is your love and it is right at times to express this love sexually. This passion, if you do not control it, is like a wildfire that will destroy everything. But with wisdom, this passion will create many generations and warm thousands of lodges through hundreds of snowy winters. With reverence, this passion will give its power to your children's children's children.

Involuntarily, his hand gripped the stone, his eyes closed and his entire being contracted around a vision – an unbroken line of women from past to future passing the living warmth of the Great Spirit from generation to generation.

"Perhaps Hawk does see our path. The Great Spirit brought John Dunn to the People at the same time he brought me to your mother. There was a time of great trouble. The Whites had broken their promises again and were pushing into our sacred Paha Sapa.

When John Dunn came to our people, many in your grandfather's tribe wanted to kill him. This was in the summer of 1875, a year before the Battle of Greasy Grass. Old Dull Knife, the chief of your family saw some value in John Dunn. The old chief thought he might learn of the white man and his ways. Your mother was only ten winters but was given the task of teaching Dunn our ways and to learn about the whites.

He was dressed in the blue that scared many of our women and the young warriors hated him. He made many mistakes. Your grandfather Broken Knife told me once that this big white man would not live through the second day with us.

The Great Spirit saved Dunn's life with love, the love of a woman. Spoon Woman, a young widow, was given an elk Dunn had killed. She was to make him clothing that would not scare the people. She made him beautiful clothing and fell in love. It was her love that made the people see him differently. Then a young warrior also tried to get Spoon Woman's attention.

This young warrior was brash like young men are. He argued with Spoon Woman. Dunn knocked him to the ground with his left hook without fear even though he knew he might be killed. But it was in that moment of love and bravery that the people accepted him and gave him his name. Leftook. And it was in that moment our direction changed. Our path to walk with the whites changed that day. The Great Spirit brought this big gentle warrior to us and because of him we are here today.

And now John Dunn, Leftook, suffers because he no longer knows what man he needs to be."

The Eyes of Age
Near Ft. Wayne, Indiana July 22, 1897

You levy a straw tax on the poor and impose a tax on their grain. Therefore, though you have built stone mansions, you will not live in them; though you have planted lush vineyards, you will not drink their wine.
   Amos 5:11

There are those who turn justice into bitterness and cast righteousness to the ground.
   Amos 5:7

Hanna's dream and her reality parted ways when she felt her child move. She'd been flying. The movements and sounds from the train fit her dream perfectly. She awoke with a sense of dread but was unable to remember why. Her child's needs quickly foreshadowed all other thought.

Just before sunrise the landscape that passed by her window was lit by a rare, pearly luminescence that almost seemed to come more from within than the sun. Hanna didn't carry a watch but her baby was a timepiece. He wanted to nurse about every four hours. Hanna guessed that it was about four thirty in the morning. Time and space had taken on a new meaning. She was on a train, part of a traveling circus with a new baby. Schedule was everything.

The baby began to fuss causing Ben to wake and give her a blurry smile. "It's early. Go back to sleep." she whispered. "I'll change his diaper then go to the dining car. We won't bother anybody there."

"Why Miss Hanna, I don't need no watch with you about." Amos was up, bustling about in the dining car. He was neatly dressed in black creased trousers and a starched white chef's tunic. "Can I bring you somethin'? Coffee or some of that cider you's had yesterday?"

Hanna smiled warmly and said, "Thank you Amos. A cider would be nice." She sat where she could watch Amos work and covered her chest and the baby with a small blanket.

As the baby nursed, she began to talk. "Amos, how did you get your name?" Hanna sat up for a moment, switched the baby to the other side then continued. "I knew another Amos not long ago. You are much nicer."

Amos stopped what he was doing, looked at Hanna over his shoulder then poured some coffee for himself. He sat down across from her and gave her an unreadable look. "My mama named me after the Amos in the Good Book. He was one of them Minor Prophets in the Old Testament."

Hanna shuddered for a moment remembering her time at Carlisle. She reached across the table and squeezed the huge, calloused hand of the man sitting across from her. "Less than two weeks ago, my life was so different. It was like a Hell, but I really didn't know anything else. The Amos in that life was the devil, yet he was a preacher, a leader of the school where I was."

Amos patted her hand then clasped his on the table. He looked at her with a sad smile. "We's all had trials." He gave her another intense, unreadable look then said almost light heartedly, "The Amos in the Bible was around at a time when things was real good for Israel – a long time before Jesus. They was rich an had lots to eat. But ole Amos told em not to get greedy and treat poor folks bad. He reminded 'em of the flood. And darned if they didn't listen – lost their way and things got real bad." He stood and was about to excuse himself to go back to work then he stopped. He leaned down, put his big hands on the table and gave Hanna a very fatherly smile. "I spect you's doin just the opposite young lady. You's goin from bad to good, praise the Lawd."

With the hand Hanna wasn't using to hold her child, she reached out and covered the man's hand with hers and said, "I'm really happy here. So many people back at the school were evil – not all of them – but many. It was a dark time for me."

Amos shook his head and agreed. "All of us has a darkness inside. We's capable of doin' bad evil deeds. But we get to choose like the Good Book says. I think you's choosed to be good." Amos smiled then stood and walked back to the kitchen where he disappeared.

Hanna felt the baby stop nursing so she lowered him to her lap and arranged her top. She put the baby over her shoulder and after a satisfying burp she laid the baby on her legs. "What are we going to call you little man?" She wiggled her legs a little bit and the baby seemed to smile up at her. She looked into his deep, brown eyes and then Hanna was gone. The two of them were lost in each other's eyes in a connection that was old as time. Then Hanna jerked back to reality when she realized Amos was back, leaning over her shoulder smiling at her child.

"Looked at the map and the boss Hubert's schedule." Amos said. "We be stoppin' in South Dakota soon." There was a definite question in his expression.

"You mean..." she didn't finish.

"We's gonna be doin a show in Yankton the first part of September." He looked at her solemnly. "You's people be there!"

Hanna looked over her shoulder and caught the old porter's eyes. There was a brief connection, a flash of some ancient wisdom and pain. The implications of what was to come began to unspool in Hanna's mind when Amos stood and walked to the kitchen.

"They's always a powwow." He laughed as he began to put out silverware onto the empty tables. "The little ones always touch my skin." He finished a table and as he walked to the next he said, "I's got a nickname there. They calls me We Mahal Luaya. Means sundown." He laughed again. "Yea, I's be dark alright."

Both Hanna and Amos jumped when Kanj Coonshi spoke from behind them in Sioux. Neither of them was aware she'd come into the dining car.

"His name is one of great respect." Kanj Coonshi shuffled in and sat across from Hanna. She turned her chair so she could

see both Hanna and Amos then she spoke in broken English. "Tell my words." She glanced at Hanna, looked at Amos intently and began to speak in Sioux.

Wide eyed, Hanna listened raptly. Then she spoke the old woman's words. "Black is the color of west where the sun sets. There are four sacred colors and the four sacred directions. And the Creator made four colors of men. Sundown is the most beautiful color." Hanna smiled at Amos, looked at Kanj Coonshi with awe then said, "She wants me to tell you some words from our Creator, part of a prayer." Hanna listened to the old woman for a moment then began.

"Great Life-Giving Spirit, I face the West, the direction of sundown. Let me remember everyday that the moment will come when my sun will go down. Never let me forget that I must fade into you. Give me a beautiful color. Give me a great sky for setting, so that when it is my time to meet you, I can come with glory."

Amos came and squatted in front of the old woman. He took one of her hands in both of his and whispered, "Pilamaya, Coonshi." Hanna had not lived enough years to read the look that passed between them.

Then, as Amos returned to his work, Kanj Coonshi faced Hanna. "You hear story." The look in the old woman's eyes was not that of an elder but shy, pained. She reached behind her neck and untied a strap of rawhide. Attached to the strap was a beautifully made arrow point. She placed her necklace on the table. Then she reached into a pocket and placed a twenty dollar gold piece near the arrowhead. *"I said before that you must choose. My choice was made for me."*

Lovingly, the old woman touched each object before her then grasped the arrow point and began her story.

"Now I am old. When I was young, my name was Pretty Foe. My family, my tribe, we lived free. Soon after I became a woman, my father arranged my marriage. At my ceremony, a young hunter named Whirlwind Hawk gave my father many things. Soon, I was living in my husband's lodge. I was afraid; he was shy. We became friends.

There was a hunt. My husband came home, upset. He told me the kill was his but an older hunter claimed it. My husband told me to go with the women to butcher.

The other wives and women took our knives to the kill. The men ate the heart and liver while we worked. The older hunter had the honor of the first cut, the first bite of liver, the choice to share with the other men. As the sun went down on that remarkable day, the men sat around the central fire and feasted. The women cooked.

Before, as we butchered the buffalo, we recovered the arrows from the beast to return to the hunters. We found an arrow wound underneath the animal. The shaft was broken. Inside, in the buffalo's heart, we found the arrow that had killed it. It was my husband's arrow.

We did our work. We returned to camp with the meat and the hide. We cooked for the men. But we knew who made the kill. The men ate around the fire and honored the older hunter while my husband sat quietly in respect. But I could see his eyes. I was angry.

I stepped into the circle of men. I broke the rules. They scoffed at me and told me to leave. They said Council was not a woman's place. But I held up the broken arrow and told the truth. The chief told me to leave the men's circle and to do my work but I refused. Some of the other women stood behind me. One was the wife of the chief. I gave the broken arrow to my husband and left. The older hunter, the one who claimed the kill, came to my husband, shook his hand and gave him the spot on the right hand of the chief that night. The other men thanked my husband for his skill.

My husband gave me this arrow point in thanks. That night, my husband and I made our first son. My husband became a man that day."

Hanna laughed and said, *"That is a beautiful story."* But when she saw the old woman's eyes, she saw a depth of pain far deeper than her own. She knew there was more.

"The whites!" Kanj Coonshi touched the gold piece. *"This is their worship. They think they can own the power of the Great Spirit in this gold."* She picked it up and examined both sides. *"They lust after this gold because they think that with enough, they can buy*

the Earth. Their love of this gold breaks the Great Spirit's heart because he has given us everything we need."

The baby squirmed, whimpered then nuzzled Hanna's breast. As the baby nursed, the old woman smiled and continued to talk.

"Care for your child. Love him and let him take his own path. He will step away from you sooner than you know."

"Your family? Do you have family?" Hanna was still too young and too white to realize the history she asked about.

"Gone!" The dead flat tone of the old woman's voice startled both Hanna and her baby.

"Teach me Grandmother. Pilamaya"

"Before your mother, my people were driven onto the Paha Sapa. It was a good place, a sacred place. The whites promised us the land there was ours as long as the sun rose and the grass grew. They promised us food and that no whites were allowed to cross our land. But then Yellow Hair, the Army man Custer, came with many men. They told us they looked for a place to build a fort to help protect us but instead, they looked for gold. The whites poured into our land then seeking gold. The white army could or would not keep them out. So our warriors defended our land and caused the army to come and punish us. We killed Custer at Greasy Grass but more and more soldiers and whites came. They took back some land and gave it to white settlers. We could not stop them. They took more and more of our land and sent the men in black robes among us. They took many children away to learn the white ways. They taught that our belief was wrong and their Jesus would save us from our sin."

The old woman stopped her narrative and held out both hands, palms up. In her right hand, she held her arrow point. In the left, she held her gold piece. "One child, my daughter, died of the coughing disease. The next winter, we had no food. My baby was born dead. But my husband and I and a son and daughter still lived. We stayed and tried to keep our old ways. It was very bad. The whites came among us and took what they wanted – we were nothing to them. But then a holy man came to us from the south. His name was Wovoka and he told us that the old ways would come back if only we obeyed the whites and held to our beliefs. He said that one ceremony, our Ghost Dance, would save us. He taught our men that if they danced for days until the pain and hunger and thirst caused visions, that Christ would come back from the dead with all our dead. He said that then and only then, the whites would disappear from the Earth and we could live with the Great Spirit again in peace.

The old woman stopped again. She placed the gold coin on the table and laid the arrow point on top of it. She clasped her bony hands together and continued.

"The whites became afraid of us again because they thought our dancing would cause revolt. They came among us and said our dance was forbidden. Wovoka told us that if the men wore ghost shirts, they would stop bullets. The dancing continued.

The whites soldiers came to our camp and forced us to leave our spot and move close to their fort. We made camp where they told us to be on the banks of Wounded Knee Creek. But when our men danced the Ghost Dance again the next day, the soldiers came again to take our weapons, our tools to feed ourselves. A man refused. One gunshot became many. The soldiers became like animals. Many men died. The women and children that ran were hunted down. My husband and children and most of my tribe died that day."

"I told you my choice was made for me." Coonshi put the arrow point back in her pocket and held up the coin for Hanna to see. "My husband was a friend of Mr. Cody. Cody learned to hunt the buffalo from my husband. When Cody heard about what the Army had done, he came and found me. He gave me this coin on that day. He told me that his wealth was my wealth. He asked me to come with him to keep the spirit of my people alive."

"I don't know how to choose. What should I do?"

"We come soon to Paha Sapa. Life there is hard. Life among the whites is harder. I live here on la oya', this metal road in this make believe because it is more real than the life among the whites. But if you decide to live on Paha Sapa, find my friend Plenty Horses. He lived at your white school. He can help you."

"How can I choose?" Hanna's voice was choked with emotion, her eyes haunted.

The old woman reached out and took Hanna's hands in hers with surprising strength. *"It is not where you live – it is how you live. Always live Wakanisha."*

Acceptance
September 8, 1897

The prairie seemed endless, two-dimensional. The South Dakota land was flat, featureless except for the sage and yellowed grasses that stretched to the horizon. Hanna could see the effect of the constant wind. The shortgrass prairie moved like water in a gale. Her imagination and boredom convinced her that she was on a ship crossing a limitless sea. The rocking of the train on its rails became the deck rolling beneath her feet.

The wind, the motions, the unending panorama passing by the window was hypnotic. The one thing that kept Hanna tethered to reality was her child.

For some reason she could not explain, Hanna nursed her baby seated on the bench looking toward the back of the train. She gave the phenomenon little thought. It just felt right to look into the past, to see where they'd been as she had this intimate contact with her child. But after the child was burped over her shoulder, she placed him on the seat across from her to change his diaper. Then, instead of pulling him back, she joined him on the seat and began looking forward.

Hanna smiled at a tidbit of knowledge Amos had given her. His analogy compared a ship to their train. She sat with her child on the starboard side of the train. He taught her that port was left and starboard was right as one faced the front. And the mnemonic – the word port and the word left have the same number of letters. Then, as she looked out at the endless expanse, a Sioux prayer came unbidden. Since the train was heading due west, she looked north, the sacred direction of white, of cold wind and adversity.

Hanna and the baby stared out the window and watched the panorama. The unchanging prairie again began to entrance Hanna. She could also feel her child – it was as if their spirits were bound together and journeyed out and away. The telegraph poles became visual punctuation marks to the rhythmic sounds coming from the wheels. The endlessly repeating downward curves of the telegraph wires between the poles matched the vibrations coming from the tracks below. Hanna had no vocabulary to describe what she felt. It was as if utter boredom and joy were combined into one state of being.

Slowly the reality of their surroundings seemed to disappear - only the prairie remained. Hanna began to hear a story in her mind, not in words but in images and almost sacred connections. Her boredom was replaced with a familiarity - a sense of peace and belonging. Without thought, Hanna reached out with her free hand to touch, to connect to the reality of her waking dream, to feel the place she somehow knew was home. The hard cold glass erased the illusion.

The baby's cry echoed Hanna's disappointment. He had also been somewhere else, a place away from the boredom and the endless track across the seemingly never-ending prairie.

Hanna turned the baby to face her and kissed him on the forehead. The baby fussed a moment then became still and contented when Hanna hugged him to her chest. She stood facing the window. She swung the baby gently back and forth as she shifted her weight from foot to foot. Her eyes looked out the window without focus. Her attention was on the child, hoping he would nap.

Hanna stood in the window looking out but not seeing. She felt herself slipping back into a place her ancestors called dream walking. Again the train car and her current reality faded away - the prairie became her entire existence. Hanna imagined that she was the axle of a giant wheel and the telegraph poles that snapped past were the spokes. The car rocked slightly and Hanna placed her forehead against the glass to steady herself - her reality returned only for a moment. Then, the poles passing by became the legs of an impossibly huge spider that was walking along above her, propelling her along as it walked toward some unimaginable destination.

A tiny change in the repeating monotony destroyed Hanna's illusion and brought her back. A red tailed hawk sat atop a telegraph pole. It appeared to recognize her. Its eyes seemed to track Hanna's as the train sped past. Then it was gone.

The change in Hanna's consciousness was instantaneous, profound. Suddenly, her need to see the hawk again was her only thought. She pressed her face against the window and looked back, hoping to catch a glimpse of the bird before it receded into the infinity of the prairie.

There was a flash of feathered plumage - a powerful down stroke of wings and the hawk disappeared, hidden by Hanna's limited view from inside.

The pain Hanna felt was as real as if she had been stabbed. She ached to see the hawk again, to know what it meant, to feel that connection again.

The despair forming as a sob in Hanna's chest was instantly replaced by a joyous sense of wonder. The hawk plummeted from above the train and kept pace outside her window as it made eye contact. It flew there for only seconds but to Hanna, it was an eternity.

With one hand, Hanna clutched her child and in the other, she gripped the stone in her pocket. With her thumbnail she felt the outline of the hawk etched there. She longed to tell Kanj Coonshi about the experience she'd just had and ask what it meant. But the prairie was not finished with her.

In the distance, Hanna could see a small water hole surrounded by a herd of pronghorn antelope and several elk. The animals looked up and watched the train pass. They seemed to look at her with amusement.

Almost immediately, a badger came into view. It was digging a trap. This fierce animal looked up from its work as if to say, "You belong here."

A covey of quail and a few prairie chickens burst from cover and flew beside Hanna's window for a moment, displaying their beauty to her – showing off their flying skills in the excitement caused by the air currents of the passing train.

It was as if the land was calling to her. A jackrabbit nibbled on sage stopping its meal to look directly into Hanna's eyes. A powerful memory came to her then – the taste of rabbit and the warmth and softness of its hide as she sat around a fire with her friends in another life.

A coyote was next. It sat on its haunches and watched her pass. There was no pretense at all. The trickster was there only to smile at her and make her feel that the memories, the feelings that flooded her were simply a call to return, a beckoning for her to take her place in the sacred hoop.

Almost without thought, Hanna walked forward and opened the door to the vestibule between the cars. She stood there with her child exposed to the elements. The wind blew powerfully from the north. The smell of the sage reminded Hanna somehow of creation. The air was so fresh it filled her lungs with joy and a sense of recklessness. She leaned out over the chains that formed a barrier and began to see the little things – grasshoppers flying about, mice going about their quiet, mysterious work. It was during this moment of almost complete abandon, a wish to be part of what she was experiencing that she heard the whistle from up front and the train began to slow then stop.

Hanna stepped down onto the ruined soil that made up the track bed and looked forward. A crudely painted sign announced Meckling, South Dakota. The small collection of shacks and outbuildings couldn't even be called a settlement let alone a town. There was only one structure that resembled a building – it was part sod, part stacked rock with a shingled roof that served as the station and supposedly, a telegraph office. Nearby was the inevitable water tank on stilts to fill the steam engine and the coal shed. There was not a single tree. Meckling, South Dakota was only a short rail siding and a corral with a ramp to load cattle.

Without thought, Hanna walked out onto the prairie. She walked into the wind, the smell of the untouched soil and the pungent aroma of sage in her nostrils. Her approach from downwind surprised several small animals and somehow that feeling of ambush felt right to her. She continued, carefully avoiding the prickly pear cactus and dry sage twigs in her path.

She stopped when she heard a muted but threatening rattling sound near her feet.

On the ground in front of her was a large rattlesnake, shaking its rattles and looking at her. It was coiled, ready to strike. Hanna estimated that the reptile was as long as she was tall. The snake's face was incapable of expression but Hanna sensed both the threat and the hatred the snake somehow projected. But she also instinctively knew she was in no danger – the rattlesnake was only proclaiming its right to be.

Hanna and the snake considered each other until she sensed a shared understanding. In her mind, Hanna said, "*Aho thiblo'.*" (*Hello, older brother.*) The snake wavered then lowered its head and slid silently away. The change in the rattlesnake's posture somehow displaced the expression of hatred with grudging acceptance.

Hanna sat then. She lowered herself to the ground, sat cross-legged with the child in her lap. She dug her fingertips into the soil and felt an intense connection to the earth. It was there moments or an eternity later that Ben found her.

"Didn't you hear the whistle?" Ben stood above her with one hand outstretched. He smiled at her as if he understood.

"*Iron Eagle, we belong here. I feel it.*" She spoke in Sioux as she reached up and took his hand. They remained there for a moment as if they were deciding if he would sit or she would stand.

He squatted down, touched the baby on the cheek and smiled. "*Yes, I do feel it. But come, there is a place where we belong not far from here. Our people wait for us.*"

Less than two hours later, the train began to slow again. The sun was poised just above the skyline – it appeared as if the train continued instead of stopping, it would plunge directly into the sun as it touched the horizon.

The train slowed even further then abruptly turned onto a siding. Directly ahead the first train of Buffalo Bill's Wild West Show was already stopped on the siding. In the distance, the rooftops of several buildings could be seen. But in the immediate area, there were tipis standing, many cooking fires lit and a multitude of people milling around.

As their train slowed even further then chugged to a stop, much of the crowd of people began to gather at all the train's doorways, joyous smiles on their faces.

Hanna looked out her window in wonder. Ben stood, extended his hands to pull her up. "This is the powwow Amos told us about." He pointed forward. "There is a reservation on the other side of Yankton. These are our people. Come on!"

Hanna gathered up her diaper bag, the baby and stood. She and Ben excitedly stepped down into the crowd. Black Elk was there and helped her down. John Dunn stood there as well, talking in Sioux to a person Hanna had never seen.

The scene was happy and chaotic. There were invitations to eat. She could hear drums in the distance – the sound was both hypnotic and familiar. She felt strangely excited and peaceful at the same time. Something about the energy and ambience seemed so right. The setting was exotic and almost frightening in its intensity but she also felt like she was home.

Hanna was following Ben who was following John Dunn who was being led toward a large tipi by a man she'd never met. The crowd surged and another man, a stranger stepped between her and Ben as they all walked the same direction. Then Hanna was alone in the crowd and just beginning to feel lost and intimidated when she felt a hand on her shoulder. She turned and standing in front of her was a tall native woman dressed in a drab gingham jumper and what looked like a pale blue man's work shirt underneath.

"*Aho mithanj! I see you have more than your precious stone with you.*" The woman smiled sadly at the baby then reached out and touched Hanna near her heart.

Hanna's face lit up with joy as she whispered, "Bess, is that you?"

"*Hau Mushkay.* *You look like a Human Being. It is good to see you.*"

Hanna looked up at her old friend from another life. Bess looked the same and yet there was tenseness about her, a wariness in her eyes that was more pronounced. Only a few months had passed since they'd been students together at the Carlisle School. Yet there was a separation that spanned centuries.

There was a brief, uncomfortable silence between them – there was so much to be shared, so many life lessons that needed sharing that neither knew where to start. The throng of humanity continued to swirl around them – they were anonymous within the crowd.

"Bess, it's been less than three months since –"

"*If you want to be a Human Being, talk the talk.*" Bess said acidly. "*There are thirteen moons, not twelve like the whites. You can say Chanjwa'pe for the time now meaning the moon of many leaves. Or this is the moon the calves grow hair. The People will know when you say it.*"

Hanna looked up at her friend and smiled. "*You have not changed my friend.*"

"*Much has changed!*" Bess looked angry, near tears. Her fists were clenched at her sides. Resentment poured off her in waves.

This tense moment was broken when Ben appeared. "We thought we lost you!" He glanced at the baby then at Hanna with his usual smile. When he saw the look on her face, he followed her gaze and saw Bess. The crowd parted as Dunn and Black Elk found them.

The randomly moving crowd of humanity flowed by this reunion scene as if it was nothing more than boulders in a stream. Yet some looked up startled. There was a palpable energy emanating from these six people standing there. It was as if the powwow was a storm cloud full of potential that created a huge static charge and the family of Black Elk was the most likely place the lightning would strike.

The new baby boy with his mother and father formed one point of the sacred hoop – the red of east and new beginnings. Black Elk stood there with the power and cold of north, needing courage to continue. John Dunn, Leftook, longed for the warm winds of the south to bring healing and comfort for his wounded spirit. And Bess Little Robe stood in anger of the west, at the blackness of endings.

There was a moment of silence but not of peace. There was a furious search for synergy as eye contacts were made then broken, spirits searched for worth and judged, smiles shared in hope.

It was Bess, the outsider with courage, that spoke first. "You must be Big John Dunn?" She extended her hand in greeting but her eyes were cold, guarded.

"This is Bess Little Robe, my friend from school I've told you about." Hanna looked at the faces around her hoping to ease the tension. She also knew she was the singular point of contact between these people that she loved.

"I'm not called Bess here," she said in clipped English. "*They call me Unjkela.*"

Black Elk and Dunn shared a look and smiled. What passed between them was unreadable to the others.

Hanna was about to ask what the word meant when Bess nearly exploded in anger. "Do you think this is funny?" She had her hands on her hips and her body language was clearly confrontational. "*Unjkela means cactus! Yes! It describes me! I always poke people when they try...*"

Black Elk stepped into the center of the circle and almost forcibly took her hands in his. "*You remind us of a person from another life we loved and respected very much. Her name was Macawi – she was the strongest woman we ever knew.*" He dropped her hands but continued to hold her with his eyes. "*The Great Mystery brought us together. Let your anger go and our stories will connect us.*"

In a borrowed tipi covered in cowhide with only one pictogram painted on its side, an image of hunger, Bess told her story.

I remember freedom. I was little and I learned to live. I knew the ways of our brothers the animals. They fed us and gave us our homes. We thanked Thunkashila for our lives and I was happy. I was ten winters when I realized how our people feared the whites. I had learned the old ways and was ready to be with the People. The Great Mystery was all about me and I was learning my place in it. I lived many days on the land by myself, taking rabbit and fish to live in the snow. I came back to my family ready to take my place. It was then I hoped for a vision quest to follow. But my father told me to live among the whites, to learn their ways in order to help my people. My father was proud but feared the whites. He wanted me to learn their ways in order that perhaps one day, our people would join them in peace.

Then, for the first time in my life, I was afraid. I rode in the last car of a terrible train, hungry, with many other children. I learned the strange talk of the whites. I ate their cold, smelly food and followed their rules. I tried and was the best at every type of learning. I did their math. I learned about their Christ and his teachings. I was beaten for saying our beliefs were the same as theirs. I tried hard and learned until I was a better white than they were. But I was never praised, only punished for trying to be one of them.

I badly wanted to run away like many others. I waited for word from my father to return. But no message ever came. Twice, new children came from our tribe and told me of the sorrow that came from living on the white's reservation. But still, I waited.

And then you came Hanna. You were a Human Being but knew only the white ways and wanted to learn how to walk the Red Road. I taught you and somehow, it gave me hope. You were like the white man's story of Cinderella. You suffered like the rest of us but somehow remained pure and happy.

Then, like a dream, you found your prince. And your father came with his big white warrior friend and rescued you. Your life was like a fairy tale to me, to all of us at the school. When you disappeared that night, I knew I had to follow you. The day after you were gone, life at the Carlisle School became horrible. The whites punished us all because you found freedom. We all suffered but in our hearts, you were our hero, our dream.

Not long after you left, several of the older children were rebellious. You had given us hope. The school reported some of the children had left. But when several fresh graves appeared in the cemetery, I knew I had to leave. My anger had grown so large I knew I would kill then be killed. So I took the tiny amount of money I'd saved and on a rare day of freedom, I tried to buy a train ticket home.

The stationmaster would not sell me a ticket but told me to wait for the train. When it came, the conductor came and told me I had a spot on the train. But I was not to pay for the ticket with money - I was to be his woman, his entertainment. I agreed. I lay with him at night and then he fed me. When we came to another white city, he gave me to the next conductor on the next train. My money was taken. I got what I wanted. They got what they wanted. It was a trade I made to come home.

After many days I left the train in Yankton. I had to walk through the town and the white people there scorned me. I had to find my way to the reservation and my family. And when I found my people, my family was dead. They had little food and had frozen to death the terrible winter before.

When word came that Buffalo Bill was coming and that we might just have one last gathering of the people, I had to come. I had to find out if you had found freedom. I had to know if there was hope.

I apologize for my anger. It is all I have left.

Wačhípi

(Both noun and verb, to dance or place to dance, powwow, a gathering)
September 8, 1897

The skin tones of the people at the gathering didn't concern Hanna. It was a powerful memory that did. Here, all four colors of men seemed at ease with each other. It was that same feeling of peace that Hanna recalled from her distant childhood. Sunday dinners after church back in Kansas – heads bowed in prayer, hands joined around the table. It was a feeling of joining, connectedness, that she felt here with these hundreds of souls all joined in one place to celebrate life.

As the sun set, the prairie sky transformed from bright and harsh to awe-inspiring. The wind stopped blowing and a sensual quality overpowered Hanna. The smoke and smells of cooking meat was intoxicating; laughter and snippets of conversation came from all directions. The six of them simply wandered from fire to cooking fire. Rare slabs of meat, hot from cooking stones, was offered by the women there. They shook hands easily with those they met. At some fires, they sat in circles with others and ate hot corn cakes. The feeling of communion and utter belonging was palpable. The conversations were sometimes in English, sometimes in Sioux. Often the speakers spoke both languages, switching from one to the other, using words that worked best for the feelings being expressed.

There were no words. Not in Sioux, not in English; Hanna had nothing in her, nothing in her short life's experience to compare. As the sky to the west deepened from reds, ochers, violets and deep purples to black, the call of the incessant drumming became primal. In that instant Hanna glimpsed what it meant to be a Human Being.

The air they moved through seemed thick, utterly dark. The earth under Hanna's feet existed only as affirmation that she was not falling through a void – each step she took was an act of faith that there was indeed ground beneath her. The starlight gave only enough radiance to see others as ghostly shadows as they passed. The scattered cooking fires illuminated only small circles of the other celebrants gathered there. Some ate, some danced to the incessant drumming. Some embrace passionately then drifted off into the dark. It seemed to Hanna that all of the four colors of men were there together without barriers.

Hanna desperately tried to analyze her surroundings. At the same time she was flooded with feelings of complete release. She felt her hand clutching Ben's belt as he walked in front of her through the darkness. She was barely aware of Black Elk in the lead followed by Dunn. Hanna followed as if she had no will of her own while Bess seemed completely at ease. The baby was on Hanna's back – somehow she knew that he had long ago released the tethers and was completely in the moment. They seemed to be headed for one of the larger fires. When she looked at the flames her night vision was destroyed giving the illusion of being in space. When she looked into the dark again the starlight made her surroundings seem ghostly, dreamlike.

The ongoing scene reminded Hanna of an art book in the Carlisle library. The prints by Hieronymus Bosch conveyed the same feelings she was having now, walking through this blackness lit only by flickering firelight. She felt the same compulsion to look and yet the same fear that the book could be closed. Here, she was immersed.

They passed other people, some going the same direction, some the opposite. Faces came out of the dark, faces with smiles of greeting, others with looks of blatant invitation. Hanna had never felt such openness, such a lack of barriers between people. She was unsure and felt vaguely guilty of her own feelings – she was keenly aware of her own womanhood, her fertility. The baby at her back was proof. She was still breastfeeding and her femininity was obvious. The signals she got from passing men were clear. Yet she was confused by the notion that she felt available to respond. It was the first time Hanna had ever felt a significant disconnect between her early teachings as a Christian and the Sioux woman she was becoming.

Hanna was vaguely aware of a slight change in direction when she passed a young couple sitting on the grass. The moonlight on them gave the impression that they were lit from within, dim as if their entwined souls were fireflies. The young woman straddled his lap; her buckskin skirt was at her waist as she held him loosely with both arms and legs. His face was buried in her chest as they moved slowly together. The young woman looked up at Hanna with an easy smile and mouthed the word *peace* in Sioux. Hanna felt a brief, profound affinity with the woman on the ground as she returned the smile. The moment ended when Hanna passed by and the young woman turned her attention back to the man beneath her.

As they approached the large cooking fire, Hanna felt a rush of absolute joy. She felt totally connected to the people around her, who in turn seemed to exist without past or future. The utter and complete totality of each life was expressed in that moment. There seemed to be only joy with no barriers. The other people gathered around the fire simply parted as Hanna and her family joined the circle. Then they became part of the whole.

Hanna had no way to know she was experiencing a human ritual as old as the history of man. It felt so right! There was Beltane, Walpurgisnacht, The Penis Festival, and The Cleansing of the Virgin; there were human celebrations of the creation of life in cultures spanning the globe. Yet, it seemed that another force was sweeping away this joy of procreation and replacing it with guilt and shame. And with it whole cultures were being crushed. The multitudes of Native American civilizations were being pushed aside by the European love of ownership and control. The same year Hanna was enjoying perhaps the last true Sioux powwow, Hawaii had been annexed by the United States and Japan had been forced to accept the Gold Standard.

Hanna saw Amos on the other side of the fire. He smiled and came around the fire clockwise. He was with a woman Hanna recognized as one of the ladies from the wardrobe car.

He nodded to Dunn and Black Elk. "Boss", he said in greeting then stepped up in front of Hanna. "I's so glad you be here, Miss Hanna. These gatherin's make life worth livin'."

The casual loving way Amos had his arm around the woman's waist made Hanna smile. This easy acceptance between them extended to Hanna and her family. Hanna sensed that Amos and the woman had been lovers and yet there was nothing hidden, nothing held back. Their skin color meant nothing here. Their ages or even other existing relationships did not matter in this moment.

The seamstress disengaged from Amos and took Hanna's hand in both of hers. "I'm so glad to see you's wearin your dress. Kanj Coonshi taught me that-un years ago. She took me under her wing when I first joined up." She smiled shyly at Hanna. "Name's Hattie. Maybe we's could swap stories sometime."

"Pull up a chair!" Amos spread his arms indicating they sit on the ground. His gesture was as elegant as any ever used by a headwaiter in the dining car. Then, like a stage magician, a bottle appeared in his hand. He passed it to Black Elk. "A little confection I's picked up in Kentucky last time through."

One-by-one they sat in a circle as the bottle made it around. The first time the bottle passed, Hanna was taking her child out of the pack and didn't taste the bourbon. The second time around Hanna began to notice small subtleties. Her father declined to taste the whiskey – Bess made an obvious effort to sit next to John Dunn and looked at him with some interest. Hattie sat comfortably next to Amos, but she looked at Black Elk with an uncomfortable familiarity. Ben tasted the bourbon and Hanna immediately noticed a change in him.

Then Hattie asked, "What's your baby's name?"

It was Ben who answered. "In Sioux culture a child names himself by some deed. As a child grows, he does something or something happens that begins their story. My father called me Iron Eagle because I was always flying around and falling but never broke." He looked to Bess. "This is Bess, a friend of ours from the school. She has been called Cactus since she came here." He laughed softly at the look he got from her.

"*I've heard the people call you Leftook.*" Bess looked at Dunn with intensity.

"English please!" Amos asked. "We's a family here."

"How did you get your name Mr. Dunn?" Bess turned to face him almost as if her bodily gesture excluded the rest of the group.

A gunshot roared near the central fire accompanied by screams of fright. Startled, they all turned and looked toward the sound just as the gun sounded again. The muzzle blast pointed into the air, the same color of red as the peaceful fire.

"You's fuckin red niggers! Git back onto the rez! You's ain't welcome here." The voice seemed young male, local and drunk. There was another shot into the air as if it were an exclamation point. "JUS' GIT!"

Moments later Dunn stood in front of this young man. It was a configuration with which he was all too familiar. There were four of them. All young, in their twenties. The one with the gun was the biggest but probably not the smartest. "What can I do for you son?" Dunn stood there, arms crossed in front of his chest, hands clasped, his body turned slightly sideways. He was six inches taller and probably out-weighed the young troublemaker by a hundred pounds, but his submissive posture was meant to diffuse and not inflame.

"I ain't your son old timer!" The kid put his pistol into the holster and stepped up to Dunn aggressively. "If you's the boss man here, git these red lickfingers outta here. They's place is on the rez. Chop! Chop!"

Dunn hooked his fingers into his pants pockets and smiled easily. "Are you the sheriff here about?"

"I's the local militia – me an my boys here. Getta a move on!"

Dunn nodded respectfully for a moment then replied, "You probably know that Cody's Wild West Show is set to perform here this week. I'm part of the show and we've leased this land from the city. Surely these performers and our guests aren't a problem?"

The young man staggered back a step and looked around. "Tell ya what bossman. You git me and my boys some a this young red meat and we'll let ya stay."

Dunn didn't realize Bess was standing behind him, fuming. He started to say "Sorry son, I can't –" when Bess stepped around him and earned her nickname.

"You immature little prick! You make me sick!" She stepped up within inches of the young drunk and gave him a look of naked hatred.

Dunn stuck his arm between the young man and Bess and tried to separate them. *"You're not helping!"* he said in Sioux.

"English, Injun talk! I don't give a shit. I'll take her – she be good in the sack." the white boy said as he leered at Bess.

Dunn spun around and manhandled Bess. She had her hands out like she was going to scratch his eyes out.

"My daddy tole me about squaws like you! They all fight at first then they gets all quivery. Let her come on, old man!

Dunn had one hand on Bess pushing her away and the other on the drunken boy's chest, trying to avoid further escalation.

With one hand, the drunk threw Dunn's hand to the side and with the other punched Dunn in the mouth.

There was a brief tableau as if the firelight had frozen this scene like a Bosch painting. Bess's face was lit with anger and surprise. Dunn had blood seeping for his lip. The young bully looked at Dunn in wonder as if he'd accomplished the impossible. In the next instant, the boy was on the ground unconscious, nose broken.

Black Elk, who had been standing near leaned close to Bess. He smiled and whispered, *"That is how Leftook got his name."*

Choices
Outside of Yankton, S.D., September 8, 1897

"Boys, sometimes violence gets you what you want. Sometimes it doesn't." Dunn was backlit by the bonfire as he spoke to the other young men that had accompanied the shooter. Dunn leaned over and took the revolver out of the unconscious gunsel's hand and unbuckled the boy's holster. As Dunn yanked the belt free, the boy rolled onto his side.

For the three other 'townies' that had tried to slip away into the darkness, they experienced their own version of Hell. The moment Dunn knocked their friend to the ground, they tried to scatter. They didn't make it far. The gunfire had scared some of the celebrants away, but the ones that were enraged instead circled the fire. The boys were surrounded.

Dunn towered over these three young men. He wore faded dungarees, moccasins and a deerskin shirt. Around his neck was a thong of rawhide laced through three very large claws. "Can one of you tell me what you planned to accomplish?" Even though he had the confiscated pistol in one hand and a cartridge belt and holster in the other, his voice was friendly, almost jovial.

Not one of the young men spoke. Their eyes were huge with terror, but it wasn't the big man in front of them that they feared. His bearing was familiar, comforting – he felt like a sheriff, calm, ready to restore the peace. The young Indian woman that stood behind the big man was the source of their terror. In her eyes were an absolute feral hate and certain death. Unconsciously, the three wanted to hide behind the big man as if he was their savior.

"My name's Dunn but for now, call me Boss. I get it. You boys came out for some adventure – had a couple of snorts from your friend's bottle here." As Dunn talked, he removed the cylinder from the pistol and took all the brass and unspent cartridges and dumped them in his hand. "I guess it's up to you to decide what kind of adventure you want now." He handed the pistol to one of the boys, the cylinder to another and the belt and brass to the third. "I can arrange for you boys to join up with some of these good folks and have a meal – some hospitality." Then he tilted his head toward Bess. "Or, if you like, you can see what Cactus Girl has in mind. What'll it be?" He glanced at Bess with a look that was hard to read.

It was as if the three young white men finally realized their situation. Moments before they had been slightly drunk, bulletproof and in charge of their adventure. The next instant this huge man had knocked their ringleader to the ground and hostile faces had surrounded them. Now the big man calling himself Boss had given them options. The three looked around them frantically, assessing.

The tall Indian girl glared at them from behind the big man's back with naked hatred. Behind her was an Indian man wearing faded jeans and a light blue work shirt – he had a slight smile on his face as if this incident was familiar. Beside him was a young Indian couple holding a baby; they watched the scene in wide-eyed wonder. And the baby! The child's eyes seemed to narrow their perception. There was no judgment in the baby's face, no hostility, only peace. It was as if by looking at this child, the hostility surrounding them no longer mattered.

"What'll it be?" Dunn's voice seemed to come from a far away place. Had these young men the vocabulary to describe what they'd experienced in that moment, they would have told of a sensation like tunnel vision where all they saw, all they experienced were the eyes of this child. It was as if they were falling into a place where hatred didn't exist, a place of peace and acceptance.

"Huh?" The boys looked at each other then one said, "We could eat –". He hesitated. "If you's would share."

Dunn smiled. "Good choice boys. He turned around and motioned. "Amos, why don't you help these young men get settled in someplace."

Amos stepped into the circle of light and held out his hand. "Welcome to Buffalo Bill's. Lets get you –"

One of the boys interrupted. "Hey, I ain't goin no place with no n..."

The look on Dunn's face and the very minimal way he raised one hand at waist level signaling *STOP* was all it took to silence the boy.

Amos continued as if nothing had happened. "What'll it be boys? We's got some ribs an beans or I can find you a decent steak and corn." He tilted his head at the unconscious hothead on the ground and said, "Pick em up and bring em along. He might be hungry in a bit."

Amos chuckled as the boys organized themselves – one of them ended up with all the gun parts and the other two carried their wounded friend in a clumsy fireman's carry.

As Amos left with the young men in tow, Bess turned her ire on Dunn. "Welcome to life on the reservation!" She stared at him balefully then continued in Sioux. *"They come! They take what they want! Our women are not safe! And when a red man confronts them, he's beaten – or worse."* She stepped closer to Dunn aggressively and put her hands on her hips. *"You should have let us deal with these Wasicans. They would have just disappeared."*

"At what cost?" Dunn looked down at Bess much like a father would have done with a misbehaving child. When she didn't drop her eyes, he said, *"I am Akíčhita here. You are a woman!"*

As the two of them stared at each other, a subtle change came over Bess. Her look softened and her hands fell to her sides. A look of thoughtful respect crossed her face then she reached up gently and touched Dunn's swollen lip. She smiled at him wistfully and asked, "If I had some whisky, I could disinfect your cut."

"It is nothing," Dunn continued in Sioux but he did not look away.

"You said it. I am a woman. I will take care of the man that stood for me." She looked into his eyes with a frank invitation. *"Take me to your train so I can care for you."*

Another look passed between the two as Hanna, Ben and Black Elk looked on. The air between Bess and Dunn seemed charged like just before a lightning strike. Whatever it was that was passing between them was so palpable that the baby even seemed aware of the psychic energy nearby.

Without speaking, Dunn turned and began walking toward their train. Bess followed, a discreet step behind him in a manner classically modeled by Sioux couples for millennium.

Ben gave Hanna a knowing smile and began to lead her toward the nearby fire. Black Elk stopped them. *"We should follow. This is our family and we should be there to counsel each other. Come!"*

As they left the light of the fire and walked toward the train, the blackness of the late summer evening engulfed them. In the distance, Hanna could see the interior of the train cars softly lit. She wondered about what she had seen and had experienced. She was confused about the way she felt. She wasn't sure if she was jealous or happy if Dunn and Bess were to somehow connect. She knew there was a significant age difference between them but somehow that felt unimportant. Ben and Black Elk weren't talking so she asked, "Papa, what did Dunn mean when he called himself *Akíchita*? I don't know this word."

"It is a term of great respect and more. It means warrior but the one called Akíchita is the lead warrior, the head of security for the tribe. Dunn is that to us."

The horses nickered happily when Black Elk and his family entered the stock car. A kerosene lantern softly lit the space and the air was sweet with the smell of green hay. Dunn sat on a bale; Bess knelt in front of them. She held a bandana and was dabbing Dunn's face. He had a bottle of whisky in his hand. Bess was softly chiding him for taking a swallow. Both Bess and Dunn looked up and smiled as the rest of the family entered.

"I was just telling Mr. Dunn here that whisky is only good for one thing – cleaning wounds. Otherwise, its poison." She smiled sadly at the big man again and once again wiped Dunn's lip with her cloth.

Hanna felt almost disoriented watching Bess and Dunn interact. The scene was so domestic, their conversation so familial it seemed to Hanna that they were an old married couple. Yet only moments before they had been at each other's throats. And they had only met that evening! It was hard for Hanna to grasp. These two people that she loved, these people from two very different portions of her life now seemed somehow together. Then, when she remembered that Dunn had been there at the very beginning of her life, a life she couldn't even remember, her knees just wouldn't hold her. She sat next to Dunn and sighed.

The baby fussed and nuzzled Hanna's chest. Hanna leaned back, unbuttoned her blouse and began to feed her child. She'd been self-conscious about nursing, but now it just seemed natural. She tried to follow the conversation as the topics flowed back and forth. Hanna heard a version of one of her father's many visions, the one about the cup of water and the bow and arrow, how one gives life and the other the power to destroy. She heard Dunn comment that he didn't see how punching a young drunk fit that wisdom and Bess contradict Dunn by saying that it fit perfectly. Hanna heard Ben laugh and describe the looks on the boy's faces when Dunn lectured them. They all laughed good-naturedly including Bess when Dunn said that the boys were more afraid of Cactus Girl than they were of him. Hanna looked down into her baby's eyes and the conversation became background noise. She heard the sounds but the content had lost meaning. The voices were happy, comforting, and dream-like. She pulled her knees up on the bale and leaned back sitting curled up around her child. Then as the baby fed and looked up at her, she drifted into that timeless, holy place shared by infants and their mothers.

Everybody jumped and the baby squeaked when the door banged open suddenly. Dunn was the first to speak. "Morty, any problems?"

"No Boss! It's all good. Ain't no townies makin' trouble. I'm just waitin' on Jimmy to take my watch. Sorry I disturbed you. Just heard talkin in here – doin my job." Morty returned the double-barreled shotgun he was carrying to an informal port arms as he left.

It was during this vacuum, this break in the conversation that Ben dropped the bombshell. His question brought to the forefront the painful subject they hadn't discussed. "Bess, Hanna and I came here to live on the reservation. What's it like?"

Bess spun and looked at Ben. The pain in her eyes pierced him to the bone. "It..." she hesitated to gather her thoughts. She put one hand on Dunn's shoulder in a distinctly possessive gesture and used his stability to push herself to a standing position. She turned to face Ben with the whisky soaked bandana gripped in both hands.

"Our people are owíhaŋkekiya! Destroyed! Their will has been taken and only their bodies remain. Our holy ceremonies are forbidden. Our men no longer hunt – we are not allowed to feed ourselves. Our women are given dirty wooden houses in which to live. Our girls have no recognition of womanhood – instead some of them go off with white men and live in places for the white man's pleasure. There, they live a better life for a while. only to be thrown away. Then they are trash to both the whites and our people."

Bess turned and ripped the whisky bottle out of Dunn's hand and held it like it was a poisonous snake. She was nearly vibrating with passion – her face was terrible to see as she made eye contact with each person there. "*Our young no longer learn the skills of their parents. Boys run in packs like dogs and treat the drunken men with disrespect for being fools, yet drink this themselves whenever they can get it. Our girls try to be white and are shamed by both our people and the whites.*" She stopped again as if to find an answer to Ben's question. "*Live here with the people on this train. Look for a place where you will be treated like a human being. In the meantime, your children will learn pride.*"

Ihánbla

On the tracks outside Yankton, South Dakota, September 14, 1897

There's a wordless moon that's watching tonight
There's a garden that's left to grow wild
There's a sound with no name when a far away train
Cries like an unloved child.
    Buddy Miller

"Papa, she came to my dreams again last night. She was sitting on a wire by the big locomotive. When she flew, the steam whistle seemed her voice. She looked back at me as if to say. 'Follow'. She flew west toward the sun until the tracks joined in the distance - she didn't grow smaller. She didn't use words but the feeling I had was family; that I was to take my family and be with this family."

The train car in which they sat stretched from west to east. The sounds coming from the huge engine up front spoke of departures, of readiness to travel. The hiss of steam escaping as safety valves vented extra pressure; the calls of the porters and the conductor doing checks, the clang of the fireman's shovel as he fed another shovelful of coal into the firebox. Outside the early morning light caught tendrils of smoke from the dying fires. Not one person inhabited the field that for nearly a week had been a joyous gathering of the people.

Both Hanna and Black Elk jumped when the train whistle made a loud, plaintive shriek. Hanna looked at her father briefly then down at her child. The child smiled up at Hanna and when the engineer gave the train a single tug, the baby laughed.

"The white man has a word for what this might be - fate." Black Elk looked at his daughter with eyes that were both joyous and sad. "*We also have words, maya owicha paka, that means the same thing as fate or destiny.*" He smiled and continued. "And it is also slang for being pushed off a cliff." He looked at his hands clasped on his lap. "What made you decide to stay with us? I know *you dreamed of living with our people on the reservation - that somehow your life would have been better there than at the school."*

Hanna's eyes were haunted, guarded. Rather than answer with words, she sobbed helplessly, her eyes filled with tears, her body language signaled near complete defeat.

Black Elk looked at his daughter and suddenly saw her not through his own eyes, but through the eyes of what her life had been. He had lived his own horrors, had lost much. He had experienced the near complete cultural destruction of his people. But he grew up Red and had had those experiences. His roots made him the man he was - is. He had started out walking the Red Road and continued to do so in the limited way that was open to him. But this young red woman before him, the daughter he'd searched for her entire life, began her life the day her mother had died. She had grown up Red in a white home, was taught a religion that called for peace yet warred against all those that were different. When the whites fought for their freedom and independence, they celebrated it as a righteous rebellion. When the Red Man fought for his freedom, the whites called it an uprising and it was crushed. When the whites won a battle, they called it a victory. When the Red Man won a battle the whites called it massacre.

Black Elk changed seats and sat down with his daughter. He put his arms around her and pulled her close as she cried herself out. "*I know you had a dream of your family, but I am glad you're here. Life on this train is not the life our people once had, but we have many freedoms our people on the reservation do not.*"

Hanna looked up at her father, rubbed as much grief out of her eyes as she could and smiled at him tentatively.

"*I think I know the reason you decided to stay.*" Black Elk glanced out the window for a moment as if he were looking at an alien culture just on the other side of the glass. "*I know you grew up in a white man's house. I know you were treated like an outsider in that little town. I know the school they sent you to be a w'owanjke, a horror. And I know that Bess told you much about life on the reservation.*" He reached down and gently turned her face to face him. *"I think your mother talks to you, guides you."* He smiled at her sadly.

She held his gaze until both felt that the outside world disappeared and nothing existed but the tunnel of understanding that flowed between them. Then softly, she whispered, *"Yes Papa."*

It was as if the baby sensed the flow of love between father and daughter. He made a happy sound and reached out and grabbed Black Elk's shirt.

He smiled and took the baby out of Hanna's arms and held him in the crook of his arm. *"Before you were born, our people were fighting the whites. I left your mother and went back to my own tribe for a while. We were separated for five winters. Even when she was alive, her spirit came to me. And she dreamed of me. Perhaps the most important reason for a iháŋbla, a vision, is that it helps us to realize our oneness with all beings, to know that all things are our relatives. In behalf of all things, we pray to Wakan-Tanka that he may give to us knowledge of Him who is the source of all, yet greater than all things."*

From far ahead two long whistles sounded. They heard the lead train pull away. Somewhere near the front of their train they heard a loud *all aboard*! Minutes later, the conductor came through the door and asked Black Elk, "Your crew all accounted for?"

"Yes Boss. I made the rounds this morning early. They know to get to Calgary on their own by October 1 if they miss, but I think they're all accounted for. Any stops in Montana?"

"Possible one-nighter in Billings and another in Helena. We gotta stop for supplies just over the border. We might get a couple vacation days in Regina, if we're lucky. I could use a night in a saloon." The conductor winked at Black Elk, tipped his hat to Hanna and was gone.

When the conductor left the car, the baby began to nuzzle Black Elk's shirt and fuss. "Hanna, your mother and I were never able to give you a name. *You were born and in less than a moon our lives were torn apart. I watched you ride away in a wagon and I didn't even have a name when I prayed for you."* The pain in his eyes was a terrible thing to see. "*I know our customs tell us to wait, but I wish for a name to call my Thakóža, my only grandchild.*" He handed the child back to Hanna.

It was at that moment that the train whistle made one last plaintive call that cars began to move. Much passed between father and daughter in that instant. It was yearning and pain, the moments and years that should have been, their unrealized dreams, the cultural divide that hungered to be sealed. They felt the core of the father–daughter bond. It was a bond, which had been interrupted so early when Hanna was a tight bud that later, flowered so differently. It was all there in their eyes and more. It was a circle that desperately needed closing.

The baby's incessant fretting pulled her attention away from her father and Hanna began to feed her child. The animal joy of nursing seemed a pale light against the darkest grief Hanna had ever felt. The steel rails were taking her away from her dream of walking the Red Road with her people. Tearfully, she looked up again at her father.

His eyes held pain of a different sort but joy also, and hope. Black Elk's smile was reassuring. Then something caught his eye.

Hanna followed his gaze and there atop a pole passing by the window was a red-tailed hawk. There seemed no doubt of the bird's intent. It looked directly at both of them in turn. Before the train could pull them past this vision, the bird took flight. It flew just outside their window and with each powerful down-stroke of its wings, a palpable sense of family, of Wakanisha, of future and past, of possibilities filled their hearts. Then, with one last thrust of its wings, the hawk flew skyward leaving them with a sense that she's always been there, guiding.

Hanna looked up at her father again, her grief replaced by a sense of wonder. In his eyes she saw that he'd shared in this experience. A feeling of joyful anticipation filled her being. She looked down at her child and it was completely clear the child had also shared.

Hanna lowered her face to her child's until her cheek was touching his. She breathed in his smell and was overwhelmed by the fierce, protective love she felt. She inhaled again and knew there was no richer smell, no stronger feeling, not in nature or the world of man that was more powerful than the love she felt in that instant. A vision opened up inside her that somehow she knew had been passed to her from her mother hawk a moment before. She heard voices in the train car with her, but the sounds had no meaning. Instead, she was only aware of an infinite prairie that stretched to the horizon and beyond.

She seemed to be flying, looking down as if she were a bird. And below her, a line of red skinned women stretched to infinity in both directions. Some of the women were childless; some had many children at their feet. Directly below her was an empty spot next to a small, intense young woman with deep brown intelligent eyes. Hanna joyfully realized that her mother was there. On the other side of Hanna's spot in this unbroken line was another young woman that Hanna somehow knew was her daughter. Downward she spiraled until Hanna stood in her spot in this line of women, her relatives. Hanna looked downstream at the woman standing there next to her, a complete stranger but completely familiar, her daughter whose essence was connected into this age-old voyage of spirit. Hanna smiled at her daughter and saw beyond to her daughter and far into the future. Hanna noticed a strange thing as she turned to look behind her, at her own mother. Hanna was wearing skins and all of the women behind her were dressed the same. Hanna's daughter and perhaps ten generations were dressed in the clothing of the whites then her relatives were dressed again in skins. Hanna turned and looked into the eyes of Itunkala, her mother. Those eyes were so deep, so penetrating that Hanna felt as if she were falling into a place where only spirits could dwell. Her mother reached out, put her hand on Hanna's shoulder and said –"

"Hanna! Hanna, what do you think?"

She blinked, looked up and there was Ben. He was standing beside her in the aisle, his hand on her shoulder He looked at her expectantly. Abe Hubert was there, sitting across from her, talking with her father.

Hanna's return to her current reality was painfully abrupt. She looked across at her father who gave her an understanding smile. She had a vague memory of grief as she smiled back knowingly. Her child still nursed, the train rolled on but instead of grief, Hanna felt as if a gift awaited her and it brought her quiet joy.

"We've been discussing what name we should give our boy." Ben was his usual, vibrating good-natured self. Your father reminded us of Sioux tradition and Mr. Hubert here says there's an advantage to naming our baby now. He even has a suggestion." Ben nodded toward Abe Hubert who sat there smiling.

"Consider this the prattling grandfather, not your employer." Hubert gave her a hard smile, a nod and continued. "You Indians aren't the only ones who've been pushed around. I'm from the Tribe of Israel – I know you've read about us in your Bible." Hubert nodded at Black Elk and said, "Your father has been gently pushing me around. He wants me to hire your friend Bess, who now seems to be a new close associate of Dunn, your Left Hook. It seems they're spending time together. But that's another story. I'd be honored if the first name you give your son were Abraham. Little Abe! In my tribe that name means *Great Man, Gift of God*." He paused and looked at each there. "And it was me that put your little rescue party together. "He put his hands on his hips and looked at each person there. Then in a voice that was almost childlike, "And, I'm the oldest person here."

Hanna smiled up at Hubert and said, "She's really good at math." She blushed thinking about Bess and John – she wasn't sure if she approved.

Hubert laughed. "Just like your father, change the subject." He grinned at Black Elk then glanced back at Hanna. "I already hired her. You're right, she is good!"

Hanna looked at this intelligent, intense and demanding man. She made eye contact with Ben then with her father and the acceptance was there. When she looked into the eyes of her son, the readiness was there. "Hello, Abraham. Little Abe." she whispered. She looked up at Hubert and turned the child to face the old man. *"Hello little man, meet your Thunkashila."* She stood and handed the child to the old man. Then in English she said, "Abraham, meet your second Grandfather."

Body and Soul

On the tracks somewhere near the North Dakota, Montana border – Fall, 1897

"Dammit woman! Why do you keep following me around?"

Bess's reaction was immediate and forceful. Dunn was so startled by the fierceness of her response that fear showed in his eyes momentarily. She'd stepped around him, spun to face the big man and shoved him in the chest with both hands. "You know why I'm here!" she whispered with such intensity the words seemed shouted. She put her hands on her hips, stood on her tiptoes with her eyes scant inches from his. "We had an instant connection the moment we first saw each other. You know it! I know it! You act gruff and distant, but your eyes say something else." She dropped her hands to her sides, looked down sadly and said, "Our spirits want each other."

There was no movement in the stock car except the gentle rocking from the rails. The horses stopped feeding and stared at Bess and Dunn. There was an animal intensity between the two the horses understood. The two humans glared at each other defiantly.

Bess sat on a hay bale and looked at her hands for a moment. When Dunn sat across from her, she looked up and saw the pain in his eyes. "Kanj Coonshi stopped me in the aisle of her car yesterday. She sat me down and just looked into my eyes. It felt like she saw my spirit. You know what she said? 'You can heal him.' That's all she said. I tried to hide my feelings from her and answered, 'Who?' She touched my heart with that boney finger of hers. She wasn't fooled. Then she said, 'You can do this child.'"

Dunn stood and started to walk away.

Bess grabbed the big man by the hand and pulled him around facing her. "She didn't use the Sioux word phiyÁ meaning heal like a doctor. She used kiyáphA which means to heal by sucking out poison." She dropped his hand and smiled wistfully.

"You're right." Dunn said with more authority than he felt. "I am drawn to you. So, are we talking about us as a couple, as mates? There are so many reasons it shouldn't be that I can't believe I am even talking to you about it. Look at me! The gray in my hair, my knees ache – I'm probably twice your age. It would be like father, daughter. You're this bright, young woman in her prime. "I'm –" he looked down at himself, "old!"

Bess reached out between the space that separated them. "Take my hand. Please. And tell me what you feel."

"I don't need to." He smiled sadly. "Even when you shove me, I feel your spirit."

She turned her palm up and looked at him pleadingly. "Please."

Reluctantly, Dunn took her hand and immediately felt a sensation like a pleasurable shock. He looked into her eyes and his consciousness narrowed to what seemed like a tunnel between them, where a nonverbal communication linked them. He had been there before. He felt the same link he'd had with his woman from several lifetimes ago. The remembered pain offset the hope and joy he felt. He'd cultivated a deadness of spirit to simply survive.

For Bess, the experience was reversed. It was the first time she'd ever experienced hope and joy in expectation of togetherness with a man. Every man she'd ever experienced, the relationship had been coerced or forced. It was the first time she'd ever touched and been touched by a man that hadn't brought bitterness and anger.

This moment between them seemed timeless; it might have been seconds or years. It was the sound of Dunn's horse nickering that brought them back to the present. Somehow both Dunn and Bess heard the horse's approval.

"Bess, there are so many reasons that we..."

She reached across, gently put her fingers to his lips and sat next to him. "Shhh. I know some of your story. I know there was a woman you loved from before. I know she died and..."

"She killed herself because I wasn't there." Dunn stifled a sob. "Our camp was attacked. Black Elk and I were the only men that survived. Itunkala, Hanna's mother was killed. Most of the other women were raped by the soldiers, as was my wife. Her name was Spoon Woman. Because I was in uniform, I was chained for desertion. The soldiers took Hanna, who was only days old, with them back to their fort in Kansas so Black Elk would be cooperative. The rest of the tribe was sent west to Ft. Laramie in Wyoming. They took me to Kansas to punish me. A young couple in a small town outside the fort adopted Hanna. Days later, the soldiers just let me go. I spent a few hours in the home of the young preacher that adopted Hanna. I told them her story and gave them her precious black rock. Then I followed my tribe west to Ft. Laramie, hoping to be with my wife again. Just days before I got there, the soldiers took all the children away. Hanna's aunt, Itunkala's sister and my Spoon Woman just gave up; they died together. I was too late."

Dunn looked at Bess with haunted eyes. "It took a miracle and Abe Hubert to put what's left of my family together. I'm bitter, scarred. I would not be a good man for you. I don't know if I can love again."

Bess took Dunn's face in both her hands, got close and whispered, "Hear my story!" She leaned against him, put her head on his shoulder and began. "The first time I was with a man, I was a young girl. It was my first day at the school where you rescued Hanna. A bunch of us got off the train and were taken to the school. We were separated from the boys, taken to a room with showers. We were told to take off our clothes, our hair was cut and we were sprayed for lice. After the shower, a man came in and just selected me as if I was some animal to be bought. He took me to his room and raped me. Then, for years, he sent for me. It was always the same. He told me what a good girl I was, made me show him my body, then he just took what he wanted. When I finally got strong enough to refuse, I was punished." She gave Dunn a sad smile. "You call me Cactus Girl. Now you know why."

The two sat there together, lost in their own bitter memories. Then there was a subtle change. Warmness began to flow between them where their bodies touched. Bess somehow sensed that a few cracks were opening in the walls Dunn kept up to protect himself. Dunn could feel the anger in her bleeding off into an acceptance, a peace within her. Finally, she whispered, "John, will you please hold me?"

Dunn leaned back against the hay bale that was part of his reading chair. Bess stood for a moment and sat between his legs with her back to his chest. Tentatively, Dunn put his hands on top of hers and wrapped her arms along with his around her stomach.

"How's that?" Dunn said softly into her ear.

Her answer was not verbal. She seemed to melt into him.

At first, they experienced a sense of comfort that before had been impossible, oppositional. The comfort transitioned to a feeling of quiet intimacy. It felt as if the cloth that separated their skin no longer existed and their spirits were separated only by the thinnest of membranes. The horses nickered their approval again, but neither Bess nor Dunn was aware of anything except the growing closeness of their individual selves. It was as if their inner beings were trying desperately to merge, to become one; but that final step still needed some blessing.

They both thought it was the other who moved first. It didn't matter. Slowly, their entwined hands moved up her body until their hands cupped her breasts. Neither knew if it was his hands that gently squeezed and molded her hands to her breasts. There was mutual assent. To Dunn, it seemed as if she encouraged him, wanted him, and initiated this intimacy. For her, it felt as if his barriers were falling and he was losing himself in her. For both, their heartbeats increased together until they had no awareness except for the shared intimate closeness. Nothing else existed.

Their right hands, entwined, moved as one like their nervous systems had become melded. Together and frantically, their hands were beneath her skirt. Bess knew her body well, had relieved her longings many times. But with his hand there with hers at her core, it was as if the two of them shared the experience. When she cried out in release, she felt it in two bodies and knew he felt it through her. It was as if for that timeless moment, they had become one.

They sat there together; time ceased to exist. What had been contentious was now acceptance between them. They felt lazy together, relaxed. He leaned his head down and kissed her on the cheek – the act seemed natural and right to both of them. Then a slow realization came to them at the same time; they had become friends.

Bess turned to face him and asked, "John, can we start over?"

He sighed. "I'll try."

Boundaries
Crossing into Canada, Fall, 1897

The land created me. I'm wild and lonesome. Even as I travel the cities, I'm more at home in the vacant lots.
   Bob Dylan

"Grandmother, soon we pass into Canada. I am so excited because I have never been in another country before. When I was younger, my teacher told stories of traveling in other lands. I always imagined these places to be different, better."

Kanj Coonshi continued to stare at the limitless Montana prairie as it passed by their window. Hanna wondered if the old woman had heard what she had said. Hanna bounced Little Abe on her knee and tried to be content watching the unending plain as the steel wheels rumbled beneath the floor.

Slowly, the old woman turned. Her eyes seemed young and angry. "*There are no countries! Only Makȟá. It is everything. If you walked on the prairie and picked up a handful of soil, it would be Makȟá. If the wind blew it away as dust, it would be Makȟá. It is the land we walk on. Only the white man makes* these owíčaǧo, *these imaginary lines on the Earth to say 'I own this.' We belong to Makȟá, to the Earth. No man can own the earth without doing violence to other men.*"

When the train finally passed from Montana into Canada, there was no change. The rolling prairie of Canada looked no different than Montana. Hanna watched a barbed wire fence pass by her window that stretched to infinity both north and south. The only other landmark was a shack that stood by a rutted wagon trail. A wooden cross arm that guarded the border between the two countries was raised. There was no guard. The American state of Montana was less than a decade old.

"*Grandmother, my man spends less time with me now that we have a baby.*" Hanna blinked and looked down, surprised that these words had come out of her mouth. She wasn't even consciously aware of her feelings of loneliness until just now.

Kanj Coonshi smiled and said, *"Let me hold the child while we talk, little sister."* The old woman sat the child on her lap facing Hanna. Little Abe gripped both Coonshi's thumbs, one in each hand. He gave Hanna a brief smile; his head was upright on his neck and he held himself steady, almost.

"Does your man give you good love?" The old woman gave Hanna a knowing smile.

"Yes, he loves me, us. He's a good man!"

"Does he make you lose yourself when he's in your bed? Do you cry out when he loves you?" Kanj Coonshi stared frankly at Hanna.

Hanna's ruddy skin turned several shades darker; she broke eye contact, embarrassed. *"Yes Grandmother, he is a good man in all ways."* she stuttered.

Kanj Coonshi's laugh was a pure, innocent contralto in comparison to her speaking voice that was harsh, throaty, commanding. *"When I was young, the women talked freely. There was no shame. We learned from each other."* Kanj Coonshi leaned forward and put one hand on Hanna's knee. *"When your baby is older, your man will be back. It is natural for him to spend more time with his friends now. Your baby takes your breasts that were his. Much of the care and love you gave him you now give your child, as you should. Some men are jealous and make trouble but Iron Eagle is a good man. He will wait till you are ready. Then, your time together will be even better. I know; my man gave me five children."* The old woman leaned back and looked at Hanna with the eyes of age. She spoke of life but, knew too much of death.

Regina, Saskatchewan was founded in 1882 on a site previously called *Wascana* (Buffalo Bones) by the Cree Indians that inhabited the area before the white invasion. Two other much better locales were considered for the center of regional government; they were covered with trees and close to water. But Edgar Dewdney, the lieutenant governor of the North-West Territories, held extensive real estate holdings in and around the railroad line that passed through a tiny settlement aptly named Pile-of-Bones. Princess Louise, Duchess of Argyll, wife of the then Governor General of Canada, later named the new community Regina, in honor of her mother, Queen Victoria. The slaughter of the bison herds to control the Indian population was not confined to the young republic, the United States.

In 1897, Regina was a small city with large dreams. The opera house, the many fine hotels, restaurants and shops sat at odds on the featureless plain with dusty, unpaved streets. Most businesses and a few homes had telephones in 1897, but electricity was still three years in the future.

Regina was no different than the multitudes of mid-western towns scattered throughout Canada and the United States. It grew clustered near the rail lines that brought it life. On one side of the tracks, the businesses became more genteel the further from the tracks they were built. The saloons and bordellos, hardware stores and livery stables sat near the tracks and sold goods and services basic to human need. On the other side of the tracks, there were animal pens, coal and water storage units necessary for train travel. Also there were the warehouses, machine shops and blacksmiths that serviced the new, mechanized society.

A flagger, a switch monkey and a rail boss met Cody's second train as it pulled into the outskirts. The train was shuttled to tracks adjacent and parallel to the tracks that held Cody's first train.

Hanna's view to the left was all too familiar – dirty black gravel, trash, broken glass. The only living things she could see were cattle penned up, their eyes empty and terrified. But to the right almost near enough to touch was Cody's train. She could see into the adjacent car's windows and it appeared to be a private car. She'd been in Hubert's car but it was unappealing because of the clutter. But this car's interior was neat. Hanna seemed to be looking into another life, a life of quiet luxury, a life of privilege.

The sun's reflection made it difficult to see detail but Hanna thought she could see a woman moving about, a flash of hair, a skirt swirling. Hanna wondered if she was looking into the private life of the show's main attraction, Annie Oakley. As she nursed, Hanna's imagination took her away. She pictured herself as the show's star, being fawned over, invited to fancy hotels at every stop and surrounded by material wealth.

"Hanna! Hey! Let's go!" Ben stood in the aisle nearly vibrating with excitement.

For an instant, Hanna saw the child in Ben, the boy and man she knew and fell in love with. Then, their current reality asserted itself. "Ben, you don't want to go into town dressed like that, do you?"

"Come on! I've got a couple of hours before Dunn and your father make arrangements for the horses. Let's go! I can change later after I help corral the horses in livery."

"But Ben, look at you!" Hanna closed her top, stood and handed the baby to Ben.

"Oh come on! I don't want to change then change again. I'll be loading hay into the feed car and moving stock. Let's just take a quick walk around town; maybe find a place to eat dinner. We can dress up later and have a nice time. Besides, I'm anxious to see what a different country looks like."

Hanna and Ben picked their way across the litter and blackened gravel until they came to the beginnings of a wide, dirt road. Little Abe rode on Hanna's back in a beautifully made traditional elk skin backpack. They walked toward the buildings in the distance. They passed the corrals, several sheds containing piled coal, bales of hay and rusted axels and wheels. Then, a boardwalk started on both sides of the street. A street sign at the first intersection they came to read Dewdney Avenue.

They stepped up on the boardwalk, happily headed for Regina's bustling downtown. They were walking in front of a large, unmarked warehouse. A white man was on the boardwalk, sweeping. As Hanna and Ben approached, the man stopped what he was doing and said, "In the road Priggers." He leaned on his broom and scowled at them.

Hanna stopped, surprised, "What?" she asked. Ben's face clouded with anger as he balled his hands into fists.

"Yea, you Prairie Niggers belong in the street. Git!"

Hanna grabbed the back of Ben's shirt and tried to pull him back. At that same moment, a large, burly man stepped out of the warehouse. "Hey Rufus, need a hand?" He stood there blocking the boardwalk, a sneer on his face.

Ben took another step forward, towing Hanna behind him. He mirrored the big man's stance. Ben's hands were on his hips, chin out, defiant. "Is there some law that says I can't be here?" The tone of his voice was incendiary.

"Ain't got no laws for you Redskins. You just ain't allowed up here with us white folks."

Ben stood his ground and said nothing. Hanna stepped down onto the dirt hoping Ben would follow suit.

"Listen boy. I can give ya two bits a day to scoop up them road apples and wheel em to the dump, but you best git down in the road or you's in a heap uh trouble."

In the background, Ben could hear footsteps behind him on the boardwalk, but he was so angry, the sound barely registered. Then he saw the change in the faces of the men blocking his way. He turned and walking up the boardwalk was William Cody dressed in his trademark fringed buckskin shirt, large hat and goatee. With him was Annie Oakley and her husband and manager, Frank Butler. Following them were a growing number of townsfolk anxious to be part of history.

Cody stopped and viewed this confrontational tableau calmly. He turned to Hanna and said, "Why you must be Hanna. I've heard your story and I must say it's incredible." He reached down and offered his hand to her. "Please do me the honor." He pulled her up onto the boardwalk. "I would love to have you and your family join me for lunch." He extended his right hand to Ben and said, "You must be Iron Eagle. I hear good things about you from the crew."

Hanna felt flustered but she managed to say, "Mr. Cody, I want to thank you for taking us on. If it weren't for the show, our lives would be very different. I never would have found my father." She smiled shyly at him. "Now I have a family."

"Please my dear, I should thank you. Your courage, your stamina are an inspiration to me. But please allow me to correct your thinking. Many people call us the Wild West Show but it's not. It's my wish that what we present be called an exposition. What we do is not entertainment but educational. We re-enact our nation's history. It's entirely up to the audience to interpret our efforts on their behalf." Cody looked pointedly at the two men blocking their way. "Some people see our red skinned brothers and sisters as heathens and savages. I know differently. I have met many like you who have lived through terrible trials only to remain gracious, intelligent and God-fearing." Cody removed his hat and bowed to Hanna. "Please accept my apologies on behalf of my white brothers. Many of them are ignorant of the breadth and depth of the Indian character of which you are a fine example." Cody stepped up to the open-mouthed men on the boardwalk and asked, "Gentlemen, may we pass?"

Cypress Hills
Near Calgary, Canada Fall, 1897

History releases me from my own experiences and jogs my fictional imagination.
   Jennifer Gilmore

Now that he was older, Hubert found great pleasure in his morning routine – a routine that worried him briefly each morning. The slight worry came as he urinated in the toilet of his private car. His worry – that soon the day would come when his day would be ruined if the routine were upset. But so far, it hadn't happened. There was nothing remotely routine about this traveling circus he managed and the lives of the people that depended on his wisdom.

As always, Abe peered out his window hoping for a target. And today promised to be a grand day – not far ahead the tracks passed through a tiny town clinging to the railroad tracks for its very existence. And where the tracks intersected the town's only dirt road, a freight wagon waited to cross. With great accuracy, Hubert flushed about thirty yards prior to his car passing the intersection – he was rewarded with a perfect billow of spray beneath his car as it passed the hapless teamster. The look of horror on the teamster's face was worth its weight in gold – genuine laughter was good medicine.

Amos had a cup of coffee ready as Hubert entered the dining car – another good omen. Amos was wise and considerate. Hubert treasured their brief morning conversations. And, as usual, Amos had a newspaper from some previous stop. It didn't matter if the news was days or even weeks old. Hubert drank his second cup and read the paper as he made his second visit to the bathroom. Ah yes, it promised to be a good day. His bowels obeyed satisfactorily and a sense of well being spread out from his center lightening his mood.

Hubert whistled a tune, something in a minor key from his past life as he dressed in one of his four nearly identical suits. He couldn't name the tune or the words that accompanied it, but it pulled up vague memories of his childhood growing up in Chicago. A samovar filled with tea sat on the table – many people were gathered around speaking Yiddish, German, Romanian and Russian. Some were family but all were part of his tribe. These early memories made him especially thankful for the people that surrounded him now.

Then, as he passed into the vestibule between his car and the dining car, Hubert stopped and said a brief prayer of thanks before he took his morning walk. There were a few folks eating breakfast in the first dining car – Amos nodded graciously as Hubert passed through. The second dining car was nearly full and all there nodded or smiled and said "Good morning!" to him as he passed. Some of the girls in the wardrobe car were working – some sat together and smoked near an open window as he passed. Abe touched his hat as he walked by these amazing women and was rewarded with more than one wink. It was indeed going to be a good day.

The nursery car was especially happy today. Children of all ages and colors were playing riotously just prior to morning lessons. As always, the children shrieked and gathered around when he stopped in their midst. "Closest number to one hundred?" He smiled broadly as the children mobbed him. It was part of his daily routine - he never had a number in mind. But Abe always managed to give the penny to a new child each day.

Hubert's daily walk through his train was almost always pleasurable. He also used this time to be the boss – to tell his section leaders about the upcoming plans. That way, his people knew what was to come, what costumes to have ready, what acts and actors were needed, what equipment had to be readied. And at the end of the train, the stock handlers would know what animals were going to perform. It was there in the stock car that Hubert's day took a turn.

"Oy Vey!" Abe Hubert said as he looked around the car that Dunn and Black Elk usually called home. "Why all the glum faces?" He pushed the derby back on his head and looked around. The whistle blew up ahead as the train crossed a lonely intersection. A puff of coal smoke blew in the open window.

The six members of Black Elk's family sat on hay bales in a rough circle. Only Little Abe seemed cheerful. Ben and Hanna looked morose, Dunn and Black Elk slouched dejectedly and Bess was her usual angry self.

"None of you got off in Medicine Hat! Right?" The tone of his voice made his comment more of a statement than a question. "Yea, I heard about your experience back in Regina. They were schmoes!" Hubert walked over to Hanna and held out his hands for the baby. "L'chaim!" he said as the baby settled into the crook of his arm. Dunn's horse nickered from its stall and the baby laughed. "I'm glad somebody is happy to see me."

Dunn sat up but didn't stand. He touched his hat with two fingers and said, "We're just sick of these Podunk towns and all the podunks that live in them."

Hubert stood there looking down at Dunn, a knowing smile on his face. "My people know what it means to be an *oysvorf*. In Yiddish that means bad guy, villain, the outsider. We Jews have been outsiders for centuries. Just because your skin is different doesn't mean you're the only one that's been persecuted. It's been going on since man was created. You just have to keep going."

Dunn nodded then asked, "What's up boss?"

"Well, it looks as if we will arrive in Calgary a day early. So you and your crew will have an easy day handling the stock and putting the first act together."

"We doing Little Big Horn?" Black Elk asked.

"Nope! Cody wants to do Cypress Hills first then the Battle of Cut Knife."

"*Chesli!*" Black Elk sighed and frowned at Dunn.

"English please! But from your tone of voice, I can guess." Hubert handed Little Abe back to Hanna.

"Manure! That's what it means. We hate that show." Dunn held up his hands. "Yea, I know the Canadians love it but it's painful for us."

As Hanna sat Little Abe on her lap, she asked, "I've never heard of Cypress Hills. What happened there?"

Hubert looked at Black Elk and smiled grimly. "I need to sit down to tell this. And Bess, I'm just the messenger here!" He looked at her warily as Ben stood for him to have a place to sit. Dunn draped his arm over Bess's shoulders as the old Jew began his story.

"Back in the 70's not far from here, a dozen or so wolfers were returning from their winter hunt and camped on the Teton River, just over the border in the U.S."

"You mean they were hunting our wolf brothers?" Bess was already showing signs of her trademark ire. "Why?"

"Bess! Please let the man tell his story." Dunn took his arm from around her shoulder and he faced her. "Good or bad, this is Canadian history." When she started to protest, he held up both hands and said, "Cody tries to illustrate history. It is up to the audience as to how they see it."

"Do you still want to hear this?" Abe Hubert asked Hanna, but meant his question for Bess. "It's the Canadian version of Sand Creek."

Bess stared sullenly at the floor as Hanna nodded the affirmative. But before Hubert could continue his narrative, Bess faced the older man and in a flat, menacing voice said, "Except for Leftook, you're the only white who's ever treated me like an equal. And yet, you're telling about another event where whites destroyed creation and are proud of it." She clenched her fists and seemed ready to erupt.

Hubert squatted down until his eyes were level with Bess's. "Some advice my dear! I was young and angry once. It was not a tool that worked. Let go of your anger – know your limitations. Change the things that you know you can change and try to find some joy in that." He looked at her long and hard. "Life without joy is not life."

Hubert stood and continued. "This story is important to Canadians because it made them realize there was no real law and order in this area. It's the bad behavior of both the whites and the Natives that brought about the formation of the North-West Mounted Police."

"You mean the guys in the red uniforms?" Ben asked.

"They didn't wear red at first but yes, it was the beginning of the Royal Mounted Police." Hubert glanced nervously at Bess then continued. "Anyway, these hunters had been shooting buffalo and lacing the meat with arsenic. The wolves and coyotes that died from the poison were skinned to make coats the rich wanted back east. Many other animals and a few people died from eating the poisoned meat." Abe paused and looked at Hanna – the pain in her eyes made him want to weep.

Hubert shuddered then continued. "These hunters were camped just over the U. S. border headed for Fort Benton when most of their horses were stolen. They assumed it was the local Indians that were the thieves. And having to pack all of their cargo to the fort on their backs that made these guys mad. The soldiers at the fort refused to help so the hunters took it upon themselves to get their horses back. They followed the tracks north into Canada for three days then lost the trail after a bad rain. Anyway, they ended up at one of two whisky forts in the Cypress Hills region. Even though it was against the law to sell whisky to the Indians, these forts made a fortune trading whisky for whatever the Indians would bring in."

Bess whispered "Whisky!" with such malice in her voice Hubert stopped his narrative and all there looked at her.

"After three days of hard drinking and no horses, the hunters decided to spy on the camp of the local Assiniboine Indians camped near the whisky forts. The Assiniboine, led by a warrior named Little Soldier, didn't have the horses so the hunters went back to the fort for even more drinking. Some freighters driving wagons arrived with more whiskey and this large group of white men spent that night and the following morning drinking heavily.

The next day in a drunken rage, one of the freight haulers thought one of his horses had been stolen. He grabbed his rifle and staggered toward the Indian encampment. The rest of the men followed. They surrounded the Assiniboine's and started firing down into the camp. They used their advantage of higher ground, tree cover and superior rifles and devastated the village. Most of the Assiniboine men, a few women and children died. The surviving women were taken into their tipis and were violated until the whisky ran out several days later."

Hubert stood and looked sadly at Bess. "The Indians knew better than to trade for the whisky. The whites broke all kinds of laws, both Canadian and American. It was because of this incident and many others like it that the Canadian government realized just how lawless the North-West territories were. The incident at Cypress Hills resulted in the Mounted Police."

Hubert squatted down again and took Bess's hands in his. When she finally made eye contact, he spoke softly. "You're young and from your perspective, your people have always been persecuted. But that hasn't always been the case and hopefully, it won't always be. A hundred years ago, this country was young and everybody hated the English. Now they're trading partners and thick as thieves. Just do what you can – live your life and treat others fairly. And better yet, you belong to a tribe now that cares for you and protects you. All we're trying to do is tell stories and let people see their history." He patted Bess's hand and stood up. "And I really need your help." He turned, gently pinched Little Abe's cheek and was gone.

Ben sat down again next to Hanna. He glanced at Black Elk as if he couldn't believe what he'd heard. "What's the Battle of Cut Knife?

Dunn stood and stretched. "I'll tell it." He looked at Bess and said, "You'll probably like this story better. It's like the Canadian version of Little Big Horn. Yes, your northern brothers got some revenge."

"About fifteen years ago and north of here, there was a large population of Métis. They are a group of people that are mixed local Indians and French. They controlled a large area near Battleford, a town a days travel north of here. They organized and joined the Cree and the Assiniboine and began gathering a large force. Their plan was to march on Battleford to force the local Indian agent to give them the food they were allotted. All the local Indians were starving – then the whole thing went south."

Dunn sat down again near Bess and continued, "It was tragic, a big misunderstanding. All the local whites saw were the Indians gathering and they got scared. They all went to the fort in Battleford for protection. When all the farms and houses were empty, somebody went around and looted all the empty buildings. The whites claimed it was the Indians – the Indians claimed it was other whites. Nobody knows. Anyway, the government sent for the cavalry, the army and the Mounted Police."

Dunn paused for effect. "The cavalry attacked the Indians not realizing how big a force of Indians there were. The cavalry was utterly defeated. There was a huge loss of life on the other side. It all could have been avoided if both sides had kept their promises."

Dunn leaned back and sighed. He reached up and put one large hand on Bess's shoulder and pulled her to him. "All Cody is trying to do is get people to learn from their history." He shook his head. "I don't think it's working."

Thiyáta
Calgary, Canada, Fall, 1897

There's no place like home.
   L. Frank Baum

Some of the deer jumped to the ground the moment Ben slid open the door to the stock car. The elk were not so gregarious – they waited for the ramp to be pushed into place before descending onto Canadian soil.

The elk blinked in the sunlight. They oriented themselves to the enclosure formed by the two trains parked parallel to each other then followed Ben toward the water tank.

Ben loved this moment. The deer were so tame, the instant they were released, they gathered around him, nosing his pockets for the sweet green hay he kept hidden there.

Cody's two brightly decorated trains were parked on separate rail spurs in the Calgary train yard roughly forty yards apart. Temporary fencing strung between the front and back of each train formed a huge rectangular enclosure.

In these rare instances when the trains shaped this refuge, the white-tailed deer and the elk were allowed to roam free. Sadly, the two bison named Kurt and Maddy were kept corralled. It was as if the trains defined a small territory separate from whatever place Cody's show performed. Only one thing spoiled the freedom enjoyed by the animals and all four colors of men within this space – the human spectators that actually lived there often intruded.

Ben stopped, almost as if he'd walked into a wall. His reality flooded in and threatened to overwhelm him. His existence as a new father, an animal handler and part-time actor had become so all encompassing, his past barely intruded. It was nearly October, *Čhaŋwápa kasná wí, Leaves Shaking Off the Trees Moon,* as Black Elk called this moon. Yet a little over three months ago, he and Hanna had been virtual prisoners at the Carlisle Industrial School in Pennsylvania. Every moment of their lives there, they had been terrified of being a couple. They hid Hanna's pregnancy knowing that if found out, they'd probably never see each other again. The food was terrible and abuse was rampant. This past summer of freedom with a reunited family had been joyous.

Ben focused on his work. He and Hanna were relieved that they wouldn't have an active part in the upcoming performance of Cypress Hills. Ben's job was to help with security and Hanna would man the ticket sales booth along with Bess. Black Elk was slated to play Little Soldier, the Assiniboine chief and Dunn was to act as one of the drunken, aggressive trappers.

The next morning was busy as usual – breakfast was served early, the stock were fed and watered, the tipis and the rest of the sets were unloaded from the storage cars and stacked on wagons to be transported to the Calgary fair grounds. And during this harried but organized time, the locals were there, watching, intruding, asking questions. The children from Cody's show and the local children played together in the open area between the trains as children always do. Couples of all ages from nearby Calgary strolled around the outside perimeter formed by the trains. Children and single men intruded into the heart of the Show's contained interior.

As usual, the show began with a parade led by Cody on horseback. Annie Oakley and her husband Frank drove a fancy cabriolet drawn by matched white horses. An Indian wearing a porcupine quill breastplate and full-feathered headdress led several of the deer and elk that had been haltered and roped together. Maddy and Kurt snorted at the audience lining the street from a circus style barred wagon.

Calamity Jane told stories of the old west through a new loudspeaker device, recently invented by Alexander Graham Bell and improved upon by Ernst Siemens. The audiences settled into their seats during the story telling and were fascinated by the rope artists and the trick riding. Then the announcer said, "Ladies and gentlemen, I present to you the sharpshooting duo …".

When Annie Oakley and her husband Frank Butler stepped out in front of the crowd, the thunderous applause completely drowned out the announcer.

With her trusty .22 rifle she mesmerized the audience for almost a half hour with her uncanny skill. The act began when Frank lit a cigarette as he walked thirty paces and stood facing the audience. With one shot, she shot the ember and extinguished his smoke. Frank then took a deck of cards out of his shirt pocket, drew the Ace of Spades and showed it to the crowd. He held it out facing the crowd and with another single shot from Annie's .22, the top half of the card fell to the ground. Frank then asked if anyone in the audience had a dime. A man who responded was asked down from the bleachers and instructed to toss the dime into the air – she hit the dime in mid-air. The man picked up his dime and yelled to the crowd that it had been hit dead center. Then Frank asked the man to pick a card – Frank tossed the card into the air and Annie put six holes in it with her rifle before it hit the ground.

The crowd surged to its feet applauding and whistling as Annie and Frank took their bows. At that moment Cody made his entrance riding Charlie. The audience roared their approval. Cody let the adulation wash over him for a few moments then simply held up his hand for silence – the crowd complied instantly.

Cody rode slowly to the announcer's podium and took the microphone. He paused dramatically then began. "Ladies and Gentlemen, may I present to you an event important to your country's history – the incident at Cypress Hills."

Several brightly decorated tipis stood on the left side of the field representing the Assiniboine village. At stage right, a crudely made log fort was erected, open on one side so the audience could see the interior. Cody narrated the troubles the trappers had losing their horses, having to pack the pelts to Ft. Benton and their subsequent trip bent on revenge. As Cody told this part of the Cypress Hills story in his deep resonant voice, Indians began to appear in ones and twos in the tipi village. A child kindled a fire; a hunter walked in with a side of meat to the cheers of his kin. Women worked on hides making clothing; children played – the scene very clearly showed a simple day in the life of an Assiniboine tribe.

Next, the trappers appeared and seemed to sneak around in the distance, looking into the village as Cody explained that the missing horses were not to be found. The trappers retired to the fort and began drinking. Perhaps the actors playing the trappers were just playing to the audience, but the more drunken they acted, the more laughter came from the stands.

Several wagons appeared at the gate of the fort and more whisky was carried in. The trappers and the teamsters appeared to be conversing and soon, more whisky was consumed. They fell off their stools, they argued and were riotously drunk acting, much to the delight of the audience. And then one of the teamsters ran toward the crowd and raised his rifle. When the audience quieted, he screamed, "I thinks one of them dad burned Redskins stole my hoss!"

At this point, Cody handed the microphone back to the announcer, looked sadly at the audience and removed his hat.

The trappers and the teamsters ran out of the fort, surrounded the village and began firing indiscriminately at the Assiniboine. A warrior raised his rifle in defense but was cut down. A child ran to his father's side and fell. Several of the women tried to shield their children and were shot where they stood.

When all of the men, most of the children and some of the women lay dead, the firing stopped. Then, as if in a dream, the surviving women stood and cried as the dead rose and slowly walked off stage left.

There was a momentary tableau while not one person on stage moved as the smoke cleared. Then, with drunken laughter, the white men rushed into the village and dragged the remaining women into their lodges.

For a full five minutes there was not a sound, not a scream, not a moan of pleasure, nothing. The audience was left to stew in their own imaginations.

Without looking at the crowd again, Cody rode toward the tipis at stage left and exited. At the same time, the players in the tipis came out somberly. The Indians walked with heads down toward stage left. The trappers and teamsters walked to stage right, hats in hand.

The applause that followed was not for the performance of Cypress Hills; it was for the red-coated riders that appeared center stage. They were dressed in the uniforms of the Royal Mounted Police. As they rode past the audience, the announcer simply said, "It was the lawlessness at Cypress Hills and the newspaper articles that followed that led to the formation of Canada's Mounted Police Force. Tomorrow, our exposition will examine the happenings at the Battle of Cut Knife. Thank you for coming! We hope to see you all here tomorrow."

"Uŋkče!" Bess growled as she stormed into the stock car. She slammed the door so hard, both Hanna and the baby jumped.

Hanna laughed and tried to settle Little Abe at the same time. "I love learning new words when you're mad." She looked at her friend standing there, fists clenched at her side, surrounded by hay bales and the smell of horse. "I thought you've been trying to let go of your anger."

"*I am so angry, I don't want to even talk their talk.*" Bess blew forcefully through her nose and sat down next to Hanna.

"*The men...*" Hanna gave Bess a questioning look.

"Yes! White *wasicans*! Did you see their eyes?" Bess rolled her own eyes and sighed. "*One grabbed my hand and told me to take him to my tipi.*"

Hanna sputtered, half laughing half horrified. "*You mean he wanted you to go to one of the tipis and...*"

"Yes, he wanted me to *kichi yungka*, to fuck him!" Bess shuddered. "*If I would have had a knife, he'd be dead.*"

"*A young white man followed me as I was coming to feed the baby. His eyes were hungry; you know the look when a man wants a woman. He went away when he saw I was carrying Little Abe.*"

"I know the look all too well." A look of revulsion crossed her face. "Men can be such pigs. I wonder why the white men don't treat white women like they do us?" Bess leaned back against the hay and smirked. "Maybe white women have nothing under their big puffy skirts but petticoats between their legs!" She glanced at Hanna and burst out laughing."

Hanna gasped then joined in the laughter. "Bess, what was that word you used?"

"Uŋkče! That word?" "It means the fart noise you make when you shit! It's my new name for young white men."

Both women were laughing hysterically when Ben stepped into the stock car all of them used for their living room. "What are you two laughing at?" He looked at them with curiosity, hands full of tack.

Bess and Hanna doubled over and laughed even harder. It was a full minute before either one of them could speak.

"I'm glad you two can laugh after this rotten day." Ben said. "I was just coming to tell you that Amos cooked up a real nice meal for tonight to cheer folks up. Our shift isn't until about seven." He turned and began hanging the tack on pegs and commented, "The compound between the cars was full of whites after the show. We had to run em off." He put the last bridle on its hook and said, "During the last act, the women looked like they wanted to cry but the men - their eyes looked half crazy like a horse just before a thunder storm. After the show, a bunch of them came snooping around, looking at our women hungry like."

"I know!" said Hanna. "One followed me and another one got fresh with Bess. He's lucky to be alive."

"Who's lucky to be alive?" Dunn stood in the doorway, nearly filling up the space. Black Elk was behind him as the two walked into the car.

Bess stood and approached Dunn. As he put his arm over her shoulder, she recounted her experience. She expected - she hoped - he would erupt and try to exact some sort of judgment. His response surprised her.

Dunn was thoughtful for a moment. He looked at Black Elk who nodded. "Let's take a load off and talk." Dunn arranged a couple of bales and sat down, pulling Bess down with him.

"This happens almost every time we do Cypress Hills. These boys probably heard stories from their daddies about Indian women. That scene at the end always gets them. Anybody notice the faces in the audience?"

When all of the three young adults nodded in agreement, Black Elk began. "*We've seen this behavior almost every time we put on Cypress Hills. We had to get the local Mounted Police to take a boy away once. Another young man was happy to talk to us after Leftook here sat him down.*"

Black Elk pulled out a bale and sat next to Ben and Hanna. "*Our beliefs and the way the Whites believe are very much the same. We can call him God or Thunkashila, Wakan Tanka, it doesn't matter.*" He looked at Hanna sadly. "*Your mother believed that there really is only one Creator; we all just call Him by different names. And we feel him in three ways just like the whites. It's how we live those beliefs that make trouble. The White Buffalo Woman teaches us that the four colors of men must get along in peace. But for some reason, many whites believe those of us with different colored skin do not have a spirit, a soul. To them, we are just animals for them to do with as they please.*"

Black Elk stopped speaking for a moment lost in thought. "*The White Buffalo Woman teaches us that the power between a man and a woman, that passion, is a holy thing. This attraction between a woman and a man is part of the sacred hoop. With wisdom and respect, it can fill the lodges of our people for thousands of years. We see nothing wrong with these feelings – they are a part of us and should be enjoyed.*" He smiled at Ben and Hanna.

"The whites think these feelings are a sin. Their church teaches them that these sexual urges are wrong and it can only become not a sin by getting permission from the church. It is this sin and guilt that makes them angry. Many of them think that because a red woman has no soul, it is not a sin to lay with her. They think that they can just take what they want from us because their God will not punish them."

Abe Hubert pushed his way into this emotionally charged conversation. He knitted his eyebrows as he looked from face to face. He shrewdly knew not to ask about the discussion. He nodded to the men, touched his hat to the ladies then turned to

Ben. "The boys are having a bit of trouble getting the deer back to their enclosure. You seem to talk their language. Mind giving the boys a hand?"

Ben smiled and jumped up. "Sure, boss!" He turned to Hanna and said, "See you in a minute." and was gone.

"Tomorrow is Cut Knife as you know. We're going to pack it and do a night run. If we're lucky, we'll be in Colorado Springs by Thursday. We'll be doing Little Big Horn Friday and Saturday. Then we've got one show in Pueblo Sunday and we're done until spring. Cody's taking the trains to his ranch in North Platte – he's wintering the stock there. We'll all meet up in Denver next year, May first." Hubert noticed the distraught look on Hanna's face. He gave her a tight smile, nodded and was gone.

Hanna, as always, could never hide her emotions from those she loved; the devastating pain she felt was there for all to see. She looked at her family and burst into tears. "Ben and I! The baby! We don't have any place to go!"

Her father scooted over and took her and the baby in his arms. "You're coming with us – if you want."

"I just thought – I didn't know… ". She sobbed and continued, "I thought we live here."

Black Elk used his thumbs to remove her tears and smiled down at her. "The Show never performs in the winter. But don't worry, John and I bought a little place in New Mexico. It has mild winters – good water." He looked across at Dunn and saw that Bess had questions as well.

Dunn just smiled and said, "Just get it out – tell them our plans. Then we can talk."

"Cody and Hubert allow us to use this car over the winter. We'll get hooked up with a train going south sometime next week. We take our horses and now, we have a family to take along." He smiled down at her. "We'll take two of the tipis from the storage car – you can live over the winter like a Human Being. John and Bess can have the other one if she wants to come. I'll sleep in our little ranch house."

Hanna's face lit up like the sun. "*Hanj Ate'.*" She stood, hugged him and whispered again, "Yes, Father."

Black Elk gently lifted her face and looked into her eyes. "*I lost you once. That won't happen again. You always have a home with me.*" He reached out and put the palm of his hand on her cheek, his fingers gently behind her neck. "*Our word for home is Thiyáta. It means more than just a place. It means much more, it's a feeling.* With his other hand, he touched his heart. "*Thiyáta means to be here, to be at home. It also means to go home. Think about it. No matter where we are, we're either home or we are going there.*"

Okíni (to share)
Somewhere headed south on the tracks in Montana – Fall, 1897

"When did you plan on telling me?" Bess tried to speak in neutral tones but she knew her voice sounded angry. She stood in front of the man she at times called Leftook and at others Dunn. And in the quiet, intimate times, it was John. The space they shared was homey. It was a stall in one of the livestock cars furnished with hay bales. Small artifacts from their lives sat out, or were nailed onto the rough pine lumber that formed the space where they slept and spent private moments together.

When they'd first met, his three names had meant only one man to her. But as Bess grew to know him, the parts of his past he chose to share gave distinct shadings to which name she used. She almost felt guilty for not telling him the name her parents had given her. That name was a link to a painful, extinct past. She feared that to share her real name with him, with anybody, would strip away the rough, spiky exterior that guarded the child she was inside.

After their first night together, Bess had hung up a tiny pair of intricately beaded moccasins her mother had made for her. Hanging below the moccasins was a white, embroidered collar. When he'd asked, all she'd said was, "These remind me of the extremes of my life." She refused to elaborate. Looking back, Bess realized that his response was one of many lessons he had to teach her about sharing.

Leftook had pulled a rough cotton pouch from his saddlebags. He took out three things, a porcupine quill breastplate, a scrap of deerskin and an eagle feather. As he hung up the breastplate on the opposite wall he said, "*I got this the day I became a Human Being. And this is all that's left of the first shirt my woman made for me.*" He looked at it then up at Bess with a terrible sadness. "She made this for me the day I got my name." He stuck the feather into the breastplate and said, "*This, I can not talk about.*"

"You mean New Mexico!" It was both a question and a statement. Dunn sat down on the hay bales stacked like a bench under the open window. The look on his face was relaxed, inquisitive.

Instinctively, Bess knew she was going to have to open up and share her heart. It was something she hadn't done since childhood; the thought of it terrified her. She had distant memories of running free as a child. She remembered the confusing agony of her people moving onto the reservation, the changes, the lack of freedom, the bitter, hungry winters that were her childhood.

At that moment the train entered a sweeping left turn. The abrupt change in direction threw Bess off balance. She stumbled and would have fallen had John not caught her. She ended up in his lap, his arms around her and the familiar erotic, comforting closeness enveloped them both.

Call it serendipity or irony. Bess and Leftook were at a crossroads, a *íčhiyopteya*, a place where two people meet and might just pass by. At that instant when a word or look could have changed the course of their lives, the train varied its passage. Bess stumbled and fell into Leftook's embrace. In that moment, his arms were around her because on the day of his birth many years before, surveyors of the new Montana Territory were drunk on the job. Rather than walk back the miles to where they made their mistake, they simply made a curve in an imaginary line that should have been straight. The train, as it crossed this flat, nearly featureless expanse, was just rolling on the tracks that followed the plat lines drawn so long ago. It was that centrifugal force that kept them pressed together as Dunn began to speak.

"Bess, the decision is not mine to make," he said softly into her ear. "I hope you want to come. But we need to talk." He turned her to face him. "Our bodies want each other." He gave her a wistful smile. "We're really good together that way. And I know my spirit wants you – I can feel it every moment we're together." He stopped, lost in thought, remembering. "Bess, it's what's in our hearts that we need to share."

The train finished its long sweeping turn and Leftook gently pushed her off his lap onto the bale beside him. "Bess, you know my story. My wife, Spoon Woman and I learned each other's words by sharing our hearts. And here I am with you. We speak English and Sioux - yet we haven't really talked."

The two of them looked into each other's eyes; they saw the pain and hope there. It was Bess that dropped her eyes.

John gently tilted her head back so they were seeing each other again and said, "Bess, I hope that you want to be my *winúȟča*, my woman." He smiled. "In English I would say, I want you to be my old lady." For a moment, there was an unreadable look in his eyes then he said, "Bess Little Robe, *Thečhíȟila.*"

"John!" She stifled a sob and silently signed, "I love you, too." with her hands. She looked down at the hand she used to touch her heart and began. "John, I'm afraid. You know my story. Until you, there was only one other man that didn't hurt me. His name was Pony Boy and I think he was a two-spirit. We never..." she hesitated. "We didn't – we weren't intimate, like you are with me. He was just a good friend." Bess hesitated, glanced up with a haunted look in her eyes then continued. "My father sent me away to that horrible school. The man at the school - the one that raped me - gave me that horrible collar, made me one of his special girls." These last words from Bess dripped anger and pain. "I just don't want to hurt anymore."

Dunn put his arm around her shoulders and pulled her back against the bales. "Bess, what we have right now is enough for me. We spoke our hearts together. It's a start, a good start." He smiled down at her and pulled her close.

She responded. She unbuttoned the top buttons of her shirt for him then gently put one hand on his groin. She turned into him and tried to pull his body down to cover hers.

Dunn responded in a way she didn't expect. He turned and faced her, kneeling on the fresh hay. He put his hands on her shoulders and held her at arms length. "*It's not that I don't want you right now. I do!*" Everything about him conveyed his arousal – his breathing, the look in his eyes, the bulge where she'd had her hand only a moment before. *"We know much of what's in each others' hearts. We know the sore spots, where the scabs cover our wounds. And in time, if we stay together, we will have disagreements – all couples get angry with each other."* He looked at her very intensely. *"I promise you that I won't use something I know of your heart to win an argument, to hurt you because I'm mad. I promise!"* He stopped, searching for words. *"Love is important – we have that I think. We need to trust each other - I think you more so than me. I promise that your name will be safe in my mouth."*

"Leftook, I..." the words didn't come because they weren't needed. The love that passed through their eyes was enough.

"There are many other practical things we need to discuss." He leaned back and laughed. "You're young enough to be my daughter. I may need to spank you from time to time if you lose your temper."

She gasped, shook her head "No!" then laughed out loud.

"And" he said, "*Lol'íȟ'aŋ Wóyute*, you have never cooked a meal for me. Your corn cakes might taste like manure."

She looked at him with an evil smile. "You want me for your old lady just so I will cook for you?"

"There might be more I want from time to time."

She reached out and punched him playfully. "You snore and leave the room a mess. And you might bring home skunk and rat for me to cook. I want buffalo back strap. *Are you a good hunter*?"

He answered her evil smile with one of his own. "I can bring you all the meat that you need!" He stood and adjusted himself with his right hand.

She laughed as she stood and fondled his crotch. "Hmmm? This might not be enough. Do you think it's enough?"

He pulled her into a rough hug. "You're enough for me. More than enough!"

She sighed and whispered, "John..." and didn't finish.

"What?" He held her for a moment and when she didn't respond he asked, "Will you come to New Mexico with me? Will you come and be my old lady?"

Her answer wasn't verbal but it was a very convincing "Yes!"

Uŋspé
Near Taos, New Mexico, Moon When the Trees Crack From the Cold
(Winter 1898)

First, there was only warmth and comfort. Then came a blessed feeling of refuge, sanctuary. She felt enclosed, safe, protected. Next a memory within a memory came. In her past there had been pain and unhappiness. But the memory of that time was somehow kept from her. The skins that kept her warm also insulated her from all but this moment. In that instant, she was happy, utterly content.

Then, with the warmth came light. It was luminous, a color she loved but could never describe. It was the color of comfort, of complete trust. In that moment, her spirit was completely unguarded, open. She had a brief memory of floating warm within her mother's womb and somehow seeing a milky band of stars in the night sky.

The color brightened and something called to her, a voice beautiful and familiar. There was movement when the warm buffalo hide that covered her face was pulled aside. Kneeling there was a woman looking down at her with eyes that seemed deep, timeless. Within those eyes Hanna felt she could see the stars - and beyond.

The woman smiled then and Hanna knew – there was the spirit she'd felt countless times the hawk had visited. The woman's smile made Hanna feel the connectedness to all things. The woman touched her own heart then looked toward the rising sun. As Hanna sat up she marveled at the iridescent colors reflected from the feathers that were her mother's garment. Her mother! "Mama!" Hanna spoke that universal word in her heart and Itunkala, her mother turned, smiled then pointed toward the east.

The buffalo hide wall held there by thirteen lodge poles glowed that color she loved. The natural pigments painted on the outside walls seemed to live. Some scenes she and Ben had painted together, some she drew herself. But the pictographs were not static in her dream – they moved as if Hanna was seeing passages of her life. "I'm dreaming." Hanna realized. "If I wake, will it also be a dream?"

She seemed the observer as Ben gave her the black rock, a treasure she believed stolen, gone forever, now engraved with the picture of a hawk. But the pain was not in this living scene, only the rapturous joy of its return. She looked to another picture and saw the rock come to her hand the first time - the time her white father gave it to her as an early Christmas present. The joy and wonder was there again as Rev. Cliff Parnell gave her the real gift, the story of her red birth, of her connection to The First People. Hanna looked at another picture she had painted alone. It was simply her hand holding her precious black rock – part of the hawk engraving was visible. Hanna blushed briefly knowing her mother knew, could see the passion of this image. Hanna relived the wondrous intensity the moment this picture captured – she and Ben were naked in their bower, their hiding place. She held the stone as they moved together with such force, such abandon that they cried out together in one voice. The animal in them and their spirits had joined in this act of creation. In her mother's heart, she knew in that instant their first child had joined them. Reluctantly, Hanna looked away and saw the moment in that terrible room when her life was delivered to her. The picture somehow showed inside and outside. Leftook stood in the doorway like an avenging angel. Her father was outside waiting; waiting to lead her to the Red Road, his hand out in total acceptance. Then another picture appeared. It puzzled Hanna because she knew it had not been painted there on the wall of her tipi. In this picture, there were two hands; old, wrinkled, twisted by time. Then Hanna knew – Kanj Coonshi was there. One hand held Hanna's black rock and the other, a white man's gold coin. Suddenly, the eastern light was gone. In her dream, Hanna sat near her hearth, the fire barely smoldering. She knew she still had to choose one; she could not have both the gold and the rock. But there, kneeling on the floor of *her tipi, was Itunkala. Her mother held a gift. Hanna saw the stars in her mother's eyes again, felt as if she were falling into a welcoming void. Then Hanna saw the gift her mother held. In her hands was a cooking stone that had belonged to her mother, her mother's mother and back to a time that her people were new. Itunkala set the stone near the embers, reached across the warmth and touched Hanna's heart.*

The instant between sleep and consciousness felt like falling. Hanna awoke, unsure if the spasm she'd experienced was real. Her dream was so fresh that her surroundings and the images from her dream fused. When she felt the touch near her heart again, she smiled to herself. Her mother had visited her yet again. It was an almost daily occurrence. A red tailed hawk seemed to always be nearby. And there were flashes of knowledge that were not memories but more like ancient wisdoms. Hanna silently mouthed *"Thank you Grandfather, thank you mother,"* as a prayer, like she had done every day of the nearly three moons they'd been here.

Hanna and Ben were spooned together, her chest against his back. Her back faced the embers of their fire. Little Abe was snuggled in the warm hallow between them. The awareness that had passed between mother and daughter was replaced by a powerful, instinctual joy Hanna felt when she saw her son smiling, wanting her breast.

Hanna could see her breath in the air as she adjusted the heavy buffalo skin over herself and her child. She knew it was cold; probably the coldest morning they had experienced since their first night in their tipi. She smiled inwardly as she remembered that first night – the floor didn't move and rumble beneath her feet; it had been so quiet the night sounds had frightened her. The animal skin blankets had been slightly repulsive. But she had learned so much.

Moon When the Leaves Turn Yellow (Fall 1897)

Taos had been terrifyingly new, yet so interesting. Hanna had felt hyper aware the day they arrived over three moons ago. She remembered feeling fiercely protective when strangers approached, strangers that seemed to know her father and Leftook. The train had stopped in this tiny town that somehow reminded her of her long ago home of Larned, Kansas.

To Hanna, Taos was similar to the countless little towns lining the rails that crisscrossed America. It had the charmingly built railroad station surrounded by blackened gravel, trash and tattered outbuildings and storage bins that accompanied the reality of train travel. To the west were the shanties and livery stables, hardware stores and lumberyards. East, down the main street were more livery stables, saloons, hotels and nicer shops. In the distance were one and two story homes, some wood framed, some adobe.

Then, as Hanna waited with Little Abe near the corrals, something about the locale touched her. Beyond the shanties and clutter of the rail yards lay a small verdant valley with dramatic badlands beyond. Behind her to the west was a range of mountains that seemed to loom over the town, both threatening and beautiful. Even in the early fall, there were patches of snow near the peaks. And the air itself was different - there was a clarity and a dry fresh fragrance that somehow seemed as if there was a color present one could not quite see, just feel.

Their rail car was disconnected and shuttled to a small siding by a team of horses driven by a tiny red skinned man - he also seemed to know her father and Dunn. The three men had been laughing and talking when she and Ben had shyly stepped down onto the reddish soil of New Mexico.

That first day in Taos had been a blur to Hanna and Ben. The horses were skittish in this place of new smells and sounds. Dunn saddled his horse Kangee in the rail car and rode him down the ramp. It took a good deal of coaxing and bucking until Dunn's roan settled. The horse was then tied to the rail car and as the two other horses were led down the ramp, they calmed when tied next to Kangee.

All three horses shied and pulled at their tethers when a large cargo wagon approached. The same, small red skinned man from before was at the reins. Beside him in the sprung wooden seat was a young woman.

The wagon rolled by Hanna; the driver hardly noticed her. But the young woman turned and made eye contact. She had a broad, strong face and wide set intelligent eyes. She was simply dressed - fringed deerskin leggings and boots, a simple deerskin top with a drab, brown woven skirt. Her hair was in two long black braids framing her strong jaw. She had a brightly colored blanket wrapped around her shoulders. The young red woman was a total stranger to Hanna but something passed between them; there was an uncanny familiarity as if their spirits had already met. Taos - dirty cinders where she stood - the child in her arms ceased to exist in that moment that felt like an eternity. Hanna saw a story in those eyes that mirrored her own - sadness, terror and separation, abuse, shame, joy. In that instant, both knew the other's life was a mirror, dissimilar yet the same. Then a word seemed to speak itself in her mind. "Mitȟáŋka! Sister!"

Ben removed the ramp to the rail car and the wagon pulled along side the open door. Ben, Leftook, Black Elk and several locals quickly piled hay bales in the wagon two deep. The lodge poles and hides were stacked on top and lashed down. The tack and saddles came next and were thrown on the ground. Then, what few personal possessions Black Elk and his family had stored were brought out and carefully stowed.

Hanna watched with interest as the other two horses were saddled. Black Elk mounted his horse while Bess climbed up and sat bareback behind Dunn. Ben mounted and rode up to Hanna and said "Climb on."

"Not carrying Little Abe. I'll ride in the wagon." Hanna waved as the riders led the way.

The ride was so rough on the wagon's tailgate that Hanna climbed with Little Abe up onto the bales. But when the wagon left the dirt streets of Taos and followed a wagon trail west towards the mountains, Hanna jumped down to the ground and walked. Moments later, the young woman was walking along-side her.

"How coula." Hanna was the first to speak. Her traditional greeting in Sioux brought no response, but a quizzical look that meant, "I don't understand."

"Hän sóe!" The young woman looked at Hanna questioningly.

Hanna smiled and shook her head. She pointed to herself and said, "My name is Hanna." She pointed forward where Black Elk was riding next to Dunn. "He is my father."

The other woman gasped and a momentary flash of wonder crossed her face. She looked over at Hanna with an intense, new interest in her eyes. "My name Maria. He, my father." She glanced up at the drover and smiled shyly. "His name Tall Horse. He not tall." Her English was clear but with an accent that Hanna couldn't place. "I live on - I live with father on Boss Dunn ranch."

Hanna excitedly asked, "Maria, where did you learn to speak English?"

The other woman suddenly stopped walking and faced Hanna. "Today we meet. We talk today, tomorrow. Not yesterday – yesterday gone. We no talk about." There was a momentary flash of pain in her eyes then she smiled. "We learn together." Maria reached out and with one finger she touched Hanna's heart.

As they walked along behind the bumpy, dusty wagon, Maria would point to a plant or bird then name it in Tewa then in English. Hanna happily introduced Little Abe to her new friend then said, "Wawíyekiya – baby. A baby old enough to recognize people." They walked along together, happily naming things, laughing at something the other had said, sharing. Then, without conscious thought, they became lost in their own thoughts.

Hanna's next awareness came when she realized Leftook and Bess were riding next to her. The landscape had changed significantly. They were walking near a small, clear stream that meandered through what looked to Hanna like a canyon. In places the rock walls were nearly vertical. They followed a small uphill path that wound through a narrow expanse of sandy ground. Some wildflowers still bloomed even this late in the year. The slopes were covered in places with lush green grass, willows and cottonwoods. She looked up at Dunn and was about to say how beautiful this place was until she saw his face.

"You two were dream walking." There was a look of wonder on Dunn's face but a deep sorrow shown in his eyes. "There is much more you need to learn about your mother." He nudged his horse with his heels and was gone.

As she watched him ride ahead up the canyon, Hanna nearly stumbled with the intensity of an image that came. It was like a powerful memory she had of walking like this many times in the past but the memories were not her own.

Minutes later the canyon opened up into a small valley. The valley floor was nearly flat. There were a few large boulders dotting the landscape but mostly the ground was rich pasture. In the distance, Hanna could see several structures including a small wood frame ranch house with a very steep roof. Off each side were less steep shed roofs with cozy windows and doors cut into the walls of the structure. Smoke rose lazily from a single stovepipe. Near by there were several barns, corrals and a fenced garden. On the periphery she could see a variety of smaller homes, some adobe, others of framed wood and a few tipis. There were many cattle happily grazing the lush grass. Several horses nickered at their approach. Then there came a happy shout from the house and in ones and twos, people in all the four colors of men walked toward them in welcome.

Moon When the Trees Crack From the Cold (Winter 1898)

Hanna sat up and tried not to disturb Ben. She put Little Abe on her lap and wrapped them both in a blanket. Everything was in its place. The firewood she'd collected the day before was stored just left of the door opening just as she'd been taught.

Everything else in the tipi was neatly stored in its proper place as her father and Bess had taught her.

She smiled to herself remembering the day they first arrived. Bess quickly took over from Black Elk and supervised the erection of both tipis. Bess had shown her trademark displeasure when she discovered that the tipis each had only a dozen lodge poles. Bess explained the significance of thirteen poles. The woman owns the tipi and has thirteen menstrual cycles, as there are thirteen moons in a year. She sent Leftook and Ben to the surrounding mountains for two new poles. Then Bess, Hanna and Black Elk had been in hysterics when her father told the story from long ago about when Itunkala had won the tipi-erecting contest.

As Hanna counted her lodge poles which she did every morning, she wondered when Little Abe would stop nursing and she could start her blood cycle again. She bunched up the heavy buffalo skin and put Little Abe against it so he couldn't tip over. She stood and reverently walked clockwise to her pile of fuel. She knelt down, arranged some smaller pieces of wood on the coals and coaxed a flame. She stacked more wood onto the flames, retrieved another armload and stacked it close to the fire.

Hanna sat next to the baby and held her hands out toward the fire. As she sat there contentedly watching, Little Abe let out a man-sized belch. Hanna smiled to herself again as Ben began to stir.

"Híŋháŋni Híŋhaŋni lahči Híŋhaŋni wašté." Ben said as he sat up and smiled sleepily. "Good morning and a blessing – I wish my dad had taught me to say that." He turned and scooted close to the fire. "Pilamaya for the fire. It's cold out." He turned, picked up the baby and sat him close to the flames.

Little Abe babbled in excitement and waved his arms around enjoying the heat and movement, but Hanna was not so happy. "Ben, that's too close!" she said crossly. She reached across Ben and pulled the baby away from the fire.

Before she could sit back down, he pulled her onto his lap. He wrapped both his arms around her just under her breasts and kissed the side of her neck.

Instead of pulling away, she melted into him. "Good morning, handsome." she whispered.

He kissed her again in the hollow of her neck, nuzzled her breasts and quietly said into her ear, "I want you."

She turned and kissed him deeply as she found his erection under the elk skin breeches he was wearing. "I want you too." She kissed him slowly then said, "Soon." She smiled, then nodded toward their bed.

"Let's snuggle little man." Ben said as he scooped up the baby and pulled Hanna under the warm buffalo blanket. They lay there happily together, the baby on Ben's chest, as the fire warmed the space within their tipi.

Outside, they heard a dog bark, footsteps and the sounds of the communal fire being tended. Ben sat up, threw more fuel onto the fire and said, "*Leháŋl uŋkíye uŋspé.*" He seemed proud. "If I said it right, it means, 'Today you and I learn.' I've been practicing my Lakota with your father. He calls me his son." Ben smiled happily at Hanna then asked, "What are you doing today?"

"Bess, Maria and I plan to forage. Bess wants to show us rabbit snares. If I understand Maria correctly, she's going to show us where to harvest pine nuts and…" Hanna shuddered, "she knows where to catch rattlesnakes now that it's cold." She shook her head. "She says the meat is delicious."

"Sounds tasty! Today, if we get lucky, I'm going to take an elk further up the canyon." Ben patted the knife at his waist. "Your dad and Dunn are going to show me how to dress out the kill. They even taught me the prayer. Your dad says that's the most important part of the hunt – to thank the spirit of the animal as I send it back to the Creator." He handed Little Abe back to her and said, "I need to check the horses. I'll be back for some of your corn cakes." He smiled and was gone.

Hanna pushed her cooking stone into the fire. She briefly put her palm on the still warm surface and said a short prayer of thanks for her friend Maria.

Maria had appeared early on the second day they had arrived in the protected valley. She had walked the three miles from Taos carrying the cooking stone and the stone mortar and bowl used for grinding corn.

Hanna remembered Maria's words. "Belonged to my sister. Now yours, my new sister. Together, we learn."

Author's note

Wetu: *The Moons of Renewal and Growth (spring)*
Magzksicaagli Wi - *Moon When Ducks Come Back*
Wihakata Cepapi Wi - *Moon of Making Fat*
Wojupi Wi - *Moon When Leaves Turn Green*

Bloketu: *The Warm Moons (summer)*
Wipazuka Wasti Wi - *Moon of the June Berries*
Canpasapa Wi - *Moon When the Chokecherries are Ripe*
Wasuton Wi - *Moon of the Harvest*

Pyranyetu: *The Moons of Change (autumn)*
Canwapegi Wi - *Moon When the Leaves Turn Brown*
Canwapekasna Wi - *Moon When the Wind Shakes Off Leaves*
Waniyetu Wi - *Moon of the Rutting Deer*

Waniyetu: *The Cold & Dark Moons (winter)*
Wanicokan Wi - *Moon When the Deer Shed Their Horns*
Wiotehika Wi - *The Hard Moon*
Cannapopa Wi - *Moon When Trees Crack from the Cold*
Istawicayazan Wi - *Moon of Sore Eyes (Snow Blindness)*

Primal

Ben sat cross-legged on the earthen floor lacing his boots. The buffalo hide near his face glowed from the early morning sun. He looked at the pictographs that he and Hanna had painted on their tipi and smiled. Each image was such total reminder, a memory so physical that the events shown in these paintings flared up in his consciousness as real as the experience itself. *"Thank you Grandfather,"* he said as he stood and pulled on his jacket. Then he turned to say goodbye.

Hanna kneeled on the hearth near their fire. In one hand, she held a stone bowl filled with corn she had soaked overnight with some ash from the fire. In the other, she held her crushing stone. Little Abe sat naked in the warmth on a rabbit skin. She looked up at her man and spoke.

The words she said to him didn't register as words. The total rightness of what he saw and felt was so overwhelming, he put one hand over his heart as if somehow, he could keep his emotions from leaking out. His woman was smiling at him, making a meal for him. His child was laughing near their fire. It was as if the earth where he stood flooded him with a primordial, fierce, protective love. His feelings were so intense he walked directly across the earthen floor to his family and pulled them close. He was dimly aware of her words, "Ben, your manners, your boots!" Then he felt her warm breath as she laughed into his neck. The baby pulled his hair. He held them and wished this moment could be their eternity.

Finally, he stood and said, "Sorry!" as he walked clockwise around the outer wall, tiptoeing as if it mattered if a bit of mud fell from his boots. Then he opened the door flap and spoke in Sioux, *"Thečhíȟila."* and stepped out into another extraordinary day. He heard her whisper, "I love you too," as he closed the flap.

Ben stepped out of their tipi the moment the sun peaked over the rim of the earth and flooded their valley with light. He shielded his eyes from the glare then turned and looked down the valley. He gasped involuntarily at the beauty.

It had snowed lightly during the night. Every tree, every bush, every blade of grass was covered with hoarfrost. The early sun christened every frozen surface in colors without names. Tendrils of smoke rose from each chimney, every tipi. A light fog followed the brook as it made its noisy way to a far away ocean. Ben, who never tired of the splendor of this small, protected valley, was so overcome with this new beauty, he wept.

A soft whistle pulled Ben out of his reverie. Several older men sat around the communal fire, wrapped in robes, smoking their pipes. One of the men waved to Ben, motioning him over to join them. Ben waved back then held up one finger as if to say, "Wait."

He squatted down, opened his door flap and looked inside.

Hanna said, "What?" then saw his face. She wrapped up the baby and joined Ben outside. No words were said – none were necessary. They had no vocabulary to describe the wonder of creation.

Black Elk was wrapped in a heavy buffalo robe. He stood and left the communal fire. He walked to his family but said nothing as he pulled them close and wrapped the robe around them all. The warmth between them and the love that surrounded them was a gift more precious than any gold.

Finally, Black Elk spoke. *"Thunkashila has blessed us as always. Our game will be easy to track this day."* He paused momentarily. *"And he shows us his presence when we feel these things."*

Dreamily, Hanna asked, *"What things, Ate?"*

"When we see beauty, when we feel love between us, then we know truth. We cannot know beauty, love or truth without the spirit He has given us. Wakan Tanka, he is the creator. We see His work and experience the beauty He gives us. We feel love in everything, yet can't understand His works. That is the Great Mystery." Then somewhere close by, a hawk called as if adding an "Amen" and an affirmation.

At that moment, the silence was broken again. From Bess's tipi came a peal of laughter in a pure contralto. That was followed by more laughter in a robust baritone. Hanna turned to Ben and said, "I've never heard either one of them laugh."

The tent flap of Bess's tipi opened and Dunn stepped out. He turned to say something but grunted when she reached out and grabbed his crotch.

Dunn jumped back and said "Enough woman!" Then, as he passed the spectators, he failed miserably to look dignified while he jogged toward the common latrine. Moments later he walked past Hanna's tipi and said "Mornin'!" as if nothing had happened.

Dunn stood outside his woman's tipi and asked, "*May I come in?*" It was hard to tell if he was being sarcastic, humorous or just being respectful to Sioux etiquette from the tone of his voice. When Bess answered, "*Enter.*" Dunn reached inside and pulled his rifle from its spot by the door. Without another word, he walked over and stood in front of Black Elk and his family.

Dunn made eye contact with Ben; his look was serious. He handed his rifle, a Winchester 92 .44-40 to Ben and said, "Tonight we feast." It was then that he smiled.

Ben sensed that he was being watched, measured. It was a feeling he knew well. Back in his Kansas hometown and later at the Carlisle School, other boys and men had sized him up. Some had challenged him. The boys with bleeding lips and broken noses respected his skill as did the football coaches that saw his talent. Ben knew his own strengths within himself and was confident as a man. But Hanna's father and Leftook were different. Ben understood these two men were alpha. He tried hard to earn their respect. Had he been raised red instead of white, he would have recognized this process as the natural order of things.

As the three men walked toward the corral, the horses nickered happily. It was as if they knew they'd be part of this rite of passage. All three men were dressed warmly. Ben carried the rifle; it felt more like a talisman than a weapon. Black Elk was dressed entirely in skins and carried a bow and a quiver of arrows. Dunn wore his Colt .44-40 pistol, a cartridge belt and a large knife at his waist.

Dunn stopped Ben at the corral gate and asked, "Your knife sharp?" When Ben nodded the affirmative, Dunn pulled a small whet stone from his saddlebag and declared, "If we get a kill today, we'll need this." He turned and began to saddle his large roan.

When Ben stepped into the corral, his small chestnut mare came to him. He was vaguely aware again that the other two men had observed this exchange, this relationship. But for Ben, it seemed natural. He had grown up around horses and knew their ways.

Ben's horse made eye contact first. Ben looked back into the eyes of this creature that had no spoken language except to express primal urges such as fear and aggression - hunger. But in the eyes was an undeniable spirit. To Ben, his horse clearly conveyed, "I see you." And Ben's eyes reflected the same understanding and respect. "I see your spirit as well." Then, as if the two had said hello, the horse leaned in to Ben much as a human would shake hands. Ben leaned in also and placed his forehead against the warmth of the horse's jaw. In this short, skin-to-skin contact, vast understandings were passed. It was during this sharing that Ben missed another evaluation – Dunn and Black Elk made eye contact, smiled briefly to signal their own understanding and approval of this young man.

The sun began to warm the valley floor as the three men readied three extra packhorses. As the three riders followed the stream higher and higher through the twisted canyon, the air grew colder. They quickly reached an altitude where the narrow canyon floor was still covered in snow. And in the snow were the tracks of the elk they were hunting.

"We stop!" Black Elk whispered. "They hear us and smell us. They're moving up the canyon – staying out of range. We wait here." He jumped off his horse, tied it and the three packhorses to some brush and drank directly out of the stream.

As Ben dismounted he couldn't help notice how much his father-in-law looked like a superb animal – there was no wasted motion; he was completely at home in this natural environment. "What now?" Ben asked.

Black Elk held a finger to his lips and whispered, "If we wait, the Great Spirit will reward us. Soon, the sun warms the valley floor behind us. The air will rise. Then the air in this canyon will flow downhill like water. We will be downwind then. He gives us an advantage if we are wise enough to use it."

The three men positioned themselves in a sunny spot and sat on boulders. The horses waited patiently tied to some juniper. The easy silence was broached when Ben spoke. "I know you watch me, judge me," he said quietly. "I will learn what you teach me."

Dunn and Black Elk looked at each other and smiled. "You go." said Dunn.

Black Elk rose, walked to Ben and sat on his haunches so his eyes were level with Ben's. "*Hau Coula my son. I would give my life for you. We watch you just as you watch us. We do this to know each other well – it is our way. We watch each other not to judge, but to know what is best for our people. You are strong and becoming wise. You know things you have not been taught. We watch to learn from each other. I have learned that anger can be a useful tool from watching you. I would ride with you always.*"

Dunn stood and put his hand on Ben's shoulder. "That day back at Carlisle. I slammed the door in your face – I yelled at you. You pushed back just as hard. Had you not knocked on the door again and again, we would not be here. Happy Seed would not have her father. Little Abe most certainly would have been sent away from you. We all played our parts." He squeezed Ben's shoulder and reached to pull him up. "My thanks to you and to the Great Mystery." He laughed. "Let's hunt some elk! Tonight we celebrate life!"

As Black Elk predicted, a slow cold breeze began to flow down the canyon. They mounted up and followed as Black Elk slowly and quietly rode ahead. At each bend of the creek, he dismounted and using cover, peered around each turn until he spotted the small herd of elk about 200 yards ahead of them. He held up a fist and tied his horse to some brush. "Quiet, we go on foot from here."

Ben and Leftook dismounted, tied the horses and joined Black Elk. Ben quietly levered open the rifle and checked that there was indeed a cartridge in the breech. He then checked the safety and followed.

The terrain undulated, following the streambed. Up ahead, a small oxbow was partially hidden by a ridge of rock that came nearly to the water's edge. The elk were barely in range, but the rock outcropping gave the herd cover.

Ben stretched out prone on the ground, the rifle aimed uphill. But he only got glimpses of the animals as they moved about, grazing on the lush grass that grew there. "I can't get a clear shot." he whispered. "I have to get closer."

Black Elk signaled by pointing at his own eyes with two fingers then pointing at Ben. He put his fingers to his lips then silently climbed up the slope until he was hidden from the elk. He put his bow on the ground, removed an arrow from his quiver and placed it near the bow. He got up on his knees, undid his breeches, urinated on the arrow and winked at Ben. Black Elk nocked the arrow and fired it high overhead. The arrow landed upwind from the herd.

Almost immediately, the herd began to move downstream, away from the smell of human.

Ben's heart began hammering as the elk drew nearer. Then the herd disappeared behind a ridge. Moments later, the herd crested the ridge, presenting perfect targets.

Ben slowed his breathing, blew half his breath out, felt his heart beating. Then, he selected his target, waited to squeeze the trigger between heartbeats, and fired.

The sound of the rifle was deafening and almost instantly, the young elk jumped and disappeared behind the ridge. Somehow, both Dunn and Black Elk were beside him yelling, "GO! GO!" In that instant, Ben became the young new hunter while his elders ordered him. He obeyed!

All rational thought left him. He was up and running. Ben was dimly aware that his knife was in his hand and he may have been screaming as he ran. He wasn't sure. His only awareness was that of a predator pursuing its prey. There was bloodlust in his heart as he ran; he had a dim picture of himself in his mind holding a piece of raw meat to his mouth. He ran, his breath was ragged, but he felt a fierce brutal joy that far surpassed sex. This visceral emotion possessed him completely. It was pure animal survival.

When he crested the ridge, Ben found the young elk on the ground, thrashing and terrified. Ben grabbed an ear and was prepared to cut the elk's throat, to end it. Then came eye contact. Ben felt the tender spirit of the elk as the two regarded each other. He saw its fear and agony. Ben also saw the spirit there not unlike what he saw in the eyes of his horse, the many dogs he'd known, a spirit akin to the people he loved. He put the knife on the ground and put his palm on the elk's chest. He felt its spirit, he felt the heart slow then stop; he felt the last shuddering breath. He felt the spirit leave.

When Black Elk and Dunn arrived seconds later, Ben was sobbing, his head on the elk's chest. The two older men made eye contact yet again. They nodded to each other, acknowledging the worth of this young man.

Black Elk knelt near his protégé. *"The prayer! Now is the time."*

Ben raised his head, looked around as if lost. *"I didn't know it would feel like this. I hurt – in my heart – like part of me died!"*

"Release it. Let him go, son." Black Elk knelt across the elk's body and put his own hand near the elk's heart.

Ben looked up from his first kill; the pain was evident in his eyes. *"Thank you, brother, for your life."* He stopped and looked skyward. *"Your spirit is now with Wakan Tanka, but your body stays here to feed the people. Thank you for your life."*

Dunn knelt beside Ben. He put his huge hand on top of Ben's and Black Elk's joined them. Each silently said a prayer – each wish was vastly different, yet the same.

"Before we eat first meat, you must know that this is the animal that gave me my name. Elk, *heȟáka,* means forked horn in our language. *Heȟáka Sápa,* Black Elk. My name came to me when I was much younger than you. And yes, I wept as you did."

Dunn stood and pulled Ben to his feet. "This next thing we do – you'll probably have a problem like I did the first time." He nodded to Black Elk as he handed him the large knife.

Black Elk positioned himself so he was kneeling near the elk's abdomen. He lifted one of the elk's back legs and handed it to Ben. "Here, hold this steady while I cut." With the tip of the knife, Black Elk carefully slit the elk's belly skin from anus to neck. Next, he cautiously cut the thin muscle tissue starting where the elk's ribs spread and made an opening large enough to insert both his hands.

"Here, take this." Black Elk handed the bloody knife to Dunn then looked up at Ben. "Lift the leg as high as you can. We don't want anything to touch the ground." Black Elk reached inside the open wound, tugged, repositioned himself then extracted the liver. He stood and held the steaming organ out toward Ben. "You first! This is your first kill."

Ben was aghast and took a step back. "What do you mean?"

Leftook stepped in, carved a small piece of liver off with his knife and said, "This tradition is old! Your ancestors believed the man that made the kill got first choice. He takes the best cuts. Here!" He held the bloody morsel out.

Ben clenched his fists at his sides. A part of him was disgusted. The dark bitter killing, the blood and guts, the evisceration made his stomach roll. But a deeper part of him recalled the memory of mindlessly running, the bloodlust, and the dark animal part of him that did just that, held a bloody piece of flesh up to his mouth. Timidly, Ben took the meat between one finger and his thumb and held it up to his mouth. Then the smell took him. His mouth flooded with saliva as he took a tiny bite.

The look of wonder on Ben's face made the other two men laugh as the younger man took a larger bite with obvious enjoyment. Leftook stepped up, put his arm around Ben's shoulders and said, "*You are now a true Human Being.*"

Time lost its meaning for these three apex predators. They fed until they could eat no more. Then the butchering began, the preparation to return from the hunt with provisions for their kin.

"I'll talk you through this." Black Elk said to Ben. "But first, you should know that you choose the cuts you want. It's your kill."

Ben accepted the knife, but looked uneasy. "I don't know. Please help me out here. What would you take?"

"If it was me, I'd take the rest of the liver and the heart. When we get back, you should give my grandson a tiny taste of the liver – he's about ready for solid food." Black Elk nodded at Ben's discomfort. "The backstrap for sure – that's the best meat there is. And you made a good choice with this yearling. White men kill for big horns and eat tough meat. The next best meat is the –"

Down slope they heard a laugh and a loud "EHAW!" Dunn was downhill about fifty feet, motioning for them to join him.

At Dunn's feet was another yearling elk. "Damn son, that was a hell of a shot. Went through the first and got this one almost square between the eyes." The big man looked at Ben with new respect.

"Well, this changes everything." Black Elk looked down at the second elk. "We have work to do." He looked up a Dunn and asked, "John, if you would bring the horses, Ben and I will start getting this feast ready to move."

While Dunn was gone, Black Elk sat cross-legged on the ground and said, "We have a problem, a big problem, but a good one. Since you made the kill, you decide – but please allow me to tell you my opinion."

Ben sat across from his father-in-law and simply nodded.

"*When the People were hungry, we wasted nothing. Now we have plenty – too much to carry. If I were you, I'd take the good cuts and leave the rest.*"

Ben answered in Sioux. "*If we leave without taking it all, won't that be a waste?*"

"*If we take the four backstraps only, that would feed everybody at the ranch a fine meal. But if we take the backstraps, two hearts, two livers, the hides and four hind quarters, we will have meat for a two day feast and enough to share with our brothers at the Pueblo.*" Black Elk smiled and continued. "*And think of our horses. If we take only the good cuts of meat, it will weigh three times as much as our friend Leftook.*"

Ben's face was troubled and he began to speak, "But..."

Black Elk laughed and interrupted Ben. "*The Great Mystery wastes nothing. Our four-legged brothers will find what we leave and have their own feast. The insects will find what the four legs leave and have their feast. And the bones will feed the trees. Life is a cycle – nothing is wasted.*"

When they reached the ranch, the sun was high overhead. It didn't take long for word to spread. A small crowd gathered around, laughing and congratulating the men, praising the hunt. Preparations were made for cooking fires as the meat was unloaded and further broken down into manageable pieces.

Hanna approached Ben in a moment that nobody else had his attention. "You are a good man – a good hunter." She took both of his hands and looked up into his face with pride and happiness. "Come!" she said urgently and pulled him toward their tipi.

"Where's Little Abe?"

"He's sleeping. Come!" Her smile was feral – her eyes urgent.

"The meat. I should –"

Hanna pulled Ben inside, quickly checked the baby then in one quick move, pulled her garment over her head.

Ben stared, transfixed. His woman had never looked more beautiful. Her hair looked like liquid stone – some fell down her back and the rest partially covered her small, swollen breasts.

"Come," she said breathlessly, "I want to feed you." She reached for him and when he stumbled to her, she pulled his head to her chest.

Her milk was sweet and in an instant, he had never felt so aroused. The taste, the close warmth of her, the sounds she made when she held him brought a realization. He knew this gesture she'd made for him was a signal, but her breasts were for their son. He lifted his head and kissed her deeply. And when she responded, he reached down to her warm core and felt her shudder.

"Ben..." was all she said as she pulled him under the warm buffalo cover beneath them.

He entered her then and she rose to meet him. Ben lifted himself on his elbows and looked into her eyes. Neither moved. Their connection was hot, intense and completely overwhelming. He felt as if he were falling into a warm, starry expanse within her eyes. Nothing else existed. It was as if their bodies had become one where they were joined in heat and passion. And in their eyes, their spirits had joined in a joyous reunion. Then he felt her first contraction and saw her face. She smiled. She had never been more his. She pushed up harder as he tried to enter her even further. Her eyes widened as her contractions came closer and closer together. When she felt him release she whispered his name once again closing her eyes as her entire body arched up against him. Then blackness took them both.

Moments or centuries later, they became aware of each other again. Neither had moved. He held her head in his arms and she still had her fingers pressed into his back. He rose up again and looked down into her face. "Hanna, you are..."

"Shhh. We don't need words." She pushed up against him suggestively and said, "Go! Do what you need to do, then come home to me." She pulled him out of her and gave him a gentle squeeze. "I'll be waiting."

The sun was already behind the mountains when Black Elk and Ben returned from the pueblo. Small cooking fires dotted the common center of the ranch. The smell of roasting meat was intoxicating.

Ben was vibrating with excitement when he found Hanna cooking meat outside on a small fire. Dunn and Bess were there along with a few men Hanna barely knew.

Love and pride shown in Hanna's eyes. Every person around Hanna's fire had stopped eating and looked up at him in admiration. Dunn said, "The mighty hunter has returned," but the words didn't sound sarcastic. The big man seemed genuinely proud. Bess mouthed "Pilamaya!" She gave him a look of esteem that, coming from her, meant everything. In ones and twos, people from other fires drifted over to thank Ben or offered congratulations on the hunt.

Hanna patted a spot on the ground next to her and said, "Here, sit. Let me feed you." The smile in her eyes and the look on her face gave Ben an erotic thrill because of the double meaning in her words.

Ben sat next to his woman and soon after she held out a steaming chunk of elk loin fresh from her stone. For the second time that day, his mouth flooded with saliva as he took his first bite. The meat was slightly charred on the outside yet barely warm at the core. The blood and juice filled his senses. The taste, the awareness of nourishing his body, the visceral response his body sent his spirit was so intense that in that instant, nothing else existed. Almost without thought, a groan of pleasure came out of him that was loud enough for all there around the fire to hear. The laughter and grunts of agreement from all those around the fire were so right and so connected, no words were needed.

As they fed, Ben told his story.

"When I got to the pueblo, some children and a few old men came out to see why I was there. When I unloaded the first packhorse and opened up the hide, more people showed up. Those two hindquarters were heavy – probably two hundred pounds. By the time I unloaded the second packhorse, I think everybody that lived there was standing around cheering me. Black Elk just stood there telling the elders my story."

"Then, when I told them that they could keep the hides too, several women came up and thanked me in Tiwa. I tried talking to them in Sioux but nobody could understand me, so we talked in English."

Ben laughed. "They gave me a new name. They called me Ben Two Elks. Anyway, the meat and the hides just disappeared, but the elders invited me into the dark underground room they called a Kiva. Only the men were allowed in. Some of them did an Elk dance, thanked me again, and then gave me this." He held up an intricately carved doll with antlers. "It's a Kachina Elk doll. It's for Little Abe. It seems as if some of them knew my story."

Ben stopped talking when Hanna offered him more meat. It was then that he saw a silent conversation happening between Dunn and Black Elk. It was Leftook who spoke.

"Ben Two Elks. That is a good name for you. And it is traditional that you have earned this name. Look around. We are having a gathering because of what you did. But…" Dunn stopped talking in English and spoke in Sioux. *"You must realize that your new name came to you because you helped the People. The People, Ben Two Elks. But when you told your story, you used the pronoun Miyé which means 'I, me, I'm the one.' You were speaking only of yourself."* Dunn hesitated, searching for the right words. *"When you begin to use the pronoun Uŋkíye that means 'us, you and I, the group whenever you act, then you will be a true Human Being."*
"You will be Ben Gregor when you think only of yourself," Dunn said in English. *"But when you work for the people, you will be called Ben Two Elks."*

The moon rose late – the tiny sliver crescent gave almost no light. Stars burned brilliantly but gave scant illumination to the gathered humans below, certainly not enough to illuminate the differences in skin color. The scattered cooking fires were mere embers and barely lit the faces of those that were still part of this gathering. Only the central fire still burned bright. Nearby, a handful of drums sounded. A few danced near the drums, some as couples, some joyfully alone. The children still present slept near the drums in a complete defiance of logic. Around the periphery of the large common area, a few buildings had the lights from candles and kerosene lamps burning in windows. The tipis and other native enclosures were dark. Couples left hand in hand seeking darkness and privacy to join in the joyous act of creation.

Leftook lay on a blanket, his hands on his stomach as if to signal that he could eat no more.

Bess was snuggled against him, barely lit by the dying fire. She had one leg and one arm thrown over his torso as she kissed his neck, the side of his face. She unashamedly ground her pelvis against his leg as one hand explored his body.

He had half-heartedly tried to discourage her then gave in to the pure animal pleasure of simply being loved. When she whispered into his ear, he did not respond.

Finally, Bess mounted him, took his hands in hers as she moved her body against his in a highly erotic way. She tugged his hands saying "*Hiyóhi*, come please."

Then, without a word to anyone, Bess and Leftook stood and walked hand in hand to their tipi. When their tent flap closed, the signal to all was obvious.

Ben, Hanna and Little Abe were spooned together – Hanna had the baby in her lap with her back against Ben. He had his arms around both. Nearby, Black Elk sat alone but close to his family.

When Bess and Dunn left, the three adults left at their fire smiled in understanding. There was no judgment. They were happy that these friends had found love.

Then Hanna stood, smiled sadly at her father and said, "Ate, please hold your grandson. I want to thank my man for providing." She put Abe in her father's lap, kissed them both then held out her hand to Ben.

Black Elk sat there on the cold earth, warmed both by a dying fire and the body of his grandchild. He felt a bitter loneliness and a joy at the same time; his grandson babbled his joy at being outside under the stars, watching the fire burn to embers. It was at this moment that the first coyote cried out in discovery. Moments later, the call was returned as more and more coyotes joined in. Black Elk listened in envy and wonder as the cries of the coyotes and the cries of passion from the tipis joined into a hymn of thanks. *"Listen little man, brother coyote has found the elk we left for him. He calls for his mates to share. His spirit is good. He shares for the good of his clan."*

At that moment, Little Abe grabbed his grandfather's thumbs as if joining in the spirit. He leaned back and rested his head on his grandfather's chest.

Black Elk leaned forward, kissed the child and pointed to the sky. *"Look little man, see that band of stars. That is the Ghost Road. Itunkala, your grandmother is there. She is one of those stars. She watches over us even now."* He wrapped his arms around the baby and said, *"Once, when your grandmother was little like you, she sang to a rattlesnake."*

The Business of Survival
April, 1898 Taos, New Mexico

Extinction is the rule. Survival is the exception.
  Carl Sagan

Dunn pushed through the double swinging doors and walked into the bar at the Columbian Hotel. Even though he pretended not to notice, there was a noticeable lull in the chatter. Dunn removed his hat the moment he stepped inside. He was dressed casually in a planned counterbalance to the stuffy suits, vest, and variety of stylish hats the other men wore. Dunn's dungarees were faded to near sky blue; his deerskin pullover shirt was unadorned but perfectly cut. The huge Colt .44-40 on his belt looked proportionate to the man; he nearly had to turn sideways to come through the door. His elk skin moccasins made not a sound.

"Afternoon Johnny! Everything ready?"

"Yep! They're all waiting for you down at the other end of the bar, Mr. Dunn." The bartender tilted his head toward a gaggle of over-dressed men.

"OK if I leave this here?" Dunn asked, indicating his hat. The barkeep just nodded.

John smiled broadly as he approached the waiting men. They were so easy to read – they smiled back but to a man, each radiated disapproval and feigned superiority. "Gentlemen! Good afternoon! Sorry I'm late."

The men at the end of the bar collectively shrank back as he approached. To Dunn they were like a group of sheep that had banded together for strength only to be confronted by a large, hungry wolf.

"Bring your drinks if you wish. Johnny has set up the back room for us. Follow me please." Dunn politely opened and held the door to a nicely furnished room adjacent to the bar and lobby of the hotel. A large, round table filled the center of the room. The chairs were neatly arranged, and on the table was a bottle of the bar's most expensive bourbon. At one seat, there was a cigar box and another lockable metal box. A shot glass sat at each place.

As the men filed in, not one took the spot that already had been designated as the head of the table – the chair that had its back to the wall and faced the door. The men shuffled around like a bunch of puppies trying to be dominant, but also being careful to arrange themselves in the proper pecking order. Finally, the bank president, Mr. Giles Hollis, took the seat on Dunn's right, the obvious place of dominance next to Dunn.

Dunn got a vivid picture in his mind of a pack of dogs, pissing and marking their territory – smelling each other's butts. He laughed out loud.

"Something funny?" the banker asked peckishly.

"No. I'm just glad we could have this little meeting. Please help yourselves." He smiled at the men around the table. He took careful notice of how they arranged themselves. It was identical to a Sioux counsel's pecking order. The grocer sat at Dunn's left. *"They always treat the man that feeds them as their inferior."* Dunn thought glumly to himself, remembering having the same thoughts inside a tipi in another life. He stood behind his chair while the other men sat. He smiled around the table, enjoying their unease.

When Dunn didn't speak, the short uncomfortable silence resulted in uneasy glances, hands clasped or dropped into laps. Then the grocer to Dunn's left took off his hat. Like lemmings, the rest of the hats came off in a rush. Dunn grinned inwardly and began his spiel.

"*Wahóši*," Dunn said in Sioux. He looked around and saw that every man there was looking at him, slack jawed and ready. He opened the cigar box, took one, cut it and lit it and passed the box around.

"That, gentlemen, was a traditional Sioux greeting at counsel. It means news; I bring you news and I want a word with you." He stood behind his chair, leaning slightly into the circle, hands on the back of his chair.

As the cigar box and whisky bottle passed from hand to hand, Dunn watched their faces as they admired the expensive whiskey and Cuban cigars.

"Thank you, Mr. Liebert, for the use of your fine establishment." John smiled toward the man sitting across from him. He knew full well that the hotel owner was completely in the dark. Johnny, the bartender, had set up the meeting.

"I have a proposition that hopefully will be beneficial to all of us; but before we start, a little about me. My name is John Dunn. I'm a former Army officer from the War Between the States. I lived with the Indians for a while and now William Cody employs me as a performer, advisor and general roust about."

The man sitting next to the banker blurted out, "Did you wear the blue or the gray Mr. Dunn?"

Dunn took his hands off the back of his chair, leaned forward and put them in the middle of the table. Dunn's face was inches from that of the judge. He kept his tone neutral, but in his eyes was a look that said, "I've killed better men than you." When the judge dropped his eyes Dunn continued. "Mr. Haag," the big man said softly, "We're all on the same side now."

Dunn stood, scooted his chair out and sat down. There was a collective sigh of relief around the table as this huge, larger than life man finally sat and joined the circle. The force of Dunn's will was so strong, it seemed as if the only space left in the room pinned the other men to the walls like the hides of small animals hung up to dry.

"Before we start, I'd like to welcome each of you and be sure I'm right about your role in our little town." Dunn took a pull on his cigar then continued. "I know you have your questions about me. I showed up here a few years ago and paid cash for my little ranch up the creek." There were polite chuckles around the table at Dunn's double entendre.

"Mr. Lloyd Haag, owner of the lumber and hardware store. And our judge, correct?"

"Correct!" Mr. Haag said and quickly broke eye contact.

"And Mr. Hudspeth, I love your place. The St. Vrain Mercantile has a little of everything. You put on a good breakfast."

The man smiled warmly at Dunn, thankful for the recognition.

"And Mr. Tresner. You're our lawman hereabouts?"

The sheriff simply nodded and looked at Dunn skeptically.

Dunn smiled warmly at the man at the end of the pecking order. "Mr. Neeley, I applaud your efforts to keep our little town fed. I hope you and I can do some business soon. I have cattle that we will soon butcher, and the elk on the ranch are especially good. I'm sure I can supply your grocery with some quality meat."

"And Mr. Hollis. Your bank stands to benefit from my proposal – that is if we can all agree on some basics." Dunn looked around the table. "I'm Mr. Hollis can verify that I keep a decent amount on deposit at his bank. And, he will also tell you that I keep a large lockbox in his vault." Dunn looked pointedly at the banker and asked, "Do my deposits at your bank indicate that perhaps all of you might just be interested in my proposal?"

And when the banker nodded the affirmative, Dunn opened the metal box in front of him and took out a handful of gold coins. "And speaking of money –" Dunn stood and placed a twenty dollar gold coin in front of each man. "Here is a little something for your time today."

Every man reacted the same. They all leaned forward, their eyes on the coin in front of them. They placed their hands on the table, palms down as if the gold was a magnet that drew their very being toward it. Only their eyes were different. The banker Hollis looked slightly peeved that this small coin would attract him so. Haag the judge looked at his coin suspiciously as if the gold was bait in a trap. The three businessmen, Liebert, Neeley and Hudspeth were like kids on Christmas morning. The sheriff was pragmatic. He was the first to pick up his coin. He looked at both sides then put it in his pocket. Twenty dollars was more than his salary for a month.

Dunn watched, satisfied that these men would favor his deal. One by one, the coins found their way into the pockets of these men that held the future of Taos in their hands. There was no contract but these men had been bought.

"Before I get down to brass tacks about you and I making money together, I need to let you know what I've learned working for Mr. Cody." John looked around and saw that he had the group's attention. "People all over the country pay hard money to see history, gentlemen. They come to see history relived. They come to marvel at Annie Oakley and the rest of the show. But what they are most curious about, what really brings them in is one thing. They come to see the Indians. They come to see what has disappeared from where they live. The names remain, the legends get told, but many people now have never seen a real live Indian."

Dunn looked around, saw the questions then continued. "What you have here is a rarity. You see Indians every day. You see their pueblo and marvel at their primitive ingenuity. But to you, they are just background color. I propose to change that."

Hollis scoffed. "The local Indians don't contribute. Sometimes, they sell a little corn or some of their baskets or pottery on the street. But we don't really see any of that money. They mostly just cause trouble."

"Do any of the Indians that live around here have any money on deposit at your bank?" Dunn asked.

"They're not citizens. They don't have an address. No, they don't do business with us." The banker's smug, self-important persona began asserting itself.

"Mr. Liebert, do Indians ever stay at your hotel?"

"Mr. Dunn, you know better than that. They're colored! We don't allow coloreds on the premises."

"Mr. Neeley," Dunn asked, "do the Indians buy groceries from you."

"No! They can't come in the store." Neeley answered sheepishly.

"Why not?"

"Well, it's against the law I guess."

"What law?" Dunn looked at the Sheriff. "If I'm correct, New Mexico is not a state, right? It's a territory of the United States. So there are some general understandings, but are there specific laws prohibiting Indians from eating in a restaurant or staying in a hotel?"

"Look, I'm a city employee. I get paid to keep the peace." Tresner looked a bit uncomfortable being the crux of this line of questioning." "I just do what I'm paid to do."

"Allow me if you will." Dunn said. "Just so we all understand the situation, let me paraphrase." No one spoke so Dunn continued. "New Mexico is a territory. Taos is a town without a courthouse, yet I have a deed that says I own property. I paid cash for the land in your bank, Mr. Hollis. Mr. Haag, your signature is on my deed guaranteeing ownership."

Dunn looked around at the men at the table. He leaned back in his chair, the back of his head rested on the wall behind him. "You, the men around this table, are the city fathers so to speak. You are the city council, the judge and jury; Taos is yours. Is that a fair assessment?"

No one spoke because they didn't have to.

"Good!" said Dunn. "I'd like to join you!" He looked around at the shocked, suspicious faces. "Hear me out!"

"I plan to build a large trading post at the edge of my property nearest town." Dunn immediately saw the negativity in the faces around him. "And!" he said loudly to Mr. Haag, "I plan to buy all my building supplies from you." He turned to Neeley. "Any grocery items we'll order through your store. And the local Indians can trade their wares for real U. S. currency; that in turn can be used to purchase goods and services here in town. And if by chance, some of them become prosperous, they might just deposit their cash in your bank Mr. Hollis."

As expected, the banker showed some interest when deposits were mentioned. "For the sake of argument, Mr. Dunn, what would make us change our policy?

John leaned forward aggressively. His chair banged on the floor. "You already have Indian money in your bank!" He sat back, crossed his arms over his chest and waited for the others around the table to quiet down.

Dunn looked around at the faces of the men he needed to convince; their attitudes ranged from indignant to curious. It was the banker Hollis that Dunn knew he had to convert.

"Look!" said John. "It's fairly simple. Let me just start at the beginning and give you some history of how we ended up here. When I'm done and you have questions, I'll answer them all. OK?" When Dunn saw the nods of agreement, he began.

"My partner and I joined Cody's Wild West Show back in 86. The show pays in cash and we live on the train – no place to spend the money. Anyway, the show performs from April through the end of October. That means that we're on our own for the five winter months. Our train stopped here on our way to Mexico that first year. We walked around town for an hour or so while the train got coal and water. I ate a great lunch at St. Vrain Mercantile." Dunn nodded to Mr. Hudspeth and continued.

"My partner couldn't come in because he's Indian, so he made friends with a few of your Indians at the pueblo. And that's how it started. His name is Black Elk. He bought a beautiful basket and a couple pieces of their pottery. When we got back to the show, everybody was impressed, especially my boss."

"In '87, we stopped in again and bought as much pottery and baskets as we could carry. We even took a few of their Kachina dolls. We planned to put them out on the midway for sale, but that didn't happen. The day before a show in Baltimore, our business manager went into town and came back with a curator from a museum there – bought the entire lot."

Dunn looked around at the men sitting near him. He definitely had their attention. "So here we are over ten years later." Dunn said. "Now on paper, I own the ranch free and clear. But I have lots of partners. Many of the other performers on Cody's trains have bought in. The Pueblo elders know what we plan to do. But we need you, the men around this table, to be a part of this."

Dunn hesitated for effect. "Museums and collectors know where this incredible art is coming from. They will start coming here to buy – they want to see for themselves how these people live. And when they do..." Dunn looked at each man there, "and when they do, they will need a place to stay. And they will need a place to eat. They'll need help getting around." Then Dunn looked directly at the banker. "And they will have money, lots of it!"

Hollis interrupted. "What's in it for you Dunn?"

"I'll be in the middle. The artifacts will be sold out of my trading post. I take the money, pay the artists and get a small commission. In return, I'm the white face that can legally do business with you." Dunn looked at the banker with hard eyes. "The Indians don't trust you! They're not welcome in this town. I'm here to try to change that."

"What are you implying, Mr. Dunn?" asked Judge Haag.

Dunn stood and paced around the room as he talked. "The Pueblo Indians are a peaceable people. They are incredible artists. Their culture goes back thousands of years, way before the Spanish arrived here. The Spanish enslaved them and took what they wanted. And now us whites are here and the Indians have no rights. Technically, they don't even own the land where they live."

John sat down again and continued. "Try to see it from their perspective. The Indians make beautiful art that white folks want to buy. But they don't really have a place to sell their art. They don't own stores – the notion of real estate is foreign to them. The white people in this town don't really see the value of their art and only pay pennies for it. What would you do?"

"Hell, I'd leave!" said the sheriff.

"Right!" answered Dunn. "The Pueblo people know that they can come to my ranch and live. But that's not really a good solution. Look! You have the railroad, the telegraph, the hotels and restaurants. The Indians have what lots of people want. Buyers will come here for the art. And they want to come here and see how these gentle, disappearing people live. You have an amazing treasure here – I'm just trying to get you to see it."

"Mr. Dunn!" Judge Haag said indignantly. "Do you expect us to just let these redskins in our shops, in our homes? The people in this town would ride us out on a rail."

"Change takes time and work." Dunn's demeanor changed; he seemed real at that moment – vulnerable. "It is you, the men at this table, that will make Taos what it will be in the future. Maybe, after a few visitors have come and brought money to town, maybe one day a week, the Mercantile could have outside seating and serve your Pueblo neighbors. And, Mr. Hollis, maybe my foreman could open an account for the people working on my ranch. If the men in this room could slowly, over time, change attitudes and open a few doors, the town's people will follow."

"You've given us some food for thought, Mr. Dunn. We'll see what develops." Hollis was not completely contrite when he said this, but he did want to seem in control by signaling the end to this uncomfortable meeting.

Dunn stood, shook hands all around and said his thanks. He walked to the door like one properly dismissed. Then, at the door he turned "One more thing gentlemen." Dunn said softly. He made eye contact with each man there. "I leave in a few weeks. I'm taking some of my people back to Denver to meet up with Cody. We are spending this coming summer in Europe touring, so I'll be pretty much out of touch. There are a fair number of people living at my ranch now. Some of them are a different color than us. These people are friends of mine. I care for them like they are family. And they are my employees." He paused and unconsciously put his hand on the butt of his pistol. "If anything should happen to my friends while I'm gone, that I will not forgive. And I will hold some of the men in this room responsible."

Steerage
On the Atlantic Ocean, Spring then Fall, 1900

When Cody's company boarded the steamer *State of Nebraska* in early spring, Hanna and Ben were filled with a sense of wonder. The sea was so vast! In comparison, the Mississippi was awe-inspiring – the railroad bridge was over a mile in length. But the ocean - it completely filled Hanna's senses.

Like eager children, Hanna and Ben explored carrying Little Abe. The crew on deck ignored them. They ran from stem to stern, looked at the lifeboats, watched as supplies were lifted by crane and lowered into the hold, chatted excitedly with other passengers. But when they stepped into the enclosed hallway leading to the first and second-class cabins, a white-coated orderly brusquely told them that their place was below decks.

To his credit, Ben did not show his temper to this English-accented servant. He just nodded curtly and escorted Hanna back into the open air.

It was then that Dunn and Hanna's father found them. "Ben! We need all the help we can get." Dunn said breathlessly. "We have to get all the livestock below decks. The horses are used to this, but the buffalo sometimes need to be blindfolded. Meet us on the dock as soon as you can get there. We'll be taking the horses up the ramp near the stern, then down into the hold. It might go well and be over in a couple of hours or we might be here until tomorrow. If we have to crate the buffalo and elk, we might be late in sailing. Let's go!"

While Ben was busy, Hanna wandered below deck to claim a space for her family. The steerage compartment was directly below the salon deck where the first and second-class passengers were housed. Above that was the wheelhouse. The ceiling of steerage was festooned with pulleys, cables and a series of gears that controlled the ship's rudder.

The steerage compartment was a dank, foul smelling place. The room, which was hard to make out in the gloom, was rectangular, perhaps forty feet wide and sixty feet long. The only light in the room came from two bare electric lights and the open portholes along the hull.

There were a few others from Cody's troupe wandering around, claiming places to sleep. Chains in six-foot intervals hung from the ceiling near the hull. Attached to the chains on one side and to the hull on the other were canvas bunks. These platforms were stacked three high without ladders to reach the middle and top beds. A row of narrow rough lumber tables were lined up down the middle of the room – similarly made benches were pushed under the tables. The rest of the floor was strewn with straw-covered wooden sleeping pallets with very narrow walkways in between.

Hanna heard a thud from the other end of the room followed by a loud, familiar voice. "*Kichi yungka! Siksil hung'! Wasicans!*" Hanna laughed out loud when she recognized Bess' voice – she'd heard her friend curse before, but never quite this vile. "Bess! Let's find bunks together!" Hanna yelled as she carefully made her way through the darkness.

"Oh! What do you think, dearie? Do you want a cabin nearest the ball room or the theater?" Bess said in a terrible English accent. Hanna laughed at her friend's attempt at humor, but could hear the anger underneath.

"It's only a week." Hanna replied. "This isn't much worse than Carlisle. "Hopefully, the food is better."

"Don't count on it!"

Bess and Hanna dragged six pallets together near one corner of the cavernous room. Their choice quickly revealed advantages and problems. They had no one else on one side of them but they were close to the stairs and the unlighted washroom. And the foot traffic was continuous. Being by the stairwell was both a blessing and a curse – the fresh air was welcome when the doors were open, but the ocean air was bitterly cold, especially at night. And when the seas were rough, the portholes and doors remained closed, making the stench unbearable.

Ben found them late in the day shortly before several stewards arrived with boxes of bowls and spoons. One steward stood on the first step and gave instructions. "Meals will be served twice a day from these steps. Your bowl and spoon are yours to use while you're here; wash them after every meal. Any questions?"

Ben stood and asked, "Where are the bathrooms? There are only sinks in the washrooms."

"You can pick up your buckets topside – one per family. Be sure to toss the contents overboard downwind." The stewards' laughter echoed in the stairwell as they made their way up to fresh air and their own sense of freedom.

"And the water in the faucets is cold sea water!" Ben yelled after them. There was no reply from topside.

Hanna's father seemed unfazed when he arrived. "This isn't really so bad." he said. "It will be much more crowded on our return voyage. There are many people immigrating to the United States."

But Dunn was visibly angry and trying not to show it. "Look at this!" he said quietly. He had a sheet of paper in his hand. "I took this off the captain's chair when we got the tour. He probably would have me thrown overboard if he knew I had it. Listen!" Dunn stepped under the bare bulb and began to read. "*State of Nebraska* passenger and cargo manifest - "83 salon passengers, 38 steerage passengers, 97 Indians, 180 horses, 18 buffalo, 10 elk, 5 Texan steers, 4 donkeys, and 2 deer."

Black Elk showed no emotion at all. Bess' face flared into a hateful sneer, while Ben and Hanna looked at John questioningly.

"Us Indians are listed after the steerage passengers but before the livestock. I wonder if the fucking English see us as a lower class than the peasants or as high class livestock?" He wadded up the paper and threw it against the wall. "I have a bed in one of the cabins upstairs but I'm staying down here with you." He sat and put an arm over Bess' shoulders protectively.

"John. John." Black Elk said softly. "We carry our freedom with us here." He touched his chest near his heart. "*Maya owicha paka*. It is fate." He looked around at his family and smiled. "Daughter, may I hold your black rock?"

Hanna pulled her rock from its special pouch saying, "*Ate', I carry it always.*"

Black Elk held the stone in both hands, appeared to pray for a moment then began. "We ride in this English vessel. And the white men that have our sacred land in America speak English. Yet the name of this vessel is The State of Nebraska, an American state is named after an Indian word meaning flat water." He stopped and looked around him, hoping for recognition. "The flat water the Indians called *Nebrathka* is the Platte River."

Black Elk looked at his family again and knew his story held them – the fetid darkness was forgotten. He felt their spirits and saw the wonder in their eyes as he spoke directly to Hanna. "This rock came from the Platte River. I met your mother there on that river a year before the Battle of Greasy Grass. Your mother began to teach John Dunn to walk the Red Road there in the state of Nebraska many winters ago. Kangee, our Shaman gave this rock to your mother near that river." He looked down and rubbed a thumbnail over the likeness of the hawk that had been etched there. "*Your mother, my dear Itunkala, guides us still,*" he said in Sioux. "If our path is to spend a few days together in this darkness, we must learn what wisdom she teaches."

Hanna and her father stood near the bow talking. They were well into their seventh day of sailing on the way back to America. "Ate'? Do you remember that first day we sailed away from the United States?"

Black Elk said nothing. He realized that his daughter needed to talk.

"When the ship started to move, I was so excited. But when we started to pull away from the dock, when the land got farther and farther away, I got scared. I ran as fast as I could to the back of the boat – I don't know, it just felt like I was losing everything. I remember crying – I thought about jumping off but couldn't. Everybody I love was on that boat. But where we lived, home, was just going away. It was an awful feeling."

Black Elk turned to face his daughter. "I felt something like that the first day I went to live on the reservation." He said nothing else when he saw the depth of his daughter's understanding.

She smiled at him sadly and continued. "You and Dunn had Ben down with the animals somewhere. I ran down to the hold where the animals were and you weren't there, so I just stood there near the buffalo pen and cried. You know the big old male, the one you call *Tȟáŋkaya*. He came over to me and looked at me like he knew. I reached through the bars and touched his face." She looked up at her father; she struggled to not let him see the tears that were forming.

"Ate. You came and found me there. I hugged you and told you that I felt sick. You just smiled at me and brought me here. You said, 'Watch the horizon.' Now I come here every day. I come here in the early morning to get the smell out of my nose. And I come here at sunset and say my prayers." She leaned against him, put her head on his shoulder and said, "*Pilamaya Ate'*."

Father and daughter stood there together as the prow split the Atlantic in its push to reach the American shore again. The cold late morning wind blew past them, but the closeness of their spirits warmed them.

"Ate? Are we all the same? I mean, our teachings say that the four colors of men must learn to live in peace. But at home, the whites never seem to be at peace – they take what they want from us – they take what they want from everybody." Hanna hesitated, searching for words. "The English loved our shows – they clapped and cheered just like the American audiences. But finally Ben and I stopped trying to see the English towns – we were made to feel like we didn't belong. The Germans were just the opposite – we had a hard time being alone. They followed us around, wanted us to come home with them. They acted like we were somehow better than they were. The French – they just went about their business. They never paid much attention to us when we walked around, but they never offered any help either. And the Italians – " Hanna laughed. "Well their women are sweet but the men, they –" Hanna blushed.

Black Elk laughed out loud. "The last time we came to Italy, some of our women loved the men – others hated them." He smiled at Hanna. "I understand."

The two of them stood there not speaking. The cloud cover broke a bit as beams of sunlight pierced the skies. Finally, Hanna sensed a change in her father; his focus seemed different. He stood a bit taller. Then he spoke. "See that smudge on the horizon? That's home. We should be in the harbor before nightfall."

They stood there, not talking for what seemed a long time. When Hanna could finally make out that what she was seeing were not clouds on the horizon but actual land, she spoke. "Ate', is that really home? We live on a train that goes from place to place, doing make believe shows for white people that hate us."

Black Elk looked down at his daughter with pain in his eyes. In some respects, he lived in the past before the white man came or in the future when hopefully, the prophecy of the White Buffalo Woman would come true. He looked back out to sea then spoke. "They say the early white explorers were afraid to come ashore. They reported smelling Indian cooking fires hundreds of miles out to sea. Then, legend has it that a terrible disease swept through and killed many as it did in Europe during the time of the Black Death. The early white explorers came at a time of great weakness."

"Ate'. I don't know what will come, but I am glad that we can be a family." She put one hand around his waist and held Little Abe in the other. He had his arm around her shoulders as New York Harbor came slowly into view.

It was early evening when The State of Nebraska sailed past Liberty Island. Lady Liberty stood tall, her lamp shining out for all to see.

Hanna turned to see the multitudes of immigrants pouring out of steerage to watch as they steamed past the Statue Of Liberty. Hanna was dumbstruck at the beauty – the skyline of New York glowed backlit from the setting sun. Electric lights blazed in many of the tall buildings, adding to the surreal feeling that this scene was a mirage, a made up thing like an iridescent bubble floating on a pond.

Then, Hanna turned away in disgust from this scene of white culture. She trudged tiredly to her spot in steerage to pack her things. An indelible feeling took her, made her want to cry out at the unfairness.

The immigrants that crowded the deck to watch Lady Liberty welcome them to their New World - the immigrants that had filled all the available space down in that stinking hold - the immigrants that tried to take the meager rations from others that were weaker or smaller - the immigrants that had molested the young women and girls that spoke different languages. It was Leftook and her father, the other red men that maintained order in the hold, made sure the weaker, older and the children got their share of the dismal gruel the English fed to their passengers. It was John Dunn who stole fresh water from above deck. It was the red women that helped the other women with their children when they were sick, when buckets needed emptying. It was her people that maintained what little humanity was left to the unfortunate souls seeking a better life in America.

Hanna was joyous that the voyage was almost over, but she returned to steerage with a heavy heart. It was the realization that these immigrants would have more freedom the instant they set foot on American soil than her people who had been there since before history.

Author's note:

William Cody and his traveling exposition made many trips to Europe in the years between the mid-1880's and 1906. Cody's troupe traveled to England aboard the *State Of Nebraska* in 1897 to honor Queen Victoria's Golden Jubilee marking the fiftieth anniversary of her ascension to the English throne.

The author chose to fictitiously set this chapter on the vessel *State Of Nebraska* for obvious reasons.

Two Moons

On the rails headed West somewhere in New Jersey, fall, 1900

"Evenin' Boss. Don't usually see you around here this time of night." Amos continued to tidy up the dining car; then he saw Dunn's face. "Coffee?"

Dunn sat down and looked out into the night as if he could see the countryside passing by in the dark. "Got anything stronger?" The look on the big man's face was a rarity – he looked vulnerable.

Amos pulled a large, unlabeled bottle and a shot glass from behind the serving bar. He placed the glass in front of Dunn, poured it neat and overflowing then went back to work.

"*Pilamaya mithkȟolá!*" Dunn said in Sioux and drained the glass. Immediately, Dunn slammed his palms on the table, coughed and squinted his eyes. "Woo Damn! That cleaned my horseshoes!" He coughed again and asked, "What are we drinking?" His voice was almost unintelligibly raspy.

"That, my friend, is what my brothers in Newark calls rum." Amos poured another glassful and sat down. "You wanna talk?"

"No need to, Amos this varnish is all I need." Dunn raised the glass, took a sip and shuddered.

"What did you say a moment ago?" Amos asked. "You were talkin that Indian talk."

"I said 'Thank you my friend,' in Sioux. It's used when talking to an honored friend." Dunn saluted Amos with his glass and took another sip.

Amos sat down across from Dunn and looked at him closely. "If you's got a misery like I thinks you do, this rotgut ain't gonna help."

"Thank you, amigo. My woman is in a mood. I'm just getting some air." Dunn took another sip and smiled. "If you don't mind, I'll just sit here with you a bit. Let things cool down. Need some help?"

"I's 'bout done. Just sit tight and I'll have a nip with you."

As Amos put the finishing touches on the dining car, Dunn stared out the window into the New Jersey night. There was the occasional glimmer from a passing farmhouse, then the train rolled through some small village. The crossing gate was down across the only street that intersected the tracks. The stationmaster waved sleepily as Dunn passed by, ready to raise the arm again and return to his cozy office.

John was lost in thought and gazing out the window; he didn't hear Amos pour himself a shot and sit down.

"Oogy Wawa!" Amos clicked his glass against Dunn's and raised it to eye level.

"Huh? What?" John appeared startled. He looked across the table at Amos and asked, "Come again?"

"Oogy Wawa! Means cheers in Zulu where my people come from." Amos clicked his glass with Dunn's again and took a sip. "Drink up my friend – cool down."

Dunn picked up his glass and was about to take another drink when the door to the dining car banged open and Ben walked in.

No words were spoken; none were needed. When Amos and Dunn looked at the expression on Ben's face, they nodded understanding as Amos stood and fetched another glass.

"Sit down son." Dunn said as he patted the chair beside him. "Amos and I were just solving the ills of the world. Join us."

As Ben sat, Amos placed a third shot glass in front of the young man and filled it with rum.

Dunn put his arm around Ben's shoulder and said, "Some advice. Take a deep breath, hold it in and take your medicine."

Ben eyed the glass with some trepidation, looked at Dunn suspiciously, then glanced across the table at Amos.

The old porter simply smiled and nodded his head.

Ben did as he was told. He took a deep breath, downed the dark amber liquid in one gulp and breathed out. Ben gasped at the same instant he was propelled backwards almost as if he'd been kicked by a horse. Had Dunn's arm not been around his shoulders, Ben would have fallen over backwards in his chair. Ben gasped again, coughed twice then held one hand to his chest. "Oh fuck, it burns!" was all Ben could say for a moment. Then slowly, a light seemed to come on his eyes and he smiled. "You boys come here often?"

There was good-natured laughter as Amos topped off all three glasses. Then the three began to talk.

"I'm so glad to be off that boat!" Ben said. "Those big European cities were pretty amazing. It was really interesting to see where you white folks came from." Ben nodded toward Dunn then took a sip.

"I'll take a tipi and rare buffalo backstrap any day." Dunn answered as he took a swallow himself.

"Speaking of food, it was terrible down in that hold. Hanna told me it reminded her how the food was at the Carlisle School." Ben looked at Dunn wide eyed. "What would it have been like down there if we hadn't kept the peace? It must be Hell for the immigrants coming over!"

"That's how it is with most whites, Heaven or Hell." Amos drained his glass and topped off all the glasses again. "You have no idea how bad some men treat their brothers. I've heard tell how it was in the belly of them slaver ships. Makes our little trip seem like nothin."

"What was it like topside?" Ben asked. "You went up a few times didn't you John?"

Dunn snorted mirthfully. "I was in the bar with Big Abe having a drink. This English chap walks up wearing his starchy uniform all covered in with gold braids and his silly hat. Anyway, I'm dressed like I usually am, comfortable. So the Englishman stands next to Hubert who's dressed in his three-piece like he usually is and the English just ignores me. He introduces himself to Hubert as the Purser or the First Mate – anyway he's polite at first – asks Hubert how he's enjoying the cruise, talks about the weather. Then he asks Hubert how it is to travel with 'Those Indians.' Abe said something like, 'Some of them are my good friends.' Then, this English Gentleman," Dunn's voice dripped sarcasm, "starts talking about Canadians so he's not openly talking about us Yankees. He says something like, 'The Scots and the Irish, even the French are having half-breed children with those Indian women.' Hubert can feel me starting to get irate so he puts a hand on my arm to keep the peace. Then that self righteous prick says, 'You'll never find any English half-breeds.' You know what Hubert said to this guy?" Dunn raised his glass and said "To you Big Abe!" and drained his glass. "He said, 'That is not surprising! The Indian women have to draw the line somewhere!'"

After Ben stopped laughing he asked, "Did you know that Columbus started off with four ships but one fell over the edge? Columbus didn't know where he was going, didn't know where he'd been and did it all on somebody else's money. The white man has been following Columbus ever since."

Dunn choked on his drink, he was laughing so hard, but Amos crossed his arms and asked seriously, "Why you boys here?" He looked at Ben and Dunn and continued. "You have damn fine women. You could be all wrapped up warm and tight but you's here talkin to me. What gives?"

There was in uncomfortable silence as Ben and Dunn regarded each other. Ben started. "I'm worried about Hanna. She's been a little moody. Tonight after we got Little Abe to sleep, we were sitting quietly on our bed talking. She got this odd look on her face, hiccupped, sneezed then farted. We both got a good laugh out of it but she didn't stop – she couldn't stop. She was almost hysterical. She was laughing so hard she puked into her hands. Then immediately, she was crying. I tried to talk to her, find out what was going on. Finally, she just told me to leave her alone – and here I am."

Amos regarded Ben for a moment then asked, "Your babe still nursin on her?"

"She stopped a month or so ago. Why do you ask?"

Amos ignored Ben's question and turned to Dunn. "How's your woman tonight?"

Dunn pursed his lips for a moment, thinking how to respond. "Well, you know Bess has a temper. I pretty much can ignore her outbursts and wait her out. She doesn't stay mad long. But tonight, she got scary. Instead of eating in the dining car tonight, I took two plates back to our place because she'd said she didn't feel like being in a crowd. We were eating and she said, 'Is your food cold?' and I said, 'No, mine's fine.' She jumped up and threw her plate against the wall so hard pieces went everywhere. I don't scare easily but when she told me to leave, I did."

"Boys" Amos said, "My missus sometimes got in a mood 'bout half-way through her cycle. She also tole me that sometimes women that lives close get sort of matched up – start havin' their days together." He topped off all the glasses and raised a toast, "I 'spect that 'bout the time you boys get back to your winter spot in New Mexico, you could both make a baby." He raised his glass, took a sip and said, "Havin' children is part of the Good Lord's plan. Here's to fathers!"

Nightmares
On the rails headed east, April 1901

The show in Marietta, Ohio was practiced perfection. Ticket sales were excellent. The livestock were corralled outside for an overnight stay. The trains were packed and ready for an early morning departure. Cody and most of the show's management spent the night at The Levee House to enjoy a restaurant meal with cigars and brandy later in the bar.

By the time Cody arrived back at the trains the next morning the livestock were loaded, the engines had been fired up to pressure and coal and water were ready for the next leg of the show's push east to New York City. The trains crossed the Muskingum River Bridge as the sun illuminated the new spring foliage.

Hanna and Bess were busy counting tickets and the money from yesterday's show when Hubert arrived. "How's Little Abe this fine morning?" he asked. The man was obviously in a good mood. He whistled tunelessly as he sat and slurped his second coffee.

"He's fine," Hanna said without looking up. "He's in the nursery car."

Hubert looked at Hanna then spoke to Bess. "You keeping Big John out of trouble?"

Bess didn't look up from her work either. She didn't even reply. There was a distinct tension in the room.
"Oy Vey!" Hubert leaned back in his chair with an ominous squeak. "You two are gloomy today!" He stood and walked across the car to the south-facing window. "Look out there! It's spring. The countryside we're passing through is luscious – wildflowers everywhere. That's a true hardwood forest. Who could be unhappy on such a lovely day?"

Bess and Hanna were sitting side-by-side. Hanna continued counting the money and making ledger entries while Bess counted ticket stubs. They gave each other nervous glances but did not look up.

Abe came and stood between them. "Finish your count, then we talk!" He gave them each a stern unreadable look and sat down.

Hanna and Bess shared a tortured glance as the smoke from Abe's evil smelling cigar wafted through the car. Then for the next half hour, the women lost themselves in the purity of math.

As Hanna was entering her final figures in the ledger, Abe spoke. "You two saw the schedule, right?" His tone of voice made it a statement, not a question.

Hanna put her hands in her lap and looked down as she nodded. She looked more hurt than angry. Abe scooted his chair over so he was close enough to touch. "It's been almost four years. You're women - not little girls. And Carlisle is just a town. Why does it still have power over you?"

Bess was up, fists balled at her sides, fuming. She sputtered, but all she could get out was, "Because it was..." She stood there looking like she might either scream at Abe in anger or cry like a little girl. She did neither – she glanced down at Hanna in utter anguish.

Hubert was unfazed by the intense emotion around him. Hanna stood and put her arms around her friend as if Bess might fly into pieces.

"Talk to me. Tell me why this place hurts you so."

Hanna hugged Bess then sat facing her boss. As Hanna struggled to find words, Bess stepped away from this painful conversation and looked out a window with her back turned.

"Every town has its secrets," Abe snorted. "We have to go through Pennsylvania. The tracks lead through Carlisle." He paused and put his hands on his hips. "We play New York! We can't just detour because Carlisle is a bad place. Look, we've played Chicago lots of times. I grew up there and have scars." Hubert took a deep breath, realized that his tone of voice was strident. "No matter how bad things get, we always have a choice. Every morning when you wake up you can decide to be wounded or you can choose happiness."

"Mr. Hubert, back in Chicago - are your people there? Does your tribe still exist?" The look in Hanna's eyes was both pleading and angry.

"I have cousins there. When we play there, I always go to Temple, if there's time."

"Bess and I have no village to go back to. She was raised Red with all their beliefs and ceremonies. That's gone for her. I was raised in a Christian home, then just thrown away when my fa..., when the man that adopted me died. Bess and I and all the other children at the Carlisle School were like animals in a cage. The men used us girls like..." Hanna sobbed and couldn't continue, but she didn't drop her eyes. The communication between them continued at a much deeper level.

Hubert reached out and took Hanna's hand in his. He stood and pulled her over to where Bess stood watching the Pennsylvania countryside pass by. He pulled them both into a rough hug and said, "You have a village here with us."

Bess was stiff in his arms, then slowly softened. As if her release was a signal, Hubert said, "When we stop in Carlisle, meet me up in front of the train. I want to show you something."

As Cody's train rolled into Carlisle, Pennsylvania the landmarks were painfully familiar. Hanna recognized the road that led to their old swimming hole. Sadly she couldn't remember the name of the creek, but fondly recalled the feelings of freedom there with her friends. Their train did not stop at the station but continued on to the large maintenance yard that housed the water tower and coal sheds. Many townspeople were milling around Cody's first train. A few curious spectators jogged to the second train as it chugged to a stop.

The first stop was beside a coal shed and as the fuel was being loaded many white faces peered into the windows. But there were no red faces and thankfully not a single person looked familiar.

"What are we afraid of?" Hanna asked. She and Bess stood at the top of the steps in the vestibule between the cars. Two stairs separated them from the familiar comfort of their rolling home and the soil of Pennsylvania.

"I feel so stupid!" said Bess. "There's nobody here! There's nothing that can hurt us, but I'm terrified. Why don't we just..."

Hanna grabbed Bess's hand and stepped down, causing Bess to stumble and nearly fall. The two of them stood there on the ground, big-eyed as they looked around. Then they laughed more out of relief than from the comic scene they'd just performed. They were two young Sioux women, very pregnant, and acting like kindergartners on the first day of school.

A shrill whistle followed by a loud, "Up here!" made them look forward. Hubert stood near the front of the engine waving for them to join him.

When they walked past the engine, it was like being in the presence of a fire-breathing dragon. It clanked, belched steam, hissed and radiated a heat and smell that somehow reminded Hanna of the Hell her stepfather had described. Hubert waited for them in front of this black iron monster.

The front of the locomotive towered over Abe as he stood there. He faced forward down the tracks - the cowcatcher pressed against the backs of his legs. He pulled Hanna and Bess in between the tracks and had them face him side by side. Smoke and steam poured from the stack above him; hundreds of small, inexplicable noises arose from the machine behind him.

Abe wore a kippah on his head and around his shoulders was a long white cloth like a shawl. He looked like some Old Testament prophet. He stood there, eyes blazing, hands outstretched, palms out. Behind him was the icon of mechanized white supremacy, a symbol of power and authority, it's headlamp shining like a beacon for believers and non-believers alike.

Hubert reached behind him and held up a bucket full of water. "Ladies," he said, "This bucket I got from the kitchen.

The water is just from the faucet." With the other hand he showed them the fabric around his neck. "This is a bar towel I borrowed from Amos. There's no magic here. But there is faith!"

"When I was a little boy back in Chicago, there was a ceremony I watched in Temple a couple of times. It's called Mikveh – a ritual cleansing of hands. Since we're here in this place that holds such bad memories, bear with me. This might just be a bit of theater on my part or it can be more. It's up to you." He paused, looked skyward then began in a completely different voice.

"Blessed are you, Adonai or Jehovah or Thunkashila or the Great Creator, our God King of the universe who has sanctified us with His commandments and has commanded us concerning the elevation of hands."

Hubert gave them each a fatherly smile then said, "Please hold out your hands, palms up." He leaned down, immersed his own hands in the water then picked up the bucket. Slowly he poured a small amount of water on the hands before him. "We wash our hands of all the sins, all the hurts, all the injuries and injustices that have been done to us." He set the bucket on the ground and dried his own hands then those of Bess and Hanna.

"Again please." And as Hanna and Bess held out their hands a second time, Abe wet his own then poured water over theirs. "We wash our hands of all the sins, all the hurts, all the injuries and injustices that we have done to others." He then dried all their hands again.

"And again." And as he poured the water on their hands the third time he said, "We wash our hands again in order that we can receive the blessings of you, our Lord whatever your name may be. We lift up our hands to you for the sanctuary you give us. We bless you and thank you. Amen."

There was a moment of quiet joy most days that Hanna had become so accustomed to, she just accepted it without savoring it – until now. Little Abe was finally asleep above them in his bunk. She and Ben spooned together, warm, the familiar rumbling wheels below them. It was during these intimate moments that she and Ben could communicate – sometimes a single word, a touch, understandings from skin to skin contact; even an unvoiced sigh spoke volumes. It was during these intimate moments that an almost unrealized pain dropped away.

"Ben?"

"Uh huh."

"Something happened today."

"What?"

"I told you about what Big Abe did - the ceremony."

"Wish I'd been there."

Hanna rolled onto her back and held Ben's hand on her pregnant, distended belly. "I described what Big Abe said – what it looked like." She pulled Ben's hand to her lips and kissed his palm. "I told you what happened, but I didn't tell you how it felt."

"Tell me." He put his toes under her foot and gently pushed up – an unconscious affectionate little habit they'd developed that needed no words.

"Like right now – you and I are together – not our bodies exactly – we're together – like I don't have a wall up – I don't need to guard myself. I feel safe."

She felt Ben's answer in the language of souls.

"Later, Bess and I walked around Carlisle. It was like a little pain in my heart was gone. The towns people still looked at us like they always do but it didn't matter any more." She hesitated, feeling Ben feeling her. "I can't explain it exactly – I just felt open. I saw other people as just people, like we were the same."

"I'm not sure I understand."

"Ben, you're strong. People sense it. You radiate this confidence that comes from knowing -." She wavered, struggling for the right words. "You get respect because…" She hesitated again. "You know that you'll win in a fight."

"So, you have to be tough…"

"Ben! Look through my eyes!" Hanna realized she'd raised her voice. She continued in almost a whisper. "I'm a woman. I'm small. And I'm red. All my life, I've felt insignificant. And it hurts to be taken advantage of." She shuddered.

"Hanna, I've always treated you…"

She interrupted him again. "Ben, today something happened inside me. I feel different. Open. After Big Abe did his ceremony, I allowed myself to feel equal."

She rolled onto her side and faced him in their narrow bed. There were no words, no dominance. Their bodies and their spirits joined so completely that they lost awareness of them. Only stars remained.

Ben lay there watching Hanna sleep. Very pregnant with his child, she no longer had the slim body that filled him with lust. What Ben realized fully in this instant was that it was her spirit that was beautiful. It was their spirits that had made love moments before. He realized that the memory of this time with her was a treasure he would carry in his heart always.

There was no horizon, only fog. The prairie was utterly flat, monochromatic. She was only aware of the cold because she could see the frost; it covered the sage and short grass with rimes of ice. She turned and looked south behind her. A small village of tipis stood there barely visible. Smoke from sage fires streamed away in the north wind. The sky above was tinged in a warm welcome yellow, the color of a summer sun.

She faced north into the wind afraid of the harsh white. Behind was her life, her people. And it was her time to guard, to stand between her kin and the threats that blew in from the relentless north. Ice rattled against her elk skin clothing. Sleet like needles assailed her. She wanted so badly to close her eyes, to curl up on the prairie but it was her time.

A tumbleweed blew out of the fog. It rolled swiftly toward her village, her people. Instinctively, she knew it contained a threat and moved to stop it. She placed her body between it and her people. When it struck the force and the malevolent curse it contained nearly blotted out her consciousness as it shattered against her like a thin glass ball. As she bled from a multitude of tiny cuts, she felt warm knowing the buffalo would come; her people would eat another day.

Weakened but determined, she again faced the north. Eddies of snow swirled about her feet and obscured her vision as if the north was her enemy. A maelstrom of white accompanied the fog. Huge snowflakes blew into her face, churning, hypnotic and hallucinatory. It was as if the north was a huge hungry beast that would devour her on its way to her people.

Two figures appeared in the distance obscured by snow as they approached. At first, they appeared to be men dressed in skins as she was. They were comfortingly familiar. But with each gust, each white out, these men changed. There was a howl of wind and the men were white, dressed in cavalry uniforms, their intent obvious on their faces. She saw into their hearts and felt fear and anger in equal measure. It was both memory and premonition – she watched as one drew a knife by the door to her tipi. The other stood behind, sliced it open with his bayonet and fired his rifle into her living space. She felt a momentary pain in her breast, then watched the eyes of her newborn recede as her essence rose above her ruined body. Then she looked into the eyes of the Old Woman Who Judges. They stood as if on a high precipice, surrounded by a multitude of women, looking down as men in blue overran her village.

"I have been waiting for you." The old woman's elk skin dress was simple, but beautifully beaded. She looked impossibly old, but her eyes were alive with a powerful spirit. The ancient woman touched the young woman's heart and said, "Uŋkíye yuhá ól'ota tȟawóečhuŋ." (We have much work to do.)

The younger woman felt a stab of sadness and regret. There in her heart was a distant, residual memory of her past life, a life unrealized now. She pictured the handsome face of her husband - felt the *yearnings of a body now gone. She saw the love of her child who now would grow up motherless. She turned sadly to the old woman and asked, "Work? I am the child here."*

The old woman did not speak; she only pointed to the changing scene below. The sage and yucca bloomed. The paintbrush and thimbleweed flowered in riotous color. Two young hunters appeared, hungry and desperate. One pointed and both then watched in wonder as a beautiful young maiden approached them dressed in brilliant white.

The young woman glanced up from the drama below, her eyes questioning as if expecting an answer from the Old Woman Who Judges. The old woman didn't speak - the answer was in her eyes as she pointed again. "That is you. That is us - all of us."

She regarded the young men in front of her through the eyes of all women, as these two young men perceived her as the two spirits of men always do. One was shy, fearfully respectful of all that she represented. The other was filled with lust as he saw the beauty of her outer form. The shy one looked at her with awe and reverence as the other reached under her skirt and touched her where husbands touch their wives in love.

A black cloud covered the lustful young warrior – lightning struck him, a snake ate his flesh. Soon, his bones fell black upon the prairie.

The snake, with its hard, lipless face, seemed to smile up at her as it wrapped around her ankle. Then, in a lovely pure child's soprano, it sang the traditional song of happiness as it crawled away back to its lair.

Then she was running blissfully across the prairie with the perfect abandonment of a child. She was racing with a young warrior, a boy on the cusp of manhood. The two of them shared a new love, a friendship untested. They won the race and stood by a wide river to accept their prize. A shaman, kind yet intimidating, reached into the river and pulled out a black stone. The shaman handed the stone to the young man and said, "You may have questions, but there are only choices."

Far to the north, the sounds of battle and a bugle called to them. Again, the Old Woman Who Judges pointed. They were on an impossibly high precipice, observing but not participating. The young woman looked into the eyes of the old woman and saw pain and hope. Then she looked in the direction the old woman pointed. She recognized their sacred Paha Sapa with a multitude of blue-coated white men there in battle with her people.

Then she saw him – her new friend, the young warrior was there. He was now in full young manhood, riding swiftly into battle. When he fell wounded onto the prairie, she felt the bullet that he took as if she was in his skin. The pain she felt in her heart was a realization of her love for him. But the battle continued. Many warriors fell, as did the men in blue. Then, in a final, blistering attack, the battle was over. A white man with long, blonde hair fell. Many arrows pierced him. When the white man's sword was taken from his hands a great cry went up. This cry of joy rang like a bell, slowly diminishing over the next few years as the white hoard continued to push her people aside. When she saw her man, her love riding back to her, she and her people were in hiding.

This time, the old woman did not point – the terrible sadness in her eyes left no option but to look and know. On the prairie outside a small white man's town, she saw a young man whose spirit matched her young son's. He was beaten bloody, head lolling to the side, hanging from a barbed wire fence as if crucified. Instantly, she was by his side, crying hysterically. She reached out to put her hand on his shoulder, to rouse him, to feel. But he was cold.

A hand on her shoulder awoke her. She thought she might have screamed when she awoke. Her first impression upon awaking was of tears on her cheeks.

"Hanna, you were having a bad dream." Ben moved his hands from her shoulders and used his thumbs to push her tears aside. "What were you dreaming?"

Hanna shuddered unable to speak. Finally she managed to say, "Hold me." The fading memory of the dream was just too terrible to even think about.

"I have to go soon." Ben smiled and got up, concern in his eyes. "The parade starts at noon and we have to have everything in place. We've got wagons to unload, stock to be fed and ready to move out. I'm going to grab some breakfast then find Dunn and your father. Maybe see you after the show this afternoon. Be careful out there." Then he was gone.

Hanna sat up and tried to shake off the feeling of doom her dream had left her. She leaned down and scooped Little Abe off the floor. He'd been playing with a doll and immediately wiggled out of her arms in protest.

"Mama. I don't like it!" Little Abe stood on the bench seat and looked out the window.

"What don't you like, Little Man?" Hanna sat across from Little Abe, her arms crossed over her pregnant belly.

"I afraid. I no like outside."

"In our language you would say *Miyé ikȟóphA*. It means *I fear* or *I'm afraid something will happen*."

"No!"

"What do you mean *No*, Little Man?" Hanna tried to keep her voice neutral but she knew there was a frown in the tone she used with her son. "That's the language of our people."

"Oskar say it stupid."

Hanna sighed and looked out the window. "Oskar speaks Cheyenne. Our people speak many different languages. And the Cheyenne were our friends before the white man came."

Hanna could not reconcile the scene she was currently seeing with the vision she experienced in New York harbor. A year ago, New York had looked like a mirage, a vision of shining towers, lit from within by electric lights. It was beautiful and rivaled the cities of Europe. Here was the polar opposite. Three and four story tenements surrounded the blackened cinders of the rail yard. The only natural color was the blue of the sky. The rest of the picture was greys and blacks. There was no green at all – not a tree, a flower, nor a blade of grass. The only living thing Hanna could see was the occasional passing of an armed railroad guard walking by to keep the trains from being ransacked.

"Let's go get some breakfast then get you ready for the day." She grunted as she hoisted herself to stand. "I have to go to the bathroom – want to come with me?"

"No mommy. I stay here and play wif Sally. Daddy took me."

Hanna worried as she walked down the aisle to the bathroom at the end of her rail car. Her son preferred to play with a small ceramic and cloth girl doll with changeable clothing that the women in the wardrobe car made for him. For some reason she couldn't quite grasp Hanna wished her son would play with the stuffed bear or even his toy wooden wagon.

Later, after breakfast, Hanna was getting Little Abe dressed for the day. "Come on, Little Man. Auntie Bess will be here soon. We're going into the big city – it should be exciting."

"Aw, Mommy! I want stay here. More fun."

"Auntie Bess and I have to go to the fairgrounds and get everything ready. We sell tickets and take money – that's our job. If we don't do our job, we can't stay here on the train. We've talked about this before." Hanna tried to put the boys shoes on as he squirmed and fought her.

"Please Mommy. Can I stay in dress car? I like the nice ladies."

"It's called the wardrobe car, Little Man. You pester the girls there too much. Come on – stay with me today. We'll have an adventure."

"Do I hafta?" he whined. "I like playing dress up. I have fun in the dress car."

Hanna looked at her son and smiled. "I'll ask. OK? But if you stay there, you can't leave. You have to wait until I come back. And you have to do what the girls say. OK?"

Little Abe laughed and hugged her legs. "Thank you mama – I be good."

"Why don't you ask them to make you a little warrior costume? Your dad can make you a bow and arrows."

"Naw – I like dressing up like Sally. When I wear skirts, I feel special."

The Damnation of Frank Lynch
Swearing Creek, North Carolina, October 29, 1901

Even uncomfortably pregnant Hanna felt more contented than she could ever remember. She and Ben were spooned together – his arms were around her holding Little Abe near their unborn child. A full moon lit their way as Cody's trains rolled north toward Danville, Virginia. Their sleeping compartment was cramped but cozy. The sounds and motions from the track below were comforting.

The chaos of show business, the irregular schedule, different towns that seemed the same, all the tiny last minute emergencies were everyday occurrences. Everybody in Cody's troupe accepted the unpredictability with grace and good humor. The very randomness of life on the rails had become comforting and predictable.

"Ben, do you think we've passed into Virginia?" Hanna lay there in her tiny cocoon of warmth and love. They cherished these moments of private togetherness. It was during these less stressful times between shows when the two of them could talk quietly before falling asleep.

"Probably not. Hubert said it was about 140 miles from Charlotte to Danville. The map shows Danville just over the border. We'll probably cross over into Virginia about sunrise."

They lay there happily conversing without words. Ben reached under Hanna's garments and put one hand on her distended belly. Almost immediately he was rewarded by a kick from inside. They laughed quietly together and then he nuzzled her neck and whispered "*Thehíla*."

Hanna didn't move physically, but he felt her spirit move closer to the thin membrane that kept them from becoming one. "I love you too, Iron Eagle Ben Two Elk," she said sleepily.

Even though both of them felt a delicious fatigue, they were still too excited to sleep. "One more performance." Hanna said quietly, as much to herself as to Ben. "After Danville, we're off for the winter. It reminds me of school but better."

"*Chesli*, anything is better than good old Carlisle."

"Ben!" Hanna laughed, "We want the little man to learn good words."

"What's wrong with the word *chesli*? I load bales of green hay then feed it to the livestock. Then I shovel out the *chesli*. It's a great word! It keeps me busy. Smells good, too!"

"Ben, he's learning words so fast – we need to be careful what we say."

"I thought you wanted him to learn our language." Ben gave her a squeeze and said, "Tomorrow I'll teach him road apples and turd. Those are good English terms. Then I'll get him his own shovel!"

"Ben, don't be ungrateful!" Hanna immediately regretted her tone of voice. She sounded almost as angry as Bess. More evenly she said, "We have a good life here. The last few days have been wonderful. The whites in Charleston were friendly. Then we got our pay and even a bonus because of the show in Charlotte. Bess and I processed more than 30,000 tickets. Remember yesterday while we were shopping in Charlotte – the townspeople treated us like royalty. The weather has been perfect. We only have one show left to do in Virginia, then it's off to New Mexico and our beautiful life there. We should be back in time to have our baby. Imagine, our baby born in a tipi. Seriously, I feel so lucky."

"Hanna, I'm sorry. It's just that shoveling shit seems so ordinary. I know that I'm part of a world famous act, but it's become routine. Yeah, I know, we see people every day from our train windows who are much worse off than we are. It's just that at the end of the day, you count tickets and I shovel shit. Did you picture our lives like this?"

"Ben, from my earliest memories from back in Kansas people hated me because I was red. The only person who loved me was my dad. My teacher was good to me but she died. Then it was my dad. If it hadn't have been for you, the Carlisle School would have defined my life. Ben, we have a good life. Be thankful! I am." And then she slept. And dreamed.

She was walking. The prairie was vast, so immense that she was dimly aware of keeping its enormity at bay with an act of will. She realized she was herself in a pool of spirits. As she looked through her eyes, her feminine ancestors looked with her, shared the experience, felt the power that was older and more powerful than all the human souls that had ever been.

The landscape was foreign yet totally familiar. Hanna had never been in this place but the joyous feelings of home flooded her, pulled her into the collective spirit that keeps us all. She nearly wept at the overwhelming connectedness she felt. With each step she took the earth welcomed her, joined her, was her. The soles of her feet told her of recent rains, the life in the soil, last night's fog. The air was alive with sound, smells, and the essence of the living things around her. There was so much knowledge carried to her by the wind, she stopped to sample, to feel, to know. A lark called for a mate and the beauty of it's voice made her wet with longing for her own mate.

Again, the vastness threatened to conquer her with its beauty. She stopped, overcome. The only rational feeling she had was to surrender, to give thanks. She faced east and felt the wind full on her face. She felt the light, new days, beginnings. Knowing the power to start over unburdened the sorrows she knew would come.

She turned and the west welcomed her with sunsets that spoke of endings and beautiful colors.

A warm wind greeted her from the south. She felt its soothing warmth, the comfort that comes from the ease of summer. She knew she would find rest from her weariness there, a renewed connection to the sacred web of life.

A bitter cold from the north chilled her, but gave her the courage and endurance for all that is cruel in life. The north spoke of a deep love that gives strength to face the things in life that hurt, that are harsh and make you squint.

She walked then, knowing she was expected; others were waiting.

In the distance she saw a village. Many tipis were there; all but one were ghostly, transparent. The central cooking fire was cold; not one human being could be seen from this distance. But one tipi, not the largest or the closest to the central fire, glowed from within. Unlike the rest of the structures in the village that seemed transparent, hazy, this tipi that called to her was vibrantly painted in scenes from scores of millennia past. At the top, tied to four of the thirteen lodge poles were banners representing the four colors of men. She saw the history of her people painted there – she saw a trek across ice from another continent, pictures of her people hunting massive hairy elephants. The pictures seemed to move as if she were actually there experiencing the intensity of the hunt. She saw her people living and adapting to every ecological niche on this new land. She experienced each belief system her people devised to help them live and respect every part of the sacred Earth in which they lived. She saw and knew that within this one tipi was the feminine force that connected her people.

The tent flap was open – a clear invitation to enter. She hesitated for a moment, turned and looked behind her to the east, to the light of new beginnings, then stepped inside. When she stepped through the threshold, she moved west toward the direction of endings, beautiful colors, sunsets.

The transition from outside to in was jarring, yet beautiful. Outside, the spirit of the world and its vastness was so overpowering she was lost in the oneness of it. But the single step into the tipi brought closeness, intimacy. Seated around the tipi wall were generations of her mothers and those yet to come. Each was familiar; she felt her connectedness to this chain, this lineage of spirits that stretched into the past and future. Outside her spirit had felt the enormity of creation, an infinity of space. Yet inside, it was as if she were returned to the womb where time was a thread that bound her to the women around her.

She looked at the wise friendly faces that looked up at her and saw a beautiful tiny woman with her hand holding a space for her to sit. This woman smiled and patted the spot next to her. Hanna saw the hawk feathers woven into this woman's long hair and knew. This was her mother, her guide. The two fell into each other's eyes and experienced their lives together in a world where Itunkala had lived and raised her as a daughter.

Itunkala reached out, took Hanna's hand, and sat her down in the circle. When Hanna felt the earth beneath her, her mother on one side and the spirit of the daughter she was to have on the other, she knew that the circle would go unbroken.

No words were spoken; none were needed. The spirit of their linage, the seamless connection between their lives stretched to infinity both to the past and into the future. It was as if the mother-daughter bond was the continuum of a singular soul that was punctuated only by time and space. Hanna could almost feel the spot at the other side of the universe where her line met, began and ended.

Hanna felt a change, a different focus of the energy she felt. There was an expectation like a collective breath taken and held, waiting for what was next to come. Then another woman stepped into the circle. She was young, beautiful – she wore a lovely beaded deerskin shift. Hanna felt an immediate joy when she recognized this woman – it wasn't the lovely youthfulness of this woman but the spirit beneath that was so familiar.

Standing there was Kanj Coonshi wearing what she wore on the day she married. She smiled down sadly at Hanna, extended both her hand, inviting her to stand.

Hanna stood face to face with the woman she knew only as Old Grandmother. Yet, the woman was youthful and still full of the same joyous wisdom. And in her eyes, Hanna saw the stars.

"It is your time little sister. Mine is past. Your tasks now are the choices you must make. There is nothing else." Then as Hanna watched, Kanj Coonshi rapidly aged and shrank until there was nothing but the smoke from the sage fire.

Hanna watched the smoke swirl up through the opening at the top of the tipi as the four banners in the four colors of men fluttered in the wind. Then a new star appeared in the Ghost Road.

Hanna was up and clutching Little Abe protectively even before the sounds and sensations registered. The train was braking hard. The wheels were shrieking against steel rails. The deceleration threw her against the wall of their sleeping quarters. Ben was up, wide-eyed, looking out the window when the crash occurred. The forward momentum of their car stopped almost instantly followed by the sound of an explosion from forward. Their car continued to move but sideways in a sickening way; the wheels thudded rhythmically as they rolled across the wooden railroad ties beneath them. Then the car jumped the tracks entirely, began to slide down an embankment and finally came to rest tilted dangerously against a large tree.

There was a momentary silence followed by the screams of people and animals alike. Hanna and Ben dressed quickly and stepped down into a moonlit nightmare.

Many of the wooden cars lay splintered into shards. Several had fallen into a creek, while the remnants of others littered the bridge that crossed a small waterway. It was hard to see in the light of the full moon, but the pitiful noises coming from the shattered stock cars were sickening.

Ben led Hanna and the baby to a hillside above the bloodbath. He left them there so he could go and give whatever assistance he was able to give.

Moments or hours later, local farmers and townspeople from Lexington and the surrounding countryside arrived carrying torches – trying to help. Hanna watched horrified. She was reminded of the scenes of Hell she'd seen painted by

Hieronymus Bosch. She began to shiver until the shaking was almost uncontrollable. A wave of nausea took her. She put the baby down, fell to her hands and knees and vomited.

Hanna sat there feeling less shaky when a man she'd never seen walked by. He was nearly hysterical and muttering, "It's my fault! It's my fault." He was dressed much like the engineer of their train but he was bare headed with a nasty gash on his forehead. His hands and knees were bloody. In one hand, he kept waving a piece of paper. "It's my fault," he said again. "I thought it said train." He looked down at Hanna, shrieked, "I'm sorry!" dropped the paper and wandered off murmuring to himself.

"Hey! Stop!" Hanna turned as Abe Hubert walked up, flustered. He looked as if he'd been crying. "Who is that man?" Hubert asked.

Hanna just shook her head, not trusting her voice. Then she picked up the paper the man had dropped and handed it to Hubert.

"It's a telegram," he said and read it silently. His face turned red, he sputtered for a moment and exclaimed, "That must have been the other engineer that caused this mess. It's probably just as well that he wandered off. Cody is looking for him. I think he plans on killing him." He held out the telegram to Hanna.

```
Cody wild west show northbound stop
take siding at Lexington stop
let Cody trains pass stop
```

It took more than a week for Hanna and her extended family to recover enough to board a train that would take them to New Mexico. William Cody was devastated but generous as his performers and roustabouts scattered for the winter. He gave the tipis to Black Elk and his family.

Hanna bought a newspaper at the Charlotte station as they waited to board their train west. It contained a detailed article about the train wreck that Hanna and her family had experienced first hand.

Buffalo Bill Derailed in Davidson County

In October 1901, two trains collided near the Linwood rail station — disrupting the reign of the famous Wild West Show. But in the midst of calamity the importance of human kindness shone through.

Two trains pulled out of Charlotte in the early morning hours of October 29, 1901, heading north on the Southern Railway. On them, members of Buffalo Bill's Wild West Show, having just entertained more than 30,000 spectators in the Queen City, rolled north toward Virginia. Danville was to be the final show of the season. But one of the trains never made it out of North Carolina.

Under a full moon, the lead train, carrying Col. William "Buffalo Bill" Cody in his own private Pullman car, moved swiftly toward Lexington. A second train filled with animals, roustabouts, and one of the show's stars, Annie Oakley, departed later and lagged behind.

Roughly 65 miles north of Charlotte, Southern Railway Engine 75 chugged out of the Lexington station, heading south with a load of fertilizer.

Critical Mistake

Southern Railway's mainline was a single track in 1901. As Buffalo Bill's trains headed north, the freight train's engineer, Frank Lynch, received a telegraph message ordering him to let the show trains pass. Lynch followed the order and pulled onto a sidetrack. But he missed the critical detail that the Wild West Show traveled on two trains.

After the first show train passed through Lexington, Lynch eased his locomotive back onto the main line. The engine picked up speed, traveling at about 45 miles per hour. As he rounded a curve, Lynch saw a sickening sight — a headlight charging toward him.

The second show train, with Engineer Bud Rollins at the helm, was traveling too fast to avoid the inevitable. Emergency brakes squealed. Sparks flashed as steel grated against the iron rails. Both crews jumped clear of the impending crash. Seconds later, near the Old Red Mill four and a half miles south of Lexington, the trains collided.

The impact knocked some of the show train's five cars into Swearing Creek. Others lay gnarled in a jagged heap of metal in a cornfield owned by Linwood resident Wesley Young.

In an instant, a single human error sent hundreds of show horses and exotic animals to their deaths and sidelined one of the greatest spectator shows in American history.

Oscar Sisk, a retired railway man, came to the scene to help. He described what he saw: "Two engines seemed to have tried to devour each other. One had run halfway inside the other, and then they reared up on the tracks like two giant beasts in deadly combat. All the cars on both trains were made of wood and were shattered into thousands of pieces upon impact."

No people died in the crash, but Cody's show suffered catastrophic losses. Among the 110 horses that died, two were the showman's personal mounts — Old Pap and Old Eagle — along with two stallions Cody received from Queen Victoria. Only two horses survived the crash. One of them was Duke, Cody's favorite.

When Cody arrived at the scene, eyewitnesses say he blinked back tears as he told his men to get their guns and, "Do what we have to do." One account says he pursued some of the freight-train crew with his gun drawn. Railroad reports show Lynch made his way to Salisbury where he hitched a ride on a train bound for parts unknown and escaped into anonymity.

Neighborly Hands

When Wesley Young's 19-year-old daughter, Belle, heard the crash, she grabbed her younger sister, Minnie, and ran down the road to the creek. As soon as they saw the disaster, they roused the rest of the family to help.

In the hours after the accident, the Young family went into action. Mrs. Young used the family's bed sheets to make bandages. She also sent Belle and Minnie to the neighbors to ask for flour. Retrieving hams from the smokehouse, Mrs. Young cooked for the group, making biscuits with 100 pounds of borrowed flour and serving meat and eggs and vegetables until she ran out of food.

By morning, word of the great train wreck spread throughout the Piedmont, and crowds began to gather. Onlookers later described the aftermath: Cowboys, some still dressed in their show regalia, herded buffalo into a nearby pasture. Willie Cox told what he remembered of the accident: "There were saddles, bridles, costumes, and other show equipment that had washed down the creek and were being gathered up and carried away by residents of the area."

The accident was not only a tragedy, but also one of the most dramatic events ever to shake the Linwood area. Belle Young was known to regale her friends and family members with stories of the accident and the days that followed. She told one reporter, "We had a big time back then. I reckon I got to know them all. They stayed there a good bit."

Cox said Cody's first concern was for the show people. According to one witness, Cody asked a storekeeper in Linwood to estimate the value of his entire stock, then purchased it, and turned it over to those who played cowboys and American Indians in the show.

"It was quite a show for the people of Linwood," recalled Cox. "Indians and cowboys camped in a pasture near the Linwood railroad station and walked back and forth to the store, carrying goods to the camp. Buffalo, horses, and cattle that survived the wreck were pastured near Linwood for several weeks."

Wesley Young and his family helped Cody and his crew in whatever way they could. In addition to feeding the group and pasturing animals, the Young's also put show members up in their barn overnight.

Cody was grateful and gave one of his surviving horses, Shoo Fly, to Wesley Young. Belle and Minnie told members of their church that it was the fastest horse their father ever owned.

Oakley's husband, Frank Butler, carried his injured wife to a railcar that workers set up as a temporary hospital. She went next to a hospital in Winston-Salem, where she received treatment for her injuries, including paralysis.

Annie Oakley, who was asleep when the accident spilled her car into a swamp on the north side of the track, was thrown from her bed and suffered extensive injuries. Early newspaper reports announced she was dead. Annie Oakley had been a main attraction of Buffalo Bill's Congress of Rough Riders for 16 years. It was rumored that the stress of the wreck caused her hair to turn white overnight.

William Cody's last words before he boarded a train to take him to his winter home in Wyoming were, "I don't know if my exposition will rise from the ashes."

Author's Note:

The above newspaper account is in part, an article written by Caron Lee Myers for Our State Magazine September 2011. (North Carolina) Ms. Myers kindly gave me permission to fictionalize her work in order that it fit the illusion of my fiction. I achieved that narrative by simply removing her references to outcomes later in the timeline. The words in the last paragraph quoting William Cody are my words alone.

Caron Myers lives in Lexington, North Carolina and has written extensively about the history of the area in which she lives. Ms. Myers interviewed at least one member of a family that took part in the rescue of the human and animal survivors of Cody's wreck. She's walked the tracks over and near

Swearing Creek and has held remnants of that wreck in her hands.

Ms. Myers is part Native American (Cherokee) and holds a deep respect for the lives that the original inhabitants of this country lived.

Aftermath
Swearing Creek, North Carolina, October 30, 1901

The wreck was like a huge black monster that had eaten John Dunn alive. He was deep in its gut, smothered, wondering if he would ever find his way out of the beast's frigid maw. He was up to his knees in mud when the sun finally found its way in the east further illuminating the devastation. What little consciousness Dunn had left of self gave him no chance of escaping the desperation. He'd become so anxious as the hours crawled by that soon he'd simply forget to breathe.

Dunn vaguely remembered standing ankle deep in the cold water of Swearing Creek. His clothes were covered with mud. His forearms were spattered with the blood of several beautiful horses he'd helped free from the wreckage, only to watch and hear them shot.

Then there was no memory. It was as if he'd awakened from a bad dream. He was dimly aware that he was kneeling at the creek washing a shoe. He had no memory of finding it, only that for some reason he couldn't recall the shoe was important. Then the daylight registered – torches and moonlight no longer lit his surroundings. He raised his eyes to the east and saw tipis backlit by the sun.

Then there was no thought except of home – to be inside, isolated with his woman, to be warm and loved. The shoe floated away downstream forgotten.

Dunn turned his back on the horror of the train's mangled remains. With the wreck behind him, the circle of tipis sitting on the level ground above Swearing Creek looked normal, reassuring. The part of his mind that was swirling with fear and grief wanted nothing else but to step into his tipi. His woman was there and by closing the tent flap, the chaos below could be blocked from his consciousness.

But the other part of his mind, the *Akíčhita* role that dictated he was responsible for the security of his people, also had to function. His path between the solace of his tipi and the disarray and madness behind was a gauntlet.

"Hey Boss! They found the safe from the Hubert's car buried in mud."

"See if you can find some locals with a team. Pull it out and get it up to the first train." As the man turned to follow his orders, Dunn asked, "Gordy, is your family OK?"

"Yea, Boss. They's stayin' with some farmers, friends of the Young's, I reckon." Turning to go he added, "Hey! Thanks for asking."

Dunn made it a few more steps uphill toward his tipi and blessed oblivion when he was stopped again.

"Hey Boss, them sodbusters got the buffalo and horses that ain't dead together in some corral. They's feedin' 'em the same. Is oats gonna' hurt them buffalo?"

"Sam, just worry about getting all our surviving stock rounded up first," Dunn said wearily. "We'll sort out the feed later." It took an act of will to not bolt uphill when he asked, "Sam, your wife OK?"

"She be a bit banged up but she's tough. She's cookin' with them farm gals. Your Bess make it?

"She's good," Dunn said wistfully. He nodded toward the tipis at the top of the rise, wishing only that he were there. "As best as we can tell now, we lost a lot of the stock, but none of the crew died."

"That's not exactly true, Mr. Dunn."

John turned toward that familiar voice. Hubert's accent was unmistakable – his Chicago roots were mixed with a tinge of Yiddish. Dunn had heard that voice angry, jovial and often philosophical. But never in the years that Dunn and Hubert shared had that voice held such pain. "Everybody's accounted for except Old Grandmother – the one you call Kanj Coonshi. I checked. She was in the nursery car that is still intact. She's just gone. Any ideas?"

"Boss, I..." Dunn just couldn't continue. The man standing before him seemed incongruous. Hubert was dressed in his usual three-piece suit. With the exception of his shoes, his clothing was spotless as always. But behind him was the utter devastation of the world they shared. Abe Hubert was the closest thing to a father figure Dunn had. And at that moment big John Dunn wanted nothing more than to have someone, anyone, hold him and reassure him that the wreckage in the creek below was no longer his responsibility.

"John. You don't need my permission go up there and just close yourself off for a while. If that's what you need to do, do it!" There was pain in Hubert's eyes, but there was more. There seemed to be some existential strength that somehow isolated Hubert, surrounded him and it kept the devastation at bay. "Hold your woman if it helps. Cry. I did. But think about what I'm about to say, then get back in the saddle. We need you."

Hubert turned and looked down the hill at what was left of Cody's Wild West Show. "John, look at the opposites. Up there is your woman in a safe place. Down there," he gestured at the splintered wreckage below, "is the reverse. You're probably feeling anger and depression, but they're not contrary to each other at all. They're the same feeling, except anger makes you want to fight but depression is giving up." He gave Dunn a long hard stare then continued. "If you're like me, you're also feeling fear and grief. Again, they're the same except fear makes you want to run, but grief just roots you to the spot." The older man put a hand on Dunn's shoulder and said, "John, take a break – think this through. We have a lot of work to do before we can put on the next show."

"Thanks boss, I think..."

"John, we're not doing Danville – you know that, right?" Hubert now seemed all business. "Tell your crew that as soon as this mess is cleaned up, we all head home for winter. Cody will probably leave here and head for Wyoming. I assume you, Black Elk and your families will be going to New Mexico, right? I'm headed up front to meet with Cody, Arizona John and Laugan, our supply agent. I'll do my best to get you the same deal – couple tipis, your horses all to Taos. Just try to keep your head on straight." Then he was gone.

Dunn's next awareness was of standing outside the tipi where Bess and Hanna were weeping softly. The tone of their voices registered more than the words he heard. It gave him a frisson of memory so poignant that he gasped. He'd heard women weeping before.

From below Dunn heard shouting. He could hear the men, but the substance of their yells just wouldn't register. He didn't care. The tipi was at his back blocking the view of the carnage – the warmth of the rising sun was on his face. Then he heard her voice, Bess' voice – his woman's voice.

Just as the shouted words from below didn't carry meaning, Bess' words were just sounds. But the timbre, the utter familiarity of her voice resonated at such a primal part of his animal being that his consciousness narrowed until nothing else existed. A coppery bloody taste filled his mouth. A series of powerful memories flooded his being. He sat to keep from falling.

He was sitting, terrified, in a tipi surrounded by many men being judged. He stood knocking outside the tipi of Itunkala his teacher. He experienced again the intimate privacy when Spoon Woman pulled him into her tipi for his first real moments of a woman's love. He once again felt the wonder of belonging when he stepped out of his woman's tipi and saw the painted faces of the Making of Relatives ceremony. Then, the bitterest of memories came and forced him to stand. He relived stepping inside the tipi of Itunkala, covering her and bringing her unnamed child out into this hostile world.

Dunn braced himself on one of the thirteen lodge poles and saw himself in a lineage of men who protected. He was outside; inside was the baby he'd carried to safety, inside was his woman and their unborn child, inside was his reason to exist. "*May I enter?*" he asked in the language of his people.

Why?

Taos, New Mexico – November 15, 1901

"Mommy! Are we there yet?"

"Abe, my name is Hanna or you can call me *Iná*. White children call their mothers Mommy or Ma. In our language, we say *Iná*."

"*Tákuwe?*"

"That's just what we do. We make up names for those we love. Like I call you Little Man. You call your father Ate'. That's like the white children when they say Papa."

"*Tákuwe?*"

"They just do." Hanna smiled to herself, knowing that her precocious son was about to begin negotiations.

"Iná, can we go in now. I cold."

"But look how beautiful it is, Little Man." Hanna sat in the vestibule between the cars with Little Abe barely on her lap. Her pregnant belly took most of the available space. She had her arms protectively around her son and her feet were on the first step down. She tried very hard not to let impatience seep into her voice, but it was difficult. Hanna felt the need to nest – she knew the birth of her second child was close. She wanted nothing more than to take that last step down from the train onto the soil of New Mexico.

A year ago Hanna had been anxious and fearful. Dunn's ranch had been a concept without images. Her mother's protective instincts had made this unknown into scenarios that kept her awake at night. Now the ranch seemed more like home than the trains that had been the third chapter of her life. The train wreck was the painful beginning of a fourth. It was as if she and her family didn't speak of it, their future might be unaffected.

"*Iná, are we there yet?*" Little Abe squirmed and tried to climb off Hanna's lap. All that separated them from the rocky soil rushing by the train's steps were two safety chains and the third step down.

She stiffened and without conscious thought she barked "That's danger! Stop!" and held her son painfully tight against her stomach.

He howled in outrage, strained forward then threw his head back.

The quick adrenalin rush and her fierce mother's instinct blunted the pain. She was up and stood on the second step, turned, and stood her son on the platform between the cars. He immediately fell on his back and proceeded to throw a full-blown tantrum. Hanna held his ankles as he tried to shake her loose. She stood there making calming noises until he began to settle.

"Your screams aren't words, Little Man." The tone of her voice did not match what she felt. She was angry, in pain and desperately wanted to be off the train and surrounded by the women that would help her give birth. "Use words to tell me what's wrong. When you cry, your sounds have no meaning."

"What words, Iná? You say talk Indian words. Oskar says they stupid. When I talk Indian to the sew ladies, they don't know what I say. Other Indians talk words I don't know. Mommy, I confused."

Hanna sat on the top step and patted the place beside her. *"Sit here, Little Man, and we will talk Lakota, the words of our people."*

Abe sat down and looked up at Hanna. She felt the familiar sensation of falling into a spirit world as she looked into those innocent eyes. *"Iná, is train people our people?"*

It was heartbreaking for her to see doubt in eyes so young. *"There are many tribes of people – most of them speak different languages. The language we speak is one of those languages."*

"Tákuwe?"

"Thunkashila, the Great Spirit, made men different. There are four colors of men and they all speak different languages.

"Tákuwe?"

"Our world has many different countries. Every country speaks its own language."

"Tákuwe Iná? Didn't The Great Spirit want us to talk to each other?"

"The Great Spirit wants us to all live together in peace."
"Tákuwe?"

Hanna sat there with her son lost in thought. The New Mexico countryside passed by in such a profusion of splendor that she felt as if her heart was torn in pieces. The valley the train passed through on its way to Taos was breathtakingly beautiful. The peaks were snow-capped, their flanks a deep pine green. The cottonwoods that lined the creek had turned – their leaves a brilliant yellow. And her son was asking questions she still hadn't answered for herself.

"Little Man, our old stories say that we should all live together and be friends."

"Tákuwe Iná?" The boy looked up at Hanna in complete seriousness. "I like live on train. Everybody nice."

'Look out there, Little Man. It is beautiful. This is fine place to live." She looked at her son closely, desperately wanting to know he believed her. She wasn't so sure. Hanna stared deep into her son's eyes and saw utter childish trust. It hurt because she had lived a history of good followed by bad. The death of her beloved stepfather resulted in the revulsion she had experienced at the Carlisle School. Her fairy tale rescue from the school by her father had just ended in a horrific wreck. Could she and her family actually live happily ever after here on this idyllic ranch? She desperately needed to be able to ground herself in a future that was predictable in order to convince herself and her son that everything was going to be fine.

"This will be a perfect place to live, Little Man. You can help me stand our tipi. We can point our lodge poles at the stars and I can cook for you. We can be safe and cozy this winter when your little brother or sister comes. We can live in the old ways. When you grow up and have children you can tell them stories about us and how we lived. Yes! That will be a very good way to live."

It was Friday afternoon when the train pulled into Taos. As always, a few curious locals came to watch the drama – a stranger on the train always sparked speculation and gossip. Ben, Hanna, Black Elk and the baby were the first off and drew little interest but when big John Dunn stepped off with his pregnant woman, a crowd gathered in a hurry.

"Read about the wreck in the paper, Mr. Dunn!" said the breathless ticket agent. "We's mighty glad to see you. Me and the misses prayed for you after we heard about Cody's circus." The agent seemed to speak for the crowd. "We'd sure love to hear about what happened."

Dunn smiled grimly at this little well-meaning man. "Thank you Mr. Krey for your prayers, but right now I need to spend time with my family. What you could do is round up some help. We need to unload and get to the ranch. We've had a rough time of it."

Unloading in Taos was the opposite of Cody's well-practiced team. While Black Elk, Ben and Dunn unloaded the horses and tack, Bess and Hanna supervised the unloading of the family supplies. The helpful volunteers managed to get the tipi poles, hides and the rest of their possessions out of the boxcar without the sense that a wagon was needed to move them later. When Tall Horse finally arrived with Maria, there was a brief but joyful reunion between the women.

After the total contents of their lives were packed onto the wagon, their horses either saddled or in tow, the family of Black Elk stood together in the New Mexico dust with an unsure future before them.

The six of them formed an uneven circle – a nexus with visible gaps near the two pregnant women as if the unborn held a space. No one spoke, but each there became acutely aware of the equality between them and the spirit world that swirled about them. Their past and their future awaited a choice as always. Their feet were planted in the Earth's soil, but it was their spirits that stood upright and became the conductor between massive opposing energies. It was Bess who spoke for them all.

"*I'm walking!*"

Dunn jerked as if shocked then said, "*It's almost three miles. The wagon will be so much easier on you.*"

"The wagon is too rough. I want our child born with women around, not sitting on that buckboard." Bess glanced at Hanna and saw the affirmation there. She nodded at Dunn and said, "The women will walk. We won't be far behind. When we get there, we will help arrange our tipis. You men can set them up after you unload."

"But that's women's work..." Dunn didn't finish when he saw the thunderous look on his woman's face.

The tension turned to laughter when Little Abe spoke the truth. "She boss, Uncle John!"

Tall Horse sat tensely on the sprung wagon seat and snapped the reins angrily as he spoke. "Boss, I don't like it. Those gunsels from the court house traipsed all over our place."

Black Elk rode on one side of the wagon and Dunn on the other. They took turns asking questions. "What did they want?" Black Elk spoke evenly, trying to keep the worry out of his voice.

"When they showed up, I told em to go piss up a rope. They had this deputy with them – showed me some official paper. Said they had the right to go all over and drive them damn stakes in the ground."

Dunn rode silently for a moment then asked, "Were they surveyors?"

"I don't know what that is!" Tall Horse snorted. "Bossy – they acted like they owned the place. Just pushed us around. I didn't like it one little bit."

"Did they have little telescopes on a tripod with another man with a long, marked stick off in the distance?" Dunn was also nervous. He spoke with a confidence he didn't really feel. "Tall Horse, you're the manager when we're gone. You did the right thing. We'll work it out."

"Yep! Went clear up to the headwaters of our creek – we followed 'em. Dragged their crap up to the tree line on both sides of the valley. I guess I shouldn't have been so pissy. I'd like to see the map they drew."

"The white man likes to draw lines on the Earth." Black Elk's tone was flat and angry. "They believe they can own the land. They draw lines then fight with their neighbors." He shook his head sadly. "Ownership always means violence."

Dunn patted his saddlebag. "I have the deed to our land right here. I'll ride into town in a day or two and knock a few heads together if I have to. Our land is bought and paid for."

The dust from the wheels arose reddish brown as the wagon pulled away from the women. Little Abe happily kicked up clouds of his own as they walked toward the ranch and hopefully a quiet peaceful winter. They all were lost in their own thoughts.

Little Abe stopped so suddenly that Bess had to step over the child or trip.

Hanna said, "Careful, Little Man."

The boy ignored them both as he examined a rock. "*Look Iná! I find pretty rock. Can I keep it?*"

"Abe, Maria doesn't speak our language so to be polite, we have to talk English while we're around her."

Little Abe gave Hanna a look of intense sarcastic irony that was adult in its complexity. Hanna steeled herself for an equally mature rebuke, but Abe defused the moment when he asked, "Auntie Maria, will you carry me?"

Maria already had the boy in her arms before Hanna said, "Please!"

The boy kissed Maria on the cheek, looked at Hanna and mockingly said, "*PhiláyA?*"

Bess burst out laughing at the look on Hanna's face. "You're going to have your hands full!"

Before Hanna could answer, Little Abe said, "Mommy no have hands full – Auntie Maria do." He wiggled his little bottom in her hands.

Their good-natured laughter seemed to bond them, ease the tension. They talked as they walked – the conversation never staying on one subject too long.

Maria with her limited English joined in more and more often, helped by Little Abe's newly acquired vocabulary. She asked about both Hanna's and Bess's pregnancies and admitted a wish to be a mother some day.

The three women hugged and shared tears when Maria asked if she could help with the birthing when it came. They cried again when they talked of Hanj Coonshi's death and the many wisdoms she'd taught them. Little Abe walked some of the time and was carried whenever he asked. But walking or being held, the boy was part of the conversation – always as an equal. It was as if his childish innocent perspective made him wise far beyond his years when talking the talk of women.

There was a lull in the conversation and Little Abe was starting to fall behind. He reached out and tugged on Maria's drab orange, rough wool skirt. "I like your skirt better than boy pants." he said. "Carry me please, Auntie Maria." He held up his arms to her. He hugged her and kissed her on the cheek. "I love you, Auntie. You dress like a boy and a girl together. I want to be like you."

As the three women walked together, they exchanged knowing glances. Then Maria asked, "How hard is being teacher to baby? They change so fast."

"I'm learning!" Hanna said pensively. "Its like he's a tree that's growing and I'm growing along with him except that I'm taller. I have to protect him and let him grow but at the same time allow him to have more than his share of the sun. We grow together – I just have to stay a little ahead."

She smiled to herself. "It's difficult because he's so smart. I know it will get harder as we both get older. Last week, Ben and I wanted to have a night off and have dinner together in the dining car. We just wanted a little alone time. Who knows how long it will be before Cody's shows will be on the road again? Since we're going to be living in a tipi with two children, we just wanted one special meal alone. Anyway, I told Little Abe that he was having dinner with Black Elk, and Ben and I were going out alone. He asked, 'Can I come?' and I told him that the dinner was just for grown-ups. You know what he said? He said, 'Mommy, Amos has a baby chair in his eating car'." Hanna chuckled. "We took him along."

The women arrived at the ranch as the sun fell behind the snow-covered peaks that surrounded their little valley. Hanna took Abe in her arms and pointed. "Look, Little Man. The men have our tipi poles up and pointing at the stars. Come! Help me! Let's do women's work and make us a home."

Property Lines
Taos, New Mexico – November 16 - 1901

Where there is no property there is no injustice.
  John Locke

Dunn awoke from a disturbing dream. For an instant the residual fear he felt melded with the sensation of being lost. In the dream he'd been riding hard across the prairie. The wild flowers were in bloom and the smell of sage was intoxicating. His dream recalled an earlier dream from his youth when he flew. He was running down a hill and when he outstretched his arms, gravity no longer held him. The feeling of freedom was exhilarating. He experienced that same feeling of release with his horse. Then, he and his horse had ridden at a full gallop into a barbed wife fence. He was tangled, imprisoned, bleeding – his horse was shrieking it's last breath when he awoke.

He looked up and saw the comforting cone shape of his tipi. Bess was beside him snoring gently. She lay on her side, her pregnant belly supported by a rabbit skin pillow that was a gift from Hanna. He and Bess had not slept well. Their first night in a bed that wasn't rolling on rails always seemed off.

John slipped out from under the buffalo robe and pulled on his breeches as quietly as he could. Soon he was outside barefoot. The earth under his feet was slightly damp, cold and holy. The connection he felt to the soil through his feet was primal as if his flesh was giving thanks to the place from where it had come. He smelled the tang of mountain air testing, for threat and pleasure. The wind on his skin told him more about the day than a calendar ever could. As he walked toward the small copse of trees, he thanked the Great Spirit for every sensation, every small ache, for the absolute beauty around him, for his life. He thanked the Great Mystery for allowing him to be completely in this moment as a magnificent animal with a spirit that was a gift from Wakan Tanka. As he urinated, the primeval satisfaction he felt in this simple act filled him with a sense of well being, of reverence and thanks to the earth. The water from the earth that gave him life he returned in a holy cycle – his scent marked his presence as if to say *Pilamaya - I'm here.*

As he pulled the buffalo hide door aside to return, he whispered, "*May I enter?*"

"*Come!*" Bess grunted softly then said, "*I think today is the day.*"

Dunn ducked as he stepped into the tipi. "What makes you think...?" He stood and was unable to complete his thought. He was completely overcome by the rightness of what he saw. Bess sat near her cooking stone pushing small bits of kindling into the coals. She had the buffalo robe over her shoulders and was leaning in, puffing on the embers trying to coax a fire to warm their home. The early morning sun illuminated the eastern wall of their tipi. The pictographs painted outside shown in counterpoint to the creamy yellow of the sun-warmed buffalo hide walls.

The scene was so common, so normal, yet transcendent in its beauty. Dunn felt the connection to thousands of generations of human beings that had experienced this very setting. It was in that moment that he saw his place in the divine plan. He lived. He loved. His woman cooked for him and was with child, his child, a child that would in turn carry another. He sobbed as he sank to the floor next to Bess. He held her then and wished that this moment could be their eternity.

"John, what's wrong?" Her voice was sharp, concerned. Then she saw his eyes.

They leaned in, touched their foreheads together and sighed. He rubbed her belly, then as one they rocked gently side-to-side. No words were needed.

Small sounds from outside intruded – a dog barked, a morning dove cooed from across the compound; someone was cursing softly trying to get a horse in harness.

"*Mi thehíla* (My love) I think the baby comes today."

Dunn reached for a handful of twigs for the fire. "Why today? How do you know?"

She gave him a look that would become very familiar to him in the years to come. In her eyes were the beginnings of a prairie thunderhead with the lightning, thunder and wind to follow. *"I'm a woman! Yesterday I felt frantic – I spent all evening arranging our tipi. This morning, I'm not hungry."* Her face changed and there he saw exaltation, fear and joy. *"I can feel him. He wants to see his father."*

"So it's a boy?" Dunn put his hands on his hips as he stood and faced her.

Bess looked up at him with an expression that both agreed with his statement and was an answer to his question. She went back to feeding the fire.

She watched as Dunn buttoned up his shirt, pulled down his cartridge belt and holster from a peg by the door. "Are you leaving? Today?"

"Tall Horse told me yesterday that surveyors were here marking the land. Those Wasicans, the banker and the judge – they're up to something. If they are drawing lines on the land, they've figured out a way for it to benefit them and not us." He winked at her as he strapped on his gun belt. "I'm just going to make a few inquiries. I'll be back soon."

As Dunn rode down the main street of Taos he generated some attention. Many folks nodded and smiled and more than a few gave him hostile glares. His first stop was the St. Vrain Mercantile.

The building looked the same except for one addition – a lean to had been added to the south side of the building. Underneath were rough tables and benches where several men sat there eating breakfast.

Dunn tied his roan and sat down at one of the empty tables.

Almost immediately a teenage girl stepped up and said, "Good Morning, Mr. Dunn. What can I get for you?" She was simply dressed in mixed Pueblo – white clothing. Her skirt was a pale yellow of loosely spun wool. On her feet were boots that were of the same rough wool but dirty white. A single thick braid hung down over the blue check gingham blouse. Her face was red, but her English was nearly unaccented.

"Do I know you?" Dunn asked, smiling.

"Everybody knows you, Mr. Dunn. I met you once when I was a little girl. My name is Pakwa. Tall Horse is my uncle."

"Well, I'm really pleased to know you Pakwa. I didn't know…"

"Hey Frog! More coffee over here!" A shabbily dressed man with a beard at another table yelled out.

Both Dunn and the Pueblo girl stopped talking and looked angrily at the group of men that were chuckling.

John started to stand when Pakwa put a hand on his shoulder and pushed him back down. She turned and gave the men a dark brown look.

The men at the other table laughed good-naturedly. The bearded one said, "Hey Tadpole, could we PLEASE have some more coffee over here?"

Pakwa laughed with the men and said, "I'll be right back." to Dunn. She pulled a coffee pot off a tiny pot bellied stove and poured a round of coffee at the other table.

When she came back, Dunn just starred at her incredulously.

"Those men are my regulars. They come here almost every morning. When I first started they were rude. They treated me like most folks around here regard us Pueblos. I know one of them has a daughter, so I asked him what he would do if someone talked to her like they did me. It's become a joke."

"Why do they call you Frog?" Dunn's respect for this young woman was rising steadily.

"That's my name. Pakwa means frog in our language." She smiled. "They think its funny, but in my culture the frog and the tadpole are sacred." She looked down, embarrassed. "They're symbols of fertility."

As Dunn ate, Pakwa talked. "I was too young to understand what was going on when you had that meeting with Mr. Hudspeth and the others. I guess I should thank you because things have started to change around here. Three years ago, I couldn't even step up on the sidewalk. Now I work here at the Mercantile. I still can't go inside when white folks are there but out here, I'm the boss." She hesitated and looked around as if somebody else might be listening. "The rich folks won't eat out here. They don't want us Redskins even talking to them, but they sure like the money we bring in. Mr. Hudspeth says that maybe someday it won't matter what color you are."

Dunn pushed his plate toward the middle of the table. "I'd sure like to talk to him before I meet the banker. Is he here?"

"Nope! Sorry. Saturday is his day off."

Dunn left a five dollar gold piece under his plate.

All conversation stopped the moment Dunn stepped into the bank. Inwardly he smiled. He knew his look intimidated these gentle town folk. His faded blue dungarees said working class – the moccasins and the deer skin shirt screamed heathen, as did his bear claw necklace. But it was his saddlebags that drew the bankers' eyes. They knew the bags held gold.

There were customers at both windows. Both tellers cowered and hoped the other one would finish with their customer first.

Dunn put his saddlebags on the small reception table in the bank foyer. There was a metallic clink as the contents shifted. Dunn waited patiently.

Finally an elderly woman finished her business and eyed Dunn suspiciously as she walked past. He touched one finger to his forehead and said, "Ma'am."

The young teller was a complete opposite of Dunn. He was short, thin and his hair was parted fashionably down the center. He wore garters on his upper arms to keep his shirtsleeves from covering his hands. His circular glasses fogged a bit as the young man began to sweat. He cringed as Dunn approached his window.

Dunn stood at the window and looked down over the glass that separated them. "Mornin' young man. I've got a couple things you can do for me. I need my lock box from the safe and I need to talk to Mr. Hollis."

"Sorry, Mr. Dunn. I can't help you with either." the young teller stuttered. "Mr. Hollis is busy and he's the only one here that knows the combination."

"That's alright son. I reckon I can take these…" He plunked his saddlebags on the counter in front of the young man with the unmistakable sound of gold coins. "…to Santa Fe on the afternoon train. Their strong box is safer than yours anyway." He turned to go.

Before John had crossed the floor, the door to Hollis' office opened and the bank president said, "Welcome back, Mr. Dunn. I can see you now."

Dunn turned, winked at the teller and stepped into the important man's office.

"I assume you want to make your usual deposit – half in your account and the other half in your safe box." Hollis sat as he said this without inviting Dunn to sit at the chair in front of his desk.

Dunn dropped his saddlebags on the floor, sat and put his feet up on the banker's desk. "Your assumption is correct, Mr. Hollis. But the gold is unimportant – it's just a tool like my gun. What concerns me are all the surveyor's pegs on the land where my family lives." He paused, dropped his feet to the floor and leaned forward. He kept his voice even - the menace in his eyes was unmistakable. "You know anything about that?"

"You have the luxury of traveling the world while day to day disputes crop up here in our little town. People are moving here, Mr. Dunn, with some thanks to you. People are building homes. New businesses are cropping up. However, there was a killing this year when two neighbors got into an argument about their property lines. There have been many more fist fights and court filings. The town and the county are simply trying to get accurate ownership documents. Like the rest of the country, we're trying to bring order to the growth that's happening."

"You will give me a map of my property, Mr. Hollis! I paid you cash for the land and Mr. Haag signed my deed. My Indian brothers have a very different notion of ownership. I will have any documents necessary to show ownership! Do I make myself clear!" Dunn stood and leaned in over the desk to make his point.

"You'll have to go to the land office at the courthouse and request a plat map. The bank has no dealings with our elected officials." Hollis blinked – Dunn did not.

"Hurry, Princess Itunkala, we have to get ready for the ball."

"Oh! I'm so excited! Should I wear the blue satin or the beautiful deer skin with the beads?"

"Oh, the deerskin! You are an Indian princess after all!"

"But I want the satin gown. You always get to pick first."

"Well, you can't. I'm the main princess – you're just my servant."

"That's not fair! I want it." Hanna frowned slightly. She put down the doll she was holding and flipped the corn cakes frying on her stone. Little Abe shifted impatiently, waiting. Talking The Girls was his favorite game. He had an impressive collection of girl dolls and dresses all made by the wardrobe ladies.

"Ben, why didn't you go with Leftook this morning?"

"Come on mommy! We're going to be late for the ball!"

Ben looked up and smiled contentedly. He was sitting with his back to the tipi wall directly across the circular floor from their tent opening. Their tipi was warm from the morning sun and the fire. The air inside smelled of corn cakes and the solvent he was using to clean his new rifle. "He had business at the bank." He rubbed his face. "Last year, red skin, not welcome. Remember?"

"Mommy! Come on!"

"Maria said things had changed – a little bit." Hanna began putting the warm cakes on a plate and started frying strips of venison. "Abe! Put your dolls down – we can play again after lunch."

"Mommy!"

Hanna looked up annoyed when the tent flap opened – permission had not been asked.

"Hanna!" Bess stood there in the opening awkwardly. Her eyes were wide, frightened. "*My water came. The baby...*" She paused, her face seemed to fall then she stood there sobbing.

"Ben! Help her inside! Then go get the women." Hanna struggled to stand – her own pregnancy as obvious as her friend's.

"Mommy! You promised!"

"Abe! Go with your father!"

"I wanna' stay with you!"

"Little man, your father needs your help today. Auntie Bess is going to have her baby. He needs to get the women together so they can help Auntie Bess. Then, he needs to take the wagon into town and find Uncle John and Maria. Can you do that?" Hanna was saying this to her son but meant it for Ben. She looked up at him sharply – he nodded in reply. "Some day, Auntie Bess's baby will play Talk the Girls with you. But you really need to help. OK?"

"OK, Mommy!"

Hanna managed to get her friend sitting near the fire, but Bess wasn't rational. Her eyes looked like those of an animal caught in a trap.

"Bess hold my hand. Breathe!"

Bess was hyperventilating and almost non-responsive. When she finally looked at Hanna, there was no cognition – only fear.

Hanna scooted around until she was shoulder to shoulder. She put one arm around her friend's back and with the other, held her hand. Then she began to speak. "*Soon a HokšíyuzA, our midwife will come. She will know exactly what to do.* Hanna shook Bess gently. "*She will help you when the baby comes. But now, just breathe – that's right. Hold your breath then let it out slowly. Look at me. Good.*" Hanna smiled at her friend, squeezed her hand and continued. "*The women will build a shelter for you near the creek. It will be beautiful. There will be a fire and they will burn sweet herbs and your baby will know it is time to come. Other mothers will be there – they know – every one of us has been where you are now. They will tell you what you already know – what your body already knows – you are young and strong and soon your baby will take your breast. Then you will feel a love like none other.*

Black Elk was sitting outside smoking a long pipe when Dunn came galloping up the road to the ranch. He stood and held a hand up in greeting while the big man hurriedly tied up his horse. *"Sit. Smoke with me and let the women bring your baby to you when it comes."* Black Elk had been in battle with this big man – had hunted large animals – had seen Dunn in situations where other men had threatened death – but he had never seen fear and anxiety in his friend's eyes like there was now.

Dunn strode to the opening of the tipi almost as if his friend didn't exist. When Black Elk said, *"Leftook, our traditions – men should not bother the women during birth."* Dunn pushed him out of his way and stepped inside.

The buffalo hide, the membrane that created the home within the tipi, was no thicker than two fingers. Dunn had stepped through the opening that separated outside from inside countless times. But today the contained energy, the sense of ownership, was so palpable and different he paused, uncertain.

Eight women sat in a circle around the fire; eight sets of eyes confronted him as he intruded into an ancient ritual as old as man. Bess smiled tentatively – the rest wordlessly signaled awáȟtani, trespasser, transgressor - one who has broken with tradition. The power emanating from this gathering of women stopped Dunn cold – his fear and anxiety instantly became embarrassed confusion.

A middle-aged woman Dunn had seen many times but didn't know stood and made eye contact. And there it was, that implacable will, a sense of authority emanated from her so strongly Dunn saw the face of Macawi from another life. He took off his hat and dropped his eyes as if he were a schoolboy with the wrong answer. "Get firewood! You help!" she ordered.

Dunn glanced at Bess then said sheepishly, "Yes ma'am." to the woman in front of him. Moments later, he stood outside with Black Elk with door flap closed behind him. Black Elk smiled but said nothing.

Moments later the clatter of an approaching wagon disturbed the quiet of this extraordinary day. Ben pulled up the horses; Abe was on his lap helping with the reins. Maria and several other Pueblo women were in the back, breathless. Abe was excited at having helped steer the wagon at a gallop all the way from Taos.

Hanna stepped out of the tipi and gave her father a kiss on the cheek and Ben a clumsy hug. Dunn snuck a quick glance through the open doorway and was rewarded with a smile from Bess. Then Hanna gave Maria instructions. "Take the men and a few women to the clearing above the ranch. Build a simple lean to so the back faces the wind. Get a small fire going and hang a pot so we have hot water when the time comes."

Maria led the men and a few women to a gentle oxbow near the stream above the ranch. She drew a rectangle in the soft sand of the bank and asked the men to bring larger branches. Even before the frame was assembled, the women were laughing at the men's attempts to build a shelter. Finally, Maria said to Ben, "Go smoke. We call if help needs."

Black Elk and Ben were happy to leave the women to their work. Little Abe was glad to be near the central fire – he loved to find things to burn. Only Dunn was nervous, ill tempered. The men got their robes and settled in around the fire. While Little Abe played, and the men smoked, Dunn continued to nervously watch his tipi.

Finally he asked, "*I know both of you have been through this.*" He glanced at Black Elk. "*For you this is your second time – once with Itunkala then again when you became a grandfather. And Iron Eagle, you were like me when Hanna had Abe on the train.*" He looked up uneasily. "*So you know how I feel. Any words of wisdom?*"

Black Elk took a pull on his pipe and began to talk. "*You have noticed that everything an Indian does is in a circle, and that is because the power of the world always works in circles; and everything tries to be round. The sky is round. I have heard that the earth is round like a ball and maybe so are all the stars. The wind, in its greatest power, whirls. Birds make their nests in circles for theirs is the same religion as ours. Even the seasons form a great circle in their changing. They always come back again to where they were. The life of a man is a circle from childhood to childhood and so it is in everything where power moves."* He took another puff and continued. *"When I was younger, Itunkala taught me that..."*

A loud commotion came from the tipi where the women were talking. Dunn jumped up and ran to the door just as the midwife stepped out. "What?"

He stood there, rocking from foot to foot anxiously waiting. "Is she alright?"

The midwife smiled. "Tell Ben his woman make water. We today have two baby."

The beauty of the sunset was lost on Ben. Dunn was oblivious to everything except the groans and cries of his woman in the shelter by the stream. The words of encouragement and the news reports the women brought him were not enough to ease his fears. Even the easy conversation he heard between Bess and Hanna as they waited for the ever-increasing contractions to peak did nothing to calm him.

Both men paced back and forth as close to the shelter as the women would allow. Black Elk brought Little Abe down to the creek from time to time for updates, but for the two expectant fathers nothing existed except the drama they could only hear, not see.

Then, as the sky was giving way from vermillion and oranges to indigo, the cries and grunts from the lean to became urgent. The words of encouragement were insistent, demanding. *"Push! Pant! Hold your breath! PUSH!"*

Ben and Dunn were frantic. There were moments that the women attending Bess and Hanna had to physically restrain the men from intruding.

When the silence came it was almost worse. The two anxious fathers-to-be looked at each other with alarm. Then came laughter, exclamations of delight, happy congratulations.

Almost simultaneously, the sound of two crying babies filled the air. The men held each other and wept.

The mid wife stood, walked to the stream, washed then approached Ben and John. She dried her hands on a towel then put her palms on the two men's hearts. "One boy. One girl. A circle. You blessed be." She smiled and was gone.

And standing there were Bess and Hanna, each holding a tiny bundle wrapped in fine deerskin.

"We have a son." Bess handed the bundle to John.

Dunn was vaguely aware that Ben and Hanna were hugging and laughing quietly as they walked away. His eyes were only for Bess and his child.

Bess came and stood beside him, leaned in and said again, "We have a son John. Hanna had a girl. The babies look like brother and sister."

Dunn looked down into the eyes of his woman then at the bundle in his arms. Gently, he uncovered the face of his child and looked into the eyes that seemed to be filled with stars. Dunn touched the child's cheek as the two of them regarded each other. Then, there was nothing else except the sensation of falling into those eyes. A connection like an electric current filled his senses as a wave of protectiveness washed over him. His only cognition was to give thanks, but the connection to his child was the prayer, was everything. The circle that John Dunn, Leftook, had searched for all his life had just closed. Finally, he felt complete.

Okȟólakičhiye
Taos, New Mexico – March 14, 1902

It is often safer to be in chains than to be free.
  Franz Kafka

"*Mišnála ikȟópȟA!*" Dunn reined in his big roan and stared straight ahead.

Black Elk stopped his paint next to his friend's horse and looked for threats. There were none. It was a pleasant spring like day - the willows were greening up and the grass near the stream was lush and full.

"I'm not even sure how to say it in Sioux. I'm afraid. I feel something like fear." Dunn wrapped his reins around his saddle horn – a sure sign that he wanted to stop and talk. "I've seen it in men's eyes before they died. I've felt it when I thought the bullet was going to find me. Some men were defiant before I killed them but the fear was there. But I don't have words to tell you what I feel." The big man sighed and looked down at his hands. "I have this ache, this compulsion. It feels like fear but its not."

Black Elk reined his horse around so the horses were side-by-side and the two men faced each other. He smiled and said, "It is a *wóyawašte*, a blessing. Grandfather put this in your heart." He put his palm over his heart and said in Sioux, "*You feel it here – it came with your son?*"

Dunn stared at his friend quizzically. "*Yes! The first night we slept together as a family – our son was between us. He was warm and his new life connected Bess and me like never before. I had never felt so complete. But the next morning I passed by a pile of lumber beside the barn. Someone left a nail in a board and I became obsessed – I knew it could hurt my son so I forgot breakfast and got a crowbar. I pulled every nail. Then I saw a broken bottle – it was the same. I see things that are a threat to my son and I can't rest until I fix them.*" Dunn looked at his friend of decades with haunted eyes. "*I feel like I'm obsessed, going witkó* – crazy!"

"*My friend you now are a parent, a Huŋkáke. The Creator put this feeling in your heart like he did in the hearts of our four legged brothers, the birds – even the fish. They care for their young. Remember the teachings of the White Buffalo Woman. 'This fire that burns at your center is your love and it is right at times to express this love sexually. This passion, if you do not control it, is like a wildfire that will destroy everything. But with wisdom, this passion will create many generations and warm thousands of lodges through hundreds of snowy winters. With reverence, this passion will give its power to your children's children's children.*"

Dunn sat back in his saddle and thought for a moment. "*Did you feel this?*"

Black Elk laughed easily and said, "*I feel it still. The years when Hanna was not with me were a torture – you know this. Now that she is here with her family, I feel it also for my grandchildren.*"

"I love him so much it hurts. I'm afraid all the time that I'll be a bad father. I worry about being too old – I worry that the world will hurt him. I…"

"John, you're feeling what almost every parent feels. There are some men who just leave – don't care for their children. It is these children that lose their way. Think of yourself as a tree – you're tall and your son is a sapling growing near you. All you can do is stay strong, shelter him, but give him the sunlight to grow. He will find his way as you did." Black Elk paused. "*You have only one child – think what a man feels when he has many. Think what a chief must feel when the entire tribe are like his children. The Great Spirit expects us to do our best. What else can we do?*"

Even though Black Elk was over fifty he still rode bareback. He slid off his buckskin and landed easily in front of the Mercantile as if he were a teenager. Dunn's saddle creaked as he dismounted and tied his roan to the railing. The two men smiled at each other as if they shared a joke the other diners hadn't heard. Dunn held the door for his smaller friend as the two walked into the St. Vrain Mercantile. Gene Hudspeth, owner of the Mercantile, met them just inside the door.

"I'm sorry! Mr. Dunn – Black Elk, why do you put me through this every time you come here?" Hudspeth wiped his hands on the apron he was wearing. "If it was up to me, I'd serve anybody in here." He smiled genuinely, but his eyes looked pained as he attempted to escort the two men out of his store.

"Gene, you're a father – I'm a father. You tell me how you'd feel if your child was told to leave a public place because – well, just because." Dunn watched as the storeowner looked down, embarrassed. "People in this town call my son a half-breed, but he's no different than a kid that's half German and half English. Right now he wouldn't be allowed in here because his skin is a little redder than yours. Do you think that will ever change?"

Several towns people sat at the inside breakfast counter and watched this painful drama between these three very different men. They stared at Black Elk with unguarded distaste.

Black Elk stood nearest the open door and seemed the least affected by the prejudice that permeated the St. Vrain Mercantile. It was his nobility that set him apart. Had the customers there analyzed their feelings instead of succumbing to group bigotry they would have recognized his forgiveness. Instead they viewed his skin and his humanity as a thing to revile, a thing to set them apart.

Dunn stood there towering over the two other men. His aggressive stance, his size, his assertiveness also gave the customers at the breakfast counter reason to feel superior. They secretly envied and hated Dunn at the same time. They saw him as a better man, but his choice of alliance with redskins made him suspect, an outsider. The more Dunn advocated for the Indians, the more they held him at arm's length.

Gene Hudspeth, the storeowner, was caught in the middle. He was the first businessman in town to openly serve the local Indians, albeit only outside. He also employed one of them – Pakwa was a bit of a stigma in town. The young woman that worked for Hudspeth was a puzzle for many of the residents of Taos. She was red therefore inferior, but the men secretly wondered what it would be like – she was physically very attractive. She was also obviously smart – she never wrote down orders and never made a mistake. She also tallied the bill and made change without paper or pencil. She just didn't fit the profile of a dumb Redskin.

The white customers at the counter huddled together like sheep near a wolf feigning safety in numbers. They clung to their perceived superiority and at the same time were relieved that Hudspeth was having this confrontation instead of them.

It was Black Elk that ended this stalemate. He stepped through the door into the morning sun and said, "I'd rather be outside anyway. It's a beautiful day and I love talking to Pakwa." Once outside, he said to Hudspeth, "Grown men like us can learn from very little children for the hearts of children are pure. The Great Spirit shows them many things which older people miss."

Hudspeth stepped outside and closed the door. He glanced up at Dunn then spoke to Black Elk. "You two come here every Friday and put me in a bind." He looked up at Dunn again, rubbed his forehead as if there was a pain there then spoke to Black Elk. "I see you as a man." He hesitated, looking for words. "I see you – that's the best way I can say it. I can feel your spirit. My priest asks all of us to just see men and not their color. I sit with Mexicans at Mass – there are even a few local Indians that come. Here in town, there's laws." He looked down as if the eye contact was too difficult. "I feel ashamed. I'm caught between the law to not do business with the colored and the teachings of my church. I follow the town laws so I can make a living." He clenched his fist at his sides and looked up at Black Elk. "I'm sorry!" Then he was gone.

Pakwa was there as the two men sat at a table in the morning sun. "The usual gentlemen?" were the only three words she said, but her eyes spoke volumes.

"Excuse me sir. Mr. Dunn?" John looked up as a young man approached from the Western Union office across the street. "Telegram arrived here a couple of days ago for you." He held out an envelope to Dunn.

"Why didn't you deliver it when it got here like you're supposed to?" Dunn looked up from his flapjacks, annoyed.

"If it was up to me, I would of brought it out, but the fellows up in the courthouse have a new bee in their bonnet. They got this new rule that mail and telegrams don't get delivered to places without an official address." The young man handed the telegram to Dunn.

"What new rule?" Dunn asked as he slit open the envelope.

"The Feds passed this new law called the Newlands Reclamation Act. Then about two months ago the governor sent out some statute that is changing the way the courthouse is doing business. I don't really know what it all means."

When Dunn saw the message, he forgot about the young Western Union messenger. "Thanks!" he said absently and waved the telegram at Black Elk. "It's from Hubert. We're back in business. He wants us in Wyoming by the first of May. Listen! Muster Cheyenne May one. Stop. First show New York May 25. Stop. Tour Europe in fall. Stop. Reply soonest. Stop."

"What do you think Leftook?"

John pushed himself back from the table and said, "*We should talk to the women I suppose.*"

"What about the new white law the telegraph man talked about?"

"It's probably some bureaucracy to make us pay some new tax. It most likely doesn't concern us. What do you think about another season with Cody?" Dunn stood – the excitement in his eyes showed his obvious interest in doing another season.

"*Leftook, the word for bureaucracy in Sioux is okȟólakičhiye. It means how the tribe is organized for the best of all the human beings. A bureaucracy is not one person; it is a group of people working together. If history has shown us anything, when the whites organize something, they say it is for the common good, but usually the good is reserved for just a few.*"

Blood on the Land

Taos, New Mexico, March 29, 1902

Property is theft.
 Pierre-Joseph Proudhon

A light mystic snow covered the valley during the night. The morning dawned clear and cold without a hint of wind. One by one, tipis and shelters began to emit the pungent smoke of mesquite and pine. Breakfasts were cooked, plans were made, children begged to go out and play. A communal central fire was lit on the ranch commons. Some of the men gathered around the fire wrapped in thick buffalo skins, colorful blankets and the hides of deer and elk. One man produced a pipe and they settled in for a long warm visit. They smiled at each other and said a brief prayer of thanks. Tracks left in the snow would make any hunting easy – this day was another gift.

Hanna sat near her fire – the baby lay happily on a small blanket of rabbit fur and Little Abe played with his dolls. She smiled to herself and said *"Enter,"* when she heard Ben's voice outside.

The welcome aroma of corn cakes and fresh venison sizzling on Hanna's cooking stone greeted Ben as he entered. He said a silent prayer of thanks as he shook the dusting of snow off his boots. He and Hanna made eye contact. No words were spoken – none were needed. Huge amounts of understanding passed between them as he stooped and picked up the baby.

Hanna picked up a small package and sat on the floor cross-legged in front of Little Abe. When he looked up she unwrapped a small piece of deer hide. Inside was a slightly rusted metal knife sheathed in beautifully beaded elk leather.

"Iná, I was talking the girls!" Little Abe said irritably. When she held out the knife to him his expression changed. He stared at the knife in his mother's hands then looked up at her gravely. On some level he realized his status was about to be altered. As long as he could remember he'd been shielded from anything

even somewhat dangerous – fire, horses, the vestibules between train cars, even flowing water. He resisted the urge to grab the knife because he sensed there was more.

"When your grandmother Itunkala was your age, she learned to take mashtíncala, rabbit. I had no family to teach me so I didn't learn until I was almost a woman. You are now five winters and today is the perfect day." Hanna placed the knife in her son's hands.

"Will I make the rabbit die?" The look in the boy's eyes was unreadable.

"If Grandfather is willing, we will release the spirit of rabbits today," she said softly. "Their bodies will stay to nourish us. You will learn to thank the Great Spirit for the lives of your brothers the mashtíncala and we will eat the meat you provided for our family. Hanna smiled indulgently then continued. "And I will teach you to make true Sioux dresses for your dolls with the skin of your rabbits."

"God damned hypocrites!" Dunn fumed as the train pulled out of Taos. "That was the same peckerwood ticket agent that took off his hat and told me that he prayed for us after the wreck on Swearing Creek. Then he had the balls to say you couldn't ride in the first class car with me."

Bess was also furious. She had tried hard not to give anybody cause to deny her access to the train. She was dressed as white as the other women at the station. She wore a gingham dress and matching small checked blue and white bonnet. Only the color of her face belied the fact that she wasn't a proper wife and mother to the white man's child she was holding. Her husband was the one that looked Indian. As hard as she had pleaded, John wore his deerskin shirt, faded jeans and moccasins. He even wore his bear claw necklace. Had she not been so angry about being denied a train ticket, she would have laughed at the irony. She was embarrassed that her husband looked more native than she did.

Dunn stood and closed the sliding door to their first class compartment. He reached down and took the baby out of Bess's arms and sat down facing backwards. For some reason he could never explain, he always felt more comfortable facing away from the direction of travel. The familiar rumble from beneath the floor calmed him somewhat. When he looked into the eyes of his child, the unfairness of the world seemed to evaporate. "When we get to Santa Fe, we'll get a room at a good hotel; have a nice dinner. I can't see the lawyer until Monday, so tomorrow we can walk around town, do some window shopping – maybe buy you a new dress."

"Let's buy you a new suit." Bess snorted. "Then maybe you won't always look like you're about to rip somebody's head off like that poor ticket agent. I think he may have wet himself when you grabbed him by the shirt." She laughed her beautiful contralto. "And you keep telling me to not loose my temper." They laughed together as the familiar sensations of train travel took them to a shared place. Bess looked at the baby asleep in her husband's arms. "I think he remembers the feeling of the train from before he was born. Unlike us, he seems very contented."

"I don't like it a bit. That clerk at the railroad office said he thought Dunn is off to Santa Fe to see a lawyer." Giles Hollis, the bank president, was visibly upset. The mood in his office was tense and unhappy even though the day was sunny outside. "He can't find out about our plans – they are necessary for our survival."

"That's a bit overstated don't you think Giles?" asked Lloyd Haag, the only judge in Taos. "You control the money, I'm the law and Sherriff Tresner here is enforcement. What could go wrong?"

"It's Mr. Hollis when we're doing business Mr. Haag!" snapped the banker peckishly. "And this is business!"

Haag leaned back, lit a cigar and asked the obvious. "This seems a bit personal. Mr. Hollis!"

The banker glared angrily at the judge then replied. "Mr. Dunn is going to learn his place here Mr. Haag. And you and Mr. Tresner here are going to help me do that. In the meantime, you must understand that Dunn and his ignorant group of

Indians and circus performers" he said with obvious contempt in his voice, "are the single largest depositors in my bank. We need to snap our little trap shut before he finds out or my market share might be compromised. Understand?"

Haag nodded, but the sheriff looked puzzled. "Look, you'd better fill me in on the details so I can play my part." Sheriff Tresner said.

"Mr. Tresner, what you are about to hear is to be held in the strictest confidence." The banker's tone of voice left no question of who was the alpha in the room. "What that means Sheriff is that you tell no one! Is that understood?"

Tresner pursed his lips, nodded then dropped his eyes.

Hollis continued. "There may be a few uncomfortable situations for you in the next year or so when doing your job. If my plan succeeds, you will be handsomely rewarded. You will be able to retire and live well." When the sheriff looked up greedily, the banker knew his pawn was firmly on the board.

"Last year the Federal Government passed a bit of legislation called The Reclamation Act. This act allows for the sale of public lands to finance irrigation projects. The act is written in such a way that funds will be made available for improvements for the distribution of water. The wording is quite vague about repayment of those funds." There was an evil gleam in the banker's eyes as he rubbed his hands together unconsciously.

"Mr. Dunn holds an imprecise and ambiguous title to the land and headwaters of the water supply to our little town. I facilitated the cash sale of that land and Mr. Haag here signed the deed. Because of the passage of the Reclamation Act, Taos wants that land back. Are we clear so far Mr. Tresner?"

"If Dunn owns the land, how…"

"Mr. Tresner, we are a nation of laws." Hollis smiled an indulgent, superior smile." Statehood is not far off for New Mexico. In the meantime, we are the law here. What's going to happen to Mr. Dunn will be perfectly legal." The banker looked down on the sheriff as if speaking to a child. "The City Council and the County Commissioners have passed ordinances that can be used in our favor. Unpaid taxes can and will result in forfeited properties. And in that event, you will earn your pay. It is the Sheriff's duty to repossess properties for delinquent taxes."

"And you and Mr. Haag are on the City Council and are County Commissioners, right?" the sheriff asked with some dawning of understanding.

"It is our civic duty as leaders in the community to be sure our town grows and prospers." Hollis said proudly. "Only you, Mr. Haag and I are privy to this plan. Hudspeth, Liebert the hotel owner and Neeley the grocer only know about the ordinances – and they are not to know! Do I make myself clear?"

The sheriff nodded thoughtfully.

"Dunn and his crew will leave soon. And after they run away to their little circus, the only threat to our plan is Pakwa, that little red bitch that works for Mr. Hudspeth. She's smart and can read. The rest of the heathens up there on Mr. Dunn's property are ignorant – especially the man he leaves in charge." Hollis smiled to himself as if he had checked off every item on a list. "They have no address therefore cannot get mail. If their mail is not delivered, there tax notices will go unopened. And if their taxes are not paid, the land becomes the property of our municipality."

"What then?" Tresner asked.

"An astute question sheriff," Hollis said smugly. "Absolute beauty happens. The bank buys the land from the municipality to pay the missing taxes. The bank then applies for a loan from the Federal Government to develop an irrigation system and public water supply. Then the loan is forgiven because of technical difficulties with the language of the Act's language." Hollis stood and dismissed the two other men in the bank's office when he said, "Not one word to anybody! Am I clear?"

Tresner stood and nodded compliantly while Judge Haag just sat and smoked his cigar. After the sheriff left, Haag asked, "What else?"

"You have friends in Santa Fe, right?" When the judge nodded with a smile, Mr. Hollis said, "I want you to catch the Sunday morning train to Santa Fe and see what you can find out about Mr. Dunn."

"This mila, our word for knife, is a gift from your Ate' and me. We will use this mila to take the spirit of the rabbit. Do you accept this gift?"

Little Abe looked at the knife, glanced up at Hanna then stared at the knife again. He held out his hand and Hanna placed the knife in his hands. Had Little Abe not been so serious when he nodded his head the scene might have been comical. The blade was nearly as long as the little boy's thigh.

Hanna made eye contact with Ben for a moment then adjusted the leather thongs attached to the sheath and tied the knife around her son's waist. She then used the leather thong at the bottom of the sheath to tie the tip of the knife around the little boy's left leg.

Little Abe reached across his body with his right hand, drew the knife. He held the blade in front of his face and looked up and down the blade. "I accept this gift. Pilamaya."

Hanna and Ben fussed over how Little Abe was dressed. He had a robe similar to Hanna's, but his was made of deer hide. After the hide was tied over his shoulders, Hanna asked him, "Can you draw your mila easily? Is anything in the way?" Little Abe drew the knife easily, resheathed it and tried again.

Hanna knelt down again. "This mila will be at your side all your life. Care for it. It will help feed you; it will help make your tipi when you are a man. And in a time of danger, it will protect you. It is a powerful gift."

Little Abe reached out and nearly toppled his mother as he hugged her. "Pilamaya Ina!"

Bess and John sat in the open courtyard of the La Fonda Hotel as the sun set on this extraordinary day. The baby lay cooing in a fancy perambulator they'd bought at the concierges' urging. They laughed together; neither could remember a better day they'd ever had. The hotel was full of gamblers, travelers, gold miners and politicians – all sorts that seemed to have plenty of money. There was another mixed race couple from some place in South America. The hotel staff, the people Bess and John met in the shops, folks on the street never once alluded to the fact that Bess was red skinned and some sort of second-class person. They had been treated with elegance and respect. John had been fitted for a new suit and Bess had bought two new dresses and several bolts of material to take back to the ranch.

An elegantly dressed waiter appeared silently at their table and politely waited for a break in their conversation before he spoke. "Good evening. My name is Tomas and I'll be your waiter tonight. I hope to make your dining experience pleasing. May I take your order, Ma'am?" He wore black trousers, a crisp white shirt and a black half apron. His skin was less red than Bess's and also contained a lovely light chocolate color. His accent was indeterminate and could have been either Native American or Spanish.

Bess looked to John. She'd never ordered in a restaurant before and her unease showed.

"Just tell the man what you want dear. He's here to serve us." Bess gazed at the menu self consciously as John politely became her role model. "I'll have the mixed grill," Dunn said confidently. He handed the menu to the waiter and smiled at Bess as he did.

"Very good, Sir. That's an elk chop and a strip of buffalo loin, char grilled in a Madeira wine demi served with wild rice pilaf and fresh seasonal vegetables. Do you have a preference how your meat is cooked?"

"Tell the chef to cook it like he was cooking for himself. Thank you!"

"Ma'am?"

With more confidence than she felt, she ordered rainbow trout.

"Oh! Excellent choice, Ma'am! The rainbow trout is roasted and served whole in pasilla chili-burnt orange butter sauce. It comes with grilled fingerling potatoes and fresh seasonal vegetables. Do you have any special instructions for the chef?"

Bess laughed her lovely contralto and said, "No, you've been very kind. Thank you."

Hanna and Little Abe walked into the slight breeze across the prairie. Hanna stopped and knelt down. "Look behind you. What do you see behind us that you don't see in front of us?"

"Our feet made marks in the snow."

"Can you tell how many people made these marks?"

The boy smiled. "There are two of us."

"Not us. Look at the marks, the tracks we made. Can you tell from the tracks how many people walked here?"

Abe nodded. "Two. I see two tracks."

"Good." Hanna slipped off one of her moccasins and made a footprint. "Now look closely at this track. What animal made that track?"

Little Abe smiled. "You made that track Mommy."

Hanna knelt and looked directly into her son's eyes as she spoke. "You must watch carefully. Each animal makes its own track. A deer track is different from a raccoon. A rabbit is different than a prairie chicken. If you watch and learn, you will find food for your family. Your great-grandfather was the best tracker in his tribe. Listen to the stories I have to tell. Listen to your grandfather Black Elk. Listen to Auntie Bess. They know much wisdom about how our people lived. They can teach you how to be part of the Great Mystery, how to live and love. Now, watch the ground and tell me when you see a track that is different from ours."

They walked on and soon they flushed a rabbit and it loped away. Hanna stopped and whistled quietly. The rabbit stopped and turned its large ears in their direction. "When you learn to use the bow or the rifle, remember this trick. Rabbit is curious and will stop and listen to a sound he does not know."

They walked over to where they had spotted the rabbit. Hanna let Little Abe find the rabbit tracks. He began to follow the tracks when Hanna stopped him. "Now follow the track back; you will find where our friend rabbit was hiding."

Hanna showed Little Abe some gnawed sage bark and cropped prairie grasses the rabbit had eaten. Nearby, they found rabbit pellets. "Now we look for more tracks. The rabbits follow a trail. We will set our snares on their trail."

"Watch how I set my snare. Then, you will set one further down their trail." Hanna instructed. The two had found a concentration of rabbit tracks in a thick stand of sage. Hanna set her snare in a spot where the trail was narrow. She tied a slipknot into a noose from the strong, thin cord made of deer gut. The noose was circular, large enough for two fists to easily fit through. She suspended it a hand's width from the ground directly in the rabbit trail. She tied the other end to a thick sage branch nearby and used twigs to hold the noose open and steady. "Can you do the same, little one?"

Little Abe nodded. "I think so Ina'."

Hanna showed the boy another good spot several yards down the trail. Little Abe set his snare very well for a first try. Hanna helped him make a few adjustments, and then they set off for home.

As they walked back across the snow, Hanna continued her lesson. "Our friend rabbit guards his spirit as we do. His ears are big. That is why we must be quiet. He can smell us. That is why we walk into the breeze. He also hides or runs very fast. These are the ways rabbit guards his spirit. He does not want to be our dinner."

The sun was close to the western horizon when Little Abe and Hanna returned to their snares. The Creator was smiling on them. Each trap held a rabbit.

Hanna solemnly looked at her son. The rabbit was trembling, pulling at the cord around its neck, frantically trying to get away. Hanna pulled her knife, grabbed the rabbit by its ears and said, "Thank you, Thunkashila, for this life. Thank you mashtíncala. Your flesh will feed my family; your fur will keep me warm many winters. Pilamaya." She quickly drew the knife across the rabbit's throat. Its life gushed out onto the snow. "Pilamaya!"

Little Abe looked at the rabbit, dead in the snow, surrounded by a spray of red against the white. His eyes were big in wonder and curiosity, not fear or disgust. "Where is the rabbit's spirit, Ina'?"

"Every living thing only borrows its spirit from Wakan Tanka. One day, every spirit must return to be with the Great Spirit. Rabbit's body is here, but its spirit is now home." Hanna walked over to the snare that Little Abe had set. She pulled her blade and began to repeat the process.

Little Abe stepped in front of his mother, drew his knife and said, "I'm going to do this myself."

Moments later Tomas appeared carrying a tray with two bowls of soup and warm bread. "The soup is a house specialty this time of year. The chef digs the new asparagus himself I've been told." Discretely he leaned down and whispered to Bess "Your soup spoon is on your right – the one farthest out." He then stood and apologized. "I forgot to mention our wine list. Or would you prefer something else to drink with your dinners?"

"Son, I'm not much of an expert on good wine. Please bring us something you think would go with our meals."

Thomas nodded with a smile and asked, "We have a very pleasant Medoc from the Bordeaux region of France sir. It's a 97 Lafite Rothchild – a bit more expensive and will compliment your meals quite nicely." When Dunn nodded his approval, Thomas left to fetch their wine.

Bess looked happier than Dunn had ever seen her. She was dressed in a new cream-colored taffeta one-piece gown. Aside from the ruffles on the short sleeves, her dress was unadorned. It was tight at the waist and made her look taller, yet softer. Many of the other diners smiled at them as they made their entrance.

When Bess gushed over how delicious the soup tasted, John replied, "I prefer your corn cakes," and laughed. He reached across the table and took her hand. "Living in the white world is like living make believe. This is fun, but I am happiest when we are in our tipi and I can touch you and the earth."

Thomas returned with the wine, opened it expertly and poured a small amount in each of their glasses and bowed slightly at the waist. "I hope your stay at the La Fonda is pleasing. Your meals will be out shortly." Then he was gone.

John raised his glass, looked down into the stroller at the baby sleeping then at Bess. "Here's to us and a real life."

When Bess raised her glass, the expression on John's face changed – his eyes were on something behind her. "What is it John?" she asked, concerned.

"That's Judge Haag checking into the hotel," he said coldly. "The woman with him is not his wife."

Bess turned to look. "John, she's younger than me. Does he have a daughter?"

He looked at Bess quizzically. "What do you think?" He waited a moment then stood. "I'm going to take a look."

As Judge Haag and the young woman walked up the stairs to the rooms, John approached the desk. "That man that just checked in – he looks very familiar," he said to the clerk behind the desk.

The young man looked up and replied, "Yes, that's Judge Haag and his wife. They're regulars here. Do you know him?"

"Quite well. I hope you don't mind." Dunn ripped the page from the hotel register."

"Sir, you can't do that!" protested the clerk.

Dunn ignored the young man behind the desk and read the signature, "Mr. and Mrs. Lloyd Haag."

"Sir, I need you to return that page. Our guest's privacy is paramount."

Dunn leaned over the desk slightly until he towered over the young man behind the desk. "Son, we all have to make choices in life." He reached into his pocket and held out a five dollar gold piece. In the other hand he held the paper with Haag's signature.

The clerk took the gold.

Inside – Outside
Cheyenne, Wyoming – April 30, 1902

No problem can be solved from the same level of consciousness that created it.
   Albert Einstein

Black Elk stood and rubbed his eyes. He freely admitted to himself that his vision wasn't as sharp as it once was. He pulled a straw from a bale, marked his page and closed the Bible he'd been trying to read. Outside the stock car window his view of the rail yard near Cheyenne was familiar – dirty black cinders, dilapidated sheds, a small steam engine noisily shuttling freight cars about. But in the distance were the mountains, snow capped and majestic. "Why?" he thought to himself. "Why can I look at the beauty of nature and feel the Great Spirit, but not when reading about him in the white man's Bible?"

In the dark places at night when he couldn't sleep, Black Elk bitterly missed his life from before. There was so much absent from his life since the whites had come that he endured a constant deep loneliness. And it wasn't just that he missed Itunkala terribly – he did. He was also acutely aware that his connection, his relationship, to the Great Spirit, like his vision, was beginning to fade.

He sat down again and opened his Bible to Luke and the parable of the rich fool. He read it out loud trying hard to connect to the words.

"And one of the company said to him, Master, speak to my brother, that he divide the inheritance with me. And he said unto him, Man, who made me a judge or a divider over you? And he said unto them, Take heed, and beware of covetousness: for a man's life consisteth not in the abundance of the things which he possesseth."

Black Elk much preferred to hear the word rather than read it. He knew his English reading skills were remedial at best, but the use of unexplained pronouns and the arcane language in the Bible was infuriating. He longed for the stories Kangee the shaman told. The oral histories lit up his imagination in full color. Reading the Bible was confusing in its shades of gray.

Itunkala's face was as clear in his memory as if he had just been with her yesterday. He remembered her often questioning, *"Is the Great Spirit and the God of the white man the same?"* It was the memory of her that drove him to visit white churches. He felt that if he could somehow feel that holy connection more strongly, he'd feel her presence more acutely as well.

Over the past several years Black Elk had attended church services in the towns and cities wherever Cody's show happened to be. Often he'd been asked to leave because he wasn't white. Other times, he'd been treated as a Thŏg, an outsider. He smiled grimly to himself at a memory – he'd arrived early and sat in a pew waiting for the service to start. As the sanctuary filled up, not one person sat within ten feet of him- he felt like the bull's eye on a target. Other services were terrifying – the preacher yelling about death, damnation, sin, ever lasting fire – Hell.

When Black Elk visited his first Catholic service, somehow it felt like home. The cathedral architecture was awe inspiring and overwhelming, much like being in the presence of a canyon or waterfall. And the homily reminded him of the oral stories he remembered as a child. He closed his eyes and smiled, thinking about the story of *The Prairie Mouse and the lazy cousin*. He thought, "That is a parable I can understand." In his memory he could here Kangee telling the Lakota story that perfectly paralleled the English story of the Ant and the Grasshopper.

Black Elk heard feet on the stairs so he put his Bible down expecting Leftook. But instead, a stranger stepped into the stock car.

He wasn't a big man – he was probably an inch or two shorter than Black Elk. But where Black Elk was stocky and powerfully built, the stranger was thin, wiry. His shirt was too new; his Levi's too blue. And the buckle on his belt was huge. His spurs jingled as he stepped into the car. He had his hat in his hand submissively as if he was to meet the boss for the first time. The spurs, the lariat, the knife on his belt, the swagger all looked real but didn't feel authentic.

Black Elk stood, extended his hand to shake and said, "Good morning. You must be one of the new…"

"What the Sam Hill is you doin' here, radish? Git!" The stranger put his hat back on and did his best to act like a cactus. "Git off to yer own place, Injun. This here's my spot."

Black Elk dropped his hand and appraised this probable new hire for the show. He pictured him standing next to Dunn who was almost exactly twice this man's size and he smiled at the thought.

"What cha laughin' at ya red Nigger? Git!"

Black Elk sat on the hay bail behind him and looked up at this bristling little man. "Tókheškhe yaúŋ he? Toníktuha he? Taŋyáŋ yaúŋ."

"Don't be talkin' that heathen jibber jabber at me. Git to you own spot." He took a step toward Black Elk and assumed an aggressive stance.

"Aŋpétu wašté yuhá yo." Black Elk smiled back pleasantly.

The young cowboy's voice went up an octave and he put his hand on the hilt of his knife. "Ya heard me, ya fuckin' heathen! Beat it or I'm gonna…"

"You're going to what?" Dunn rumbled as he stepped into the car.

The new cowboy spun around and looked up to where the voice came from. The anger and aggression in his eyes immediately turned to fear.

"Son, if you plan on living and working with us, you should know that the man you were calling a heathen is your boss."

"But…"

"He's forgotten more about horses than you'll ever know."

"But…"

"Son, hand over your knife. If you've got a gun stashed somewhere, hand it over too." When the new hire hesitated, Dunn held out his hand.

Timidly, the young man pulled his knife from the sheath and handed it to Dunn butt first.

Dunn handed the knife to Black Elk then sat on another bale. "My name is John Dunn. You can call me Mr. Dunn or Boss. This man you were just calling a heathen is my partner. When you speak to him, you can call him Black Elk or boss." There was a quiet moment where Dunn let the words soak in, then he said, "Understand?"

When the young man nodded his head in the affirmative, Dunn stood and said, "Son, let's start over and pretend you just walked in." He held out his hand to shake and said, "My name's John Dunn. This is my good friend Black Elk. You must be a new hire. Do you mind telling us what you'd like to be called?"

"Reggie. Reggie Goetz." He looked back and forth between these two very different men as if reality had slipped its tether.

"Reggie, nice to meet you. Shake hands with Black Elk; then I want to take you on a little tour."

Reggie glanced up at Dunn as if he'd been asked to do something distasteful. The look in Dunn's eyes left no choice.

Dunn led the new hire out of the stock car forward towards the front of the train and stopped in the vestibule between them and the next car. "Reggie, before we go any further, I need to explain something that may be difficult for you to grasp at first. And if you can't or won't learn what I'm going to show you, you won't make it. Understand?"

"Mr. Dunn – boss, I don't understand."

"Picture a tunnel. See it! This tunnel reaches to cities and towns all over this country. It even reaches over to London and Paris. And when you're in this tunnel, things are different. Step out of the tunnel and you're back in your old life. But in here, the rules are different!" Dunn leaned over the smaller man to make his point.

"I'm not sure I…"

"Son, this train and the town where we perform make up that tunnel. We're in it now."

"Mr. Dunn. I can sort a picture it, but I don't reckon I gets it." The look on Reggie's face matched his words.

"Let's try some examples of what I mean." Dunn ran his fingers through his graying hair then continued. "When you were hired, did you meet Mr. Hubert?"

"Yea, a boss man. Wears a suit. Not a big guy, but I got the feeling I'd better do what he says."

"That's him!" Dunn smiled. "He's a natural leader. He's also the man that handles all the money. He's my boss."

Reggie didn't say anything. In his eyes, Dunn could see a bit of submission like a deer in a spotlight.

"That's Abe Hubert, my boss." Dunn hesitated for effect then said, "He's a Jew!" Dunn saw Reggie's eyes widen momentarily. "What do you call Jews where you come from, Mr. Goetz?" The words Dunn said were a question, but his body posture and the tone of his voice made it clear that the wrong answer just might be dangerous.

"You want me to say the word or just say I know a word?"

"Good choice, Reggie!" Dunn stood. "All of us are careful with the words we choose when we're on the train. Let's take a walk."

The first car they entered was full of long painted panels that provided the backdrops for outdoor scenes. There were pegs on the walls that held tools; there was tack, bolts of cloth, boxes and a large cupboard attached to a wall with labels on each drawer indicating the hardware it contained. Tucked into one corner was a small table with two chairs and two sleeping pallets on the floor.

On the opposite side was a workbench with a vice and lots of hand tools spread about. At the bench was a large, heavily built man working on a sewing machine.

"Morty. How goes the battle?" Dunn looked over the man's shoulder at the eviscerated machine and the various parts scattered across the workbench.

"It didn't like all that North Carolina mud – should be fine now." Wiseman turned and glanced at Reggie. "Who's this?"

"Morty Wiseman – Reggie Goetz. Reggie is a new hire."

As the two men shook hands Dunn said, "Morty here is a jack of all trades. He's our chief mechanic, a great baby sitter and he plays Sitting Bull in the show. You should see him in costume."

"You mean a white guy plays an Injun?" Reggie smirked, then blanched when he saw the look on the mechanic's face.

"People see what they want to see, Mr. Goetz." Wiseman said and turned back to his work.

"Any idea when Standing Wolf is going to join us, Morty?" Dunn asked.

"Soon I hope!" Morty answered without turning. "I really miss him."

Dunn stopped Reggie in the next vestibule. "Standing Wolf plays Custer."

Reggie laughed. "That's rich! Got a white guy playin' an Injun and the other way round."

"Remember what I said about being in a tunnel. Things are different in here. Like Morty said, people see what they want to see." Dunn put his hand on Reggie's shoulder. "Morty and Standing Wolf stay together in the mechanic's car when we're on the road. They're a couple."

"I thought Standing Wolf is a guy."

"He is, Mr. Goetz." Dunn watched Reggie's face react and then continued. "All of us here on Cody's train accept each other as we are. If you have some crude word in your vocabulary that describes a relationship between two men, I suggest that you keep it to yourself. Understand?"

When the two men entered the next car, they were met with the joyful, noisy chaos of children. Dunn stood back as Reggie looked around. He saw the faces of children happily playing together – faces that were in four colors. Dunn led him slowly through the car toward the doors to the next vestibule. Sitting near the door was a young Indian woman unashamedly nursing a baby. She smiled warmly up at Dunn, and then looked into Reggie's eyes with a look that could only be interpreted as challenging.

"Reggie Goetz, I'd like you to meet my wife, Bess Little Robe."

Goetz, who had been staring open mouthed at the nursing mother, turned a beet red as his teeth clicked together. He managed to stammer, "Pleased to meet cha." then Dunn led him into the next vestibule and down the steps to the soil of Wyoming.

"Son, you're going to come in contact with all sorts of folks here in Cody's show; some are white, some are yellow. Amos is the guy that runs our dining car, and he's a fine black man. They're just people. I'd suggest you hold off on judging them for a bit. Put away those words you use for people who are different away while you're here. Believe me, they know words that they might use to describe you like Honky or Gringo or Red Neck Hayseed or Wasican. Somebody might even call you a Gunsel looking how you're dressed. But here in the tunnel, we're all just people. Let's go. There's somebody else I want you to meet."

Instead of leading the young cowboy back to a train car, Dunn took him to the makeshift corral. Black Elk was there passing flakes from the bales of sweet green hay to the horses. The horses nickered and focused their eyes and ears on the approaching men.

Without saying a word, John opened the gate and ushered Reggie into the corral. "The big roan – that's Kangee – my horse. What do you think?"

Reggie didn't answer at first; he walked around smiling. "They're beauts." he said dreamily. "Who's the paint belong to?"

Black Elk slipped between the fence slats and as he touched the paint he said, "He and I go way back." and rubbed the horse's jaw.

Dunn and Black Elk watched carefully as Reggie interacted. The horses, which are better judges of characters than humans, leaned into him, ears erect, happy and curious. Black Elk and Dunn shared a quiet smile of understanding. Dunn tilted his head toward the fence indicating the men should talk.

"The religious teachings of my people come from the Legend of the White Buffalo Woman. She told us that there will be peace when the four colors of men learn to live together." Black Elk handed Reggie's knife back to him.

"Son, think you can let down your guard a bit and live among us as equals?" Dunn reached out to shake the young man's hand.

The Beast
New York City – April 21 – May 3, 1902

The difficult Indian problem cannot be solved permanently at this end of the line. It requires the fulfillment of Congress of the treaty obligations that the Indians were entreated and coerced into signing. They signed away a valuable portion of their reservation, and white people, for whom they have received nothing, now occupy it.

They understood that ample provision would be made for their support; instead, their supplies have been reduced, and much of the time they have been living on half and two-thirds rations. Their crops, as well as the crops of the white people, for two years have been almost total failures.

The dissatisfaction is wide spread, especially among the Sioux, while the Cheyenne have been on the verge of starvation, and were forced to commit depredations to sustain life. These facts are beyond question, and the evidence is positive and sustained by thousands of witnesses.

Telegram sent from General Nelson Miles from Rapid City, North Dakota to General John Schofield in Washington D.C. on December 19, 1890 concerning the conditions on the Sioux reservation.

"Ladies and Gentlemen! He survived a devastating train wreck less than a year ago! His locomotive exploded! His train cars fell, crushed to splinters! Many of the finest horses in the world lost their lives during that terrible accident in North Carolina! But, like a phoenix, he has arisen from the ashes! Please allow me to introduce to you former Pony Express rider,

Indian scout, buffalo hunter and the most famous showman alive today, Mr. William Fredrick, Buffalo Bill, Cody and his..." The roar of the crowd drowned out the rest of the introduction.

Cody cantered to the center of the arena from behind a painted canvas backdrop. The audience stood as if it was a single organism, the whistles and cheers were deafening. The crowd's adulation washed over Cody like a tide cresting solid rock. He sat in the saddle modestly, seeming humble and unpretentious. Then, when the noise of the audience peaked and was just beginning to diminish, Cody stood in the stirrups and removed his hat. In a well-practiced move, he bowed to the crowd. In that same instant, Cody's horse Duke raised one leg and lowered his magnificent head. The audience's response was frenzied. If the stadium seating had not contained the crowd, it could have surged forward and engulfed Cody and his horse like iron filings drawn to a powerful magnet.

Like a kindergarten teacher in front of a noisy class, Cody held up one hand palm facing the audience. The crowd immediately sat silent, compliantly. He nudged Duke with his heels, snapped the reins gently and slowly walked the horse to the announcer's podium where the electric sound system was waiting.

As the announcer handed the microphone to Cody, the crowd took a collective intake of breath and awaited the first word from the man it had paid hard coin to see. But Cody didn't speak immediately. He pulled the reins to the right and Duke complied. The horse and rider turned to face the audience. The sound of that movement was clearly transmitted to the crowd.

Cody's saddle creaked as a deep almost subsonic thud of hoof hitting earth passed to the viewers. It was a prelude to a practiced authentically staged frontier experience. The audience was there, ticket in hand, ready to experience a genuine adventure without having to soil a petticoat or spat in the process. The audience, like a barely caged beast, knew from the newspapers the story it was about experience. It was there to see a version of the tale it believed to be true.

Cody held the microphone up to his mouth as the beast in the stands held its collective breath. "*Maya owicha paka,*" he said in passable Sioux. Cody smiled at the effect – the audience exhaled releasing the tension. Frowns could be seen on individual faces. The crowd wanted to be fed the story it paid to see.

"*Maya owicha paka* is a Sioux term for fate, calamity. It means destiny and to be shoved off a cliff." Cody hesitated and looked at his customers to judge the effect of his introduction. "Fate visited me last October on Swearing Creek in North Carolina. Yes! Destiny intervened. It humbled my little enterprise of presenting the history of our great nation. Calamity, fate if you will, injured Frank Butler and his famous wife, the great Annie Oakley." Cody paused dramatically and removed his hat. "Miss Oakley is at this moment in a hospital bed and cannot be here to share her legendary frontier skills with you." There was a loud groan from the beast and it expressed its disappointment.

"But ladies and gentlemen, you are here on a historic occasion. You are here on this fateful Monday, April 21st, 1902. It is our first show since that disastrous wreck. This afternoon you will see brave pioneer men and women as they make their way west across our magnificent continent. You will see them interact with Indians, the people already here. You will see horsemanship unlike you've ever experienced in your life. Western and Indian riders will compete for your attention and judgment. You will see ropers use exceptional skills as they control domestic and wild animals alike." Cody paused again for effect as he scanned the crowd.

"And ladies and gentlemen, for the first time ever, you and your children will marvel at the Cheyenne Indian creation story. Then our players will present this afternoon's main event, the reenactment of the most decisive military battle of our time, THE BATTLE OF LITTLE BIG HORN!"

The beast surged to its feet in a throaty roar as Cody rode off stage left and disappeared behind canvas panels painted to look like snow covered mountains in the distance.

The moment Cody passed from view the thunderous sounds of hoof beats appeared from stage right. Two riders appeared. One was clad in skins riding bareback on an appaloosa with an elaborate feather headdress trailing behind. Galloping hard and trying to catch the Indian was a slim wiry cowboy riding a beautiful chestnut mare. There was a loud collective groan from the crowd followed by an even louder "AHHH!" as the cowboy took the lead. As the riders circled the arena, often the cowboy seemed to be winning. Other times the Indian was ahead as this scene played out for the crowd. It ended when a third man appeared on the track with a flag. As the flag dropped and the cowboy won the race by a nose, the crowd was deliriously happy. The two riders dismounted and shook hands. Then, with great humility, the Indian removed his headdress and handed it to the cowboy. The two bowed toward the beast to thunderous applause.

One by one covered, wagons appeared from stage right led by a very large man riding a roan stallion accompanied by an Indian man riding a pinto. The wagon master shouted directions and appeared to ask directions from his scout; the wagons rode the same circuit as the racers before them.

On the third circuit the wagons pulled into a circle. Families appeared. Children played. Fires were lit; dinners cooked. A man with a collar blessed the meal.

The audience howled its dismay when the Indians attacked. When a white settler fell there were cries of outrage from the crowd – when an Indian fell, cheers. The young pastor climbed into the bed of his wagon and repeatedly fired his rifle as the Indians rode past. Then, with great drama, he clutched his chest, fell from the wagon and was about to be scalped. His wife picked up her husband's gun and killed the heathen. The crowd in the stands was on its feet screaming in bloodlust.

Children reloaded their parent's rifles. The wagon master rode his stallion out and fought the Indians with a cavalry sword. A pretty teenage girl wearing a bonnet and a red checked gingham skirt swatted a passing Indian with a fry pan.

The crowd of New Yorkers in the stands was in total hysteria as the symbols of their hope and their hate battled it out on a landscape completely alien to them.

Then, as quickly as the attack began, it ceased. The players, both settlers and Indians once dead now rose. The entire troupe came together facing the audience and while holding hands, bowed deeply to the crowd.

As the wagons, Indians and settlers alike exited stage left to applause and cheers, a single Indian man appeared and walked solemnly across the field. He was huge, not tall but thick and powerfully built. His broad face was intelligent and primitive, regal, yet alien. The charisma that radiated from him both entranced the audience and made it uncomfortable. Had he been dressed in a suit from a New York tailor, the audience would have applauded. Instead, it muttered its discomfort.

The announcer waited for silence then spoke into the microphone. "As promised, I present to you an old Cheyenne warrior with a story to share. Ladies and Gentlemen, the Cheyenne Creation Story."

The Indian faced the stands and in a surprisingly gentle Bronx accented voice he began:

In the myth How the World Was Made there was an All Spirit named Maheo. He was alone in the dark void.

According to the myth, Maheo decided to create a world. From there, he created animals to help him create more life. He created land from mud and placed it upon Grandmother Turtle's back to carry. Her hair became wonderful flowers and plants and eventually he saw her as Grandmother Earth.

He did not want her to be alone and so he created a copy of himself. He pulled a rib from his right side and it formed into the first man. He, also, did not want this man to be alone, so he pulled out a rib from his left side. This rib formed into the first woman.

He sat back and thought. He decided to gift his creation with a buffalo to fulfill all their needs from food to warmth to clothing.

A few people within the crowd applauded as the Cheyenne took his exit but the collective had its way. By the time the storyteller had exited stage left the stands were silent.

The audience viewed as a singular creature is fickle, has a short attention span and in some cases, is dangerous. In the scant seconds between the disappearance of the Cheyenne warrior and the next entertainment, murmurs of discontent were quite evident. But the beast settled happily as new distractions appeared before it.

Indian women leading ponies dragging travois appeared. Cowboys in garish outfits began rope routines. Trick riders appeared. For the next ten minutes, the crowd in the stands was deliriously distracted from its own reality. The cowboys competed with each other for the crowd's adulation. The trick riders and their antics drew the beast's attention. Little attention was paid to the main attraction, the tipis. A small Sioux village just seemed to appear by magic. The tipis were erected with practiced ease by a few women while the crowd was entranced by the smoke and mirror antics of a few acrobats.

A small girl started a fire using only a bow and a few twigs. Women appeared from the tipis carrying jugs of water and wearing lovely articles of deerskin clothing. A few men gathered around the fire to smoke. Indian children played tag.

The first attack came from stage right. Major Marcus Reno led a squad of cavalry toward the Sioux encampment at full gallop firing indiscriminately. The trick riders and cowboy rope artists fled as the bugle sounded. The crowd cheered as the first Indians fell.

From within the tipis, a full war party of Sioux warriors poured out. The battle raged for minutes with great drama. Then, with howls of anguish from the audience, the Sioux began to drive Major Reno and his cavalry back toward stage right.

When General George Custer led another squad of men and attacked the Sioux village from stage left, the crowd stood cheering deliriously with calls to "Kill them all!" Custer's cavalry circled the tipis firing at braves, women and children.

Then, as if the spectators knew what was to come, a large number of Sioux warriors in vivid war paint appeared in the battle from stage right. Simultaneously, scores of warriors, women and children appeared from the tipis all carrying weapons.

The battle raged. Sioux braves shot from below their ponies' bellies. Trick riders did cartwheels jumping on and off their horses. A cavalry officer stood on horse back at a full gallop firing at the Indians. Hand-to-hand combat broke out. It was swords against tomahawks – arrows against the famous Colt 45's.

General Custer seemed to be everywhere at once, firing from the back of Comanche, his favorite horse. His blonde hair flashed in the sun. When his first pistol ran out of ammunition, he threw it dramatically and pulled the second. Custer fired his second pistol until empty, clubbed a young brave with it and then drew his sabre.

By ones and twos, the soldiers fell, dying with great drama. General Custer fought on alone until he was completely surrounded. The throaty cheers from the audience seemed to keep him energized and on horseback. Finally, he was pulled down from his horse, but still he fought on. The buckskin shirt he wore was cleverly made. Spring-loaded arrows seemed to appear in his chest. And with each arrow strike, the great man would stumble and still fight on.

A hush fell across the battlefield. The audience let out a collective gasp. Slowly and with great grandeur, Sitting Bull appeared, played by the same actor that told the Creation Story. Screams of protest and derision came from the stands as Sitting Bull strode across the killing field. He walked directly to General Custer who was now held from behind by many braves.

General Custer appeared nearly dead but when Sitting Bull approached, the great general stood tall and defiantly thrust out his chest in a show of bravery and masculinity.

Very slowly Sitting Bull pulled out his knife and held it poised to strike. As the warriors cried out in joy and the audience wailed in protest, Sitting Bull stabbed the American hero with a downward stroke of his knife. Custer fell.

The warriors swarmed around tight to this scene hiding Custer's body from the audience. Then Sitting Bull leaned in. There was a great cry from the warriors as Sitting Bull waved the blonde wig above his head.

As the audience surged to its feet and screamed out its hatred in utter fury, the entire troupe, cavalry and Indians alike returned to life. They stood, faced the audience and bowed to the beast that had paid hard currency to experience this fantasy.

There was a moment in the noisy dining car when Black Elk and Abe Hubert made eye contact. The sound of excited voices discussing the events of the day's show seemed to mute for a moment as the two experienced an exchange that went far beyond words. Black Elk was there happily with his entire family – Hanna, Ben and Little Abe plus Dunn and Bess. The two babies were tucked together in a bassinette. At Black Elk's side was a woman he'd met at a Catholic service the day before.

Hubert sat at the bar on a stool and Amos was behind the bar leaning on his elbows. Amos whispered something into Hubert's ear and both men laughed good-naturedly. "Before we start our critique," Hubert looked pointedly at Black Elk, "would you please introduce your guest."

"Everybody, please be on your best behavior." Black Elk looked down at his guest then continued. "This is Anna White. I met her yesterday at a beautiful cathedral not far from here. She told me she wants to run away with the circus."

There was much friendly laughter and shouts of, "Welcome Anna!" in several languages.

Then Hubert got down to business. "Today was our first day back in the saddle. How'd it go?" He looked around expectantly.

"For our first show of the season, it was great!" a voice came from the back of the car.

"Couple of the new guys were a bit off during the cavalry charge, but all in all, it was good," one of the trick riders spoke up.

A middle aged Navajo women laughed and said, "Morty, you get all the fun. When you scalped Custer, I thought the crowd was going to come out and kill you."

"Hey, it ain't no laughin' matter!" Morty replied. "That crowd today – they scared me."

Dunn waited for the chatter to subside. "When the audience gets like that, we call them *Uŋȟčéǧila*. That's the Sioux word for monster or bad spirit." When he looked at Hubert, he wasn't smiling. "Maybe we should tone it down a bit when the audience is a big mob."

"Anything else?" When there were no takers, Hubert continued. "Listen to what the New York Times says about us." He shook open a newspaper and began to read. "Buffalo Bill's Wild West and Congress of Rough Riders certainly lived up to expectation. Their depiction of Little Big Horn seemed so real to the audience that the fear and anger was palpable. The crowd was as dramatic as the players." He turned the page." The paper goes on to mention our various acts. Good publicity."

Morty blurted out, "We ain't doin' Little Big Horn again tomorrow, are we?"

"Nope!" Hubert said. "All the acts tomorrow are the same except the finale. We're doing The Battle of Wounded Knee, just like we rehearsed."

"That should make the *Uŋȟčéǧila* happy," Ben quipped. "It was a hungry beast today." Many there nodded their agreement uneasily.

"Oh, for you new folks, our own Black Elk was an active participant at both Little Big Horn and Wounded Knee," Hubert said from the front of the car.

Anna White looked at her new friend in wide-eyed wonder. Black Elk smiled and nodded self-consciously.

"You should ask him to show you his scar sometime," Dunn said loud enough for those around to hear.

There was a round of good-natured laughter then, Anna asked, "Were you really wounded at Wounded Knee?"

"I'd have to pull down my pants to show you the scar."

Cody entered the arena from stage left seven minutes late, unannounced. He had waited behind the painted backdrops with the rest of the troupe – listening, judging. It was April 22nd and their second performance in New York.

The audience, some thirty thousand strong, sounded at times likes a huge flock of geese feeding contentedly at a river's edge. At other times it resembled some massive carnivorous animal roaring, guarding its kill. As the minutes ticked by past the official start time, the tension mounted. Somewhere in the crowd a person began clapping. Others joined in raggedly, then others until the crowd reached a synchronicity. Foot stomping began echoing the clapping until all order was lost – the sound transitioned to what sounded like an avalanche, then descended to utter auditory chaos. The sonic span created by the crowd bridged human hearing from bass sounds that weren't heard as much as felt to pitches so high they could only be sensed as anxiety. It was at this moment Cody chose to appear.

The audience, lost in its senselessness, did not see Cody at first. One person yelled out, then two until the chain reaction was total. It was as if a huge barrel of pebbles was slowly tipped onto a snare drum – the sound of the first few stones was discernible then, as the drum is engulfed, the sound devours all.

As ugly as the sound was that immersed Cody, he reveled in it. He was a showman and as entertainers are, addicted to adoration.

Cody rode Duke slowly toward the announcer's stand as the sound level grew exponentially. He sat up straighter in the saddle, his mood lightened as the psychic energy from the crowd turned from dark and moody – dangerous – to festive. Cody also felt his mount relax beneath him, as if Duke could assess the power emanating from this huge mass of humanity. Duke, whose primal instincts earlier had sensed the need for possible flight, stepped easier now that the beast in the stands was jovial.

Cody took the microphone, turned horse and rider toward the crowd and began. "Ladies and gentlemen – New Yorkers. A gracious welcome to the second of ten depictions of American history, presented to you as unbiased, as unvarnished in truth as closely as my troupe of players can manage. Yesterday, the New York audience experienced the Battle of Little Big Horn as it happened, very near the one hundredth anniversary of this great country's Declaration of Independence from an oppressive English rule." The crowd roared its patriotism at the mention of independence from tyranny, yet seemed oblivious to the irony.

Cody waited patiently, and then silenced the crowd with one hand. "Today, you will experience an event of a very different tenure – The Battle of Wounded Knee." The crowd erupted in sound again – it reminded Cody of the coughing snarl a cougar makes when guarding its kill.

Cody interrupted the audience by speaking loudly into the microphone. "Little Big Horn and Wounded Knee are both significant events in our country's history – both involve the Plains Indians, the Sioux, the Cheyenne and others. Both battles were based on misunderstandings." Cody stood in the saddle to stress the words that followed. "The Indians were my former foe! Today, they are true Americans and my friends. Little Big Horn, Wounded Knee and every other Indian outbreak I have ever known were a result from broken promises and broken treaties by our own government."

Faces in the crowd showed anger. Huge numbers of people in the audience turned to neighbors to voice what seemed like disagreement with Cody's pronouncement. The muttering from the stands conveyed the same implied threat as that of hornets about to erupt from their nest.

Cody quieted the beast again by announcing, "LADIES AND GENTLEMEN! The history of our American west as presented to you by the CONGRESS OF ROUGH RIDERS OF THE WORLD!"

Cody exited stage left as the horse race began. The beast roared its approval when the white man won the race. But there were scattered "Boos" in the audience when the Indian surrendered his feathered headdress.

The screams of joy and anguish from the stands during the attack on the settlers in their covered wagons sounded identical to the day before. But when the troupe bowed to the crowd, the audience was strangely silent.

The spectators seemed thoroughly entertained by the trick riders and rope artists. When the seemingly white members of the troupe left the arena the audience seemed restless. When a single, powerfully built Indian began dancing slowly to a hidden drumbeat, there were more "Boos" and loud calls of "Where's Annie Oakley?"

Cody galloped Duke to the center of the arena and stood in the saddle as the crowd quieted. He then rode to the announcer's podium and seized the microphone.

"Ladies and Gentlemen. The events that transpired at Wounded Knee spanned several days. In order that you, our New York audience, can experience this historic incident in perspective, our players will compress the events into one single act. I will narrate to hopefully clarify misconceptions you may have learned by reading inaccurate accounts in your newspapers."

"Wovoka, a Paiute spiritual leader, had a vision. He taught that if the Plains Indians could live by the teaching of Christ, love one another, not lie or steal, work hard and not practice war, the white man would leave them in peace. In his vision Wovoka saw the land full of game and all people, Indians and whites, living at peace with one another."

Cody turned and pointed to the lone Indian still dancing slowly at the center of the arena. "To pray Wovoka taught that the circle dance practiced by the Sioux and many other tribes was a way to show God their reverence."

Cody watched the Indian silently for a moment then continued. "The dance, now called the Ghost Dance, spread rapidly throughout the plains. The red people were disillusioned, hungry and badly wanted a return to their once plentiful life. The Ghost Dance and what it promised was powerful medicine – it was their form of prayer."

Cody paused again and pointed to the Indian dancing tirelessly at the center of the newly erected tipis. "To our red brothers this dance, this prayer, was a wish for peace and prosperity. But to the Indian agents and those sent by the American government to manage the reservations, this dance was threatening – terrifying. They saw it as the beginnings of an uprising. And they responded with force."

Six Indians wearing police uniforms appeared from within the tipis and struggled to stop the dancer. Other Indians joined the fray trying to interfere with the police. The Indians acting as Reservation police dragged the dancer into the tipi closest to the audience. Then, a single gunshot rang out.

"The death of Sitting Bull was devastating to the Sioux." Cheers from the crowd rang out before Cody could complete this important part of the narrative. He stood in the saddle and waited until the beast quieted. "The assassination of Sitting Bull and the effect it had on his people could be compared to the dismay and disarray we Americans felt when Abraham Lincoln was shot at Ford's theater. The entirety of the Sioux reservation reacted to their leader's death with demonstrations of grief and disbelief. But to their white overseers, these demonstrations appeared as if there was indeed an uprising."

The cavalry appeared from stage right and surrounded the village. They were armed with pistols, rifles and small cannons. A small contingent of soldiers walked into the center of the tipis and began forcefully taking the Indian's weapons. One Indian resisted and his rifle discharged accidently. Within seconds, the soldiers were firing into the village indiscriminately.

"Ladies and gentlemen! On that fateful December day, as many as three hundred Sioux died – many were women and children. Twenty-five of our soldiers died and thirty nine were badly wounded, often by fire from their own white brothers." Cody stood and removed his hat. "This senseless massacre happened because of a simple misunderstanding."

The crowd stood and cheered.

Author's notes:

Duke, William Cody's favorite horse during the time period depicted in this chapter, was a gift from General Nelson Miles shortly after the disastrous train wreck in North Carolina. (See telegram below chapter heading)

More than twenty U.S. Cavalry soldiers were awarded the Congressional Medal of Honor for acts of 'Bravery' and 'Heroism' during the 1890 Battle of Wounded Knee.

In defiance to the Second Amendment, the cavalry's goal was to disarm the Indians at Wounded Knee and relocate them by railcar to an area away from their home. The picture below from after the battle at Wounded Knee is a chilling precursor to events in Europe 50 years later.

at the Battle of Wounded Knee S.D.
North Western Photo Co
Chadron Neb

Crossings
December 1902

Not like the brazen giant of Greek fame,
With conquering limbs astride from land to land;
Here at our sea-washed, sunset gates shall stand
A mighty woman with a torch, whose flame
Is the imprisoned lightning, and her name
Mother of Exiles. From her beacon-hand
Glows world-wide welcome; her mild eyes command
The air-bridged harbor that twin cities frame.
"Keep, ancient lands, your storied pomp!" cries she
With silent lips. "Give me your tired, your poor,
Your huddled masses yearning to breathe free,
The wretched refuse of your teeming shore.
Send these, the homeless, tempest-tossed to me,
I lift my lamp beside the golden door!
     Emma Lazarus

Lady Liberty stood tall in New York harbor oblivious to the judgments of men. Made from copper, she initially was much the same color as the original Americans. As the S.S. Ivernia steamed past Liberty Island, the famous statue was green from patina and streaked with rain.

Hanna stood at the railing, less awe struck than she had been two years before. "*Look, Čík'ala Wakȟáŋ.*" she said to the baby in her arms. "*She welcomes us to the land of liberty.*" The Statue of Liberty was majestic but as a symbol, it paled in comparison to the black rock she carried in her pocket. And the skyline of New York and its promised riches stood in sharp contrast to the conditions in the ship's steerage and the slums hidden within the city.

"*Ina, why do you call the baby Little Angel?*" Little Abe reminded her so much of her father when he was vibrating with curiosity, anxious to explore.

"It's the same reason we call you Little Abe. In our tradition, you will earn a name when you do something worthy." Hanna smiled at her son." "Your Lakota is good, but Wakȟáŋ means a person with special powers. Angel is close."

"Mommy, why is that woman sad?"

Hanna looked behind her, and then down at Little Abe. Every passenger seemed to be looking at the statue in reverence as the ship steamed slowly past Liberty Island. "What woman, Little Man?"

"Her - the big green lady! She's frowning and the rain makes it look like she's crying."

Hanna reached down with her free hand and tousled her son's hair. "You're right – she does look a little sad."

"Why?"

"Why?" Hanna pointed at the torch. "She's called The Statue of Liberty. She was built as a symbol to the people of America. Her torch is supposed to light the way to freedom and liberty. When you grow up you'll realize that some people are more free than others. That's why I think she looks sad."

"Mommy, look!" Little Abe pointed to a large dingy being rowed by six men. Another man stood in the bow with a megaphone and shouted, "Ahoy Ivernia!"

There was another loud "Ahoy!" from the wheelhouse. Then several-uniformed crew members pushed through the crowd on deck yelling, "Make way! Make way for the pilot." They pushed several passengers aside near Hanna and removed two short chains that served as a deck railing. They pushed a coiled rope ladder over the side and stood guard as the dingy pulled alongside.

Moments later a large man with an impressive red beard hoisted himself onto the deck and began walking toward the wheelhouse. He stopped abruptly, turned toward the crowd and yelled out, "Anybody here by the name of Black Elk?"

Hanna was too stunned to speak for a moment then she raised her hand. "He's my father. Is there a problem?"

"Tell him that a woman named Anna White has been coming to the docks for weeks asking when your ship was arriving. She's dockside now." The pilot turned and climbed the ladder to the wheelhouse.

As the S.S. Ivernia made its way slowly through the channels of New York Harbor, Little Abe was hyperactive after more than a week at sea. Hanna finally passed her son off to Black Elk and the two of them went off to explore.

When the tug met the ship, Black Elk and Abe ran forward to watch the action. Hanna stood at the railing holding her baby, lost in thought. She watched her son and father play. She smiled at their childlike innocence. In the distance she could see a solitary person standing near the gangplank on pier 17.

As the ship neared the pier, the fog and drizzle swirled around both boat and land, giving the scene a dream-like quality. The tug struggled – short blasts from steam whistles echoed. Then, almost as if her father and the person on the pier shared the same thought, the two waved to each other. It was almost possible for Hanna to see the connection between her father and the apparition on shore.

Hanna saw the eagerness in her father's eyes and tried to understand her own feelings.

The woman waiting on the dock obviously cared for her father. She had waited long months while Cody's troupe had traveled in Europe. Now waving both arms she rocked from foot to foot, conveying a joyfulness that Hanna envied.

Hanna knew she should also feel elation for her father, for it seemed that there was the possibility of a woman's love for him after all the years. She knew he'd had many encounters with the women in the show, but never once had there been any connection except proximity and convenience. She had seen the wardrobe ladies flirt, and some performers blatantly invited him to their cabins, but never once had he brought one of them to the family.

Hanna knew what she should feel but instead, she was jealous, hurt. She'd had a father's love from a very distant part in her life only to have it stripped away. Then at the Carlisle School the men that should have been trusted figures were extreme opposites. When she'd finally found her real father, a sacred circle had closed in her life – she felt blessed, complete. Somehow, the appearance of this woman on the shore represented a rupture of that circle that enclosed her life and kept her safe. In a dim, primal part of her heart, Hanna felt hate. Confused, Hanna walked and stood near her father at the railing as the ship closed the distance between one reality and the unknown.

"Ate, tell me about her."

When Black Elk turned and looked at his daughter, his love was still there in his eyes. "*When you were tiny like Little Angel, your mother and I called you Happy Seed.*" He smiled down at the child in his daughter's arms. "*Then your mother was dead and you were gone. I spent years lost, seeking.*" He switched to English. "Her name is Anna Brings White. She had two children and both died. She is also a seeker. When we met at the Catholic Church, it was as if our souls recognized each other." He looked back at the woman waiting for him on the dock, waved and turned to his daughter. "She completed something in me the moment we met." He touched the pocket that held Hanna's rock. "*When we came out of the church that first day, a hawk was waiting on the building across the street. I believe it was your mother's spirit. She gave me her blessing.*" He put his palm on her cheek and gently held her. "*I hope you do the same.*"

As a crewmember lowered the gangplank, Hanna watched the flow of humanity crossing from one reality to another. Her father with Little Abe in tow was the first. When the woman on the other side hugged her father passionately then stooped to greet her son, Hanna felt pulled in two. Her jealousy was intensely visceral. The fear of coming change flooded her mouth with a coppery taste like blood, but her spirit self seemed calm, content. This was just another crossing like stepping off the train – at the top of the steps was safety, family – acceptance. But stepping down onto the soil of another state, country, reality – the rules changed and roles reversed. This was nothing new.

Hanna stood at the bottom of the gangplank like an unmoving stone making ripples in a stream as it passed. She was only aware of the scene taking place a few yards away as the other passengers flowed past her. Her father was chatting happily with this other woman – her son completely at ease. When Little Abe held up his arms to be picked up and was scooped up by this woman, Hanna moved forward without conscious volition.

The moment Hanna began to move with the crowd, the woman holding her son made eye contact. Challenges older than memory flashed between them – the other woman dropped her eyes.

Black Elk revealed nothing except joy when his daughter's spirit enlarged the circle. If he was aware of the emotional dissonance that swirled about him, he gave no hint. Instead he radiated complete acceptance. He stood there surrounded by the people he loved – his daughter, two grandchildren and a white woman that felt red. To him, they were equals.

"Kahí, this is my daughter Hanna and my new granddaughter. You've already met Little Abe." He reached out and touched the cheek of his grandson.

Hanna gave her father a tight smile then turned, the gentle challenge still in her eyes. She did not extend a hand in greeting. "Little Abe, I need you to come stand by me." In a distant part of her mind, Hanna knew she was like a mother bear but couldn't stop.

Little Abe protested. "Mom! I can't see down there," as he was put on the ground.

"Kahí? I thought your name was Anna." Hanna's voice, though not unfriendly, was guarded, businesslike as she put her free hand on her son's shoulder.

"Hanna, in the short time I've known your father, he's mostly talked about you." Kahí looked directly into Hanna's eyes – her look was both submissive and assertive. "Your story is amazing – I believe you have a guardian angel. I want to see the rock you carry sometime." She paused. "But I have my own story. Please don't judge me until you've heard it. Please!"

A rail worker's strike delayed Cody's show for five days. Instead of a seamless move from ship to rail, the livestock had to be moved to a corral – the many sets and wardrobe crates had to be moved by wagons to a warehouse. The entirety of Cody's enterprise was sprawled about on Pier 17 in New York Harbor in very uncharacteristic disarray.

Dunn, Black Elk and many of the other men tasked with the physical movement of the entirety of Cody's enterprise had many angry encounters – some with teamsters that raised their prices after goods were loaded – some with dock officials who refused permits unless their palms were greased.

Had it not been for Abe Hubert who seemed to understand the bureaucracy of big city dealings, Dunn might have landed in jail. Dunn and the other men had roped many of the horses together. They were trying to cross a causeway toward their assigned corral when an officious little man refused to let them cross without either a bribe or some permit. Hubert simply stepped between the men, shook the official's hand and transferred a five dollar gold piece. Hubert then turned to Dunn. "Secure the horses; take some time. Feed your family and get some sleep. Relax!"

As the sun set on this frustratingly, yet extraordinary day, Black Elk's entire family followed Anna to an oyster bar not far from the docks. They were the largest group there, seven adults including Big Abe and three children. They were shown to a small alcove room adjacent to the main hall.

The oyster bar was raucous. Waiters carried huge platters of steaming oysters, slabs of cooked fish with mounds of fresh white bread. Bar maids carried flagons of beer, sometimes six at a time. The tables were crowded with a cross section of New Yorkers. One table held several men wearing tuxedos – another dockworkers and sailors. All of the four colors of men were there eating, drinking, laughing together.

The noise from the floor paradoxically guaranteed the privacy Anna felt that she needed when she stood after their meal. "My name is Anna Brings White." She stopped, looked at

Black Elk for support then continued. "This man gave me the nickname Kahí because it means 'bring' in your language. But I understand that it means much more. It means I bring something to the group, the family – something valuable." She stopped again, looked at Black Elk sadly and continued softly. "Let me tell you what I bring – I bring nothing – no wealth, nothing except my belief in the Spirit. I had a husband, a house and two children. But my children died of consumption, and my husband left me because he believed our troubles were my fault. All I have to bring is a need to be part of something larger, a family." She made eye contact with each person there then sat.

Hubert stood after Anna had finished. "We have a long hard day ahead of us tomorrow. All of you get some rest." He smiled sagely and handed out three hotel keys – one to each of the men there. "I'll be on my way. It sounds like you have some family business to discuss."

Kahí stood and glanced at Hubert, then faced Hanna. "We may not need a key." She smiled tentatively at Black Elk, then faced Hanna again "I have a small apartment not far from here. I'd like to invite your father to my place." It was both an invitation and a question.

"Why, good mornin' Miss Hanna. You's up early this fine day."

"Are you always cheerful, Amos?" Hanna sat at the table nearest the service bar in the brightly lit dining car.

Amos chuckled and poured two cups of coffee. "Lots a cream, two big sugars, right Miss Hanna?" He put the two cups on the table and sat near the window across the table from her.

"And you drink yours black – you always remember. Thank you."

"Bein' cheerful is a choice Miss Hanna – just like how's you take your coffee." Amos took a sip from his coffee and smiled. "Yep! Why choose to have a dark brown look when you can smile?"

The two of them rode along in comfortable silence and watched the Wyoming plains roll by the window. Small patches of snow were still evident on the shaded side of rock bluffs and sagebrush. The sky was still too dark to make a guess about the day's weather.

Amos took another sip of his coffee. He studied Hanna's face as she looked out the window.

"What's on your mind, Amos?" She turned and looked at her old friend. "I can always tell when you're about to give me some advice."

Amos laughed. "No advice – I's just watchin' what goes on."

"Come on Amos, you're not fooling me! What's on your mind?"

Amos laughed in his wonderful unaffected baritone. "I's just, well, I met your father's new woman. I likes her. What's he callin' her?"

"Kahí. Her name is Anna Brings White, but he calls her Kahí. It's a Sioux word that means 'bring' but a lot more. I suppose he would have called her by her name, but saying Hanna and Anna together sounds silly."

Amos took another sip of his coffee and asked, "What's you think of her?"

Hanna didn't answer right away. Instead, she wrapped both hands around her cup and looked down.

Amos smiled at her sadly, reached out and wrapped both his hands around hers like a father might do for a daughter. "I's known your dad nigh on twenty years. I saw him come alive happy when he found you." He paused when she looked up and made eye contact. "You's right. I's got some advice for you. Walk on down to that stock car he calls home. See what this woman brought on-board from our stop yesterday in Scottsbluff. Might warm your heart."

Hanna knocked softly on the stock car door. She knew the sounds from the rails made the gesture meaningless. She peeked in and there were only bales of hay and bags of feed in the open common area. Then, when she stepped in and quietly closed the door, she saw it. In the corner of the room beside the door was a small Christmas tree.

The sight of this tiny evergreen decorated with bits of ribbon didn't register at first – she simply recognized it for what it was. But then a small memory of her first Christmas seeped out of her consciousness. She saw her adoptive father, the Rev. Cliff Parnell, decorating the mantle of their tiny Kansas home with some green vines. That trickle of memory opened a floodgate of emotions and Hanna sank to her knees.

He turned and said, "No Wee Pea, Santa Clause is not Jesus' father, God is. Santa Clause is just his helper." She couldn't remember what she had said – her memories of being a four-year-old were hazy and confused. But one memory was crystal clear. Rev. Parnell gave her a wrapped present. Inside was her black stone. It was at that moment that the life she was to live began.

"Hanna?" "Hanna, are you alright?"

Hanna resurfaced and found herself on her knees, weeping. Her black rock was in her hands, as if it were the origin of distant memories.

Kahí stood near her wrapped in one of her father's old blankets. "Hanna, what's wrong?"

Hanna looked up unsure. The memories of her life back in Kansas were so real, so primal it was like waking from a dream and not knowing where she was. She'd remembered the love she had for her adoptive father, the school and her teachers, the bitter fear when she was forced onto the train that took her to the Carlisle School. She remembered the trajectory of her love of Ben – from being protected by him when she was little to the passion of first love.

"The Christmas tree – it brought back memories from so long ago I'd forgotten." Hanna took the hand Kahí offered and stood.

"Me too," Kahí said sadly. It reminds me of happier times."

It was then that Hanna saw the terrible sadness and vulnerability in the woman that was a rival for her father's affections. Somehow, Hanna could see the pain in this woman that was deeper than tears could ever cure.

"I just can't let the season go by without a Christmas tree. Somehow, I think it would be sadder if I just let the day go by." Kahí looked at the stone in Hanna's hands. "From what your father says, that rock must be a powerful gift. All I have are my memories."

It was then that Hanna noticed two well used stuffed toys under the tree.

Kahí followed Hanna's eyes and said, "For your children – can't have a Christmas without something under the tree for the little ones."

"Where did you…"

"They belonged to my children."

Hanna turned then and looked into this other woman's eyes and there were stars.

They hugged then and cried together until their emptiness united them.

Hanna began with "Kahí, I'm sorry that…"

"I'll never replace your mother, Hanna. But maybe, could we be sisters?"

"John, what if this doesn't work?"

"Then I kill those bastards and we head out for *Paha Sapa*."

Bess and Dunn stood at the back door to the Taos Municipal Court. Above the door was a sign that read *Coloreds Only*.

Bess was uncharacteristically subdued – there was far more fear in her eyes than anger. "Suppose they kill you! I don't want to raise our son alone."

"Look! We're lucky we got back when we did. If we had stayed in Wyoming with Cody for Christmas, they would have just taken the land. We still have a chance." John gently touched the cheek of his sleeping son on Bess' back. "Let's just see how it plays out."

"John, I'm scared!"

Dunn took his woman's hand and looked down at her sadly. "Yeah – me too." He nodded solemnly as Pakwa and two other women from the pueblo entered the courthouse, then turned back to Bess. "Wish me, wish us luck."

"All rise! The Honorable Lloyd Haag Municipal Judge for Taos, New Mexico Territory presiding.

Haag walked in wearing a black robe. He sat at the podium, banged the gavel and said, "Court is in session. Please be seated." He looked around the nearly empty room and smirked. The second floor gallery was packed with red faces but only Hollis the banker, Lee Tresner the sheriff and a young lawyer were in attendance except for Dunn. "Let's dispense with the formalities. Mr. Dunn, do you understand why we're here?"

"I understand exactly why we're here," Dunn said coldly. "You and your cronies are taking away my land, and you're using the law to do it. It's a familiar story."

"Mr. Dunn. We are a nation of laws. When a person fails to follow the law, there are consequences. Do you have anything to say before I rule?"

Dunn stood and glared at Hollis. "I'm loosing my ranch because I neglected to pay the property taxes. Is that correct?"

"That is correct, Mr. Dunn. The procedure is clearly spelled out in Taos statutes."

"You do realize that not one piece of correspondence was ever delivered to my representative – not the tax notice or any of the delinquent tax notices. Can you explain why that happened?"

"You have no current address listed, Mr. Dunn. You've been an absent landlord. Had you kept up with your duties as a landowner here in the New Mexico Territory, we wouldn't be having this conversation."

"Bullshit!" Dunn stood and said angrily, "I know about the Reclamation Act."

"Language, Mr. Dunn. I can have you removed from this courtroom or even jailed for contempt. Do you have a statement to make before I rule on the tax foreclosure I have in front of me?"

"Sure, Judge Haag. You may want to talk to me privately before you rule."

The young lawyer sitting with Hollis stood and said, "Not without the plaintive present, your honor."

Haag snorted then said, "You two approach the bench."

Dunn stood in front of the judge and completely ignored the young lawyer standing near him. "Judge," Dunn said softly, "I saw you in the lobby of the La Fonda last march. Did you enjoy your stay?"

Judge Haag blanched, then banged the gavel. "There will be a fifteen minute recess while I confer with the defendant in my chambers." He gave the young lawyer a withering stare. "No objections!"

Haag escorted Dunn into his office and slammed the door. He sat behind his desk and glared at Dunn before he spoke. "I have a mind to have you jailed for contempt. This had better be good!"

Dunn reached into his jacket pocket and pulled out the hotel register. "Mr. Haag, whatever a man does is on his own conscience, but I have a notion that the people who voted you into office may not approve of this." He pointed to the signature on the register. "And the woman I saw you with was not the woman that lives here with you. What would she think?"

Haag sat down heavily with a grunt. He ran his hands through his hair then looked up at Dunn guiltily. "What is it you want?"

"I keep my land. You can make that happen." Dunn sat down and put his elbows on the desk.

"And if I can't?"

Dunn stood and hooked his thumbs in his pant's pockets. "Let's just say that this town drastically needs a change in leadership. The people here deserve better. All the people."

Judge Haag sat for a few minutes thinking. "If Hollis doesn't get something, I'm out and your problems get worse. He wants the land but what he's really after is control of the water. The stream up on your ranch is a key to the growth of Taos." Haag thought for a moment longer. "If you give Taos first water rights, maybe an easement for possible diversion later, Hollis just might be satisfied. If you keep the land and share the rights to the stream with our municipality, could you live with that?"

"In chambers, Mr. Dunn pointed out that our postal system is a national endeavor and not subject to local jurisdiction. Also, the telegram is a privately held company and even though it may be subject to local laws, Mr. Dunn's access to its services might cause a conflict of interest to shareholders." Judge Haag banged the gavel and said, "I find for the defendant in that he was unduly hampered from getting official notifications. If he can pay his back taxes and any penalties in a timely fashion, any foreclosure proceedings will cease. Mr. Dunn informed me that he would pay his taxes in cash. He will also forego payment of any fines and penalties by entering into an easement arrangement giving our municipality free access to the stream that flows through his property."

Fever

Hanna did not question – she just was. She passed among the people unseen. Beneath her the earth spoke its ancient secrets. Her awareness connected her to what seemed entirety, eternity.

The village was large with many tipis. Hanna moved knowing she was beckoned but did not hurry because each sight, each sound, each touch was a lesson to carry. She looked in wonder at the hands she did not have, but knew she would carry these lessons in her heart. She had no feet and she moved surely toward the center of this gathering of the people.

Hanna passed several women, young and old alike, talking happily as they scraped the hide of a buffalo. In that instant Hanna was there – she knew each woman, their story – their joys and pain. She knew the men that had released the buffalo's spirit. She could taste the meat they had provided the people with their bravery. She knew the buffalo as a calf and its mother and its mother's mother. She knew the soil the buffalo had trod – knew the birds that picked the insects from the animal's hide – felt the itch from the insect's bite and the intimate relief as the bird had pecked away the insect, as surely as if her lover had rubbed the small of her back.

She passed a young couple near the river as they moved together in the shade of a cottonwood. She felt their joy and yearning as they cried out together in passion – she felt their child begin in the girl's womb and knew its story.

She felt the pain in the old woman's swollen hands as she cooked a tender piece of backstrap for her man. He was old and gray and almost unable to walk, but his pride was strong. Hanna saw this couple's life together. She saw their many children and grandchildren. She knew their childhoods, their meeting, and their growing love. She wept with them as their parents died and returned to The Great Spirit

– she knew which stars in the Ghost Road this old couple watched at night. She knew they hoped to soon join their family in the stars.

She felt the parent's pain and the soaring joy of the child's spirit as it talked to Maya Owichapaha, the Old Woman Who Judges. The words the shaman spoke to the small body suspended on its platform filled Hanna with a totality of comprehension so vast, nothing else existed in that instant. The Shaman's wisdom described a closed circle with no loss, only change. "The earth and the stars are brothers – one came from the other. From the earth we stand up and to the earth we return. Our spirits are eternal, as are our bodies that return to feed the earth. That we are always - that is the Great Mystery."

On Hanna moved toward the center of this large gathering of human beings. Not one person looked at her, but the spirit within each acknowledged her as she passed. It was as if it was more than learning and remembering, each spirit outside herself she experienced, she became. The more she moved toward the center of this vast circle, the more its existence became hers. She felt like she was taking on the weight of each soul she passed, yet the closer she got to the center, the lighter and more fulfilled she became.

In the distance Hanna could see the peak of a massive tipi, taller and larger than seemed possible. It was the center, the place of power to which she was being drawn. She felt an urgency to the call, but she had more to learn, more dwellings to pass, more spirits to touch, more lessons to place in her heart.

Although she was not frightened, Hanna could feel a loss, a disturbance that pulled her along faster and faster. It was as if she were a single dandelion seed in a maelstrom. Each structure she passed was larger than the last, and the faster she was pulled along, the further her destination became.

A tipi flashed past, its thirteen lodge poles pointing toward the stars. Inside was an ancient HokšíyuzA teaching a younger woman the arts of healing. Hanna's spirit touched the spirit of this old midwife and marveled at her knowledge. Hanna saw this wisdom grow and be passed on from woman to woman back until the earth was covered in ice and the men hunted huge beasts with tusks and long noses. She learned the soothing that came from tree barks and berries, roots and herbs and how to store them, where and when to find them. She saw cactus buds and mushrooms that gave visions. She learned of carefully guarded herbs that gave older men the power to make children and others that helped women choose when to not make a child. The knowledge being passed concerned the very essence of life itself and when needed, death.

She paused, curious. Before her was a tipi not covered with buffalo hide but with whitish grey tree bark. The paintings outside were of a strange design but she understood them completely. Inside a shaman sat staring into his fire, pondering a question. Hanna wanted badly to answer his question, but the center of power called to her. The old shaman looked up startled as Hanna touched his mind. She hurried on knowing the countless winters of history from her people as an epic story to be told. She knew of her people coming from another land, crossing a bridge of ice. She saw her ancient ancestors all speaking the same tongue on this journey of discovery. As some of the people stayed to conquer different places, she saw a thousand different languages emerge. These different tongues were needed to describe the animals, plants and spirits her people found in every ecological niche on two continents.

Hanna felt powerfully drawn to another tipi. She was amazed at the pictographs painted there. Side by side were pictures of battles and weapons, bloody victories and defeats mixed with scenes of love, family life and the gentleness of women. Inside Hanna touched the spirits of a husband and wife sitting by their fire. His spirit was that of a fierce warrior and the protector of his people. His mind carried a perfect map of the land for a thousand miles in every direction. He knew where his tribe's friends and enemies lived, knew their tactics and strategies. He understood the leaders of these other people with minds like his own. He had killed many men and led his warriors to do the same. Hanna saw in him the balance between the commands of *the Great Spirit to protect life and the need to take life to protect his people. Near him sat his wife, a woman with a spirit as big as his, yet the opposite. She acted as the Coonshie, the grandmother to the people. Her soul was soft and tender and was the holder of the knowledge from all things feminine, life giving and loving. These two powerful yet opposite souls complimented each other perfectly – they loved each other for the spirits within the other. They were an example for their people.*

Hanna was drawn further toward the heart of this village. She felt anxious and fretful, wanting to experience the center, the place of power that called her. That nexus was there just ahead – she could see it, she could feel the sovereignty, the authority. She knew that her questions and the answers, some completeness awaited her there.

Hanna's sense of wonder turned to impatience, for she had surrendered her will to the pull, the movement. Now, with her destination so close, she wished for a body to command, feet to run. She pictured herself arriving at the unimaginable place just ahead out of breath with her spirit and body in their familiar connection. She wanted the comfort of customary sensations – thirst and fatigue, fear and elation. She wanted to be in a body that sank to its knees in the wonder at what was to come. She needed a body to hide within when she came face-to-face with the power that was just out of reach. Her spirit was not ready for it did not know how to show deference and submission. She had no eyes to look down, she had no hands to seek forgiveness; she had no body to throw to the ground in complete surrender.

Hanna's attempts to assert her will compelled the power that pulled her forward to stop. She felt a gentle nudge and knew she had yet another lesson to come. The largest and most powerful tipi was just ahead. She could see it and could feel the power within, but she was not moving. She felt rooted to the earth, unable to move, powerless to take that last step to be in the presence of... She didn't know.

A sound, a movement nearby drew her attention to a small lodge built close to the one of power. The paintings on its sides were unrecognizable but beautiful. They told a story of the spirit world with scenes of wisdom and dreams. The door flap opened and a man beckoned to her. He was tall and straight with striking, womanly features. The spirit that shown in his eyes was open and unguarded, with the promise of true friendship. He was dressed partially in men's garb, but much of his clothing was feminine. He was a combination of the handsomest man and the most beautiful woman Hanna had ever seen.

For an instant Hanna felt dizzy and confused. The spirit within this being was attractive, encouraging. She could feel that he would offer comfort and advice. She badly wanted to share her questions, get answers and be reassured. But when her body responded to him as well, when she knew absolutely that she would take him as a lover, she realized her dream had changed. When he extended a hand, her hand shook his in greeting. When he invited her to enter his tipi, her feet carried her. She looked down and saw she was corporeal again. Her body was familiar, but the feelings and desires she felt were not.

Inside, the tipi was vast. It seemed to be a space with no walls that encompassed the entirety of creation. In the distance, a small fire burned. This spirit apparition led Hanna across a prairie in full bloom. The Indian paintbrush and gaillardia lent riotous oranges and reds to the verdant grasses. There was no sun. Light seemed to come from within each living thing. The sense of being inside and outside simultaneously was disorienting yet pleasurable.

He sat near the fire in the place of power facing what should have been the door. In the distance, Hanna could see a distortion shimmering in the air where the tent flap should have been. Outside, she sensed a completely different reality. She knew that this door had been left open as an invitation for any and all to enter.

"I have so many questions," Hanna spoke not knowing or caring if she had been impolite. She felt like a child here to learn.

He patted the earth beside him and waited for Hanna to take her place by the fire. When she sat, he took her hand in his.

"Why do I feel this?" Where their hands touched there was an intensely pleasurable sensation that aroused every desire Hanna had ever known. *"Why am I here?"*

"Hanna, you can call me Siŋsíŋ if that will make you more comfortable." He released her hand and turned to face her. *"What we are called in this place is not important. Who we are is. I am not a man or a woman; I am both – a two-spirit. Some in your world might call me a wíŋkte or a berdache. My job here and in your world is to be the bridge between the dream world and that of waking."*

"Here? Where am…"

"A part of you is with your earth family. You have a fever and your spirit is here in this place – this is your dream."

Hanna looked at Siŋsíŋ – her eyes huge with wonder. "Is none of this real?" She put her hands on the prairie and dug her fingers into the soil. She could feel the dampness – each individual pebble. She held her hands in front of her face and looked at her fingertips coated with earth.

Siŋsíŋ took her hands in his and rubbed the soil away much like a parent would do for a child. "At first we believe that our body is who we are – we believe that the body defines us. And yes, it is part of us." He looked at his hands for a moment then rubbed them together. What looked like tiny glittering stars fell from his hands back onto the prairie. *"You asked if this is real. That is your choice. Your Christian father from long ago would have called it free will."*

"Is he here?" The joy and wonder in Hanna's voice was heartbreaking.

Siŋsíŋ *smiled and touched her cheek.* "Hanna, often the answers to our questions are defined by our choices – what we choose." *He looked at her intently with eyes that suddenly seemed ancient.* "When the Great Spirit made us, he gave us a body and a spirit." *He stood and continued.*

"Our bodies come from the earth and they are related to all living things. Our bodies can make choices for us. The need to eat, to drink, to make a child are powerful. Often our bodies force us to choose these things. We share these urges with every living thing. Remember, the White Buffalo warned us about these urges when she spoke about the two warriors and the nature of man." *He stopped and touched her heart.* "The body you live in is temporary – all of its parts will return to the earth and be used again by Wakan Tanka. It is your spirit that doesn't die – it lives forever. The life you live on the earth is a time to grow until your spirit is the part of you that makes all of your choices."

From the tone of his voice, Hanna sensed that Siŋsíŋ had said what he needed to say. She had been sitting cross-legged so she changed positions and was on her knees preparing to stand. Then she asked, "Did I choose to come here?"

Siŋsíŋ *smiled and held out one hand, palm facing her, as if both blessing her and signaling her that her lesson wasn't quite finished.* "We asked you to come but yes, you did choose to come."

"We?"

Siŋsíŋ *didn't answer in words. He turned and with his other hand he reached out and grasped what at first seemed to be just the air. Then, in one fluid motion, he pulled aside one reality and replaced it with another as easily as pulling a curtain. When he completed a full circle, the endless prairie had vanished and they were inside a beautifully kept tipi.* Siŋsíŋ *was no longer a man but an ancient woman dressed in a blindingly white deerskin dress with intricate* beadwork. "Hanna, I am Maya Owichapaha. Yes, I am the old woman who judges. Welcome! You sit in the place of honor."

Hanna looked into the eyes of this woman and felt total peace and acceptance. It was as if this old woman had reached into Hanna's being and one by one, removed the tiny scars from her heart – gone was the ache of loneliness that came when her adoptive father died – gone was the humiliation of being red in a white world – gone was the shame that she was barely able to contain from the abuse she had endured at the Carlisle School. Hanna placed one palm over her heart and realized that the venom she carried from life's injustices was gone. The pain she had grown accustomed to was suddenly missing. The absence of it felt like a blessing she would carry forever.

It was then that Hanna felt a presence. She turned and there beside her was a young woman. She was dressed plainly in a deerskin shift fringed with hawk feathers. Hanna's heart knew before her mind – the guiding presence was there and her mother's eyes were full of stars.

"Hanna, my daughter, will you fly with me?"

Beliefs
On the tracks in Iowa, December, 1902

"The trees. They're moving." Hanna blinked and looked again. The scene was so hallucinatory, so out of context, she couldn't make sense of what she was seeing. Even when she grasped that she was viewing the trees from behind a window, it still made no sense. Were the trees growing? Was she falling? Hanna felt nauseous and closed her eyes– the rapid movement of leaves and branches in her narrow field of vision gave no horizon, only the feeling she was spinning or falling.

Then the sound reached her, the rhythmic clack of steel wheels on tracks and memory reasserted itself. The gentle rocking of the train car gave context to the trees passing by the windows. Then her consciousness slammed full on. She wasn't flying; she was home. Hanna turned her head and smiled. They were there – her family. She pulled herself to a sitting position as the pieces fell into place. She recognized the railcar cabin.

It was day, but the bed had not yet been made into seating. Ben sat across from her holding the baby. He looked worried. Little Abe smiled at her, both relieved and curious. She heard Ben whisper, "Thank God!" Crowded around the door were Bess and her baby, Uncle John and Abe Hubert. And there, on the periphery, was Kahí. It all came back. The season was over for Cody's show and they were all going back to New Mexico. And this woman, Anna White, the woman her father called Kahí was coming along. The discomfort, the uncertainty, the compromise of it all came back. They were headed to their winter home.

"What? Where?" Hanna looked from face to face.

At the sound of her voice, the baby leaned toward Hanna arms out, wanting to be held.

Ben stood and passed the baby as he said, "You've been unconscious with a fever for two days. We're already in Iowa headed north toward Wyoming."

"*Čík'ala Wakȟáŋ. My little angel.*" Hanna hugged the baby and seemed to not comprehend what Ben had said. She reached out to Little Abe.

"*Ina, you were sick. Daddy and everybody were worried. I knew you were all right.*" Little Abe leaned in, gave his mother a hug then laughed. "You said funny things while you were asleep. Who were you talking to?"

There was an uncomfortable silence followed by a long shriek from the engine's whistle. A second later a lurch passed through the train as the engineer throttled back.

"That's Waterloo and Cedar Falls coming up," Hubert said. "Hanna, I'm so glad you're back. I telegraphed ahead – there's a doctor there near the station. I can ask him aboard to look you over. How do you feel?"

"I just feel a little weak, thirsty." Hanna answered. "I don't think I need a doctor."

"You sure? We're going to be there for a few hours taking on supplies."

Hanna smiled weakly at Hubert and shook her head "No."

Hubert leaned in and patted Hanna on one hand. "You had us all worried there for a while." He stood and said, "Let's hop to. We're taking on food and water, feed for the livestock." He looked at Dunn. "You might ask at the station how long this is going to take – might want to ramp down and walk the horses. We've all been cooped up here for awhile."

"Back to work," Dunn said as he stood. "We're glad you're with us." He winked at Hanna, and stepped away and into the vestibule.

"I'm helping in the nursery today – want me to take the baby for you?" Bess stood there in the aisle bouncing her son on her hip. "These two love being together."

"Maybe later," Hanna answered tiredly. "I have a story to tell that I want Little Angel to hear."

"Just send word if you need help." Bess looked at Hanna with a curious smile then was gone.

"What story?" Little Abe sat near her and began bouncing on the cushions.

"I had a dream while I was asleep. I want to tell it while I still remember."

Kahí pushed Black Elk in Hanna's compartment and said, "I'm going to the dining car and see if I can rustle up some soup and a big glass of water for you." She smiled at Hanna, gave Black Elk a peck on the cheek and was gone.

Black Elk sat down in the compartment with his family. They were the image of the perfect Lakota family. He bit back the lingering disappointment that they lived in this odd, artificial environment. Then he said a brief prayer of thanks for an intact family. His daughter was married to a good man. He couldn't imagine a life without his two grandchildren.

"I was called – that's the only way I can describe it. I remember feeling sick – Bess took the baby. Then I was there." Hanna looked around her. Little Abe seemed excited like he always did at bedtime just before a story. Ben looked distracted, dubious at what he was hearing. Black Elk watched her intently. The baby played with her toes. *"I was in a huge village where there were many tipis and other kinds of dwellings. The village was set between two mighty rivers, one on the north and one on the south. The village was round and divided into four sections like the symbol of the four sacred directions."* She paused and looked up, trying to remember.

"At first I was a spirit – I didn't have a body. I felt like a child being taught. Everything I saw or touched, I understood completely. I met many of the people there and I knew their stories fully. I passed some women scraping a buffalo hide and it felt like I had been there. I watched a young couple make a baby and I knew it's whole life. I was with an old couple that wanted to join their relatives in the Ghost Road. There was a family whose son had just died. The mother and father were grieving and I could feel their pain. But I was also there with the boy's spirit when he talked to the Old Woman Who Judges - he was happy. For an instant I became a married couple and had both their spirits in me at the same time. He was a fierce warrior that had killed many men, but his wife was kind and loving – a life-giving person. It felt right to be able to take lives and protect the tribe from enemies, yet be loving and affirming at the same time.

Hanna paused, shifted the baby to the other arm and shook her head in disbelief. *"I touched the mind of an old shaman and saw the story of our people's journey from another land across a bridge of ice. I saw them slowly fill every possible corner of the land. I saw our ancestors hunting huge hairy elephants. I was shown the wisdom of the women healers who showed me herbs and bark, berries and roots that healed and gave visions."*

Hanna stopped and blushed. She remembered how badly she had wanted to lay with the two-spirit when her body returned to her. She continued her story and kept that longing close to her heart. *"I was stopped just before I reached the tipi at the center. I was suddenly in my body and couldn't move. Next I was invited into a very small tipi by the berdache who lived there. When I followed him in, the inside of the tipi was the whole world. He told me that all human beings are two parts, their bodies and their spirits. He said that our reason for living here on the earth is to learn to let only our spirit make our choices. He turned into Maya Owichapaha, the Old Woman Who Judges."*

When the train stopped, Ben stood, his impatience obvious. "I have to help Uncle John with the horses. Kahí will be back soon. Will you be alright if I leave?"

"There wasn't much more – we can have dinner together in the dining car tonight and I'll tell you the rest." Hanna smiled up at him and he was gone.

Black Elk stood ready to leave. "I should help with…"

"Ate'. She was there." She looked at her father solemnly. *"She had much to show me."*

"She?" Black Elk asked, but in his eyes, the answer was there.

"Itunkala, my mother. She told me that we have much work to do. She asked me to help you understand."

"Did she…" He sat heavily, eyes full of wonder.

"Ate', we didn't talk – I just understood. I could feel her love and the love she has for you. There was no need for us to talk because I could feel from her the answers."

"What did she say?" Black Elk's eyes were full of hope and pain.

"She was dressed in feathers. I only remember her saying, 'Will you fly with me?' She was a hawk and showed me many things. Some I understood, much I didn't."

Hanna took a deep breath and began.

"We flew together and I was very happy. She wanted me to hurry. I enjoyed flying as a bird. Then a huge silver machine flew past us making a noise like thunder. It scared me and I nearly fell. She looked at me sadly and flew higher. When I joined her, she wanted me to look down. The prairies were gone. There were machines everywhere digging and planting. There were white towns connected by roads that were covered with what looked like large moving beetles. The towns and roads covered the earth. At night, the cities seemed like beads of fire that formed a necklace that completely covered the land. Machines dug into the earth – dams stopped the rivers. Our friends the four legs were nearly all gone. There were millions of cattle living in cages to feed the whites. None of the whites hunted. They lived in boxes and bought all their food in stores. Great clouds of smoke came from buildings. The water from these buildings flowed black into the lakes and the fish were all rotting. There were many places that stored terrible poisons under the ground to be used as weapons. It seemed as if every country wanted the rest of the world dead." Hanna stopped, her eyes haunted.

"Then she flew with me so high we could see all the world. She flew me above the Paha Sapa and made me look at a terrible and wonderful thing."

"The Black Hills, the Sioux reservation – is that what she showed you?" Black Elk asked.

"Yes! In the middle of the reservation was a great fenced circle. It may have been hundreds of miles wide. Inside were several villages of our people living the old way. The fence kept in the buffalo and the elk, the deer and antelope. There were no roads or bridges. The people that lived there promised to live as our ancestors did. They had to learn how to live like our ancestors from books and stories. They wanted to give up the easy life the whites offered. Many of them died at first, but more came until the land within the circle became balanced. Inside the circle was a hard but beautiful life."

"What happened next?" Black Elk asked intensely.

"It was terrible!" Hanna sobbed. "The lights went out. The whites ran out of food and began doing terrible things to each other. Soon, white people from the towns came to the Paha Sapa. Our people from outside the circle tried to help the whites at first. When the food was gone, the whites wanted inside the fence. There was a terrible battle. Our people, both from outside the fence and inside, had many guns. Soon, there were no whites left alive."

"Then our brothers pulled down the fence and freed themselves and all the four leggeds. Right?"

Hanna looked at her father in wonder. *"How did you know?"*

Black Elk stood and sat near his daughter. *"I had a bad fever when I was very young. That is when my visions came."*

Hanna took her father's hand in hers. *"The understanding I got from the vision my mother showed me is that sometime, the White Buffalo Woman will return and the four colors of men will live in peace. It is inside the circle from where this beginning and the end is to come."*

Epilogue

~

Ten years later

Goodbyes
November 1912

Change is the end result of all true learning.
   Leo Buscaglia

"Hanna, he's almost sixteen. What were you doing when you were his age?" Black Elk stopped hanging up tack and patted a bale, hoping his daughter would sit.

"I can't Ate'! I'm too frightened. Every time he sneaks off I always imagine the worst."

"Little Abe isn't little anymore. He's curious – he's trying to find himself." Black Elk tapped the spot on the hay bale beside him again and Hanna sat with a sigh.

"That's what I'm afraid of Ate'. You've seen how he dresses when he goes out. He doesn't try to blend in – wear normal street clothes. He doesn't even try to be Abe Parnell the Cody show performer. He goes out dressed like the name he gave himself – Raven Dancer."

Kahí stepped into the aisle between the stalls. "He's an amazing young man. The audience loves his act." She leaned on the broom she'd been using to clean the stall she and Black Elk used as a bedroom. Her pregnancy was just beginning to show.

"They love it too much!" The worry in Hanna's voice was as evident as the crease between her eyes she got when she was upset. "The young men whistle at him like he's a girl."

"That's his act, Hanna. He's a two spirit – the audience sees that side of him and responds." Black Elk squeezed his daughter's hand.

"Ate'!" Hanna's voice was strident. "Out there, being a two spirit is a crime. He's red, dressed like a girl – like an Indian princess. I hate thinking about what could happen to him."

Kahí looked at Hanna sadly. "I know it is hard for you to imagine, because I would trade places with you. My boys died from tuberculosis and there was just nothing I could do. At least your son is still with you."

"When I was his age, I had just come back from my spirit quest." Black Elk took his daughter's hand and gave it a reassuring squeeze. "He's just trying to discover life."

"A moment ago you asked what I was doing at this age!" she said angrily. "I was pregnant at sixteen." Hanna stood and faced her father. "I was lucky! I found Ben when… well, when I got those urges."

Black Elk sat looking up at his adult daughter. He remembered the years of angst he'd felt. She'd been taken from him while she was still a newborn and was missing from his life for sixteen years. "Hanna, Little Abe is just like the rest of us – he has hopes and fears. Remember back when you were at the Carlisle School? If you'd let your fear rule you, Little Abe and Angel wouldn't be here. You had hope and it led you here."

"Ate'!" Hanna snapped. Her fear for her son had turned to anger and Black Elk was the only target in range. "I had the other girls! I had Ben. Little Abe has nobody to guide him." Hanna took a deep cleansing breath and blew it out noisily. "He's talked to Morty and Standing Wolf about their life. And thankfully, I don't think either of them has done more with Abe than talk. I'm not so sure about Reggie. I've seen the two of them go off together a few times." Hanna looked down at her father, pain evident in her eyes. "I've tried to talk to him about his feelings. He just won't talk to me. Big Abe tried a couple of times but Little Abe was disrespectful." Hanna paused, almost in tears. "I'm just afraid what he's going to find out there." She pointed out into the night of the Chicago rail yards. "In here, our people are understanding. Out there is a different world."

Black Elk stood and hugged his daughter. She was rigid and didn't respond. He put his hands on her shoulders - she wouldn't meet his eyes. For the first time, he noticed a few strands of grey in his daughter's hair. "Hanna, you raised him well. Now you have to trust…"

"Ate!" Hanna looked up irritably, her eyes dull with fear. "You grew up red in a red world. The culture that guided you was thousands of years old. I didn't have that and neither did Ben." She sighed, searching for words. "Ben and I grew up in the white world with a few stories about being Sioux." She backed up a step and her father's hands fell away. She hugged herself. "All my son has as a village, a culture, is this make believe we live." She gestured indicating the train car. "He was afraid to go outside when he was little – now he's out there looking for love in a world full of hate."

Little Abe slipped across the train yard like a wraith. The only light came from the gibbous moon. He was acutely terrified knowing the trouble he was in, yet he was ecstatic.

He managed to open the vestibule door with a faint rumble. When he stood silently in the aisle outside his parent's compartment, there wasn't a sound. He stepped into the compartment he shared with his little sister. When she seemed asleep, he breathed a sigh of relief. When the compartment door closed, there was a small audible 'snick' and Little Angel sat up, eyes wide.

"Well?" she asked.

"Well what?" He sat, and they both laughed nervously at the familiar dialogue they'd shared all their lives.

"Did you find a friend?" When Angel said *a friend*, there was no sarcasm or derision in her voice, only love and understanding. She had grown up with Little Abe as her big brother and she had always been his closest confidant. There had never been a time in her life that she could remember when Little Abe held back his feelings – his ecstasies and fears about being a Two Spirit, his confusion as his sexuality burgeoned. She knew how badly he wanted to simply be loved for who he was. She didn't judge; she listened.

"No!" "Yes! I found a room full." There was a light in his eyes Little Angel hadn't seen before. It was as if he had had a scab over a pain that had always been there. Now that ache was gone.

"Tell me everything!" She scooted up into a sitting position and sat on her hands - a sure sign between them that she was ready to listen.

"I went to the address Standing Wolf gave me. I was terrified. I stood outside on the street listening. I could hear the music - laughing." He looked at his little sister with a curious smile she'd never seen. "When I finally got the courage to open the door, it seemed I was outside in a black and white world looking into a room that was full of color. It was amazing. I just stood there in the doorway with my mouth hanging open."

"Come on! Come on! What happened?"

Little Abe laughed nervously then smiled at the memory. "This guy, Paul, I found out that was his name later. He was sitting at the bar talking to someone and looked up and caught my eye." Little Abe shivered and raised his shoulders in a uniquely feminine way. "He got up from the bar, walked over to me and took my hand. I was just standing there, half in and half out. You know the first thing he said to me?"

"What? What?" Little Angel asked eagerly.

"You're beautiful. He took my hand, told me I was beautiful, then kissed me."

Angel's eyes were huge. "What was it like? Was it wonderful?"

Little Abe didn't answer for a moment, but the look on his face spoke volumes. "It was the most natural thing in the world except, I've never felt anything like it. It was just there – nothing in the way. The spirit in me touched the spirit in him. I just can't explain it better than that. There were no barriers. We were just there together."

"Didn't he ask your name or something?" Little Angel asked breathlessly.

"You're not going to believe what happened next."

"Tell me!"

"He didn't say a word. He gently reached under my skirt and touched me."

"EWWW!"

"It wasn't like that." Little Abe laughed. "It was more like he just checked to see if I was who I said I was." Little Abe looked down at his sister with an unreadable smile. "Know what he did next?"

Little Angel didn't speak and shook her head excitedly.

"He looked into my eyes and said, 'You ARE beautiful!'"

Little Angel made *come here* gestures with both hands, encouraging her brother to keep talking.

"The rest of the night is sort of a blur. I remember looking up when everybody in the room applauded me. Paul took me to a stool and ordered me a drink. He had his arm over my shoulder. When other men came up, he didn't mind when they talked to me, kissed me. At some point, I remember doing my Raven Dance. Some of the men whistled at me – some joined in and danced with me. Paul rubbed up against me as he danced. He was unashamed of what he was doing. At one point, there were men completely surrounding me when I was dancing. They pushed against me, touched each other and me with their hands. I know it must sound disgusting to you, but I have never felt such freedom, such acceptance. It was like I could let the real me out, and everyone there was doing the same." He looked at his sister with eyes that were shiny with happiness. "I know it must seem really crude - I've never felt more loved in my life."

The vestibule door opened with a bang. "*Chesli*, here they come!"

Ben and Hanna pushed in through the door and the familiar family constellation reformed itself again. Ben stood, fists clenched, angry. Hanna sat across from Little Abe, smothering and comforting, softly mouthing gentle condemnations and words of comfort at the same time. Little Abe sat there silent, acutely fearful and full of rebellious anger in equal measure. And Little Angel was ready as always to be the mediator, the peacemaker; the lightning rod that somehow might make the words to follow quiet and rational.

For a moment, no one spoke. Each was worried that the conversation would be a repeat of the one before and the one before that. Most often, the words never matched the hearts from where the words originated. Hanna always spoke of the pain she felt caused by fear. Little Abe was her son, her firstborn and she was a mother; she simply wanted him safe. For Ben, his responses were far less pragmatic. He understood and accepted that his son was different. Through his anger, it seemed as if he'd rather have a more conventional son – one who would play football rather than with dolls. And Little Abe perceived every word, whether supportive or not, as a rebuke of what life had handed him. Even when his parents played the age and perspective card, Little Abe always railed against them claiming his own judgment was never good enough. The family simply didn't have the cultural background to move past their own perspectives.

Not surprisingly, it was Little Angel that spoke first. "Can I tell you what he found?"

Little Abe glared at his sister for a moment, crossed his arms over his chest protectively and looked down.

"He found some friends that are also two-spirits." Angel smiled at her brother, then looked at her parents as if what she'd reported was a solution to this current crisis.

Ben sat down heavily next to Hanna. He looked at the floor and rubbed his forehead, trying to find words. "Have I told you the story of the boy and the rattlesnake?"

The vehemence in Little Abe's voice was so intense the rest of the family jumped. "You've told me this story a hundred times!" He glared at his father. "It's stupid!"

Ben looked at his son unemotionally. "You tell it. Then tell me what it means."

Abe scowled out the window – his tone of voice bitterly sarcastic. "This dumb boy was walking from the dark side of the mountain toward the sunny side. There was a rattlesnake in the path that said, 'Take me to the sun – I'm cold.' The boy said, 'You're a rattlesnake – you'll bite me.' They talk back and forth – 'You'll bite me!' 'No, I promise.' like six times. Then the boy finally picks up the snake after it called the boy brother. He puts the snake under his shirt to warm it. When they get to the sunny side of the mountain, the boy says, 'Here we are,' and starts to put the snake down. The snake bites the boy and the boy says, 'You promised.' The snake says, 'You knew what I was.' The boy dies – end of story!"

"So, what does it mean to you?"

"You think I'm like the boy in the story, don't you?" Little Abe said bitterly.

"Raven Dancer," Ben said formally. "The boy in the story knew the risk."

Hanna was acutely embarrassed when Big Abe showed up at her door the following morning. She and Ben had stayed up half the night sometimes discussing, sometime arguing about their errant son. They'd overslept and had missed breakfast. The second show in Chicago started at four in the afternoon and there were many things that needed attention.

Hanna was suddenly struck how much Big Abe had changed in the nearly sixteen years since that fateful day in Carlisle. He still wore his nearly identical three-piece suits, but he was somehow physically diminished. Where once he'd seemed jaunty in his suits and spats, now his clothing hung on his skinny frame badly. His gray hair was completely white and wispy; he now used a cane to get around. Yet somehow, he seemed larger; his spirit and intelligence had grown to offset his physical decline.

Hanna's door was open, so Abe knocked once then came in and sat. He smiled at Hanna and Ben and in his usual no-nonsense style began. "Good news and bad news." He made eye contact briefly with each of them as always, as if he was making sure they were paying attention before he dispensed some wisdom. "Ticket sales are way down – you know that, dear. Your count them every show." He hesitated. "This may be our last season." He sighed, put both hands on the head of his cane and softly continued. "I still have family here in Chicago. I'm a bit tempted to just walk."

Hanna looked up, concerned. "What do you mean, Uncle Abe?"

"You mean what I said about our last season?" Hubert's eyes were unreadable.

"No!" Hanna's voice trembled slightly. "What did you mean when you said you were tempted to just walk?"

Hubert laughed softly and put one hand over Hanna's. "Just wishful thinking. I'm old – tired." He squeezed her hand gently. "There are people here in Chicago that I'm related to. My true family is here on this train. Let's just see how it all plays out – OK?" He smiled at Hanna and continued. "There's talk that we'll join with the Sells-Floto Circus to keep ourselves afloat."

They heard muted cursing, the vestibule door rumbled open and Reggie and another roustabout carried a small strong box down the aisle. When they put it on the floor of Hanna's compartment, a distinct metallic *clink* came from inside.

"Ah, yes, the good news!" Hubert exclaimed. "This arrived from New Mexico early this morning. Thanks, Reggie."

The chest was smaller than a suitcase. Its presence seemed to fill Hanna and Ben's living space with human desires – festive and ominous.

For a moment, nobody moved. Reggie stood in the doorway open-mouthed. Ben and Hanna eyed the chest with curiosity, and Big Abe tapped the floor with his cane. "Thanks, Reggie!" he said again pointedly.

When they were finally alone, Big Abe touched the heavy paper address label glued to the chest. "I can't believe it's been three years since Dunn retired to his ranch in New Mexico."

"It's more than a ranch, Uncle Abe," said Ben as he knelt down to unlock the heavy padlock. He pointed to the return address. "Dunn's Trading Post. You should see the place – you'd be proud."

"Who'd be proud?" Little Angel appeared in the open doorway rubbing her eyes.

"Good morning, Angel. Get your brother. We're about to open Uncle John's box." Ben struggled with the lock for a moment, then it opened with a loud *clack*.

"He's still sleeping and I don't think he wants to see anybody for awhile. He was pretty upset last night." Little Angel squeezed into the compartment and sat across from Big Abe.

A brief unreadable glance passed between Hanna and Ben, then he pulled the box open. There was a soft collective gasp. The first thing visible in the strongbox was a carefully folded Navajo blanket. The blanket's design was simple geometric shapes; the reds, whites and blacks with small accents of gray were vibrant. A note was pinned to the blanket that read, "For Mr. Hubert, friend."

"Merry Christmas!" Ben said, and smiled as he handed the blanket to Big Abe.

"That's Happy Chanukah, my young friend!" Big Abe stood, put his note on the seat and wrapped the blanked around his shoulders. When he sat, he could have passed for an elder from nearly any culture in the world. He unfolded the note and began to read.

Ben pulled a thick packet of large brown envelopes all tied together with string. He stood and sat next to Hanna. Before he could untie the string, Hanna took the packet and began organizing the pile.

"Typical!" she said. "The ledger is on top."

"Ledger?" Big Abe looked up from his letter, curious.

Hanna opened the first envelope and pulled out the cover sheet. "Bess and Big John sent..." She scrolled down the page with her finger, "five pounds of gold coins to give out to the share holders."

Big Abe leaned forward and looked down into the box. At the bottom were five small canvas bags with Bank Of Taos stenciled on each one. "There's..." He stopped to think, "over $1,600 worth of gold here." He got a dull crafty gleam in his eyes. "Shouldn't we get it locked up in the safe?"

Hanna looked up from the letter she'd picked up. "It can wait. It's not that important."

"Not important!" Big Abe sputtered. "That's a lot of money."

Hanna held up a letter clearly in John Dunn's handwriting. It was addressed to Abe Hubert. "Uncle Abe, what would you rather do right now, hide this gold like a miser or read a letter Uncle John sent you?"

Abe stuttered again then laughed. "You're right – the gold can wait."

Hanna leaned across the seat and kissed Big Abe on the cheek. "Just like you said – family is most important."

Hanna picked up the letters one-by-one. "Ben – here's one for you from Uncle John. Um, this one is mine – from Bess. Ben, here's one from Pakwa to both of us. And, oh Angel! There's one here for you from Mathó." Ben and Hanna exchanged a glance and they both smiled.

Angel's face lit up with a huge smile – she held out her hand for the letter vibrating with anticipation.

Big Abe looked up, curious. "Who's Ma Toe?"

"*Mathó* – Bear. That's what John and Bess's boy is named in Sioux. It means bear. They can't call him Little John any more. He's almost eleven and nearly six feet tall, big like his dad." Hanna smiled at her daughter. "And Little John and Angel were born only minutes apart – they've known each other all of their lives. Their birthdays are next week."

The gold sat on the floor, forgotten. There was a companionable silence as the family of Black Elk read their letters.

"This woman Pakwa – she got a husband?" The tone of Hubert's voice was so intense, everybody there looked up and laughed.

"She's younger than me, Uncle Abe! You're old enough to be her grandfather." Hanna put her letter from Bess in her lap and smiled at her boss. "What did she say to you?"

Hubert pushed his glasses up on his nose and read. "Dear Mr. Hubert. Because of your vision and foresight, my people are prospering. Collectors and museum buyers have come here regularly thanks to you. This blanket is a traditional Navajo friendship design. Even though we only know of you through John Dunn and the trading post, you are a friend of my people.

You are welcome here any time." He looked over his glasses, winked at Hanna and quipped, "Maybe I could adopt her."

"Uncle Abe," said Ben. "The first thing Pakwa would do is make you give up those evil cigars." He stole a quick look at Hanna. "You're better off being a bachelor." After Hanna elbowed him playfully he said, "Listen to what John has to say. 'After knocking heads with the local business owners, they've been making hints about me joining the City Council. That banker Hollis has been treating me with some respect. He even had a short conversation with Bess about the weather. Things are definitely changing around here'." Ben looked around and asked, "Can you imagine Leftook on the City Council?"

Hubert cackled, then pulled his watch out of his vest pocket by the chain. "We've got a big day today before our two-day run into Nebraska, but you've got to hear this." He adjusted his glasses and read from his letter from Dunn. "Amos has asked me to say hello to all of you." Hubert held up his hand for silence after everybody in the compartment began talking all at once. "That old rascal. He moved in at the ranch and is waiting tables at some local restaurant." Hubert put both hands on his cane and smiled an evil smile. "Amos wants me to pimp for him. I'm supposed to ask Alice from the wardrobe car to join him this winter."

There was more good-natured laughter around the compartment until Angel asked, "Uncle Abe, what's a pimp?"

Hubert blushed after seeing the disapproving look Hanna shot him. "Angel dear, it's an impolite word that means a man that gets a girlfriend for another man."

Ben, quick to change the subject said, "Listen, Leftook says that Mathó took his first elk in the same spot I did." He looked over at his father-in-law and read, "He cried when he said the prayer."

The sounds from outside intruded. Wagons were being readied for the parade; livestock was being fed. Big Abe started to stand and was saying, "The tickets are sold, the show must…" when Angel gasped.

"What?" asked Hanna.

Little Angel grasped her letter from Matȟó in both hands – her eyes were huge, full of joy and something else.

"Is something wrong?" Ben asked worriedly.

"He wants to marry me when we get older."

The last show of the season took place in Beatrice, Nebraska. It was hugely successful. The population of the town was just over nine thousand people, but more than thirteen thousand tickets were sold. Cody's trains pulled into the Beatrice rail yard at sunup. By ten that morning the parade had made three laps through downtown. It was a Saturday and the crowds along the main street cheered madly as Buffalo Bill led the parade. He drove a phaeton drawn by a pair of matched white Arabians.

While the parade was being organized on the blackened soil of the Beatrice rail yards, Angel got dressed and looked out her window. Little Abe was still asleep so she quietly slipped down the stairs. There were traces of frost outlining the sheds and wires that were typical of rail yards everywhere. It was a fine, clear day. The sun peaked over the tree line and promised perfect weather for the last show of the year. She stepped into a shaft of sunlight and stopped. She faced the sun, closed her eyes and let the sun warm her face. Also warming was the thought that soon, she'd be back in New Mexico with Little John - Matȟó.

Little Angel couldn't remember a day that she hadn't known Matȟó. Today was their birthday. She couldn't remember being born and the stories made her memories real – being wrapped in the same blanket with him, the two of them nursing on Auntie Bess or her mother. They'd learned to swim together, bathed together, slept together as children. Matȟó felt like more of a brother to her than Little Abe. However, the letter she'd just read changed her feelings. The thought of touching him now felt both attractive and confusing. With her eyes closed, her face to the sun, she imagined kissing him in a way that was not at all sisterly.

A window rattled open behind her and interrupted her daydream. Then she heard her mother's voice.

"*Iyúškiŋ tȟúŋpi aŋpétu! Thehíla.*" Hanna said in Sioux. "Happy birthday – I love you! As soon as the show is over tonight, we're going to have a little family party for you. Tell Uncle Abe I'll be there soon."

Angel and Hanna spent a hectic and happy day together in Hubert's office car. There was money and ticket stubs to count and accounting entries to make.

Big Abe gave Angel a gift. The moment she walked into the office, he gave her a courtly bow, said some blessing in Yiddish and put the five dollar gold piece in her hand. "Find something nice in town for your birthday." he said, handing her a box of work. "This has to be done before sundown. In the box is an envelope with each employee's name and the amount that should be in it. If there's a big "G" written by the name, pay in gold. The rest get greenbacks." Then he lit one of his foul smelling cigars and said, "Part of the end of the season speech tonight will be why the bonuses are so small. What a worthless way to end the year."

Hanna and Angel had no interest in watching the show that had become more and more repetitious as Cody's Wild West Show slowly deteriorated. Today's show was going to feature Custer's Last Stand again – by far the most popular reenactment the show ever did. Instead, the two of them worked through the lunch hour and were done just before the drovers, livestock handlers and roustabouts showed up as the show reached its finale.

The end of the season dinner was prepared and served outside. The meal was good, but not as grand as in year's past. There was quiet grumbling about the year-end bonuses and a lot of talk about winter plans.

As always, there was a stir as Cody walked through the crowd of performers, roustabouts and animal handlers. He stopped often, shaking hands, talking and giving compliments. It was painfully obvious that his age had taken its toll – up close he looked old. The crowd quieted as he climbed to the bottom step of a train car and held up one hand for quiet.

"It saddens me greatly that we have no schedule for next year. We are currently in negotiations to join up with a traveling circus. As you go on your various ways this winter, I can't guarantee your positions for next year's season." Cody paused dramatically and looked out over the crowd. "A good horse is not very apt to jump over a bank if left to guide himself. I always let mine pick his own way. And that is what I hope you all can do – find a good path for yourselves." He looked down for a second, and pulled himself up very straight. "I never could resist the call of the trail. The west of the old times, with its strong characters, its stern battles and it stretches of loneliness can never be blotted from my mind. By bringing our country's story to the people, I thought I was benefiting the Indians, as well as the government. By taking their story all over the world and giving our audience the correct idea of the Indian's customs and life, the pale faces would return to their own people and make known all they had seen." Cody stopped again and pointed to many of the groups of Indians standing there listening. "Every Indian outbreak that I have ever known has resulted from broken promises and broken treaties by the government. All I ever wanted to do was tell the tale of our country as true as I could." He waved to the crowd and as the applause, whistles and war cries lit up the night, he stepped into the train car and disappeared.

The horses nickered happily as the family of Black Elk, save one, gathered in the stock car. The familiar scent of sweet green hay and horse made Angel smile. Every birthday she could remember happened in this welcoming space.

Kahí had pulled multiple bales into a small circle and at the center was a small cake she'd bought in a bakery in town. There were a few packages wrapped in brown paper near the cake. Little Abe had yet to appear.

They talked quietly for a few minutes, waiting. Finally, Ben stood - attempting not to appear angry, but not succeeding. "I'll see where he's wandered off to – be right back."

There was a short, uncomfortable silence then Angel told Kahí of a birthday with Mathó. "We were five, maybe six. We woke up early and snuck out of Bess's tipi and tried to snare rabbits. The only gifts we got that year were rabbit pelts. We had to cook what we caught. That was our birthday dinner."

Ben came in and slammed the door. "He's gone into town. Let's start without him." He tried to smile; his anger was there just below the surface.

Kahí served the cake then handed Angel two small wrapped gifts. "I heard the stories of your grandmother Itunkala. We thought maybe these things would help you remember her." Inside the package from Kahí was a tiny crucifix on a fine silver chain. Black Elk's gift was a beautifully made knife with a six-inch blade fitted into an elk skin sheath. The sheath had two belts, one for her waist and the other to hold it secure against her leg.

Kahí helped secure the crucifix around her neck. When Black Elk helped fasten the knife to Angel's waist, he held back tears as he said, "You remind me of her."

Hanna reached behind a bale and pulled out another gift. "From your *Ate'* and me." She smiled at Angel and placed the package in her hands. "*Iyúškiŋ thúŋpi aŋpétu!* You are an angel."

Little Angel tore off the brown paper and inside was a copy of Twain's *The Adventures of Tom Sawyer*. "For your free time this winter." said Ben. "We know how much you love to read."

Angel stood and was about to hug her parents when they were interrupted by a knock at the door. Before Ben could reach the handle, Reggie stepped in followed by a man they'd never seen before. Reggie was pale and his hands were shaking. "Bad news. Little Abe got beat up pretty bad. He's in the hospital."

The man behind Reggie stepped into the room. "I'm Deputy Longmire. It appears your boy showed up in town dressed up like a girl – an Indian girl. I don't want to go into a lot of detail, but the local boys were pretty interested until they found out they'd been kissing a boy. It could have been a lot worse. The hospital is over on Ninth Street – I can take you there if you want."

The steps up to the hospital door were well lit as was the sign by the door that read VISITING HOURS 10:00 a.m. – 4:00 p.m. The door was locked.

Hanna knocked on the door - there was no response. After her third attempt, Ben stepped in and pounded with his fist.

A large woman dressed in a starched white uniform opened the door angrily. "Visiting hours are…" she blanched staring at the red faces of the small crowd wanting entrance. To her credit, she stood her ground. "The hospital is closed – come back in the morning."

"My son," pleaded Hanna. "Can I just see him for a moment?"

"Absolutely not! All our patients are sleeping and can't be disturbed."

Ben started to push his way in but was reined in by Black Elk. "Please! He's my grandson. Can you at least tell us how he's doing?"

"Dr. Hepperlen treated him about an hour ago. Your son has a broken arm – lost some teeth. There were lots of contusions and scrapes. He probably has a concussion. The doctor set his arm and gave him some morphine. He's asleep. Come back tomorrow and you can talk to the doctor. Good night!"

Hanna sat on the bed where Little Abe usually slept. Ben had held Angel until her sobs had become the soft breathing of sleep. Then his breathing synced with hers. The train yard was utterly dark – there were no sounds, not of trains or people to soothe Hanna's ache. Almost without thought, she stepped into the aisle as if the spirit of her father called her.

Black Elk looked up and saw her even before she knocked, as if he'd expected her. He put down the Bible he was reading – the look in his eyes was the only invitation she needed to enter.

The two of them stood there – his arms were around her waist – his forehead pressed to hers. There were no words either of them needed to say. Finally, she leaned back slightly and he dropped his arms to his sides. "What are you reading, Ate'?" she asked.

"Lamentations. Somehow it seems to fit my life." He sat and began to read. "I am the man that hath seen affliction by the rod of his wrath. He hath led me, and brought me into darkness, but not into light. Surely against me is He turned; He turneth his hand against me all the day. My flesh and my skin hath He made old; He hath broken my bones."

"*What of the Great Spirit, Ate'?*" Hanna asked in Sioux. "*It seems he speaks to us even in the white man's Bible. Remember the prayer you taught me – North. Make me brave when the cold winds come. Give me strength when everything is harsh, when everything hurts.*" She looked to her father with haunted eyes. "*Where do we go from here?*"

"*We go south to New Mexico. We have family there. It's a good life.*"

"*Ate'. What of your visions? What of mine? I flew over the Paha Sapa and saw our people begin again. I know it is hard, but I think I must go north.*"

"*Hanna, life with John and Bess will be easy. The ranch and the trading post make lots of money. We can be comfortable and happy there.*"

Hanna reached into her pockets with both hands. When she opened them, there was a gold coin in one and her sacred black stone in the other. "*Ate', Kanj Coonshi once told me that I would have to choose.*"

Black Elk looked down at the objects in his daughter's hands then into her eyes. In that instant, he felt a seismic shift. She was still his daughter. Her spirit had grown so much, the father-daughter bond was less relevant than the equality in their beings.

Hanna dropped the coin as if was worthless and cradled her black rock in both hands. "*You gave this stone to my mother in love. It came to me as a way to remember the sacred way of life. Of the four sacred directions, south is the easy way, the white man's way. I want our people to remember. In my dream, we go north. I dreamed that you and I wrote down our visions - we collected the ancient wisdoms so when the time comes, the people can learn to live in peace as the White Buffalo Woman taught us."*

An excerpt from

BLACK ROCK

Book Four
and conclusion to the

WAKANISHA
Series

Black Rock
South Dakota – July 2023

"Mornin' Joseph." Althea nodded to the doorman as he helped her out of the limo.

"Good morning to you, Miss *Ohítika*. I haven't seen you since the last meeting." Joseph was dressed in a beautifully made deerskin outfit carefully designed to make him look like a Sioux warrior. The guise he wore probably looked authentic to fans of western movies, except for the gold Rolex on his wrist.

Althea smiled broadly and put her hand affectionately on the man's forearm. "Joseph, you know *ohítika* means fierce and brave – it also means foolhardy." She dropped her hand and glanced up at the massive casino. "When I'm in there, I mostly feel like a *ȟleté;* you know, an idiot."

The doorman replied, "*I believe!*" These two words were said with such conviction they seemed to come from the man's spirit.

In that instant, Althea saw not a parody but a true warrior of her people. He was so sincere, so genuine that Althea blinked away tears. "*Pilamaya* my friend. How is your family?"

The doorman dropped his eyes briefly. "My boy's in treatment; think he's doin' OK. Little Lottie just turned thirteen." He sighed. "I've got my fingers crossed."

"Your family is my family." She took his hands in both of hers and said, "Our children are the future."

A small crowd gathered at the casino's entrance to see if some celebrity might step out of the limo. The person they saw did not look the part. Instead they saw a middle-aged Indian woman dressed in a simple denim ankle length skirt and a white cotton top. Her hair was long, black with streaks of grey, and tied in a ponytail with a strand of leather. She was a bit plump, wore Birkenstocks with socks, and had a feather tied to the crucifix around her neck. She looked unremarkable, much like thousands of women one might see in this part of South Dakota. When the woman turned and smiled at them, they quickly dropped their eyes and scuttled into the casino. Her eyes were a fierce icy blue.

As always, Althea's claustrophobia increased proportionately the farther she walked into the casino. There was no natural light, yet there were mirrors everywhere and they were all so clean. She hated the feeling of being swallowed up, being lost and disoriented. The sensation was the same as feeling confused while walking through IKEA when her only desire was finding meatballs and a window with sunshine.

There was no direct pathway to the elevator; she wasn't even sure if there were stairs up to the boardroom. When Althea reached the first bend in the walkway that led past the slot machines, she stopped, turned and looked back. The sunshine coming in through the massive carved doorway was a reminder of the outside with fresh air. She wished she'd taken the time to sit on the ground and feel the earth before she entered.

Even with the powerful air handling system, the air smelled of cigarette smoke, cheap cologne and desperation. The empty, rapt faces of the customers playing the slots reminded Althea of souls in purgatory. When she reached the gaming tables, the sensation of claustrophobia lessened a bit. It seemed more open, less crowded. But the faces were the same. Every customer in the building was there for one reason – money.

Althea had a brief fantasy as she passed a blackjack table crowded with players and spectators. She was standing in for the dealer. Instead of cards, she had her black rock in one hand and a gold coin in the other. And instead of calling for hits, she taught them the parable of Kanj Coonshi and Hanna's choice. She knew her great-great-grandmother's writings well.

Althea's coming of age was inexorably tied to the casino. During the late 1990's and the controversy the proposed casino caused, Althea had become a teenager. The arguments, the *Yes* and *No* signs in people's yards, the clamor for money had been of little interest to her. The immature culture of middle school, boys, and smoking pot on the weekends was her world. Then, prior to the grand opening of the casino in 2006, she had followed the Jack Abramoff scandal with some interest. She pictured herself having some glamorous career as a singer or blackjack dealer and was glad when the casino opened.

Althea's life came slowly into focus after her mother died. The cancer was brutal and inexorable. In the short time between diagnosis and her death, Althea's mother gave her several artifacts and asked for a promise. The artifacts: a five dollar gold piece dated 1897, the black rock etched with the hawk symbol and the original copies of the writings of her ancestors. The promise: live and teach the writings of her great-great-grandmother Hanna Gregor and Hanna's famous father Black Elk.

Althea remembered vividly the day of her mother's funeral. The church was full to overflowing. There were many old folks there that remembered meeting Black Elk and knew his teachings. Many more approached her, asked for a glimpse of the black rock and asked if she would continue her mother's work. The priest's homily focused on Proverbs 17.

Her memory was powerful. She sat in the small cathedral's front row as the priest spoke about her mother. Althea had the rock in her right hand – the gold coin in her left when the priest spoke these words. "The crucible is for silver, and the furnace is for gold, and the Lord tests hearts." In that instant, the world fell away. Althea stared at the two objects, the gold and the stone, and knew her time of choice had come.

Now, almost two decades later, Althea represented the Lakota Sioux as one of the casino's Seven Council Fires governing board members. She was the only woman on the board. The board's mission – how to spend a half a billion dollars a year.

Althea grimaced as she always did when she walked into the boardroom. It was so out of balance with her sensibilities that she gripped the pouch tied at her waist that held the rock. She was tempted to take it out, feel its calming black smoothness, and trace the hawk etching with her thumbnail. The garishness that surrounded her was an obscene parody. She took a calming breath and waited for the rest of the board to arrive.

The round room was huge in comparison to its need. Althea knew the space was sixty-four feet in diameter, a multiple of the sacred number four. The interior walls tapered slightly inward giving the room a discordant tipi feel. The architect was unwilling or unable to depict thirteen lodge-poles; he'd used twelve to satisfy a sense of order.

The walls were quartered by four stained glass windows designed to represent the four sacred directions. Centered in the ceiling was another window showing a red-tailed hawk in flight. The widows were beautifully done, but they were lit artificially. This huge room was contained within a square built building - a casino. The boardroom had no natural light whatsoever; its walls were all inside. The air was delivered by a high tech environmental system. The carpeting was a garish green.

Althea had voted against the funding request to build this room. She had suggested instead holding the quarterly board meetings in a real tipi. Althea had fronted the idea to the board, along with pictures of several beautiful places on the reservation where the tipi could be erected. She had passionately proposed to use the funds to build this room for scholarships instead. The vote had been three to five against.

The room's entire circumference was lined with curio cabinets, display cases and stands for Sioux artifacts. Althea loved the beautiful relics made by the hands of her ancestors. The taxidermist's art, however, was disturbing to her. She hoped that the spirits of the stuffed buffalo and bear by the door had been thanked for their lives. She reverently walked the perimeter and greeted these animals, the cougar, a badger, several rabbits, and a meadowlark, with their true Sioux names. The bear was her favorite; it reminded her of her great-grandfather, Mathó Dunn.

Althea walked around the massive table that dominated the center of the room. She slid her fingers across the velvety smoothness of this polished block of redwood. She was both saddened and awed by this piece of wood. A massive sequoia had been felled and this sixteen-foot diameter slab had been trucked in from California at great expense. Althea said a brief prayer of thanks for all the once living creations that had been brought here. The hubris of her brothers hurt her heart.

She circled the table again reading, the eight name placards near the Corinthian leather office chairs. Seven of the placards were printed in the Sioux nation orthography and represented the Seven Council Fires. These seven bands within the Sioux nation precisely represented the four sacred directions. Three named the Lakota: Húŋkpapȟa for north, Mnikȟówožu - central and Oglála for the south. Two named the Yankton Sioux from the east. The Santee Sioux from the west completed the sacred circle and the cross.

The eighth placard had no Sioux Nation designation. It only contained a name – Antonio DeLuca.

"This meeting will come to order!" Henry Lame Bull, the current council chair, rapped the gavel. "For the record, it is *Ćaŋpasapa-wi*, the month the chokecherries come ripe." Unsmiling, he glanced at the man wearing the designer suit and continued, "For you, Mr. DeLuca and the bean counters that are recording us, today is Tuesday, July 11, 2023." He pointed briefly at a microphone hanging from the ceiling.

Lame Bull smiled around the room. Except for DeLuca, the council members were dressed casually. Lame Bull wore his signature Levi's, an unironed white shirt and moccasins. The Santee representative wore a black T-shirt with a picture of Sitting Bull on the front. Across the huge table, the Oglála envoy's shirt read *Custer Died For Your Sins*. Every Sioux at the meeting wore a feather.

"Before we start," Lame Bull announced, "Lunch is at twelve sharp. I've been told that the fry bread is particularly good today." After the grunts of appreciation died down, he continued. "Did everybody have a great *Akéšakpe*?"

"English please," DeLuca said none too politely in a strong Jersey accent.

"Mr. DeLuca," Lame Bull said evenly. "All of us here are Catholic to some degree. We celebrate Christian holidays." He folded his hands on the table and gave the eighth man a direct stare. "*Akéšakpe* means sixteen in our language and is also a sixteen day holiday. Four is a sacred number in our culture – the four sacred directions – the four colors of men." He looked around at all the members of the board and continued. "This meeting is always scheduled exactly sixteen days after the twenty-fifth of June. Those sixteen days, these four times four days, are a time for us to celebrate and reflect on our heritage."

"I don't get it!" said DeLuca.

"June twenty-fifth was the day Custer wore an arrow shirt."

When Althea's funding request was next on the agenda, Mr. DeLuca had lots to say during the discussion prior to the vote. "I understand your previous requests for a million here, three million there. You bought up contiguous farms. That's strategic; it makes sense. You want your land back!" He rifled through the papers in his hand, took off his glasses and glared at Althea. "Sixty million is a lot of dough!" He tapped Althea's request loudly with his middle finger. "It says here you want three hundred miles of fencing. Then there's the trapping and transport of bison, elk, several species of deer not to mention the wells and windmills. Tell me how this zoo of yours is going to keep the investors back in Jersey happy?" The tone of DeLuca's voice and his rude finger gesture had raised the tension in the room considerably.

"Mr. DeLuca," Althea said calmly. "Tell us what you know about the Svalbard Global Seed Vault in Norway."

DeLuca thought for a moment then scoffed. "You want a bunch of animals to survive when the world ends?"

"Mr. DeLuca, there are currently almost seven hundred people living on the land we've secured. Not only are they living completely off the grid, they're living off the land." Althea watched the man's eyes for even a shred of understanding."

"I don't get it!"

Althea sighed and continued. "Consider the data! The United State's current debt is over thirty trillion. The interest on that debt costs more than every other governmental program combined including Medicare, Medicaid and defense. The current world population is in excess of nine billion, yet science tells us the Earth can only support four billion at best. And that is only the financial bad news. Every indicator of collapse is spiking - homelessness, global temperature increases, fires, extreme weather, hunger – war in all parts of the world. Mr. DeLuca, it is not a matter of if our system will collapse; it is a matter of when."

"I still don't get it!" DeLuca snapped. "How are these people going to save the world?"

"They aren't," Althea said sadly. "They have the skills to start over."

Henry Lame Bull banged his gavel and called for the vote.

Acknowledgements and Thanks

You know what happens when women get together on something? All kinds of stuff you can't explain happens. But good stuff, mysterious, but good. Usually very good. Things get solved.
   Jeremy Davies from the film Solaris

Three remarkable women contributed to this story. Two of them diligently noted the tiny errors – the out-of-place commas, the repeated words, the ambiguous metaphors – and made the story flow without the bumps I'd left in its path. The third steered the narrative as surely as if she'd had a map. It's no mystery that the Queen is the most powerful piece on the board.

My grateful thanks to Lucinda Jensen! Her meticulous knowledge of our language and its mechanics resulted in an edited version that left the story untouched but free of the tiny errors that would distract from your experience. Cindy is undeniably a student of and sympathetic to the First People.

I met Barb Ewing for coffee to give her an unedited copy of this book and made an amazing discovery. When she reads, there are no images like a movie in her mind. Instead, she sees the words. For her, the beauty is in the choice of vocabulary, syntax – the punctuation. What a perfect skill set for an editor!

And thanks to my best friend, partner and mother of our children. Without Mary, this story and my story would be vastly different. For example, when she read the ending of a draft of book one, she had me add the words that John Dunn spoke – "Take the spirit of these people with you." Those eight words became the theme of this series. And at the beginning of book two, I planned to kill off John Dunn – Leftook. Well, that didn't happen! Mary saved his life and in doing so made a course change that made this story what it is. Mary my love – *Pilamaya*!

More Acknowledgements and Thanks

The actions of men are the best interpreters of their thoughts.
   James Joyce

The actions of two men greatly contributed to this story. Their thoughts, although vastly different, positively influenced me and the story within these pages.

My son Aaron Foster is both a network engineer and an author with two young adult novels under his belt. In all probability, because he assisted me publish my third novel Aaron delayed the release of his own third book in the *Adam Undercover* series. His novels are highly entertaining, capture the angst of being a teenager and elevate imaginative technology to a high art. Thank you Aaron for your help navigating the digital world.

Thank you to my neighbor to the north and friend Robert Robinson. Robert read a brutally red marked early manuscript. And even though there were arrows, crossed out and added words, cryptic notes and edit suggestions, he found several errors after four other readers had marked the copy. He also found the beauty in this story even though the pages seemed to hemorrhage red ink. Thank you Robert for the praise and encouragement.

Made in the USA
Middletown, DE
22 January 2019